Keep Me Forever

A Novel

D1535448

ELSA WOLF

This is a work of fiction. Names, characters, places, brands, media, and incidents are either the product of the author's imagination or are used fictitiously. The author acknowledges the trademarked status and trademark owners of products referenced in this work of fiction, which have been used without permission. The publication/use of these trademarks are not authorized, associated with, or sponsored by the trademark owners.

Copyright ©2022 by Elsa Wolf
TXu 2-309-781
elsawolfbooks.com
elsawolf@yahoo.com

Editing by Faith Williams, The Atwater Group
Interior design and cover by Champagne Book Design

All rights reserved.
Without limiting the rights under copyright reserved above, no part of this publication may be reproduced, stored in or introduced into a retrieval system, or transmitted, in any form, or by any means (electronic, mechanical, photocopying, recording, or otherwise) without the prior written permission of the above copyright owner of this book.

Library of Congress Control Number: 2022911772

Wolf, Elsa
Keep Me Forever / 1st ed.
ISBN 978-1-7327774-2-2 (pbk)
ISBN 978-1-7327774-3-9 (ebook)
ISBN 978-1-7327774-4-6 (hrdbk)

United States of America

Also by
ELSA WOLF

Buried Truths, A Daughter's Tale

Dedication from the Heart

To all soldiers who have struggled with what their country asks of them and later suffer from the effects of PTSD. Some are able to continue on, while others are not. This novel imagines a new path for a soldier I once knew who lost his internal battles.

"Every accomplishment starts with the decision to try."
—John F. *Kennedy*

Chapter 1

The Train

JIM PACKED MORE OF HIS BELONGINGS THAN HE EXPECTED TO use during his trip to Savannah. The seams of his wax-canvas backpack and duffel bag strained against the load, but he was too tired to repack. As an afterthought, he pulled out the extra cash he'd squirreled away in a canister under his bed and put some of it in one pocket and the rest in his wallet. He scanned their mobile home to see if he'd forgotten anything, then grabbed the bags and headed to the main office a few yards away. Melanie was moving things around in the storage closet.

"See you in a few weeks, sis," Jim called out. She didn't respond, but they'd said goodbye the night before, so it wasn't a big deal.

By the service counter, his mama was chatting up a storm with a client. She stopped long enough to give him a quick hug and remind him to avoid getting too friendly with his father's girlfriend. He had no intention of side-stepping Suzy. It was time for him to forge a new path without being influenced by his mother's wishes. With a quick nod, Jim turned away and walked out the door toward the main road and caught the Orlando commuter bus.

Without paying much attention to anything, the time passed by quickly. He got off at the Amtrak station and made his way up to the ticket window through a crowd of people. The station's weatherboard read seventy degrees, but he felt an unnatural chill created by his inner tension. Jim wrapped his hands around his midsection to steady himself. His mind rolled back to the end of the previous night's sixteen-hour shift at the amusement park. Either fatigue had taken over his mind and distorted reality, or someone had played a cruel joke on him. Within the mist, a ghost of his sister Christina had materialized.

Her brown eyes were wide and glistening. With a smile and a wave, she'd disappeared as quickly as she'd appeared.

"Next!" the ticket agent called out in a Southern accent. "Step up, young man. Can I help you?"

"Oh, right, sorry." Jim moved up to the counter. "Sir, how long is the journey one-way with the fewest stops?"

"Six and a half hours."

"I'd like a round-trip ticket, please."

"That'll be fifty-five dollars."

He pulled out the loose bills from his pocket, along with the white liner, and snickered at the tongue-like protuberance. It looked so pitiful. Patting the right front pocket of his jeans, Jim made sure his wallet was still in place. It was a safe spot to keep it, to deter pickpockets. An old trick his dad had taught him when they'd traveled together.

"Hey, you got the money? There are other people in line."

"Sure do." Jim placed the fee on the curved metal tray under a thick glass window before shoving his pocket back into place.

The agent pulled the money through and returned the ticket with some change. The ticket got caught up in a gust of wind. He grabbed it in time and thanked God it hadn't been lost. The last time he'd traveled to Savannah, he'd been with Melanie and their mama. This was the first time he'd gone on his own and purchased a ticket without her help. During all the other trips, Melanie had been an irritating kid. Of late, he had become tolerant of her teenage antics.

By the tracks, he paced back and forth under the metal-roofed pavilion until the train arrived. The doors opened, Jim stepped in, and headed to the first available window seat. He tossed his backpack on the vacant aisle seat and heaved his duffel bag onto the luggage rack across the aisle. Hesitating, he deliberated over the letters under the flap of the backpack before maneuvering into the window seat. The letters weighed on his mind, yet he left them in place for the next hour. Finally, he retrieved them, but realized he was too tired to focus on their content. So, he folded the envelopes up, slid them into his shirt pocket over his heart, and hoped his dreams could evolve into a real-life scenario.

Out the window, the trees sped past. Thoughts of the amusement park floated into the front of his mind, along with his mama's attempt to turn their lives in a new direction that steered them away from their Catholic roots. Some days, it was hard to tell what was real and what wasn't. Her new spiritual ideas were almost impossible to live with, although he tried to keep an open mind. He reflected on what he'd learned as a child: respect everyone, and be tolerant of other religions. What a strange thing, considering people often condemned each other in the name of religion. He didn't know when or if he would join a congregation in the future. One way or another, he needed stability in his life. God tested people, and Jim believed He had an odd sense of humor. Whenever their dad came to Orlando, their mama flirted with him, attempting to reconcile. When they were all together in Savannah, it was a different story.

Jim thought about what it would be like to spend time in his father's house without his sister around. Yet, when he and Melanie went with their mama to Savannah, she put on a subdued front while attempting to be pleasant. He knew it was because Suzy had moved into their old home. She was ten years younger than his dad and eleven years older than Jim. Nothing was the same anymore. Whenever they arrived in town, their mama would go to the door with them and put on an unkind, bittersweet, "bless your heart" attitude. She'd leave within five minutes and run off to see old friends, or so she said. Every time she dropped them off, they'd go down to the river for ice cream and fishing to silently remember Christina.

As Jim dozed off on the train, he pushed his thoughts into a less personal direction to the bird-lady in Savannah. She always wore moss-colored outfits. Some days, she'd feed the birds, and others she'd root around in her shopping cart.

He awoke when the train's forward motion turned to an abrupt halt. Squinting toward the aisle, he saw the sun glint off something.

When he became more conscious, he realized the light was reflecting off a single red stone on a young woman's necklace.

"Excuse me, do you mind if I sit here? The train is packed except for this seat and another one in the back. The guy there looks creepy."

"Please, sit. Sorry. I dozed off without putting my bag away." Jim moved his backpack off the seat and placed it between his legs. He couldn't help noticing the long, luscious, auburn hair curling down over the front of one side of her shoulder. She looked about his age, or a little younger. Nineteen or twenty, he guessed.

"Much obliged."

As her slim figure settled next to him, he said, "I guess I've been asleep for a while. Where are we?"

"Jacksonville."

Her silky Georgia accent brought pleasant memories and some homesickness for Savannah to the forefront.

"I hear it's a nice beach town." Jim raked his hand through his wavy hair, attempting to appear presentable. It was strange, in a good way, waking up to such a perfect smile.

"It is. I love walking along the water. I always take the Palmetto train to travel back and forth to Jacksonville and Charleston." She sat down and placed a cloth floral bag on the floor between her legs, then held out a paper carton. "Do you want some hot French fries?"

"No, thanks. They make me thirsty." He instantly regretted refusing.

"Okay. I got these in the station. They also sell sodas and food on the train." Her thin silver bracelets clicked together over a tattoo on her wrist, which seemed to glow on her ivory skin. He was so distracted, he almost forgot to respond.

"Thanks. I'll stick with the water and sandwich in my pack. I'm on a strict diet." *More like a penny-pincher along with a low-budget life,* Jim reflected. "Where are you heading?"

"To Savannah."

"Oh, me, too." Jim realized he sounded lame.

"Are you from the South? I don't hear an accent."

"I've been away too long," Jim said.

"Oh, I guess that makes sense." She ran her hand down her hair. "I'm a student."

"Nice." He smiled. "Which school?"

"SCAD. I'm starting my fourth year in September."

"Right, the Savannah College of Art and Design."

"You know it? I'm impressed." She brought out some yarn and needles from the bag on the floor.

He noticed a monogram with the letter *S* on her bag, but couldn't decipher the rest. Next to it, he noticed her curved calves. "Are you making a scarf?"

"Sure am." She started stitching away with the multicolored yarn. Her head moved up and down between stitches during the conversation. Later, she stopped looking and fingered her way through the pattern.

His mama used to knit, so he was familiar with the movements. This woman somehow made the motions look sexy. "I know SCAD," Jim continued. "I grew up nearby, right off Forsyth Park."

"Oh, whoa, that's a fine area."

"Yes." He paused for an awkward moment while he drank in her Southern accent. "I moved away about—hmm—about six, no, seven years ago."

"A lot has happened since then. The school expanded, and the town's gone through some renovations. When'd you visit last?"

"It's been about a year."

"Oh, so I guess you've seen the updates?"

"Only some in the historic district. It's hard to keep up with all twenty-four parks, I mean squares, and all the other areas. I stick around Forsyth and a couple of other places in town." For now, Jim didn't want to get into an in-depth conversation about local history, yet he was tempted. So instead, he said, "When I'm there, I don't have a lot of time to explore like I did when I was a kid."

"So, what takes you there this time?"

"I'm visiting my dad."

"And the rest of the time?"

"I work at an amusement park." The place tended to get a woman's attention, and it got hers. She smiled. They talked about his work for a good portion of the journey.

Eventually, he moved the conversation back into her court. "What are you studying?"

"Art history, architecture, and…"

The skein of yarn popped up and out of the bag. Jim thought: *here we go.* He reached down to recover it at the same time she did. Their hands touched for a second, and a shock wave traveled between them.

"Yikes, electric. Sorry," she said.

"It's all right." He smiled sheepishly in her direction. Their interlude would end when the train stopped. Jim believed this encounter was like one of those "talk to a stranger" moments when people talk freely without ever expecting to see each other again. When they started talking, he hadn't considered continuing their association beyond the trip, but his attitude had changed.

Chapter 2

Savannah

AN HOUR AND A HALF LATER, THE TRAIN APPROACHED THE Savannah station. As it came to a halt in front of a red brick building, Jim asked her name. She rose from her chair and reached out a hand—Sara Cosgrove. He shook it with a gentle but firm grip—Jim Masterson. Before he knew it, the other passengers pushed Sara away. By the time he disembarked, he only caught a glimpse of her walking down the sidewalk. She turned in his direction and paused before getting into a waiting car. He regretted missing the opportunity to ask for a phone number and hoped he could find her on campus. To avoid carrying his oversized duffel bag across town, he signaled a taxi and told the driver to go over to Clark Hall. The building was a block away from the SCAD Museum of Art. If Sara wasn't around, he'd walk to his dad's house from there.

Jim hopped out of the cab with his bags and lingered on the sidewalk. There was no realistic way to find Sara. Nevertheless, he stepped into the coffee shop and looked around. She didn't walk into the place or even pass by the window. Meeting an attractive woman wasn't supposed to be part of the plan. Considering, he came to Savannah to see his dad and figure out how to accomplish his career goals. He'd have to get Sara out of his mind and get back on task.

Looking at his watch, he realized it was close to his dad's dinner time. He usually ate around five, so Jim needed to sit a bit longer. He knew Suzy didn't take kindly to people showing up in the middle of meals. His dad and Suzy had been together long enough to consider her more of a stepmother than anything else. Suzy was a peach of a lady. There was no other way to view her. She valued family, church, and community. Her clothes and hair were always in top form in public and often at home. Somehow, despite everything, she appeared to ignore her girlfriend status, and ran their lives as if they were married. Her situation didn't appear to bother her in the slightest, even though the people within their social circles initially disapproved.

He smiled, thinking of the good times his family experienced when he was a kid before everything changed. The board games, church retreats, camping, fishing, and hiking were treasured memories. He mulled over everything while he walked. Over the years, when he'd returned with Melanie and his mama, he hadn't had enough emotional space to reflect on the good times.

Breathing in the sweet Savannah air, he hustled past the shops, toward the park. The moss-draped trees helped him feel instantly at home. Passing by the fountain and its statues reminded him of the hours he had wandered through the grounds.

Along the walkway, he saw the familiar bird-lady sitting on a park bench. She truly was a landmark, a fixture in Savannah. When he was a kid, he and his sisters saw her sticking pins in a rag doll. Their mama had pulled them away and whispered, "Voodoo." The image had been etched in his mind, mostly because of his mother's whispers and her refusal to explain beyond saying, "You should stay away because these types of people are evil." So, at the time, he'd focused on the lion and swan statues in the park.

The woman was older now, with dark, heavily wrinkled skin. A baggy floral blouse hung over her long skirt, which was spotted with bird droppings. At least twenty birds surrounded her, nibbling on birdseed. Some sat on the top rails behind her, and others next to her hip. She leaned forward, and a squirrel took a peanut shell from her outstretched fingers.

They exchanged smiles, and Jim continued along toward his destination. Even though his mama had told him to keep away from the bird-lady, they'd always smiled at each other and waved. When he was a teenager, he'd talked to the woman from a distance. Now, he wasn't sure she knew who he was.

Farther into the park stood a man playing jazz on a trombone. In front of him sat a wicker basket for donations. Jim stopped for a few minutes to listen and tossed in a coin. The man was another familiar face who had always wandered the park. Long ago—Jim didn't recall when—he'd asked why. The gentleman had said it helped him relax after a hard day at work, and he enjoyed entertaining people.

Turning on West Park Avenue, Jim lugged his gear up the half-dozen stairs to the front porch of number 208. The conical-shaped, stained-glass lamps in the windows on either side of the front entrance were on, even though it wouldn't be dark for hours. Before knocking on one of the double doors, he drew himself up a little taller. With one deep breath, he double-checked his watch to make sure he wasn't too early.

The front door swung open before he knocked. The family Labrador, Rex, bolted out. He ran around Jim in circles before standing up and putting his front paws on his chest. It didn't matter how many months they'd been apart. Rex had a long memory and helped Jim feel at ease. Leaving Rex behind when most of his family moved to Florida was painful. The dog was getting old, yet he still had a lively spirit.

"Well, bless me." Suzy pulled him over the threshold. "James Michael, come right on in. Close the door, you're letting in all the hot air." His dad often called him James Michael to avoid confusion, since they were both James. Suzy had picked up the habit, too. Ever since they'd started dating, he'd attempted to retrain them both to say Jim, or at least Junior. Either would have been great, but it was hopeless. So, Jim was Jim everywhere except in their presence.

"I see you still have the backpack your daddy and I gave you for your high school graduation."

"Yes, ma'am. It's served me well over the last few years. Reminds me of Savannah every day." Jim put his duffel and backpack down. Rex sniffed it and dashed down the hall.

"Well, that's nice. Your daddy is in his study. He's expecting you."

"Where'd Rex go?"

"To the kitchen. Liana is in there, finishing up the dinner dishes."

"Liana must be ancient by now."

"Yes, I suppose. She's worked here on weekends longer than I've been around." Suzy turned toward the kitchen. "As for Rex, he either wants a snack or is getting a toy from the backyard. He has all kinds of treasures on the other side of his doggie door. It's hard to keep him from digging up roots by the old oak tree. Silly dog."

"Some things never change." Jim laughed. "Except, they do. There are new colors on the outside of the house. It looks good."

"Thank you." She beamed. "The blue, with contrasting yellow and cream trim, cheers the place up and lightens your daddy's mood. They are soothing and uplifting colors for people to see when they walk by the house. I've changed a few things inside, too. Have a look at your old room after you talk to your daddy."

"Thanks. I'll grab my things and take them upstairs first. I need to splash some water on my face."

"That's a good idea, darling." She briefly rubbed his shoulder. "I'm sorry you missed our Easter gathering."

"It couldn't be helped. The spring is chaotic at work."

"Yes, well, here you are now," Suzy drawled. "It's so good to see you."

"It's good to be here."

He tried to provide an encouraging nod while picking up his bags. The idea of his room being transformed from a teenage motif irritated him, and he wanted to say so. Yet, he knew harmful words could not be taken back, and he didn't want to hurt Suzy's feelings. Guessing what she might have done wasn't worth the effort. He'd see for himself soon enough. Even though he didn't want to admit things needed to change, it was time for his movie posters and trinkets to go elsewhere.

Suzy gingerly took his arm and guided him toward the staircase. "Go on, now. I'll see you when you come down." She scurried away down the hall over the inlaid hardwood flooring. The multicolored eight-pointed star in the foyer shone with an unblemished lacquer finish and was still the focal point of the space, as it had been all his life.

There was a new carpet runner on the stairs. On the way up, he bumped his toes into one of the gold rods holding it in place. At the top landing, the runner transitioned into wall-to-wall carpeting down the hallway to an open door—his bedroom. It became clear his old life only remained in his memory. The green walls were now a shade of sienna, the twin bed now full-size with coverlets making it look inflated beyond the height of the dark wood footboard. A half-dozen pillows almost completely concealed the headboard. Built-in bookshelves on the opposite wall were sparsely populated with softback books.

He opened the closet and found the remnants of his past. On the top shelf, he found a box of figurines he'd once taken hours to paint, representing various characters from *Lord of the Rings*: Gandalf and his white horse, Frodo, Legolas, Gollum, Arwen, and many others. Some of them were missing, and he wasn't sure which ones. He removed a dragon, put it in his pocket, and planned to take it to Christina's grave another day. In an envelope was a stick figure drawing of them with their old dog, Buttons, sitting between them. She'd drawn it especially for him when they were children.

Underneath the box was his portfolio filled with grave rubbings. He decided to throw them away before leaving town. Alongside the box, an old Atari game console with the Pong game cartridge still in place. Posters stood rolled up in an open-top box in the back corner. They were labeled, Jim's Pictures, in Suzy's handwriting. Long ago, they hung on the wall behind the bed. In their place hung three paintings displaying pheasants in a garden setting.

One, and only one, picture from his past remained on the wall outside the closet door. The photograph of familiar lions encircling a fountain was under a new mat. An inscription said; *The Alhambra. A courtyard surrounding these beasts is divided into four parts to represent different quadrants of the world and the rivers flowing between them to Paradise. Photograph by Yara.* Jim fixed the words in his mind and tilted his head as he gazed at the lions. He recollected the trip to the Alhambra with his parents, but not the significance of the event or why it was connected to his aunt and her home in Sintra, Portugal.

Aunt Yara was long gone. She died when he was ten years old. Not long after, Jim walked down by the Savannah River with his mama and sisters. This hadn't been an unusual outing. Except this time, she'd left him standing by the *Waving Girl* statue and stepped inside a shop with Melanie and Christina. It was one of the first times his mama had taken his sisters into a shop and asked him to wait outside. While he stood there, the statue's face morphed into Aunt Yara's smile. At the time, the vision hadn't fazed him. Thinking back, he wondered why. Until two days ago, he'd forgotten about the old vision. Seeing Christina in the underground passageways at work brought the memory back, along with questioning his sanity. Strange events were just a part of his life.

Under the window stood a new leather couch overflowing with throw pillows. Thankfully, Suzy hadn't painted the four dark wood beams across the ceiling. Jim used to stare up at them at night when he was falling asleep. The images he conjured up in his imagination soothed him. They were usually vivid outdoor scenes filled with lions, nymphs, elves, and magical beings. All were inspired, like the figurines, by hours of reading J. R. R. Tolkien, C. S. Lewis, Robert Heinlein, and Ursula Le Guin. Not to forget *The Iliad* and *The Odyssey*, which were difficult to get through. The fantastical characters seemed to have lessons to teach. The warriors on either side, whether Greek or Trojan, didn't come across as good or bad. Each side respected the other, unlike more modern conflicts, which use tactics to dishonor and demoralize one's enemy.

Enough reminiscing, he thought, and headed back downstairs to his dad's office. Jim's fist connected with the wood on the door. One rap, two raps.

"Is that you, James Michael?" His dad's voice bellowed through the paneled, wooden door.

"Yes, sir. It's me."

"Come in."

Jim opened the door and marched in with his posture erect, trying to appear confident. He saw his dad behind the Federal-style desk in his usual workday suit and a loose tie. Law books filled the built-in shelves and others rested in several stacks on the floor. A custom opening in the shelves housed a six-shelved barrister cabinet that opened on an invisible hinge. Inside was a small room large enough for a few rifles, handguns, water, and nonperishable foods. His dad had always called it the family "safe-room" for them to hide in during an emergency. A shiver traveled down Jim's spine.

His dad got up and walked across the room. One bear hug later, they stepped back and sized each other up. At least that's what Jim was doing. "Dad, the house has changed since my last visit."

"Yes, well, things have to change, don't they?" The question was rhetorical. His dad walked over to a new table with lion claw-foot legs. On a tray sat four crystal tumblers, at least six small bottles of liquor, and a bowl of nuts. Behind them was a lamp and a rectangular ceramic container with a variety of small succulent plants.

"Yes, sir. Things change. I like what Suzy's done to the place."

"I wish you could've come down sooner and spent Easter with us."

"Suzy said the same thing."

"Work and family are a hard balancing act to manage." His dad poured some liquor into a glass and swirled it around. "Son, you want a whiskey to celebrate your twenty-first birthday again?"

"I had too much Jameson with some of the money you sent last month for my birthday. It did me in. I'll pass for now, thanks." Jim fingered another bottle. "This looks like a plunger."

"Didn't come to mind when I'd picked it out. The image is disturbing. Still, I won't let that ruin the taste." His dad's laughter filled the room and then abruptly halted. "Hm, I guess it's not so funny."

"That's an interesting painting." Jim pointed above the liquor table. "Looks like different color squares put together to make a guitar?"

"You are correct. It's a Cubist work by a local artist who is inspired by Picasso. Suzy picked it out after I told her about Sintra and Peter's interest in guitars."

Jim squinted at the artist's signature, *Veasey*, and then moved away. "I noticed the photograph Aunt Yara took is still in my old room with a new frame and description."

"Yes, Veasey's painting and Yara's photo are Suzy's way of showing she appreciates my past life." His dad sighed. "She's worked hard at mixing traditional and contemporary ideas together. Overall, it's fine. Although, I did tell her my books are off-limits." Sitting back behind the desk, his dad took a swig of whiskey and peered over the rim of his glass. "Enough chit-chat. How are you?"

"Tolerable, Pop." Jim paused, thinking he rarely called him Pop anymore. "Lots on my mind."

"I'm sitting around like a bump on a log. I don't have any pro bono clients showing up tonight, so we have time. Have you eaten?"

"Yes, on the way in."

Suzy entered the room with a tray of goodies. "You boys want some pecan pie?"

"Thank you, sweetheart. We'll get to it later. James Michael and I are going to talk first."

She put the tray on a table by the window, tiptoed away, and closed the door behind her.

"Why haven't you two gotten married?"

"Long story." His dad wrinkled his nose before continuing. "Since your mama and I were married in the Catholic Church, remarrying after our civil court divorce is a bit of a problem. The church won't recognize our divorce unless we pay for an annulment."

"Annulment?"

"The church doesn't believe in divorce. They do some mumbo-jumbo to declare the marriage never existed in the first place. The process takes a year or so to complete and it's expensive."

"Money shouldn't be the issue." Jim was trying to remain calm, but he wanted to shout. "Would the three of us—Christina, Melanie, and me—be declared illegitimate by the Catholic Church?"

"Good question. I'm not sure."

"Mama never wants to talk about your split. She gets this sad, distant look on her face whenever I ask and side-steps the question. Eventually, Melanie and I gave up asking."

"We all have our ways of dealing with misfortune. I still love her. There's room in my heart for Suzy, too. Annulling a marriage seemed wrong to me, so I didn't go through with it. The priest thinks I'm living in sin. So be it. Suzy and I could have gotten married in a Protestant church, but doing so didn't seem like the right decision either. I didn't want to live alone for the rest of my life. Your mother made her choice. You know, I did try to change her mind."

"Well, I like Suzy. Maybe you could marry her at the courthouse?"

"Now, son, I'm sure you didn't come here to talk about my marital status. What's really on your mind?"

Here we go. Jim wasn't sure where to begin, but jumped right in with a positive vibe.

"Well, Dad, I'm tired of dealing with Mama's altered reality, along with working in an amusement park. I've built every prop and stage they've wanted for a little over five years. Enough is enough. Last week, one of my peers, with a higher title than mine, came by a cart I was pushing in the corridors and tossed the crap on the floor. Then he told me to pick it up. I almost punched the dude in the face. As you say down South, I was madder than a wet hen."

"As I say? You don't?"

"I got picked on in school for my Southern accent, so I adapted to blend in."

"Hmm, you shouldn't hide your roots." His dad responded with a shrug. "So, why do you reckon the guy shoved your cart over?"

"Before the incident, our boss said I could have two weeks off and the dude couldn't."

"He's no gentleman."

"I need to get out of there. I want to go to school full time and get a degree in criminology. Work my way into the FBI." Jim pulled one letter out of his pocket and pushed it across the desk. "I got accepted."

"Of course you did." His dad read the letter and handed it back. "My, my, the University of Georgia. Congratulations!"

"Thanks."

"You've never mentioned this before. Why the change?"

"I want to help people with important things. After all, you're a criminal lawyer. You can't be proud of me these days, and I'm not proud of myself. The Bureau has been on my mind since Christina…"

"Well, son, I'm pleased you've decided to move your life in a different direction." In one smooth motion, James Sr. stood, walked around to the other side of his desk, and hugged Jim. "I've waited a long time for you to make some better decisions."

"Thanks." Jim accepted the hug, took a deep breath, and let it go. His tension dissolved, and he stepped back two paces. "The main reason I came here this time was to talk to you about my options."

They sat down on the leather sofa under the bay window and dug into the pecan pie slices.

"All right." His dad gestured toward the bookcase. "I've got a lot of information I can share with you about casework."

Jim reorganized his thoughts. "That'd be cool. Back to Florida for a minute. Melanie is old enough to work and help with the bills. You never told me why Mama wouldn't take money from you."

"Believe me, I tried. At first, she accepted. However, once she got that wretched campground managerial job, she sent my checks back. It confounds me." His dad stood and paced back and forth across the room. Jim tracked the motion with his eyes. "Why she resolved to downgrade her life, and subject you and your sister to a trailer, is hard to imagine. I tried sending money again last year. She sent it back with a note saying she wouldn't take it because Suzy had moved in with me. There's a different reason every time. Bottom line—your mother doesn't want my help. She can be stubborn."

"Yeah, well, Mama's done some pretty strange things since she dragged us away from here." Jim smirked. "Our altered life in Orlando never seemed right. Last month, the campground's cat died. She sent it out to a taxidermist, saying it was her totem animal from her shaman teachings. It's in the living room now, and smelled like wet animal hair for a while. Until the scent was gone, I welcomed going to work to get a whiff of the chocolate chip cookies from the ventilators."

"I'm sorry for everything. You know that, right?"

"Yes, sir. I do." Jim wanted to steer the conversation back to the trip's original intent. "I need to ask you for a school loan. It's time to take the next step and I can't do it alone."

"Son, in many ways, we do everything alone while moving forward side by side."

"Sure, but…"

His dad's eyes seemed to drift away. "You're a man, no longer a child. I need to tell you about Christina."

"She's gone. I've known she was murdered since the day it happened. I'd rather not know the sordid details. Besides, not to sound cold—what's that got to do with school loans?"

"It's important you understand, even though she died years ago. What I'm about to tell you may affect the path you choose within the FBI and how you use your resources."

"I guess, if you say so."

"Perhaps I also need to explain some things to ease my own concerns."

"Okay." Jim drew out the word.

"Your mama may have told you differently. What I'm going to say is God's truth. You know she blamed me for everything, and I did too for a time. The day it happened—it was my turn to pick up Christina from school. I don't know why I chose that day. We were walking down by the docks. Your sister loved watching the water lap up against the side of the docks. I was indulging her instead of hurrying along in my usual way on a workday because it was the start of her spring break. We passed by a couple of guys I recognized by sight, not name. Christina waved and smiled her cute little grin. Everything was fine for the next ten minutes. She stopped by the edge of the dock and sat down. I started to sit next to her, but just as I did, she fell forward. I grabbed at her dress and missed. I watched her precious little body tumble into the river. I didn't realize right away what happened and dove in after her. The rest…"

"Dad, I know she was shot."

"Yes—the reason—I felt responsible. It should have been me instead." His dad continued to explain the long story.

"Jesus, Dad, I had no idea. The shooter's boss sounds like a twisted nut job." Jim sensed his dad wanted more of a reaction, but he held steady. Christina's death radically altered their lives, and they'd never fully recovered.

"If Christina hadn't been killed, your mama and I would still be together. Every day afterward, we pulled each other further down into despair. Then she decided it wasn't a good idea to keep you and Melanie in Savannah. She gathered you two up and left. I'm sorry for the mess I've made of our lives."

"Dad, it's not your fault." Jim rubbed his neck while trying to figure out how to get back to the topic of his school loan without further upsetting his dad.

Familiar music in the background caught Jim's ear. "Hey, who's playing Mama's piano?"

"Suzy. She played before but stopped ages ago. Recently, she took refresher lessons."

"It's a shame Mama doesn't play anymore. She has given up so much. You and Mama were involved with everything in Savannah. All the parties and community service events. Seems like Suzy has taken over everything and become a twin to Mama's old self."

"That's why I'm with Suzy. She soothes the rough spots in my heart."

They talked about his mama for the next half hour.

"So, Dad, back to why I'm here this time." Jim tilted his head left and right, listening to his neck crack. "I need money for the university. I paid for my classes at the community college in Florida. I need help to keep going."

"That's four hours from here, in Athens," his dad declared. "It would be mighty fine to have you back in Georgia."

"Yes, it would. I could move back here to get in-state tuition. What I've managed to save won't be enough."

"You can live here over the summer and use this address for your paperwork."

"Thanks. I will need more money to stay on campus at the university and pay for the rest of my tuition. Can you help?"

"I could give you enough for an apartment and food. You need to figure out how to do the rest on your own."

Jim pulled on his lower lip. "Really, Dad? Really? With your lifestyle? The tuition is ten thousand a year, and if I get a scholarship, that'll take a big dent out of the amount."

"I imagine. And you're right, I have the money. Except, I have a better idea."

"Like?" Jim didn't appreciate the tone of his dad's voice.

"Were you ever curious about why we sent you to the local military academy? Your mama always said it was because it was better than the schools in the area. I'm sorry I never explained my side. I wanted you to reap the benefits of the discipline they provided."

"Okay, and—"

"Back then, I'd hoped you would go to college and start a career in the military as an officer. Everything changed after your sister died. Now, I'd say your best option is to enlist in the Army. I know—I was a Marine, so I shouldn't tell you to do otherwise. It was because of the military that I became a JAG lawyer and eventually opened my private practice. The Army will train you, pay for your degree with the Montgomery GI Bill, and then off you'll go to the FBI. You're in good shape—you need to keep an open mind and get into a uniform and out of those jeans."

"My clothes are the least of my worries."

"True, true. Do you remember when we drove up to Washington, DC, and visited the Arlington Cemetery?"

"How could I forget? We saw the Iwo Jima Memorial, the Tomb of the Unknown Soldier, and hundreds of rows of marble headstones." The number of lost souls overwhelmed him. These and other monuments, statues, and gravestones washed through his mind, and he realized why he liked them. They helped him remember lives gone by, lives like his sister's.

"I took you, so you'd see what our country has sacrificed."

This was too much. Jim began to pace. Thoughts raced through his mind: *Why does Dad want me to risk my life? He's already lost one child. I know some countries like Israel and Switzerland have mandatory service for all citizens. There must be benefits to having firsthand experience, and perhaps less crime in the communities. Everyone gets out of high school knowing what they'll be doing next. Life sounds easier without so many choices.*

"At one point, I considered the Marines or the Navy. I dropped the idea because I want to get into the FBI as soon as possible with a degree." Jim pulled on his shoulder-length hair and didn't like the idea of it being cut off for service. It was a part of his identity.

"The military is a better route, even though it'll take extra time to reach your goal."

"I'm surprised that's your answer after everything our family's been through." Jim paused and tried not to snap. "This is all unbelievable. Mama wouldn't take your help. Instead, she used a lot of the money I earned, and now I'm stuck. I need to take a walk and think."

"Wait… don't go. I'm sorry. To make amends, do you want to do some bird hunting this weekend? I'm heading up to Statesboro."

"No, Dad. Not helpful." Jim scowled, knowing his dad's decision was likely final. "Next thing, you'll be asking me to play golf. Like I said, I need to take a walk to blow off steam. While I'm gone, please reconsider my request."

"Here's some cash to help while you're in town."

"Thanks, Dad," Jim grumbled, and left the room. In the kitchen, he called his friend Adam and arranged to meet him at the waterfront. On the way out the front door, he punched the porch railing instead of his dad.

Chapter 3

Reunion

JIM HEADED OUT INTO THE NIGHT AND WOUND BACK THROUGH Forsyth Park. He strolled, then jogged, and finally bolted into a full-out run in his jeans. They stuck to his legs and pulled on his skin, but he didn't care. He fell in stride down Bull Street.

After taking a circuitous route to extend the run, he arrived at Chippewa Square. He stopped running at one of his old favorite landmarks—the four lions sitting on their haunches wielding shields to protect the James Oglethorpe monument. He bent over, gasping for air, with his blood throbbing in his ears and his heart pounding. Trying to gain his composure while overcoming a wave of dizziness, he looked at the lion's gaping jaws, recalling how he used to talk to them. Shaking his head in disgust, he waited for his system to calm, and then started to run again until he reached East River Street.

He slowed down the pace along the water's edge and came to an abrupt halt. Christina's smiling face came into his mind when an overhead light reflected off the water's surface. Droplets of sweat moved down his forehead. The salty sweat stung his eyes, and they teared up. Wiping them off, he squinted at the globe on the top of the post. From the fixture, tiny threads of glistening light spilled out like fingers reaching up to the heavens. He'd never imagined one day's events could completely alter all their lives. His family hadn't healed. Instead, they'd pulled veils over their sorrow. Christina's death was tragic enough, but the family's disintegration magnified the emptiness.

A stray dog approached with its tail wagging. His long hair and slender legs resembled a statue from Morrell Park. Later, Jim would take a walk, or a run, to see whether the statue was still there.

"Hello, pal."

The mutt seemed to know him. Before he could make a conscious decision, he was rubbing its ears. It made a rumbling, happy sound in its throat from the attention and a drop of saliva fell off its tongue and landed in a large pockmark in the sidewalk. The familiar smell of fried oysters and sweets from the shops down the road drifted through the air. The mutt turned his head toward the sky and appeared to grin before it trotted off and laid down in front of the pet store.

Looking around, Jim noticed he was right in front of The Warehouse Bar and Grill. He brushed his hand on the side of his jeans to get the dog's oils off and stepped inside. It was early, so it wouldn't be rowdy. There was a sign by the entrance: Coldest, Cheapest Beer in Town.

He smiled, walked inside, and waited for his eyes to adjust to the dim light. At the far end of the dark oak lacquered bar, he saw Adam on a spindle-backed stool in front of a variety of beer taps. His friend's hands hugged a foaming glass of a pale beer.

Jim was in such a hurry to get across the brick floor that he caught his toe and stumbled forward. No one among the dozen clients seemed to notice.

"Hey, buddy." Adam grinned from ear to ear. "It's good to see you in person for a change. You aren't easy to reach on the phone. I leave messages and nothing happens."

"Yeah, I know. Sorry. Phone calls are expensive, and I'm not around the house much." He leaned in and gave Adam a bear hug before sitting down. "So, how's everything?"

"Changes are in the air. Check this out." Adam took a pocket knife out of his jeans.

"Nice," Jim said.

"Mom gave it to me on my twenty-first birthday the other day." Adam flipped it over. "It's engraved on both sides."

"Mighty fine, with your initials. Who's BAD?"

"Blake Adam Donnelly. Remember, he's my father."

"Right, sorry. Interesting gesture on her part." Jim thought back to what had happened between Adam's parents. His mother had left town after high school to attend UC Berkeley and returned to Savannah with a college degree, a baby, and a new last name. The name, legally changed, was for show since they hadn't married before Adam's father had died during a Vietnam war protest. Jim was sure his own parents wouldn't have approved of the situation and would have discouraged their friendship, so he kept the details to himself.

Adam put the knife away and changed the subject. In a drawn-out Southern accent, he said, "Is it raining out there? You're all wet."

"You're a joker."

"Ah, not a compliment. You've wounded me—your best friend." Adam put his hand on his heart and sighed.

"Yeah, right. I ran here full tilt." Jim touched his shirt pocket and realized his letters were damp with sweat.

"From Florida? Shit, you are in good shape."

"Bastard." Jim smirked. "I ran around town after Dad got me riled up."

"Hey, someone has to lighten up the mood around here." Adam patted him on the back. "Order some food."

"I ate already."

"A drink then."

Jim signaled the bartender and ordered a soda. He wanted to ask for something alcoholic, but his stomach felt sick from the run. He hadn't run like that since he was on the cross-country team at Benedictine. While Jim gazed across the bar at the mirror, the bartender caught a whiskey bottle as it flew off the shelf.

The guy cursed into the air and shook his fists.

"Hey, dude, what's going on?" Jim asked.

"Stuff happens," the bartender replied. "It's the ghost's idea of a joke. We're lucky he hasn't killed us with flying stuff."

"Right. Maybe the ghost wants me to have a whiskey. I'm not playing along. I'll have some rum in my Coke instead."

"I'll take a whiskey to chase my beer," Adam chortled.

"Coming right up." The bartender poured some into a fresh glass.

"How's the family?" Adam asked.

"Suzy and Dad seem fine, but it's still weird."

"I figured you'd be used to them in the house together by now."

"It's surreal. Suzy does everything Mama used to, and Mama has changed into a different person. Florida's a drag. Since we left, seven years seems like twenty. It hurt to pay for the train down here, since I have to give some money to Mama every month. When I got here, Dad suggested the military."

"Sucks for you." He lined up his index and middle finger, and pointed them at the door while clicking his tongue. "Didn't you tell me your boss did that instead of pointing one finger at things?"

"Not really relevant at the moment." Jim scratched his head and smirked. "Ah, you're trying to distract me. I'm pretty annoyed with both my parents right now. And, yeah, the two-finger thing is more polite according to my boss."

"Right." Adam switched to putting up his middle finger, laughed, and took a long swig of his drink. "Yeah, well, working at an amusement park is a better job than mine. More happy faces."

"Too many. What's up with you?"

"I'm still working at the docks, unloading whatever I'm told. Nothing new there."

"Is your mama still teaching?"

"Yeah. She's none too happy about my path. Had higher hopes for me." Adam wiped his lips with the back of his hand.

Adam's burger arrived. They sat in silence. Jim thought about his dad's words. The anger was being replaced by a sense of defeat, combined with a surge of determination. Jim looked over the bar at the hundreds of liquor bottles covering the center of the wall on multiple shelves. On one side was a chalkboard with the day's food and drink specials. The other side was plastered with beer adverts and neon signs. He wasn't sure how much more time drifted by before Adam started talking again.

"Hmm, tastes great," Adam said in between bites. "At night, this place rocks. Did you see the stage when you walked in?"

"Nah, too much on my mind."

"All right, so what happened with your dad?"

"I asked him to pay for the rest of college. No deal. He told me to join the military—said they'll pay for my degree in criminology and then the FBI would take me."

"You're shitting me? With his bankroll?"

"That's right. Then he brought up Christina's death. There's a lot more to it than I knew."

"Piling on the shit. What an ass."

"More like expressing his guilty feelings." Jim emphasized the point with a smack of his lips. "So, a few minutes ago, you gave me a funny look. What's really up with you?"

"You're going to laugh. I signed up at the Army recruiters last week. Their pitch was like listening to a car salesman. A whole new life for me. I go to boot camp in less than six weeks, for ten beastly weeks of training at Fort Benning to start. I'm going for infantry—Ranger, if I can qualify. The Army's gotta be better than here." Adam ordered another beer. "You're probably better prepared to join."

Jim let out a bitter smirk. "A couple of years at the local military academy taught me discipline and self-reliance. I'm sure I don't know enough to be in a man's army."

"At least one of us has some experience."

"Do you think they want a lightweight like me?"

"They won't mind if you can get the job done. Besides, boot camp will condition you. That'll be cool, having us both in."

"We could end up stationed together."

"Hard to say. We'll be doing a lot of running." Adam's voice elevated. "You like running, since you ran all the way here."

"Okay, so…"

"So, quit your civilian job and enlist tomorrow. It'll be great. The recruiter will give you a sales pitch and options. Find out which jobs you qualify for that'll help you in the FBI. They'll give you a practice written test to help you decide. There's a pamphlet on financial benefits and bonuses. The recruiter said I'd get some extra money if I got a friend to join."

"How much?"

"Oh, I don't know… more than my current paycheck. Maybe enough to buy some beer."

"I'm sure the girls will love it when you add a beer belly to those muscled arms of yours."

"Fringe benefits of dock work." Adam kissed his bicep. "There's a party tonight on Price Street."

"What?"

"At Mama's. She loves to throw parties for the students. You can stay in my garage penthouse tonight. You wanna come?"

"Sure. Not much happening at Dad's." Jim slapped the counter. "I'll go back there after."

"All right."

"You never told me you ended up living back at home."

"I don't advertise. Let's keep it a secret. Anyway, I needed to save money. At first, it was almost impossible to keep her away. Every night, she brought dinner over."

"She can't resist your charm," Jim sarcastically uttered.

"Whatever. That summer dragged by. Everything got straightened out once the new school year started up at SCAD—sounds like a scab on my arm. Mama had so many students that checking in on me took the back seat." Adam chugged down his beer and ordered another shot of whiskey. "The student party is at the main house. Every time she puts out a donation box for a charity, people add a buck or two."

Jim gulped down the rum and Coke. "Your mama is the best. Mine still goes off the rails."

"What's going on?"

"A little over a year ago, when she turned on the television, something set her off. She started crying and talking about the day the priest came knocking on our door after Christina died. The film had the same thing happening, except it was a policeman. Next thing I knew, she got into shamanism."

"What the hell is that?"

"Sorry, I never told you. Mama was always in earshot when we talked on the phone. It's hard to explain." Jim shrugged. "The shamans get all dressed up in colorful clothing, sing, dance, go into trances in ceremonies, and talk to the world beyond ours through human or animal forms. They say there are ninety-nine gods in the stratosphere. She's out of her mind some days, with her mystic episodes. Other times, it's hard to know what to do when something triggers her tears."

"Crap, doesn't sound like her. Is she doing drugs?"

"Yep. I challenged her, and she said something about ayahuasca. She likes the hallucinogenic experiences within the group setting. Nothing has changed since we talked."

"How does she keep her job while taking that stuff?"

"She manages. I was going to tell Dad, except it won't change anything." Jim ate some peanuts from a bowl on the bar. "After what Melanie and I have seen with Mama, we'll never do drugs."

"A good thing." Adam pushed back his chair. "Let's go. We can get more drinks at the party."

"Okay. Hang on." Jim stood. "I gotta take a leak."

When he returned, he noticed Adam had paid the bill. "Thanks."

"No problem." He started on again about his love life. "Anyway, I met Blaire at one of Mama's parties last year."

"Right, your girlfriend. You told me about her on the phone. An ambitious goddess with a brain."

"And sexy," Adam added. "Let's get out of here."

Stepping outside together, Jim moved sideways with Adam to avoid an argument between two groups of people dressed in formal wear; the men in tuxedos and the women in long gowns. Best Jim could tell, the dispute was over a girl.

They crossed the road. Jim turned back and saw an older woman standing on the edge of the group, wielding an umbrella like a sword. She was poking at them and shouting. He stopped Adam so they could gawk at the scene.

The woman's words barreled out over the hum of the water lapping up against the dock. "Life's too short—go enjoy your party—go on, get out of here, or you'll end up in jail."

Jim flinched. She was the bird-lady from the park.

Chapter 4

The Party

J IM AND ADAM WALKED OVER TO THE PARKING LOT BY THE water's edge to a dirty, dented motorcycle. Adam pulled a set of keys out of his pocket and sauntered toward the bike with a cheeky grin on his face. At the last second, he shifted over to a shiny Harley.

"Nice bike." Jim shoved Adam's shoulder.

"Want a helmet? Blaire won't ride without one, even though she says it messes up her hair. Her blonde curls tumble out every time she takes it off. She's my angel." From a side bag, he produced one helmet and left the second behind. "I don't usually wear one."

"Not a great idea."

"All right, all right." Adam put his helmet on. While standing there, he diverted into a lengthy explanation of the bike's charms, and how he took it cruising on his days off with Blaire.

He couldn't stop talking about her or the bike. Regardless, Jim couldn't help being impressed by the Harley's clean lines.

"Okay, okay, can we get going?" Laughing, Jim eyed the pink sticker on the side of her helmet. He tried to stay cool, thinking Blaire was overly cautious. Then again, maybe not. Adam had always been a bit of a daredevil. *Damn right, he would wear it.* Jim pulled the helmet over his head and fastened the strap under his chin. It was a little tight. Yet, he'd put up with the discomfort for safety's sake. One day, when he had more cash, he could buy a motorcycle. Dreams were always good.

Adam grabbed the handlebars, swung his leg up over the bike, and kick-started the engine before he sat down on the seat. Jim stepped on the peg and swung his other leg over the seat behind his friend. Before he got completely settled, Adam revved the engine, and the bike jerked forward. Jim tilted off-balance and almost fell off before he could grab the bars on the edge of the seat. The stunt exasperated him, but he didn't say a word.

When they arrived at Price Street, after careening around town too fast, Adam pulled into the side driveway. He laughed when the motorcycle's exhaust backfired. Presumably, it was his way of telling his mother he'd arrived. They hopped off the bike and headed toward the house.

The place was always welcoming, even with peeling paint on the wood siding and two lopsided apron skirts under the porch. The steps—twelve; he always counted—creaked every time anyone walked on them. Now, the steps were silent, the paint smooth, and the gates level. Along the newly painted porch floor were two equally new bench rockers on sliders. The front door was open and a fair amount of laughter and loud chatter ebbed out into the open air. Before they could go inside, Mrs. Donnelly emerged.

"Oh, my lucky stars—look who's here." She grabbed Jim and pulled him in for a crushing hug.

"Hello, Mrs. Donn—elley." The top of her head of ash-brown hair reached his chin, and the familiar smell of jasmine wafted up.

"You're such a doll. Let me look at you." She stepped back and tousled his hair. "Those blue eyes—hmm, hmm. I bet you've caught a girlfriend with those?"

"No, ma'am."

"Come on in. The house is full of prospects." It was obvious she reveled in matchmaking. "I saw your father with Suzy at the Kroger grocery last week. She was all dolled-up like your mama used to dress—oh, I'm sorry, I shouldn't have mentioned such a sensitive topic."

"It's okay. I'm not bothered."

Mrs. Donnelly took his arm. "Come along. There are so many people to meet."

Without hesitating, Jim walked along with her. Adam dodged

her skirt, winked at Jim, and beelined through the crowd. A minute later, Jim was standing with two young women. Mrs. Donnelly didn't mince words. She introduced him to Blaire Fairmont, and much to his surprise, Sara Cosgrove. There Sara stood, beyond adorable, in a denim mini-skirt, black tights, and a white T-shirt that accentuated her round breasts. She resembled a princess without exaggerated frills.

A smile of recognition spread across her face.

He hadn't imagined their connection on the train would evolve into a second meeting at a party.

Sara reached out her hand, and he shook it. She giggled and gently pulled him in for a quick kiss on the cheek. Balancing on her toes to reach him seemed effortless.

This was certainly a great beginning to the party.

"My stars—you've met before," Mrs. Donnelly crooned. "Jim, I'll leave you in good hands. I'm sure Sara can introduce you to everyone."

For the next hour, at Sara's request, Jim moved through the guests by her side. They talked to people about classes at SCAD. He hadn't remembered she was studying for degrees in dramatic writing along with art and architecture, but he'd make sure not to forget this time. She was quite precise in mentioning the details of the class while they worked their way through the room. A nerve in Jim's neck twitched. Her enthusiasm was contagious, and he soon relaxed. It helped that he had reached a life plan of his own in the last couple of hours. Both his new and old job created mixed responses. Some raised their eyebrows or smiled, while others voiced their opinions and perspectives on career choices.

"How do you come up with designs in your drafting course?" He asked as they pulled away from a group of people.

"Imagination. I think of what it would be like to be around the building and invent people who don't exist. Mix it up with some history, and I can start sketching out a plan. It's on paper, so if I don't like it, I throw it out and start over. It's fun."

"Hm, makes sense. I don't have that kind of talent."

"I've been drawing forever. Hey, there's some punch over yonder." Sara motioned to a table by the kitchen.

"Sounds good." He put his hand against the small of her back, and they wove across the room. At the table, he picked up a long-handled serving spoon, scooped some red liquid out of a punch bowl, and tipped it into two teacups on the table. He passed one to Sara.

She took a sip. The red liquid left a line across her upper lip, which she wiped off with the back of her hand. "Oh, my goodness, it's spiked. I'm not much of a drinker."

"I'm not a fan of punch."

"I wonder if a student snuck in some vodka or moonshine. It's not something Mrs. Donnelly would do."

While thinking Adam could have done it for a laugh, Jim only said, "It's a mystery."

"I won't bother trying to figure it out," she replied, and took another sip.

He picked up a card off the table. "Hmm, this says, *Terrapin Soup.* I don't eat the stuff."

Sara made a face. "Turtle? No thanks. I'd rather watch them on the beach."

"I'm right there with you."

"My favorite turtle time is watching them lay eggs. No, maybe not. What I love more is watching their babies scurry away from the nests into the ocean." She grabbed a different card. "Now this one says *Honey Bread.*"

"That's better. I like honey. My uncle has beehives." He scanned another. "This one says, *All the dishes inspired by the Junior League ladies.*"

"She probably has friends in the group. The League must be the theme for the party this round." Sara took a plate and put some spinach pie on it. "I'll pass on the jellied chicken and go for the jambalaya. Oh, I must eat some of these Irish lace cookies. And a French butter one. All delicious."

"Deviled eggs, pecan pie. The biscuits and meat look good. I'll try some of this wild boar. The flier over yonder says fried oysters are cooking on a fire out back." Jim laughed. "Adam's mama has gone wild."

Sara giggled. "You're a hoot."

"Nah, not me." Jim scooped some shrimp and grits onto his plate. He passed on the okra and fried green tomatoes. Then, as an afterthought, added some cornbread and collard greens.

"On the train, you said you were meeting with your dad. How'd it go?" Sara's voice curved up an octave.

"Not as I'd planned."

"I hope things get better."

"Thanks, I'll be fine." He put his glass on the side table. "So, whereabouts do you live?"

"Blaire and I live in an apartment in a brownstone. It works out well since we grew up together in Charleston."

"Anyone else live there?"

"The owner lives in a separate area in the front half of the building. He used to be a lawyer—now he's an artist. He makes bright colored, life-size primitive paintings, and some geometric ones. Blaire, Adam, and I barbeque in the yard with him sometimes. We all get along great."

"Cool."

"Are there lots of rules where you work?"

"Yeah, lots. Let's go outside on the front porch." Jim grabbed her hand and headed for the door. He figured taking her hand wouldn't faze her since she'd kissed him. They sat down on the two-person rocker.

"Do you know what that color means?" She pointed at the porch ceiling.

"No, what?"

"It's haint blue. The stories say the paint is mixed with lime to keep wasps and mosquitoes away—and evil spirits."

"I think the paint gets some help from sparrows—they eat mosquitoes. I'm not sure I believe a color can chase spirits away."

"Keep an open mind," Sara encouraged.

"Here's another one." He pointed to the wall at the edge of the garden by the public sidewalk. "Stone walls, once upon a time, had glass shards on top of them to protect the houses from thieves. If anyone tried to hop the wall, it became a bloody experience worse than barbed wire."

"Scared evil spirits away, too." Sara laughed. "I hear having one empty drawer—a ghost box—in your house will make the good spirits feel welcome."

"Today's been great. And Mrs. Donnelley's food is delicious."

"Yes, to both points."

"Right." He pulled his hair back into a ponytail with one hand. "I look like Robin Hood, yes?"

"No, I hope not. He's a thief."

"You're right, I'm no thief," Jim joked. "Let's see. Everyone's long hair at work must be tied up unless their characters have loose hair. If I had any tattoos, which I don't, they would have to be concealed. If I needed glasses, I would have to get contacts. Everyone wears a uniform or a costume. No sour faces permitted."

"Well, some rules make sense," Sara said.

"I suppose. Everyone who works there wants to take photographs of the up-and-coming features before the public sees them to show their friends, but they can lose their jobs if they do."

A light reflected from the porch sconce into Sara's eyes. He wanted to kiss her, but held back for reasons he couldn't explain, even to himself. "I like working in secret. The only time I'm in public is when a ticket or concession staff member calls in sick. When I'm there, I need to be 'all knowing', so I can answer the visitors' questions." He went on explaining all the nuances of his workplace for the next half hour.

"Whoa, you missed telling me most of these things on the train."

"It's not widely known, and I don't usually share this stuff." Jim winked. She didn't seem to notice.

"Now that I'm thinking about it, you told me a little."

"Did I tell you…"

"Whoa! More?" Sara giggled. "Okay, tell me. Is there going to be a test later?"

"Could be… always best to be prepared."

"Ha, ha, now you sound like a Girl Scout. Sorry, a Boy Scout."

"I know what you meant."

Sara lightly punched his shoulder for no apparent reason.

"Ouch, be gentle with me." He twisted his lip to bring out a dimple. "No need to be mean."

"Oh, stop. That didn't hurt." She moved the porch swing with her foot.

"Would you like to take a walk with me?" Jim asked.

"Mm, we'll see. Wait here." She disappeared for a long five minutes before returning with Adam and Blaire.

"Does a Tybee Island beach walk sound good?" Adam asked.

"I'm sure I'd fall asleep riding on the back of your motorcycle tonight." Blaire giggled. "And how are all four of us going to fit?"

"Now," Sara choked out the words in a hearty laugh, "that's a scary image."

Jim couldn't help but join in. A laugh came up from his belly.

When everyone had subdued their uproarious laughter, Sara said, "Land's sake, I can barely breathe. Okay, okay. To continue the beach plan—Blaire's car is a couple of blocks away. You all game?"

"Let's go." Jim looked sideways at Adam and wondered how this situation was going to unfold. They'd hung out alone, but never with girls.

They sauntered around the block, Adam and Blaire in the lead, walking side by side. Jim took the clue and stayed behind with Sara. Two blocks later, they found the car. Jim opened the door behind

Blaire. Sara climbed in and slid across the seat. He jumped in and closed the door. Adam started the engine, turned the car out of the parallel spot, and careened away from the curb. With the jolting motion of the car, Jim slid into Sara.

"Adam, take it easy." Sara straightened her skirt. "I'm turning into a pancake back here."

"Good move, man. You're making the lady uncomfortable," Jim piped in.

"Just trying to help." Adam laughed.

"We'd like to survive the thirty-minute drive to the beach." Blaire didn't sound impressed by the theatrics. "Stop showing off."

"Okay, sweetheart. Sara, has Jim told you about one of his rescue missions at work?" Adam didn't wait for her to answer. "There's a wild ride of spinning teacups. Jim was walking by with a cart full of souvenirs and heard a little girl screaming. She was trying to get off the ride when it started and her shoelace got stuck. Jim saved the day by taking the girl's shoe off before the ride sped up and dragged her around."

"It was nothing. The girl's mother thought otherwise and hugged me." Jim shrugged. "Damn, Adam, you're making me sound like a dork. Sorry, Sara."

"Hey, it's fine. I like hearing about your work," Sara encouraged without hesitation.

Jim felt he could fall hard for Sara, but he had to hold back. Relationships didn't always work out for him.

"Yeah, well, that's not entirely a true story." Jim held his hand up and said, "Adam, no more. You're such a…"

"Okay, I'll shut up and get us to the beach alive," Adam retorted.

On the rest of the drive down Highway 80 to Tybee Island, neither Jim nor Adam spoke. The girls talked about the upcoming school year while Jim listened. Outside the car's windows, on either side of the shrub-lined road, the river shimmered. Four distinct tones of blue rippled across the surface as the water took the long meandering path to the Atlantic Ocean.

They slid out of the car at the parking area near Second Street, walked toward DeSoto Beach, and crossed over the dunes. Jim pointed out a sign and read it out loud, "Venomous Snake Nesting Area." Adam, Blaire, and Sara were practically on top of him, trying to avoid the invisible snakes.

Adam gave Jim the evil eye, and they all walked single file along a wooden bridge across the dunes.

"It's a wonder anything grows," Sara said.

"The low dips in the dunes are at the water level. I guess the plants suck up what they need from there."

Light from the full moon emphasized the rye-colored grasses, bending in the breeze. When they stepped off the bridge, they turned toward the unpopulated section of the beach. Adam lagged even farther behind with Blaire, and the gap expanded to a quarter mile. Jim imagined his friend had an ulterior motive, but didn't complain. He wanted to see what Sara was like without other people around.

A light from a freight ship flickered out in the ocean. Some whitecaps closer to shore, combined with the moon's reflection, revealed a pod of dolphins breaching the surface. Taking Sara's hand, he pointed to the dolphins and mentioned how beautiful the evening had turned out while hoping she realized he was trying to compliment her. She smiled, but kept her gaze on the dolphins. Nevertheless, he was satisfied with how things were working out between them as they bantered back and forth. While they continued down the waterline, barely out of reach of the oncoming waves, he mulled over what he might say next.

"Jim?"

"Yes?"

"We met on the train earlier today, so I probably shouldn't ask if you have a girlfriend."

"Oh." Jim cleared his throat. "No, I don't. Are you applying for the job?"

"Don't tease," Sara responded. "The jury's still out."

"I sense you have more questions." Jim walked on, noticing Adam and Blaire weren't as far back as they had been. Stepping up the pace, he squeezed, and then released Sara's hand. The advance didn't go unnoticed.

In the background, Adam hooted, "Way to go! Kiss her."

"Don't pay any attention to him," Blaire called out.

"Sorry, Sara," Jim said. "He doesn't mean any harm."

"It's okay." Sara took Jim's hand back into hers. "So, tell me…"

"What?"

"About your old girlfriend."

"Old. That sounds about right."

"Oh?" A large wave crashed on the shore. Sara's voice escalated. "What do you mean?"

The recollection stung. "She's older than me. I thought she was my girlfriend, but she really wasn't."

"A cradle-robber?"

"No, not exactly. She's only five years older than me." Jim rolled his shoulders. "She—she lives near Orlando. She taught me things."

"What things?"

"Really? You want to know?"

"Sure, why not."

Jim paused. He wasn't going to talk about sex. "Okay, I'm stalling. Do you want the specifics?"

"Umm, no." Sara made air quotes. "I'm old-fashioned."

"Good to know. I don't want to be around anyone like her again."

"What happened?"

"Six months in, I found out she was married and ended it."

"Walking away from her tells me a lot about you."

"I guess." He picked up a smooth stone and skipped it across the ocean's surface. "Your turn—are you involved with anyone?"

"Nope. I've dated, but never had a boyfriend. Let's talk about something else." Sara sashayed forward, flicking the sand with her tennis shoes, and jumped over a small whitecap. "I love horseback riding on the beach."

"Oh, you are changing the subject."

"Nothing more to say about the other stuff."

"Okay, go on. Tell me more about the."

"I like to ride at a public barn on the outskirts of town. Blaire and I leased a horse named Tobias for a while. He has the kindest blue eyes, like yours."

"You're comparing me to a horse, thanks." He snickered. "There's a hotel by the river that was built on top of an old horse stable. It was a long time ago. Some of the horses hid inside during a fire instead of running out. They didn't survive. It's supposed to be haunted by their ghosts. People say they've heard hooves stomping around during the night."

"You're making me sad. Don't tell me any more ghost stories tonight."

"Okay, then here's a different kind." Jim made a horse snorting noise with his lips flapping. "My Uncle Jorge has horses in Portugal, but I haven't been there since I was a kid." He grabbed imaginary reins and trotted forward three paces. "His favorite horse, and mine, is a gelding called Rolan."

Jim left the conversation there to simmer in her mind. He knew the importance of being a horse person and hoped the connection between them would grow.

Chapter 5

The Date

EVERY OTHER DAY, HE PHONED SARA, EVEN THOUGH THEY had already set a date to meet at the end of the week. By mid-week, he had gone to the Army recruitment office. The experience was not as nerve-racking as he'd expected, thanks to the abundance of information he'd received from Adam. The recruiter seemed decent enough and said it would be at least six weeks before Jim would be sent to boot camp.

The next day, he phoned work and told them he wouldn't be returning and why. Calling his mama wasn't as easy. She was less understanding and said she'd be calling his dad to tell him off. Safety continued to be her main concern. Once she'd had time to adjust to the idea, their phone calls became more relaxed, and she consoled herself by fixating on Sara instead of his career goals.

To get his exercise program started, Rex became Jim's responsibility, which included multiple daily walks and light jogs. When he wasn't with Rex, he'd do calisthenics or wander around town. One evening, after Adam finished his shift at the docks, they agreed to start working out together in a week's time.

Finally, the scheduled day arrived to meet Sara for lunch and take a trip to an art museum. The idea of going to the galleries wasn't appealing, and he wasn't sure why he'd agreed to go during their first official date. Even though he'd read many fantasy books, which required imagination, he couldn't translate the concept into paintings. Nevertheless, he devised a covert scheme for their date. His dad's connections in the art world would come in handy, and he could set up a surprise for Sara with his dad's help. Recalling back to the family trip to DC when his parents were still together, Jim had walked with them through a few art museums at the Smithsonian. He'd preferred the guided tour of the Treasury Department, the FBI, and the Pentagon.

On his way to meet Sara, the walk across Forsyth Park was uneventful. The bird-lady was sitting on her bench and the musician was playing his trombone. Arriving at the intersection of East Park Avenue, he turned left and crossed the street over to the café, where he hoped Sara would be waiting.

She wasn't there. The hunger in his belly overruled his desire to wait for her by the door. He moved to the end of a long line and inhaled the aroma of onions caramelizing on the stovetop. Other than the smell of cooking bacon, this was his favorite. He had a hankering for meat, except the day's menu was vegetarian.

Sara popped up beside him. "Hi. I put my jacket on a chair to save a table."

"Hello. Great. Good to see you. Menu's pretty extensive." He gestured up toward the chalkboard.

"I love vegetables, but I eat meat and fish too." Sara tittered. "Oh, wait, you know that from when I ate seafood at Mrs. Donnelly's."

"I'll eat most anything on a plate, but not turtles."

"Turtles, nope… I remember."

They both ordered sandwiches with squash on the side and a large salad to share, along with individual drinks. The woman at the register passed them two trophies, each with a number painted on the side, to take to their table. She explained the staff used them to get the correct orders to each customer. They settled down in their stiff-backed chairs and waited.

"Hey," Sara whispered. "Did you see the guy in the corner with the dreadlocks? He has a cereal box next to him with carrot greens popping out of the top."

"Nope, didn't notice him." Jim glanced over.

"No, don't. You might make him nervous."

"Can't see how, but it's rude of me to stare." Jim winked. "I'm betting there are carrots hiding in there."

"Let's go to the Telfair Academy after we eat."

"Hmm, I don't know." Jim was teasing at this point because this was the right museum to visit, considering it worked into his scheme.

A woman arrived with their food. On each plate, there was a pile of broccoli, which confused them because they hadn't ordered it. Jim politely spoke up, and the woman walked off with the plates and brought them right back, saying there wasn't much difference between the two vegetables, and they didn't have any squash. She left the plates, brought back two glasses of ice water, and took the numbered trophies away.

"Imagine," Jim said, "a vegetarian menu without squash."

"Jim, this will be great."

"The broccoli?"

"No. I mean, yes, it's fine. I was talking about the museum."

"Right, sorry. I didn't catch the transition."

"Anyway, I went to the Louvre in Paris with my aunt three years ago. The tour guide was awesome."

"How so?" Jim wanted to sound supportive. He liked listening to her voice.

"The guide took us around to the paintings and sculptures. He said to look at the background of the paintings, not just what's in the forefront, and try to figure out the connected stories."

"How does anyone know what is going on when a painting's created?"

"Notes, writings, general history of the time. It's not far off from the same concepts presented in my architectural studies. Details become very important to the pieces' structure."

"Do you have any plans for after graduation? Sorry, I sound like a recruiter with all these questions."

"I don't mind. How else are we going to get to know each other? An architect would be interesting, but I'd need a master's degree. I like this city. A teacher might be a good alternative. I could combine all my interests in English, art, and history at a private or public school.

"I know we talked a little about this on the phone, but I'm sure my internship at the Smithsonian helped my perspective. If people don't learn about the past, they can't make the future better. Just about every day, when I was on breaks from the dungeon's labs, I explored the exhibits and was captivated."

"Captivated, ha, play on words—clever woman. I hope you weren't working in a real dungeon?"

"Not really. The labs were in the basement."

"Oh, dungeons sound cooler. So, what did you do? Doctoring?" He chuckled at his own humor.

"No, silly." Sara drew the word out. "Not much. I spent the summer in the Natural History Museum, setting up silk-screening for the exhibits. The studio shared space with the bird freeze-dry unit. That was creepy. The birds were found dead or donated—not killed by the museum." She put her fingertips on her chin. "I liked the work and loved exploring the art museums."

"At least you figured out what you wanted to do early on. When I visited the Air and Space Museum at the Smithsonian, I thought I liked the space part enough to go into the field. Later, I took the train down to the John F. Kennedy Space Center at Cape Canaveral, and I couldn't connect the way I'd hoped. I figured our planet had enough going on without exploring space, so I dropped the idea and stuck with my original goal."

"The FBI?"

"Right. I guess I mentioned that before."

"Several times. It's fine."

"Until recently, I'd kept the idea to myself because I couldn't figure out how to get started." Jim watched while Sara pulled out colorful bits of salad and dipped them into the cup of ranch dressing before putting them in her mouth. The motions were distracting him from his own meal. Then she washed it down with sarsaparilla soda. The drink made him think of Christina, because it was her favorite. He needed to keep his mind on the present, and refocused on the melodic tone of Sara's voice. Her enthusiasm for even the smallest things warmed his heart.

"I'm not sure I'll get the paintings and drawings. I'll do my best."

He noticed a tuning fork someone had left on the ledge next to them. Picking it up, he tapped the tuner on the table and put it into his glass of water. The fluid vibrated.

Sara giggled. "When I was a kid, my doctor used to put one of those against my knee—and my head. He made me laugh."

"This café has visiting musicians. My cousin, Peter, taught me something about music and guitars." Jim ate a bite of his broccoli, but it was too soft. His face soured. "I have an idea. We can go to a concert sometime—if you'd like?"

"Ooh, a second date?" Sara said playfully and shrugged.

"Absolutely." Jim smiled. "Let's take turns picking where we go."

"I like that idea." Sara's voice drifted away. Then, more strongly, she asked, "Wait. Where does Peter live?"

"In Portugal with his father—my Uncle Jorge. I call him Peter. His name is really Pedro and means rock." Jim impishly smiled. "He's a strong guy."

"You're goofy." Sara stumbled through Uncle's name and turned a slight shade of pink. "Uncle Hor, who?"

"Don't worry. It's almost like saying George around here, but it's spelled J-o-r-g-e. The *J* and *G* make a raspy *H* sound."

She tried again.

"Well done. You're a natural."

"Thanks." Sara jumped up and returned with a monster sized brownie from the counter. "Which side of the family is Uncle Jorge?"

"He's my mama's brother. Lives in Sintra."

"Sorry, I'm stumbling, again. Where?"

"Portugal, southern end. It's outside Lisbon. We flew over every summer. It's an unusual place. Lots of woods with mountainous terrain and historic sites."

"Is it hot there?"

"Yes, but Savannah's hotter."

"I'd like to go someday." She split the brownie and passed half of it over. "What's your uncle's place like?"

"It's right behind an estate called Quinta da Regaleira. It's a magical place."

"Wait. How do you spell Sintra?"

"S-i-n-t-r-a. It can also start with a C instead. It was named after Cynthia, the goddess of the moon."

"Have you ever heard of Antoni Gaudi in Spain? His architecture is surreal."

"Nope, never heard of the man," Jim replied. "I've heard of the word, Gaudi."

"Ah, no, that's a negative term and spelled differently. Gaudi's work has whimsical, organic shapes and is prominent all over Barcelona." Sara raised an eyebrow. "You might like it."

"I'll put Spain on my go-to list."

"Do you speak Portuguese?" She took a huge bite out of her half of the brownie.

"Some, I haven't kept up." He ran his eyes around the café. "Marmalade and molasses."

"What?"

"Sorry, I saw the containers over there." Jim nodded toward them. "Those two words came to the U.S. from the Portuguese language."

"That's interesting. I took Spanish in high school." Sara picked at a splinter on the table and it broke off. "Oops."

"Between the two of us, we are trilingual." He felt rather clever and reveled in the moment. Just as quickly, he chided himself for being pompous.

"I'm no linguist—¿Tienes hambre?" Sara said with a perfect accent.

"Not bad—let's see—there are lots of similar words." His brain was rusty. Still, he realized she asked if he was hungry in Spanish. To mix things up, he threw out a line in Portuguese. "*Não, eu não estou com fome.*"

"None of those words sound like cognates. What'd you say?"

"No, I'm not hungry." He reached over and took the last piece of brownie off her plate to contradict himself.

"Hey, I was going to eat that." She flicked a drop of her ice-water in his direction. It hit him squarely between the eyes.

"I deserved that." He smiled.

"I like spending time with you." Sara took Jim by surprise with the random compliment after his off-the-cuff remarks.

"Me, too. I'm going to miss you when I go off to boot camp in a month or two. I hope all the training Adam and I are planning will be enough."

"Have you considered running on the beach?"

"Beach, yes, but we'll also run around town since it's closer. I've learned about what we'll have to do and it's going to take more than running to keep up. I should get back to swimming. That was one good thing about my old job. They have a swimming pool I used when the park was closed and I wasn't working, except I prefer playing in ocean currents." Jim pulled himself up a little straighter in his seat. "Can I write to you when I'm gone?"

"I like the idea." Sara reached across the table and squeezed his wrist.

"How does Blaire feel about Adam's enlistment?"

"She's okay, but she worries about his safety and being apart." Sara hesitated. "Back to Sintra. Tell me more."

"Okay. Uncle Jorge taught me a lot when I was little. He's smart and a little odd at times. A year after my aunt died, he sent me a photo of his new look. He'd grown his hair out to mourn his wife's death. Both he and Peter were messed up for quite some time. Aunt Yara's death didn't affect me the same way, even though she meant a lot to me, too."

"I'm sorry. You all must miss her."

"Yes, we do. My parents didn't tell me the details until much later."

Sara pushed her chair back and stood. "Let's go to the museum. This serious talk is…"

"Sorry."

"No, no… smaller doses are all I'm asking."

They scraped their food crumbs into the trash bin and put the plates on a cart. Sara almost forgot her jacket. Jim scooped it up and handed it to her before they exited through the glass door.

Outside, a guy their age was standing on a square plot of grass with a puppy. People passed by, and he called out, "Does anyone want a puppy?"

"What kind?" someone shouted.

"Bernese Mountain dog."

"How old?" Sara asked.

"Two months. I have three more at home," the guy replied.

The black-and-white patched fur ball nuzzled against Sara's outstretched hand. Jim hadn't talked with her about animals, but this was another side of her he liked. She sat down on the curb by the grass and the puppy crawled into her lap.

"He likes you." Jim stated the obvious.

"I grew up with dogs and cats. It's too bad I can't have any in our apartment. My goldfish doesn't count." Sara massaged the pup's ear. "I don't know what Blaire would think, either."

Jim watched the scene unfold, and butterflies filled his stomach. Options raced through his head. Perhaps he could adopt the puppy and take it to Suzy. Yet, his dad wouldn't appreciate having a new animal tossed into their life. Rex would have to deal with a young one pulling on his ears. On the other hand, if Suzy and his dad agreed, Sara could visit the pup and take it when she lived somewhere else. An alternative popped into Jim's mind. He could let this pup go and become a combat dog handler in the Army. All nice ideas, but fleeting ones. Spur-of-the-moment decisions were something to avoid, and he had to stay focused on his career goals. No matter how he spun this, they had to walk away.

Sara removed the puppy from her lap while it whimpered and wiggled.

"I'll take you to meet my dad's dog at some point."

"I'd like that," Sara replied.

The puppy's owner tried to smile. "So, no puppy today?"

"No, I'm sorry," Sara said. "Give me your phone number, in case I change my mind or know anyone who could take one."

The guy scribbled his number down and passed it over.

"Thanks, and good luck," she said.

Jim reached out to help Sara to her feet. She took his hand, and once she was upright, he kissed the back of her hand. "Sorry, that can't work out."

"Me, too." She kissed him on the cheek. "You're sweet."

He smiled a tight-lipped grin and gazed into her eyes. Resisting was impossible. The puppy-kid was a few feet away, but Jim acted on impulse. He leaned in and kissed her square on the lips. She didn't pull back. This kiss was like no other. His body tingled, along with the pounding of his heart. When they moved apart, he took her hand. They walked down Price Street, away from the restaurant, the park, and the puppy.

Halfway down the block, Sara said, "You're a good kisser."

"Thanks. Likewise."

"So, tell me more about Uncle Jorge."

"Sure thing." He sighed. "I'm beginning to think you like him more."

"Oh, stop."

"Okay, I'll stop." Jim was enjoying himself.

"Humor me."

"Okay. Uncle Jorge is a burly guy, like a football player. Taking care of his horses and farm made him that way. He's also smart and has an enormous collection of books. Some of them are signed, original copies. I can ask him about anything, and he usually has an answer."

"A walking information system?"

"Yes." Jim laughed. "He's around forty-five. I haven't seen him since my parents split."

"I hope you can go back."

"Yeah, me too."

"What happened?" Sara asked.

They walked on in silence until they reached a bench in front of the museum and sat down near the gift shop entrance.

"Oops. I shouldn't have asked, since we agreed to take sad things slowly," Sara said. "Let's sit a spell."

Either way, Jim wasn't ready to let her into every part of his life. "I have a happier story. On one of my Sintra visits, buckets of rain came down over the weekend. On the way out to the barn, we heard eerie singing. Inside, there was an army of crawdads crawling into the aisle all the way up from the pond. They were our singers. Peter and I scooped the critters into buckets and put them back. Uncle Jorge didn't know why they were trying to escape, other than to avoid getting caught and dumped into his dinner pot. Crawdads aren't clever. We laughed so hard."

"I can imagine. Will you tell me about Aunt Yara someday?"

"Yes, I will. But I have a surprise for you at the museum. I found a way to get us into the area where they keep everything that's not on display. Follow me…"

"But you didn't want to come."

Jim winked and led her to the front desk. "Hello. I have reservations."

The attendant looked up at him. "Your name?"

"Masterson. Jim Masterson."

"Ah, yes. Please come this way to the museum's sanctum sanctorum."

He looked slyly over at Sara, and her eyes widened in surprise. She punched his shoulder, and he flinched in mock pain.

Chapter 6

Working Out

JIM AND ADAM HAD ALREADY RUN TOGETHER A FEW TIMES and had built themselves up enough to have regulated their breathing, which made conversation easier. Jim was glad he had a month longer than Adam to prepare for boot camp. This morning, they scheduled a run that would evolve into an intense workout. In ten days, they were obligated to gather with other recruits by the Morrell Park docks to test their progress.

Rex began whining at the door before Jim left the house in his track shoes and baggy knee-length shorts. It hadn't taken the dog long to get into the morning routine. Suzy handed Jim a leash so he could tie Rex up during calisthenics. Jim took it reluctantly, because Rex had stayed close and not been distracted by anything on their previous outings. They headed out the front door at a walk, and a block later converted into a slow jog. As planned, man and dog came alongside Adam half a mile into the run around the edge of Forsyth Park's thirty acres.

"Hey, Adam," Jim said.

"I've already run around the park once. It's only a mile," Adam replied. "How's Rex doing?"

"Great, but there's no way he can handle too many rounds at this pace." They continued, intending to go three times around and work up to six.

"We've gotta work up to seven-minute miles." Adam gestured at Jim's shorts. "Did you take my advice and wear spandex under those?"

"Yep. Thanks for the tip. Gotta keep my *boys* in place. Added some baby powder, too."

Adam laughed and wiped sweat off his own face. "Can't have them escaping. So, did you get more intel from the recruiter?"

"Yeah, he's a decent dude. I took my ASVAB pretest and qualified. I guess he's happy with me. The man said he'd drive me all the way to Atlanta for MEPS since there isn't one here."

"What? Atlanta's hours from here. He didn't say he'd drive me."

"He must like me." Jim grinned.

"That might be a problem."

"Whatever." Jim snickered. "He said there are four of us going, and he has some business in Atlanta."

"Get all the information you can out of him."

"I hope I can make it through the training."

"You'll be fine."

"Let's hope." Jim took a deep breath in through his nose and out through pursed lips. This pattern worked well until he had to speak, which he did through the exhales. The process was almost like meditating. "You'll be a great Ranger. Sucks that we'll be split up. I won't know anyone."

"I could still be on the same base, even though I'll be in a different processing area."

"Now we sound like machines—processing," Jim said.

"Toughen up, dude. More like meat processing." Adam spit on the grass.

"We're hysterical." Sarcasm dripped off Jim.

"Yeah, a laugh a minute."

"Only one per minute?" Jim signaled to Rex. "Come on, boy, keep up." The Lab's tongue hung out of his mouth, and he was smiling as only a dog can.

"Let's cut this run short and pop into the park when we hit a little over two times around." Adam looked down at Rex. "I don't want him to keel-over."

"I doubt he will, but his paws might get torn up on the pavement," Jim said.

"Rex seems fine. You might collapse."

"Oh, thanks. He's not used to running this much. We've gone out at night for up to a mile at a time."

"Looks like it's easy-peasy for him now… We've got some sit-ups and crap to do… He can watch."

They slowed down to a walk, veered into the park, and found a water fountain. Rex fell into a puddle. There was an empty dog bowl bolted to the ground, waiting for thirsty canines. Jim filled it from the spigot, and Rex lapped up half the contents within seconds. Jim took him over to a tree and tied him up near the kids' playground. Almost on cue, three kids ran over, asking to pet his smooth coat.

"Okay." Adam pulled a piece of paper out of his shorts pocket. "Let's get to it. I need the max score. Eighty sit-ups, seventy push-ups, twenty pull-ups, and—here, look at this card. It has ten different things to work on. If you train for more than you need, your test will be a piece of cake."

Jim took the card. "Gross. It's sweaty."

"The drill sergeants will expect us to do our best and then some. They'll break us down and build us up again. It's all about total self-discipline and strength, inside and out."

"This sounds a little like my time in military school. Whoopee. Yeah, the recruiter mentioned that. Let's take turns coaching each other through the circuit."

"You go first," Adam said in a commanding voice.

Jim gave Adam the evil eye and contemplated jostling his friend about, but didn't bother. He needed to get accustomed to taking orders from a drill sergeant, so this was good practice. Lying face-down on the grass, he began with twenty plank push-ups. Then he flipped over onto his back with his knees up, his heels to his butt, and his hands behind the base of his neck. Adam held down his feet and the sit-ups began. Once done, Jim got up and Adam took his place without needing his feet to be held down.

"Hey, the dock work got you into pretty good shape. Hang on, I'll get a few boulders and put them on your stomach."

"Won't even slow me down." Adam bicycled his legs back and

forth, followed by a series of crunches. A few minutes later, he was up on his feet, shaking out his hands and jogging in place. "Next task. Your turn."

"Right, let's see what else I can do." Jim squatted a few times up and down with his hands straight out in front. He didn't admit to Adam that he'd been practicing before they took on the calisthenics together. A few lunges later, Jim got down on the ground and completed the rest of the circuit.

"Hey, man, you're supposed to be out of shape." Adam slapped Jim on the back. "We still need to up our numbers to beat the PT test. Let's try the monkey bars. Looks like the kids are staying away from there."

"Did the recruiter tell you we're going to Fort Benning after MEPS?"

"Yep." Adam grabbed the lowest bars on the kid's set and pulled his chin above the bar.

"Cheater. Take the taller one." He watched Adam switch over and start for real. "Go, go, go. Two more, two more."

Letting go, Adam planted his feet on the ground. "Okay, that's twelve for me. Let's see what you've got."

"In a minute." A sort of flashback occurred to Jim. "Do you remember coming to Forsyth on our own when we were kids?"

"Sure do. Kids aren't allowed to roam without their parents anymore. Puts a damper on their imagination."

"I need less of one," Jim said.

"One, what?" Adam plucked a blade of grass out of the lawn. He put it between his interlocked palms and whistled out a shrill tone.

"A less active imagination." Jim grimaced. "There could be dried dog piss on the grass."

Adam dropped the blade on the ground, laughing.

Jim rubbed his hands on his back, preparing to leap onto the bar above his head, but then changed his mind. Instead, to avoid the inevitable, he kept talking. "You must have thought I was nuts talking to statues when we were kids?"

"Nah. Like you said, we were kids. I didn't think much of it. I talked to my plastic soldiers. Not much difference between them."

"I guess. My sisters used to talk to their baby dolls."

"Christina, poor kid. She was so sweet." Adam tilted his head forward before looking back at Jim. "Sorry, man, I shouldn't have brought it up. The thing is, we must remember the people we've lost. If we don't, it would be like they never existed."

"I'll never forget. That's the entire reason I quit my job in Orlando. I need to catch or stop the bastards who don't value life beyond their own. I'm worried it'll be a decade before I can get into the FBI, between the military and earning a degree."

"Better late than never," Adam retorted. "Take some more prerequisite college courses while you're serving."

"Good idea. I'll check into it." Jim sighed. "I also have to write Mama a check before boot camp and tell Melanie it's her turn to help pay the bills."

"You're right. There's no way to pay bills from boot camp." Adam shoved Jim. "Stop talking. Jump up and do your reps. The bar can't wait all day for your chin. Besides, those slacker skateboarders are looking over at us. We need to set a good example."

"No, they're not. They're going the other way." Jim leaped into the air, grabbed the bar, and pulled his body up. He couldn't get his chin above the bar. It felt like it was miles away, not inches. Groaning and wiggling his legs didn't elevate him any further.

As Jim struggled, Adam changed his tactic and chimed out letters of the alphabet. "Alpha is for A. Bravo is for B... M for Mike..." Before Adam got to *O*, Jim landed on the ground in a crouched position in defeat. To hide his embarrassment, he finished the cadence with Adam. "Q for Quebec, R for Roger... Z for Zulu." When the alphabet was done, Jim went over to Rex and untied him. Adam lagged in the rear and then caught up.

Jim vowed to come back to the bars twice a day to try again, knowing in time, the chin-ups wouldn't be an obstacle. While the three of them walked back down the length of the park, Adam tested him.

"What is one in the afternoon in military time?" Adam asked.

"1300 hours."

"Two?"

"1400 hours…" Jim shot them off until he listed them all up to midnight, better known as RADAY.

Adam changed gears and stated the order of military ranking, beginning with private and ending with a five-star general. Right before they headed home in different directions, they chanted out the Soldier's and Infantryman's Creed. Jim understood neither of them wanted to be caught not knowing all they could before signing on the dotted line at in-processing.

Chapter 7

More Time

IT HAD BEEN OVER A MONTH SINCE JIM AND SARA HAD MET. They'd spoken on the phone and seen each other multiple times. To prepare for their next date, Jim shaved in his old bathroom, which hadn't been redecorated, and put on a fresh set of clothes. This would be one of their last dates before boot camp and his neck was tensing up.

Downstairs, he pushed through the swinging door into the kitchen. A new Wolf gas range had been installed on the left side of the room. Its red knobs and black burners stood out from its silver casing. On the right, the cavernous hearth had a new set of fake logs and gas jets to turn on the flame whenever they wanted. Above the mantel hung an unfamiliar stag's head, complete with antlers. Knowing his dad, the rest of the beast was in the pantry in a freezer in multiple packages.

While Jim made two chocolate-malt milkshakes, Rex lapped up the water in the corner bowl and then began to bark.

Suzy popped in to see what was going on. "Good afternoon, Jim. Your outfit looks nice, but your hair's all wet and raggedy. Here, I'll fix the stragglers." She tucked a piece of his hair behind his ear and smoothed out a curl on the top of his head.

"No point. It follows its own path. Boot camp will take it all away."

"I would have only suggested a trim." Suzy opened the refrigerator. "Here you go. How 'bout some whipped cream on the shakes? Then a red-and-white swirled candy stick to turn your date's shake into a masterpiece. And use these paper cups. She'll love it. Put a straw in yours for now, to avoid suspicion."

"She?"

"As nice as you look, I assumed it wasn't for Adam."

"No, he left a few days ago for boot camp. Sorry, I didn't tell you. So, you're right, the milkshake is for a girl. I met Sara on the train."

"Lovely." Suzy handed him two plastic spoons. "Take these. They'll work better since the shakes are thick."

His dad marched into the kitchen with a manila envelope. "Son, I have all your documents in here for the recruiter."

"Wait. What?"

"Your vaccination records and a certified copy of your birth certificate. I've had a set here all along. This will be easier than bothering your mama."

"Right. Thanks. I'll run them over to their office tomorrow." Jim took the envelope and placed it on the breakfast table. "I don't mean to rush anyone, but I have to go."

"Yes, yes, he does." Suzy winked. "He's met a young lady."

"Chip off the old block." His dad slapped Jim on the back. "Have a good time."

"Dad, you crack me up. I'm not a lady charmer like you." Jim snickered.

"You'll do fine, I have no doubt."

"Yeah, I know."

His dad started to leave the room.

"Dad, wait a minute. Thanks for letting me stay here before my enlistment."

"You're welcome, James Michael. Make me proud." Both Suzy and his dad left the kitchen, with Rex on their heels.

The extra time talking in the kitchen almost made him late to meet Sara at the corner of Whitaker and East Gaston. Telling her more about his previous life wouldn't be easy, but he needed to explain in person. In turn, he hoped to learn more about her family.

"Hi there." Jim held out the milkshake. "I brought you something."

"Oh, thanks." Sara took it, stood on her tiptoes, and kissed his cheek.

He touched his face and felt the lipstick's waxy imprint. She'd left a mark on him in more ways than one. With a discreet swipe of his palm, he wiped the color off as they began walking side-by-side down the main path toward Forsyth Park.

"Oh, my, the candy stick isn't a straw." She giggled.

"Not a problem." He handed her a plastic spoon. It turned out Suzy had done the right thing. The confusion created a diversion to help him relax.

At the park, they walked toward the main fountain. Along the way, a wrought iron railing discouraged pedestrians from crossing over into the landscaped areas. At the fountain, he noticed a few fish in the water he'd never seen before. A large one popped its head up and made a clicking sound as its mouth opened and closed.

"Oh, weird." Jim pointed at the fish.

"It's a bunch of overgrown goldfish with white spots. Koi, I think. They're begging for the pellets people throw in. It's funny how big their mouths are." She picked up a discarded pellet from the ground and tossed it in.

"I didn't notice any on my last visit, and I know they weren't there when we were kids." Jim chuckled. "They look like they're going to suck up everything around them, along with the pellets."

"They're pretty cool."

"Just like our ice cream?"

"You're silly. Ooh! A brain freeze is coming on. I'm devouring this delicious treat too fast."

"Next time I'll bring something hotter," Jim teased.

"Yeah, okay. What was I saying? Right, I know. I always liked this fountain, with the centaurs blowing water out of their horns. Or maybe they're not centaurs, I can't tell."

"They are confusing. From the front, they look like minotaurs. From the back, mermaids, or serpents. I've never researched them. Did you see the small dragon near the top?"

"I did." She cupped her hand over her eyes and peered up. "Except I think it's a bird."

The cuff on her blouse slipped down and he noticed the tattoo on her wrist, the one he'd seen when they first met on the train. It was time to ask. "Um, I like your tattoo. Does it have a story?"

"Subject shift from statues? But, yes, my tattoo has a story. Everyone's does." She stretched her hand out for him to get a better look. "It's a mix between a bird and a dragon. I meant for it to be all dragon. The red in its eyes matches the necklace my mom gave me. The dragon represents my dad's determination."

"That's cool," Jim said.

"Cool? No, dragons are hot." Sara laughed and didn't offer any other information about her family. Instead, she said, "Okay, back to statues. You seem to be into them, like I am into paintings."

"Always have been. When I was a kid, I imagined they were real. I would wander around, looking for them. Back then, I went to the cemetery in town at Colonial Park. It's a strange place. It always smelled of crepe myrtle or jasmine, even when the flowers weren't in bloom. Anyway, when I was older, I went to Bonaventure more often on my bike. Talk about lots of statues to see."

"I went to the cemeteries for a guided tour with my aunt before I started college," Sara said. "There's a grave I like, made from bricks that resembles a bed. I don't know which cemetery it's in. The designs are fascinating and creepy all at the same time."

"Not to me. I know the caretaker at Bonaventure. His hair is scraggly, and he dresses in old-fashioned clothes—almost looks like the prisoner out of a Charles Dickens novel, but this guy's a harmless soul."

"A ghost?" Sara asked.

"I hope not." Jim started to laugh, then abruptly stopped. History had popped into his mind. There had been and still were large oak trees with branches like arms that spanned across pathways. From them, people had been hung for their perceived crimes. If there were any ghosts in the cemetery, they'd be from traumatic deaths.

"Why? Why do you go?"

"It was something to do, at first. Then I became fascinated by the Confederate and Spanish-American war veterans at Bonaventure. The place used to be part of a plantation. Later, I came to visit my sister's grave, and left little stones on top to let her know I was thinking of her. Who knows if spirits can sense good-intentioned tokens."

"Oh, Jim." Sara gasped and covered her mouth with one hand before continuing. "How did your sister die?"

"I'll get to it."

"I'm sorry. I didn't mean to rush you."

"It's all right. I'll come back around to her story." Jim knew he was being evasive. He couldn't help himself. "Headstones and statues intrigue me. There's at least one sphinx—a man's head with a lion's body. One that means a lot to me is called *Little Wendy*. It's bronze and sculpted by Sylvia Shaw Judson in 1936."

"I haven't seen *Little Wendy*, but I have seen the *Waving Girl* on River Street." Sara pointed at a lion statue's mouth by the fountain. "Oh, look. Odd, this spider web still has moisture on it from this morning's dew."

Jim leaned in and peered at the beast. "Nice. I've tried to take photographs of webs. They never come out right."

"They don't work for me either." Sara touched the sticky web, but no spider scurried forward.

"Also, I like Little Gracie Watson, who died when she was six." Jim paused for a breath. "I researched the younger ones because of my sister."

"That's understandable."

"There's also one with a statue of a pretty woman sitting in front of Corinne Elliott Lawton's gravestone. The statue looks a little like you, my lady."

"Thank you, sir knight." Sara curtsied. "So, go on."

"I found walking through the dirt rows between the graves with the moss waving in the trees peaceful. I only go when it's warm out in the spring and summer. There are flowers all over the grounds and good fishing in the Wilmington River." He paused long enough to take a measured breath. "Have you ever done brass rubbing?"

"Yes, in a cathedral once. Where'd you learn about that?"

"Oh, I started after I watched people put paper over the

gravestones. Some rubbed crayon or charcoal over the paper to bring up the faded words and designs. I bought some supplies with my allowance and started doing the same thing. It took a while to figure out how to get the tape to stick. The paper ripped if I rubbed too hard. After I got the hang of things, it was fun and relaxing."

"Sounds like a demented hobby."

"No, not really. The process gives me perspective on what's important when I'm wound too tight. The stones represent history, and the remains beneath them shouldn't be forgotten. We could try it together sometime."

"Well, maybe…"

Chapter 8

Reveal

JIM FELT SARA TAKE HIS HAND AS THEY CONTINUED WALKING through Forsyth Park. "My Uncle Jorge has an old cemetery at his place in the woods. Some graves go back to the 1800s. There are also unmarked graves in the overgrown field behind it. It's a potter's field."

"A what?" Sara whispered.

"That's a type of cemetery. Uncle Jorge said anyone who didn't have relatives to claim them ended up there—homeless people and prisoners—the police buried them on his land."

"Yikes."

"On a more positive side, the last time I was at Uncle's, random people came by and hung small pieces of colorful cloth on a line strung up between two trees. When I checked it out, there was a different prayer request written on each one. I'm not sure why." Jim paused. "So, here's my other weirdness…"

"You only have one?" she said.

"Good point." Jim ruffled his hair. "When I was a kid, I talked to the earth beneath the gravestones. I apologized to the dead for disturbing them. Other times I talked to the headstones."

"Yep, you're weird. But I still like you."

"Well, thank you." He walked over to a bunch of wildflowers in the park, broke off a few, and handed them to Sara. "My aunt's buried in the cemetery on my uncle's property. She died when I was ten."

"I'm sorry." Sara stopped on the path. There was a swing nearby. She walked over, backed into a seat, and wrapped one hand around each chain. "It must be so hard for your uncle to be without her."

Jim sat on a swing next to Sara. "Yes. Knowing she is nearby helps him, but he couldn't explain why when I asked."

"Does he have anyone else in his life nowadays?"

"Aunt Yara was his soulmate. I doubt he'll ever be interested in anyone else."

"It's all so sad." Sara moved her feet and the swing started up. Jim followed her lead. "What happened to Yara?"

"I'd rather not get into the details right now."

"Okay. Another family mystery."

"You must think I'm evasive." Jim stopped moving his body, and the swing slowed down.

"Nope." She vaulted off the swing, landed on her feet, then fell forward onto her hands and knees.

Jim landed next to her on his feet and gave her a hand up. She brushed the dirt off her knees, and they meandered around the park for the next ten minutes in silence. He couldn't tell if she was processing what he'd said or didn't say. "I love the riverboats," Sara blurted.

He didn't like the idea of the boats because murky waters unhinged him, so he took her hand and swung it back and forth several times in an exaggerated movement to release his tension. "My parents took me a few times."

"Let's go see if we can still get tickets?" Sara encouraged. "Or we could get something to eat at Parkers?"

"You sure you don't want something other than a grocery buffet? Like a restaurant at the City Market? Later, we could listen to some jazz by the river."

"Parkers is fine. Let's wait a while. I'm about to burst after my delicious milkshake. Walking a spell should help."

"And the music?"

"The music's a good idea." She looked up at him. "So, Jim, have you always talked to unusual things?"

"Hmm—yes." Jim almost stopped this line of conversation. The subject depressed him. "I had friends to talk to, but I still talked to the statues, to the earth—it all started after my youngest sister died."

"How? How did you lose your sister?" Sara sounded as though she didn't expect an answer, considering he'd already avoided the subject once.

"Her name was Christina. I used to have recurring dreams about her." Jim rubbed his neck, working his way into the facts. "We were with a group of people and dolphins underwater, and Christina was asleep under my arm. Then I fell asleep, too. The scene shifts, and I wake up in the real world, choking and sputtering, trying to get us above water, trying to get the twisted sheets off my body. The pillows are over my head. In reality, my sister was murdered by the river."

Sara stopped in mid-stride and turned toward him. Her lips trembled, and tears ran down her cheeks. While Jim waited, he reached into his pocket and touched the dragon figurine he'd found in his room. On his run, he'd go over to Bonaventure and put it on Christina's headstone. The last time he'd gone, there was a matted stuffed bear and a few memory pebbles left by other visitors. If she could actually see the dragon, it would make her happy.

Sara whispered, "When you mentioned her before, I assumed a different type of ending. Something less violent."

Jim rubbed his forehead hard with his palm. "Keep walking, and I'll explain. Christina's school was out for the day. Dad picked her up in front of the building, and they walked down by the river. Without warning, she was shot and fell into the water. He jumped in and got her out, but couldn't save her life."

"I'm so sorry." Sara slipped her hand in his. "Your dream, your nightmare. It makes sense, but you weren't…"

"No, I wasn't there. The nightmares stopped eventually. During this visit to Savannah, they've come back. I'm sure it's because Dad told me the entire story a few weeks ago. Someone connected to a legal case he was working on arranged the murder."

"What kind of monster would have a kid killed because of what a parent did or didn't do?"

This was a rhetorical question from Jim's perspective, so he said nothing. Sara seemed to accept his silence. They walked on for a block or two before he continued.

"Mama started watching me and my other sister like a hawk. I felt suffocated. Melanie cried a lot. I developed a kind of shell around myself. Everything bottled up inside me for about a month until I broke down in the corner of my room. I felt like a wimp. Adam said I was an idiot for thinking anyone would think less of me for crying, but I made him promise not to tell."

"Is that why you want to go into the FBI?"

"Yes, without a doubt." Jim took a few deep breaths. "Eventually, Mama ran away with us to Orlando, leaving our dad to deal with his own demons. Melanie and I had our hearts broken again. We left everyone and everything behind. Whenever we came back, it was for short visits after the men responsible for Christina's death were arrested and jailed."

Jim and Sara walked around the playground again, then the picnic area and the athletic field. As they approached the James Oglethorpe Monument at Chippewa Square, Jim noticed a penny on the pathway wedged between the red bricks surrounding the statues. Letting go of her hand, he dug it out. The markings on the coin were from several decades prior.

Jim stumbled over a loose brick. "Oops, the coin distracted me."

"Let me see." Sara examined both sides. "It's my birth year, 1961. Quite a coincidence. It must mean something."

"Well, since it's your birth year, keep it. It can be a good luck charm."

"No, you keep it to remind you of our time together." She smiled and a ray of the sun glistened off the highlights in her hair. "You were saying about your family?"

The coin was a welcome distraction. He tucked it deep into

the pocket of his jeans. "Before everything turned upside down at home, I was attending the local military school—Benedictine."

"Leaving town probably didn't help much."

"Nope. We should have stayed in Savannah. Mama was determined to take us away. The day Christina died; I lost part of my childhood. It couldn't be helped. Until then, I imagined life would never end. I was wrong. Life only goes on forever through our descendants. The Bible teachings say we live forever. It's full of stories and concepts, but for the most part, I can't relate to any of them."

"Yes, it's easiest to read the words and take them for their face value. Picking them apart and interpreting them in today's world is tough."

"Exactly. I never could figure out what it all meant beyond what the Catholic priests explained. They weren't helpful." He sighed. "Let's talk about something else. We're pretty good at flip-flopping between subjects."

Sara paused. It was her turn to rub her temples. "What were we talking about before? Oh, right, the lions. Do you think the lion statues around Oglethorpe are crying or roaring?"

"A little of both."

A fire truck passed by with its sirens wailing. Sara covered her ears and shouted, "I wonder where they're going."

"I hope it's a drill."

"What?"

He repeated himself. "I hope it's a drill."

"Me, too." Sara scrunched up her nose. "James Oglethorpe looks like a pirate with the sword and waistcoat."

"I don't think he'd like being called a pirate."

"He looks brave."

"I would be too if I was nine feet tall and bronze. I used to think my parents named me after him, and that I should accomplish as much as the real guy. The actual man came here with the British Colonists in 1733 to settle the thirteenth, and last, of the colonies.

Oglethorpe was positioned south toward the river, so he could symbolically keep a watchful eye on the Spaniards."

"Spaniards?"

"I'm not sure about the details. I can say, Daniel Chester French created the monument around 1910."

"You're a wealth of information. A family trait?"

He wasn't sure this was a compliment.

"All right, all right. I'm avoiding the rest of my family story with all this extra stuff. Back to it. Mama cried a lot, and Dad worked hard to find the murderer. One day, while we were at school and Dad was away, Mama dozed off in the living room. Her cigarette set the couch on fire. Liana saved her."

"Who's Liana?"

"Our housekeeper. She was in the kitchen, and smelled burning almonds or something weird. When she figured out what was happening, she threw a bucket of water on the couch and Mama. At first, Mama was furious about being doused with water, but got over it when she realized Liana had saved her life and the house. Even though Mama moved us, Liana still works for Dad and Suzy."

"Thank God for Liana."

"So true. Things changed so much after Christina died. Before then, Mama ran our lives by the rules of Savannah society. Soon after, she stopped dressing up and going out. She even gave up the DAR."

"DAR? What's that?"

"It stands for Daughters of the American Revolution. The women are direct descendants from people who helped our country become independent. They do charitable work. Mama was passionate about everything they did."

"Oh, wait, I *have* heard of them."

"Good, now I don't feel like such a dork." Jim rubbed the back of his head. "Melanie and I lost more than our sister. We used to hear our parents arguing through the walls, and we listened instead of hiding from the facts. We couldn't help ourselves. Almost every time in the middle of her rants, Mama shouted, 'It's all your fault.' Eventually, she stopped blaming him out loud. Then they argued about stupid things until she decided to take us away and leave Dad behind. Everything masked the real problem. Christina was gone, and she wasn't coming back."

"I'm sorry." Sara squeezed his hand.

"Thanks." Jim took some time before continuing. "The same day I met you on the train, Dad told me some things that he'd hidden for years because he thought I was too young before. A few days after Christina's murder, my dad received an envelope. Inside there were a bunch of cut-out letters from a magazine glued onto a piece of paper. It said, 'Now you can feel my pain.' The man's son was in prison for his crimes and killed inside. The family blamed my dad for their hell on earth. An eye-for-an-eye kind of attitude. The dead man's father hired someone to emotionally torture my parents by killing our sister."

"Jesus, Jim, this truly is a nightmare."

"Tell me about it." A nerve twitched in his hand. "I'm still trying to wrap my head around the facts. When I came back to Savannah, I was strutting into his office to ask for a loan."

"I imagine asking was hard enough."

"Yep, and I was hurt and confused by the time I left his office without a loan and all his baggage about Christina."

"I would have been hurt, too."

"The reason Mama couldn't handle staying in town was because she figured we'd get killed. It didn't matter that Dad had an undercover officer shadow us for months while he took legal action against the prisoner's father. During my parents' arguments, Dad said he'd lived most of his life in Savannah and wasn't going to run away like a coward. Instead, Mama ran and took us with her. We each had one suitcase and a few odd things stuffed around us in the car; the rest we left in our rooms.

"When we got to Orlando, we stayed at a friend's mansion. Mama said we couldn't live there forever, so she started looking for work. She had secretarial skills from working at the Catholic Church in Savannah, so it was easy to find a managerial job. We moved out of her friend's mansion into a mobile home in an RV Park. Her office was right next to it."

"Sounds rough. I've only camped in a tent in my aunt's backyard. What's it like?"

A fragile smile crept across his face. "It's nothing like camping in the woods. There are sections blocked off like an oversized parking lot, with trees around each labeled slot to give people a little privacy." He paused to reflect. "There's a community center with a pool, fitness center, bike rentals, and game areas."

"Anything else?" Sara asked.

"Um, public shower facilities, some picnic tables and fire pits…"

"I *meant*, what's your mobile home like?"

"Oh, the more personal spaces. It looks kinda like a real house, except there are wheels hiding underneath side panels. It has three bedrooms, a bathroom, and a living-dining room area off the kitchen. It's tiny and plain compared to my dad's house. At first, it was humiliating to live like that, but time resolved my irritation."

"Hey, we all need to live somewhere. What does your mama do all day?"

"She signs people in and out, keeps accounts straight, restocks the store, and coordinates the grounds staff. The guys do all the heavy lifting and maintenance. They make sure the place doesn't go into ruins."

"She sounds like a smart businesswoman."

"Yep, she can be. But our home life's not normal anymore."

"It sounds like she didn't notice anyone else was suffering, too."

"We were all lost for a while, but she became a different person." Jim fiddled with the letter in his pocket and couldn't decide if he should share the contents. "I helped with property maintenance when I was in high school. When I was old enough to get work offsite, I applied for a job at the park. They took me because I had some experience already. It was six miles away from home, so I took a bus to get there and ran home after my shift."

"What's wrong with your shirt pocket? You keep messing with it."

"Nothing. Nothing at all. I was thinking about showing you a letter..."

"You could read it to me."

"Yes, I suppose. I wrote it to help me clear my head after I asked Dad for a loan. There was another one before, but I burned it." He pulled the letter out of his pocket and read a few paragraphs.

"That was a good idea. It sounds like something from a journal or a diary." Sara smiled. "Did writing help clear things up?"

"Seemed to. I'm going to burn this one, too." Jim scooped Sara up and playfully spun her in a circle.

"Hey, put me down."

"Just testing my strength and trying to change the subject. Your turn. Tell me about your family."

"My story isn't happy either. My parents died in Asia when I was eight years old."

"I'm sorry."

"I have no idea why they went on that trip without me. After the accident, I stayed with my Aunt Deborah. When she sold their house, I only took some clothes and my mother's necklace. But my aunt kept a lot of their photos and told me stories all the time. Later, after high school, I added the tattoo to remember Dad.

"My aunt said I didn't talk for weeks. Instead, I drew pictures. They were all in dark colors and looked like a horror film, with flames coming out of a broken boat and demons screaming with wide-open mouths. She didn't know what to do at first. Eventually, she got through to me, and I started talking again by the end of summer. Later on, my drawings got happier. By the time I was in junior high, I'd learned to draw all sorts of things with pencils and charcoal that my teacher said were 'masterful.' By then, my aunt thought it was safe to show me the old drawings. I couldn't believe how disturbing they were. Auntie said she hadn't told me about the boat at the time and had no idea how I'd come up with the ideas.

"After I moved to Savannah and got established at SCAD, Aunt Deborah started spending half a year at a time in Wales at an organic farm. The place is off the power grid. She counsels people there. We write to each other a couple of times a month, and she phones me from a public phone near the farm. I love that she finally can do what she wants without worrying about me. The rest of the year, she's in Jacksonville or Charleston. I still miss my parents, but Aunt Deborah is wonderful, and I never felt like an orphan."

Jim was sympathetic to Sara's circumstances and pulled her into a hug. "I'm so sorry." A breeze touched them, and he took in the orange blossom scent of her hair. It seemed strange that the people he related to the best had unusual life stories involving some sort of tragedy. An older couple walked by, holding hands. Jim wanted to be that couple. Right then and there, he decided someday he'd marry Sara, if she'd have him. The unavoidable space between them during boot camp would test their budding relationship.

As they began walking again, Sara said, "Hey, look, we're at Juliette Gordon Low's house."

Jim squinted at her. "Juliette who?"

"The Girl Scout founder's house." Sara poked his bicep with her finger. "Come on, you lived in Savannah for ages. You should know this."

"Well, part of the history. I wasn't interested in girls at that age." Jim's voice crooned. "I made it to Wolf in the Cub Scouts, but I didn't stick with it after the second grade."

"Too bad."

"Hey, look, check out the downspout." Jim pointed at one coming off the building. "The dolphin is a good luck symbol for mariners. There's a piece of history for you."

"Okay, show off. They're all over town." Sara giggled. "When Ms. Low was little, the family called her Daisy. So, kindergarten scouts were too."

"I bet you were an adorable Daisy."

"Of course." Sara let out an audible breath. "Before my parents died, I came down here on a Girl Scout field trip with my mama. She said I was named after one of the Lows. I did some research when I got to SCAD. Her name was like mine, except spelled differently and she died young. A little creepy. I prefer to think of Juliette since she lived longer. But I heard she was an off-the-wall character."

"How so?" Jim asked.

"Um—one night she went fishing with Rudyard Kipling in a formal evening gown. Off-the-wall enough?"

"Maybe. What else did she do?"

"Okay, try this one. She drove her car into someone's front window, right into their dining room, backed out, and drove off without a word because she didn't want to disturb their dinner. Oh, and she wore vegetables in her hat."

"Yep, over the top, weird."

"Her house is supposed to be haunted. People say they can smell coal burning and furniture polish for no reason. I didn't notice anything when I visited." Sara twirled her hair around a finger. "Do you believe in ghosts?"

"I guess I'd better." He grabbed Sara's shoulders.

She jumped in fright. "Hey."

"Sorry. I never saw any ghosts at the cemetery when I visited. What's the story with Juliette? Is Romeo involved?"

"Funny." Sara fell into that one. "There are lots of ghosts in Savannah, or at least stories about them."

"I've heard. Sooo, how's this one go?"

"Well, it's more about Juliette's parents. They were in love in the 1800s. Don't say it again."

"Romeo and Juliet." Jim couldn't resist.

"Ugh." She smiled in his direction. "When they first met, she was sliding down a banister at Yale, fell on his hat, and crushed it. She never stopped sliding, and it annoyed everyone—not at all proper in those days. At some point, her husband died, and she followed him five years later. Right after her death, his smiling ghost, dressed in a military uniform, walked past a relative in the hall. Several people saw him in other parts of the house. They say he was smiling because his wife was going to join him. Then, at night, in our time, people have seen a woman in the window wearing a gown, carrying a candle—a ghost."

"Boo!" Jim exclaimed.

Sara only twitched this time. "Oh, stop."

"I heard there's an entire cemetery buried under a street in town."

"They're supposed to be yellow fever victims. The townsfolk lit tar fires, which poured billowing black smoke through the streets, to help clear out the sickness. It's another one of those strange things, like adding lime to the blue paint to ward off spirits and mosquitoes."

"The porch ceilings." Jim pulled his hands through his hair. "You're smart and pretty."

"Thanks. I read a lot and listen to people talking. Besides, blue was my mother's other favorite color, according to my aunt. I like it no matter where or why it appears."

"Oh, my blue eyes are a plus then?"

"Absolutely." She paused. "Jim, I'd like to make a special dinner for you before you go away to boot camp, so you'll remember I'm here."

"I can never forget."

"Good. Neither can I."

Jim kissed her and didn't want to stop. With great physical effort, he stepped back. "Adam wrote me. He said training is exhausting, and he doesn't sleep much."

"Blaire told me he can't write much, but she didn't expect to get many letters from boot camp."

"It's a busy time."

"We met last month, and they've known each other for at least a year. It's not reasonable for me to expect anything from you."

"I'll write." Jim rubbed his chin. The stubble was emerging even though he'd shaven that morning. "I feel like we know each other well already. The coin we found must be a message from a ghost."

They continued walking hand in hand, exploring the town. Farther along, they strolled past Jim Williams' home on Bull Street.

"My parents used to go to annual Christmas parties there." Jim gestured toward the property with two fingers. "Mama told me he's a colorful character."

"Those parties are surely over. Last month, Mr. Williams shot a man he knew in the house and said it was self-defense. It was all over the papers. Quite a scandal. The victim died on-site and people are already saying the house is haunted."

"Dad didn't mention any of this to me when I got back. I better ask, since they were friends."

"That's strange." Sara jolted to a stop. "I hope you weren't named after him?"

Jim laughed. "No, after my dad. Come on, there are more places to explore."

"Lead the way." Sara put her hand into the crook of his arm. "I like your spirit."

PART TWO

Chapter 9

A New Challenge

As Jim began his military journey in the passenger seat of the recruiter's car, he reviewed what had transpired in the last few months, beginning with meeting Sara and confronting his dad. Life had taken unexpected turns, but he was grateful for the changes. His restored address in Savannah had become not only his 'home of record' on his military paperwork, but a true home again. The months in Savannah had passed quickly, and it was now time to put on his boots and train to be a soldier.

Once a week, between grueling exercises that strained every muscle in Jim's body, he wrote letters and stuffed them into his trunk to send off in bundles. His drill sergeant encouraged everyone to keep their families up-to-date. The days were so long and exhausting that writing unloaded his mind, but he often fell asleep holding his pen in his hand. He'd wake up and find random nonsensical lines here and there. He called them sleep-scribbles.

The letters he wrote to his parents, one to each, were crafted to suit their individual tolerances. His mama's letters were more sensitive and his dad's more matter-of-fact. When each was complete, he wrote to Sara in a journal format. She appeared to be doing almost the same thing, except she sent him two letters each week. He admired her dedication and enjoyed hearing about her life in Savannah. Her letters got him through the daily bumps and bruises of military life.

July 1981
actual dates, not relevant
Fort Benning, Georgia

Dear Sara,

My letters from boot camp are going to be jumbled because I'm constantly distracted. When we met on the train for the first time, I never expected to see you again. I still can't believe we both knew Adam before we met. Sometimes I see him, but we're too busy to talk much. He's about to start a sixty-day Ranger program. My time here will be extended by two or three weeks because of airborne training. Lucky me.

Thank you for writing. I get whatever anyone sends me once a week via airmail. Someone flings them across the room at me, so I need to stay alert to catch them. Your letters brighten my days and remind me there's something outside of this base. Oh, by the way, don't send any food gifts. One of the guys got a bunch, and the drill sergeant said he had to eat it all on the spot. Yuck, he started retching afterward. I know this doesn't make sense. Following rules isn't optional and there are consequences if we fail. They called candy and pornography (I didn't have any) contraband at in-processing. Some things don't have to make sense.

Hang on…

Sorry, I got called away. It's an hour later. To backtrack. When my Army adventure began, I had a physical exam to make sure I didn't have any medical conditions to prevent me from serving effectively. I'm not sure how they could figure out my state of mind since they can't get into my head unless I let them.

At MEPS (Military Entrance Processing Station), we were given hearing and vision tests and had our fingerprints taken. All the acronyms are going to make me crazy. There must be hundreds of them. This one's ridiculous: POG (<u>P</u>erson <u>O</u>ther than a <u>G</u>runt). It was originally a naval Gaelic (Irish) word spelled differently. The marines got it next. Somehow, the term moved into the United States Army and now means people who are not trained for combat.

Moving on. Once we got to Fort Benning, we were given a dozen vaccines. We stood heel to toe in lines and were forbidden to talk. Had to wait until our "down-time" hours later. We talked about what we'd done before enlisting, where we'd lived, if we had siblings, and if we'd left a girlfriend behind. No depth to any of the topics. There are many accents represented: Southern, Northern, and some I didn't recognize. Some recruits used to be truckers, plumbers, farmers, and bankers. A few of them have college degrees. They opted out of officer's training. It's a total melting pot and a bit of a culture shock to get through.

So, a few days after the meet-and-greet vaccine session, most of us had snotty noses. The head honchos said our sinus troubles were caused by close contact with people from all over the States. The vaccines added to the mess. Healthy or sick, we keep going. I also got fitted with the gear I need (boots, uniforms, regulation underclothes, toothbrushes, and other stuff).

Athletically, I came here prepared, thanks to Adam. Even so, there are things I missed somewhere along the way. I didn't know I'd have to pay for some of my gear—it'll come out of my paycheck. This was probably mentioned, except it didn't sink into my brain.

Life these days is a mixture of hurry up and wait, combined with "move it, soldier," and various agitating remarks I won't mention. We are told when to stand, sit, think, talk, and sleep. I now have a set of dog tags around my neck with my name, birth date, religious affiliation, and blood type. They're to be worn 24/7. I wrote Catholic since it's on my birth certificate. The designation doesn't mean much to me these days. More later. —Jim

August 1981
(Following your lead on dates)
Savannah, Georgia

Dear Jim,

I've lost track of how many notes I've sent. Maybe this is number eight? This oversized card reminded me of you, with the statue of an angel on the front. I hope it makes you smile. Next time, I'll try to find a puppy card since we share that affection. Meeting you and spending so much time together brought a new dimension to my life. Sounds corny, but thank you for being you. I'm happy about the times we shared together. I've added a piece of paper to the card because when I start writing, it's hard to stop.

I hope you're still not too exhausted. Someone told me the other day, if you were in the Boy Scouts or a military academy, you can increase your pay grade. I wonder if that's right? Is this okay to bring up?

My classes are going well. The one on European architecture and drafting is my favorite. I've officially decided to be a teacher when I'm done with college. Oh, and I'm reading about the military. Not knowing what's going on scares me.— Big hugs, Sara

August 1981
Fort Benning

Dear Sara,

Happy 4th of July, even though it was weeks ago. I know there is a reason for all the stuff we're going through, and I'll keep encouraging myself to carry on while getting unduly harassed. Some days, I'm able to turn the verbal abuse into a bit of humor in my head. From one day to the next, I'm completely at the mercy of anyone of higher rank, which is pretty much everyone who didn't recently enlist. I'm officially a SIT (Soldier In Training). If my drill sergeant allows me to get through boot camp in one piece, I'll be grateful.

On to something else. I figure the less the drill sergeants know about me, the better. Except that's hard to accomplish when your rack is next to the office. Our spots were assigned by last name and alphabetically ordered. Even though mine starts with M, I'm still too close to the office because of the way the racks arc around the bay (the room is at least as big as a basketball court). Oops—a rack is a metal-framed bunk bed. Adam had wooden bunk beds when we were kids. I slept on the top bed. Climbing up was always awkward, with my legs and arms falling in different directions. When I was half-asleep, he'd toss up chocolate bars or whatever else was within his reach. Some of it hit me in awkward places.

Back to today. I didn't want the drill sergeants to know I grew up with Adam. For unknown reasons, he told them I was coming through training after him. Because of our connection, at least two times a day, Drill Sergeant Morgan, or one of the others, curses at me using my shortened last name—Masters. It annoyed me at first, until I realized they liked Adam and me enough to single us out as individuals instead of just another soldier going through the reprogramming mill.

The drill sergeants are subject-matter experts, even though there are always new things for them to learn from high command because things change all the time. They're not like the brown-round hats you see in the movies—screaming, with red faces and bulging neck veins. They even encourage us to write to family and friends. I think I mentioned this in a different letter. Everything is blending together in somewhat of a time vortex. From what I hear, Fort Benning is the toughest boot camp.

One afternoon, Drill Sergeant Morgan sent me out with

Miller to get two sandwiches. When we got back, we were ordered to sit in the middle of our bay and eat them in front of everyone. My response: "Yes, Drill Sergeant." An hour later, we were in the mess hall, eating again. My stomach felt so bloated. I have no idea what the point was other than to annoy us.

I've enclosed a copy of the Infantry Creed—in case you want to read it. The basics of the core values of the Army are leadership, personal courage, duty, respect, honor, selfless service, and loyalty. We have lots of cadences we chant while marching and jogging around. They can be poetic and raunchy, so I won't send copies of those. By the time we're done at Ft. Benning, we're supposed to know how to watch each other's backs in combat and move as a cohesive unit. We're being re-programmed physically and mentally. Training, planning, knowledge—it's all part of the gig.

A photographer has been trying to keep up with us. The photo books are going to be mailed out at some point. I put you on the distribution list. You'll have trouble figuring out which pictures I'm in. We all look a lot alike with our shaved heads and covers (hats). In some photos, you'll see us crawling around in the dirt, going through cramped pipes and under barbed wire. In others, we're running from place to place over poles, traversing rope courses and monkey bars, and climbing up the sides of buildings using ropes and harnesses.

Better stop now. I need some shut-eye. —Jim

August 1981
Fort Benning

Dear Sara,

Our emergency first-aid medical training is intense. I'll spare you the details. Basically, we're taught how to deal with wounds. The bosses aren't concerned about teaching us all the details we would learn in medical school. However, the terminology is the same.

Dealing with heavy backpacks while running and marching is more of a burden than I expected. My knees are sore. My feet are a mass of nasty blisters. Some are filled with fluid, some popped and flat, others torn open and raw. Topping it all off with a purplish-black nail on my big toe. The mess hurts most when I've been sitting and then have to get up. The nerves were on fire for the first five minutes. My feet feel like clubs. I suck it up, because I don't want to wuss out. I'm tending to the blisters, and hope they'll heal fast.

I'm pretty worn out at this point. I'll blame the gas mask training. We had to take the masks off in a building to understand how the gasses would affect us. I've never felt something so horrible. Everyone's noses were running and my sinuses were burning. Some of the guys lost their breakfast from coughing so hard. Crawling around through mud under barbed wire with guns firing over our heads was easier than dealing with the gas.

Sorry about all the technical stuff. Sending you a big hug. Thanks for sticking with me. —Jim

P.S. I still hate pull-ups even though I conquered them with Adam in Savannah.

August 1981
Still in hot Savannah

Dear Jim,

The garden's courtyard behind our brownstone is a great place to sit and study. Blaire and I spend a lot of time out there. Yesterday, I was staring out into nowhere, thinking of you. Mr. Veasey appeared, and I almost fell off my chair. The next thing I knew, he was making burgers on the grill. Then Blaire appeared from I don't know where.

Mr. Veasey is a sympathetic character. He often asks about you and Adam. Today, he showed us the new painting he'd started. There are two men in uniform trudging through the woods. It looks pretty good while being strange at the same time with all the unrealistic bright colors. Chuck, his "manager," is always encouraging him to paint. Especially since the canvas's sell for big dollars.

Blaire and I have been going down to the beach once a week for miles of walking. My shoes will never recover from the sand encrusted inside. Every time we go, I remember how you and I played in the waves. Collecting shells was fun, too.
—XXOO, Sara

P.S. Have your blistered feet healed? Keep telling me everything.

August 1981
Still in Ft. Benning

Dear Sara,

It's great you're still sending me two letters a week. A lot of the guys get one every other week if they're lucky. On re-reading your letters, I realized I never responded to your pay grade question about military school and the Boy Scouts. I'm not offended. It's fine and a valid point. When I enlisted, I let my recruiter know about school, and my income was adjusted accordingly. The Boy Scouts weren't worth mentioning because I didn't keep going through high school. On another point, I got a deferral from the University of Georgia. They said I can do some courses through the mail when I'm out of boot camp to get more courses under my belt.

Things are the same around here. Run, run, run, and run some more. The endorphin energy surges afterward are invigorating. The obstacle courses remind me of a kids' playground, but harder. Then there's shooting practice with different weapons (pistol, rifle, machine gun, and other stuff). From a distance, it sounds like piles of marbles dropping from my hands onto a hard floor. Up close, the noise is deafening. It's good I didn't know much about guns other than the basics Dad taught me. I didn't have enough time with him to get any bad habits. We're learning how to disassemble, clean, and reassemble them at top speed.

I'm in great shape, and eating like a horse. The food is boring, and I don't mind since it's good, nutritious fuel for all our workouts. The drill sergeants are unrelenting. They consider everything we do wrong or not good enough. Some of the challenges aren't even outside. My battle buddy (assigned partners who are supposed to help each other) and I had to scrub and re-wax the barrack's floors the other day we had to hunt for the cleaning machine. Our other alternative was to get on the floor and do the work by hand with a brush—no way, no thanks.

Last week, the sergeant declared we didn't know how to properly put sheets on our bed. For three hours, we disassembled and reassembled the frames while he timed us. There are 100 beds and around 40 to 50 guys. We didn't do it fast enough, so we lost the privilege of sleeping in them for a week. He said it's good practice for sleeping on the ground turtle-side up (belly up) with a rifle on our chests during missions. The floor was hard. We still had our pillows and blankets, so I guess that's something. I'm laughing. At least the floor was clean.

Entry 2 (a different day)

We need lots of sleep with the amount of training we go through, but we don't get enough. The endless mind games don't help. I'm not sure why we have to go through *@# like this, other than endurance and weeding out unfit recruits.

This week's new bed adventure was impressive. Six of us

arrived in the bay and found everyone's beds flipped over, with hundreds of feet of string woven between them in what our drill sergeant called a laser maze. We had to circumnavigate the maze without touching the strings around the pile of over 200 boots tied to each other all catawampus. It took about two hours to get in there and untie the boots. Then it took a week to figure out who owned which pair. I had one of my boots and one of Rodrigues's on for a day.

All the commotion feels ridiculous, but there is a logic to it all. Here is what I came up with. If we fail to work together to complete the stupid bed tasks (or whatever else we're supposed to do), then everyone will experience the consequences. This creates a silent obligation between us to do everything in our power to support each other. Some say that any given team is only as strong as its weakest link. When we screw up, we get "smoked," which means we are obligated to do extra push-ups or other types of stuff to ingrain correct behavior into us. It doesn't matter if I do something wrong or someone else does—we all can suffer the consequences. Other days, we get smoked for made-up infractions. On those days, I want to punch something and wish I hadn't enlisted. When any drill sergeant gives us a task, all I can say is, "Yes, Drill Sergeant." If I say, "Yes, sir," I could end up with extra sit-ups. Only officers can be called sir. The tiniest details matter.

Again, I have to say, the mayhem helps keep us finely tuned while keeping us balanced on the edge of an imaginary cliff. In the chain of command, if one soldier is incapacitated, the next guy must be able to step into the job.

Every day, I learn more about what an infantryman is. It's like being a competitive athlete with a group mentality. Who is the best squad, the best platoon, the best company? The squad is the smallest and the company the largest. My platoon can compete against other platoons, which create healthy rivalries and reinforces each group's desire to stick together.

Then we have individual competitions. For instance, who has the cleanest uniform, who runs the fastest, and who can take apart and reassemble their weapon under pressure. The entire process creates a constant atmosphere of self-improvement. In the end, oddly, competition isn't the right word at all. We are always supposed to be looking out for each other. I say this many times because I need to drill it into my mind.

You might ask what all the abuse is about. A summary— it's about getting in shape, working with others in difficult situations, and following orders no matter how absurd they seem (like the bed or shoe challenge). In the end, a brotherhood is formed from the hardships we experience. We learn to trust another person with our lives. The strongest bonds will be made from enduring suffering together. We are trained for war, but there's a lot of time wasted too. I hear some soldiers come back from missions and miss it while simultaneously hating the conflict. In some ways, I hope I never find out.

If I haven't mentioned. Adam went through the same training I have up until he went into the Ranger program. Each level is tougher than the last and requires more stamina. Both airborne and ranger troops take on various missions all over the world before, or instead of, sending in larger forces. Some soldiers know a foreign language that applies to the territory they're entering. My Portuguese isn't relevant at the moment.

Gotta sign off now. Goodnight. I hope to dream of you instead of soldiering. —XXO, Jim

Chapter 10

Graduation

THE LETTERS BETWEEN JIM AND SARA HAD BROUGHT THEM closer together over the last four months, and he hoped she would come to his graduation ceremonies. He felt foolish for telling her about them without inviting her.

Jim took a taxi over to the Marriott in his battle fatigues with a grocery bag loaded with his civilian clothes to meet his dad and Suzy. He didn't want to go to dinner in uniform, even though his shaven head, and the proximity to the base, made his involvement with the military obvious. He was proud of his accomplishments, but he wanted to dress like a civilian for the evening.

When he got out of the taxi and walked into the hotel lobby, he held his body straight and tall, even though his muscles ached from the previous day's activities. Across the room, he saw his dad and Suzy beaming with smiles spread across their faces. Jim limped over and embraced his dad. They stepped apart, and Suzy pulled him in for a brief hug. The three of them bantered back and forth for a few awkward moments, and agreed to go to a local Chinese restaurant after Jim changed his clothes. Jim headed up to the hotel room with his dad while Suzy waited in the lobby.

"Dad, why is she wearing Mama's clothes?"

"What do you expect? Your mama left behind fine things. Suzy is making the best of the situation. No sense throwing them out."

"I suppose. Could you ask her to wear something else to my graduation? What if Mama shows up and has a fit?"

"You have a point."

Jim dropped the subject and exchanged his uniform and worn-out combat boots for a comfortable pair of blue jeans, a white Izod shirt, and sneakers. After folding his uniform and putting it into the grocery bag with his boots, they walked back down to the lobby.

"My Lord, what's going on? You look like you're walking on hot coals," Suzy said.

"I'll tell you later. I'm good."

"No, you're not," Suzy protested. "Sit down and let me see your boots."

Jim complied with her orders while wondering if his dad had noticed his awkward movements, because he sure hadn't said a word when Jim was changing his shoes or walking to or from the hotel room.

"Jim, these won't do. What a mess."

"They're not bad."

"Nonsense. We're taking you to the military surplus store before dinner. You need a better pair before you leave this town. And some fresh socks."

The idea of an upgraded pair of boots was too appealing to object to for the sake of good manners. "Yes, ma'am. Thank you."

Within the hour, he had a well-fitting new pair of regulation combat boots and a half-dozen socks resting in a shopping bag. "Please, take the old ones back to Savannah. I want to keep them to help me remember boot camp."

"If you insist," his dad said, "but you'll never forget."

When they got back in the car, Suzy said, "Now tell me the story—about your feet."

"My boots gave out yesterday, halfway into our twelve-mile rucksack march, but I kept going. The path ended up a steep hill with the new recruits lined up along the side of the road cheering us on. At the top, there was an enormous bonfire and an oversized punch bowl with some unknown blue drink. Drill Sergeant Morgan congratulated us on our accomplishments and said we had to drink, so we did."

"No choice there," his dad said, and pulled into the restaurant parking lot. "We're here. It's time to eat some quality food."

The dinner menu was mouthwatering, and a wonderful change from the American food provided at the base. Jim ordered spring rolls, wonton soup, and Kung Pao chicken. The server brought his soup out on a tray first, spilling a portion on his leg. The curse words almost flowed out of his mouth. Squelching the expletives he'd learned to express without restraint around his military brothers was a struggle. He stayed quiet until the main dishes appeared. Once he had taken the edge off his hunger, he explained the next day's ceremony.

"Tomorrow, we won't have much time together. An hour at most. There are two separate ceremonies. One is called Turning Blue. Oh, yeah, that's why the sergeant gave us the blue drink at the top of the hill."

"Turning Blue?" Suzy's voice elevated. "Sounds alarming."

"No." Jim chuckled. "It's for infantry soldiers. We get a blue cord attached to our shoulder epaulet during a ceremony with our squad members, and drill sergeants, before the basic training graduation in the outdoor stadium. We'll walk through a pillar of smoke at the start of each event. Thankfully, there's no tear gas in the mix."

"I should hope not." Suzy cleared her throat for effect, or at least Jim thought so.

"MOPP training was awful."

"What's that stand for?" Suzy asked.

"Mission Oriented Protective Posture. When they exposed us to tear gas, they trained us with and without masks. I've never gagged and sputtered so much in my life. It was horrible. Some guys lost their meals."

"Dear Lord," Suzy exclaimed and covered her mouth.

"Oh, sorry, bad timing."

"It's all right, darling. You should be able to tell us anything, even if it's unpleasant." Suzy touched his hand. "The ceremonies—can we attend both of them?"

"Of course. The infantry cording ceremony is by my building at 0800 hours and then the stadium exhibition starts at 1000 hours."

"That's ten in the morning, Suzy," his dad said.

"Bless your heart. Thank you. I understand the military clock."

"You'll need to go through the main entrance and show your IDs to get on base for the ceremonies. I'll take you there after dinner."

"Do you remember the Revolutionary War reenactments we went to?"

"Sure thing, Dad. The smoke I'll be passing through will be like that."

"I'm proud of you, son."

"Thanks. I need to cut this short tonight. We have a curfew."

"Do you need to change back into your uniform?" Suzy asked.

"No, no. It's not required. Tomorrow's another story. We'll be in our dress uniforms."

"Well, let's be on our way," his dad said. "I don't want to make you late."

Jim slid out of the booth. Before moving away from the table, he shifted his spine and neck in opposite directions to loosen his muscles after sitting so long. Out by the car, he said, "Dinner was great. I'm glad you're here."

"We wouldn't miss this time for any reason," his dad said, and drove away toward the base.

At the main visitor's gate, Jim realized they couldn't get through. The guards said it had been closed earlier for a combat exercise and directed them to an entrance halfway around the base, which was also closed. Several gates later, they found a way in. By the time the car pulled up to the building, curfew had passed. and he needed to bolt out of the car and inside.

This time, Drill Sergeant Morgan didn't smoke anyone for being a few minutes late. No untangling of piles of boots or any other disciplinary actions. Instead, he put an old *Star Wars* film into the VHS machine. Everyone lounged around on mattresses in the center of the room to watch, and munch on vending machine snacks and sodas. When the film was over, there was a lot of hushed jibber-jabber going on and off throughout the night.

The next morning after chow, which Jim forced himself to eat, he put on his dress uniform along with the rest of the soldiers. Not long after, they headed outside and divided into designated groups to prepare for the official infantry ceremony. Jim and his training buddies grouped together among the tree line and peered across the field. On the other side, he saw the small set of bleachers where he knew his dad and Suzy were waiting with other families.

Looking around at his fellow graduates and then down at himself, Jim's emotions welled up, but they stayed contained. *One deep breath, two deep breaths.* He had done it; he had gone through grueling weeks of training with his battle buddies and succeeded. Nerves caused him to pull on the corners of his dress uniform to straighten an already pressed jacket.

Each group lined up and waited for the smoke canisters to be lit. When the billowing cloud reached its full breadth, they all marched through in formation toward the bleachers. There, each drill sergeant stood in front of their men.

An announcer in the foreground spoke a few words before inviting the families to "stand with their soldiers; their sons."

Jim watched without turning his head. His dad was in uniform, the buttons pulled against the ten pounds he'd gained over the years. Once a Marine, always a Marine. Jim stood a little taller, knowing both he and his dad had a reason to celebrate their life accomplishments, even if they were representatives of two different branches of the military.

Drill Sergeant Morgan congratulated Jim, placed the blue cord over his arm, fastened it under the epaulet, and shook Jim's hand. They concluded by saluting each other. A restrained smile snuck up from the corners of his mouth as pride swelled to almost bursting. This was a true honor, considering many of the soldiers had their parents fastening the cord on the military's behalf. Soon after, Jim and his fellow infantrymen departed to prepare for the Basic Training Graduation Ceremony. The groups would also include soldiers who were going onto other types of work or training.

At the appointed hour, Jim lined up with his platoon of thirty men. All in all, there were four platoons. They were flanked by sets of color guards. Each set composed of four men; two with rifles and two with either American or Army flags balanced in their specialized carrying belts.

Jim and his fellow soldiers stood on the edge of a football field, marching in place. He watched a soldier pull the trigger on multiple smoke canisters, but nothing happened. The second attempt worked, and the smoke slithered out into small streams before turning into a massive cloud.

The marching band moved forward, playing with gusto, with strong beats in the music. Each downbeat helped Jim concentrate on putting one foot in front of the other in coordination with the men on either side of him. One minute later, Jim's stationary marching, along with the rest of the graduates, turned into forward motion through the smoke onto the field behind their drill sergeants. The scene reminded Jim of little tin soldiers wound up and set on their way. The vision calmed the tension in his neck. When he reached the middle of the field with the other men, they all halted in unison, marched in place again for a count of eight, and then stood stock-still. The band stopped playing.

The announcer asked the audience to stand for the national anthem and Pledge of Allegiance. Jim saluted the flag, along with every other soldier. The audience members within his line of sight stood, and either placed their hands across their hearts or saluted if they were in uniform.

The crowd settled back onto the bleachers. Jim moved his saluting hand down to his side and rested his palm on his thigh. He stood unflinching while men in combat fatigues came into view with their rifles and bent down on one knee. The announcer reviewed some of the training procedures and congratulated everyone for their accomplishments over the past months.

Pride oozed out of his pores, along with the sweat trickling down his back. He kept his knees slightly bent while he stood in the blazing sun. The dark uniforms exacerbated the situation, and the men were likely becoming dehydrated. It didn't help that they'd spent an hour before the events marching around practicing their turns, and were sweating long before going through the smoke. Jim moved his eyes in various directions, without turning his head, and noticed that

Brinkley had his knees locked. He tried to whisper a warning through closed lips, like a ventriloquist. It was no use. Brinkley started to tilt to the side. Before anyone could do anything, he was on the ground. The term *heat cat*—heat casualty—came to mind. To avoid becoming the next man down, Jim readjusted his knees and monitored the men in his immediate vicinity in case he needed to prop one up. Not long after, Jorgenson, in the distant front row, started to tilt. This time, Drill Sergeant Morgan responded before the man hit the ground.

While Jim continued to stand at attention, he listened to the colonel talking about bravery and honor under adversity. This ceremony was meant to remind them of military history and values. Yet, the event had nothing to do with anything they'd do in combat. He respected the tradition, but would rather have spent more time with his family and Sara, if she showed up.

Half an hour later, the ceremony was over, and the soldiers were released. The crowds on the bleachers started to move toward them en masse. *Was his mama in the crowd?* If so, things might get complicated with Suzy and her in the same area. If things got dicey, he'd focus on something else, because he didn't want their issues to overshadow this day.

His dad and Suzy came up beside him first. After a customary salute between men in uniform, he hugged Jim. The three of them looked back and forth at each other. Suzy came in for a hug. The moment was awkward and formal, but soon he was relieved to see a welcome sight over Suzy's shoulder. Sara was walking right toward him. She was wearing a white dress with her mother's red-stone necklace, catching a ray of sunshine and reflecting in his direction. His heart skipped a beat.

Behind Sara and off to the side, his mama and Melanie were coming as well. His mama's two-piece multicolored outfit made her look like a gypsy—so unlike the formal clothing she'd worn when his parents lived together. The garish outfit, topped by a floppy hat, made her stand out among the crowd. Melanie blended in with the rest of the families in one of Mama's muted blue dresses. The three women kept coming toward him in a cluster. His mama didn't acknowledge Sara because they'd never met or seen each other in photographs. They arrived in front of Jim, and he froze in place. His mama and Suzy turned and stared at each other with forced, almost grimacing, smiles.

"Hello, Suzy," his mama said. "God bless you. You're wearing my old dress."

"Hello, Clarissa. You chose your path," Suzy replied. "It's James Michael's day. Let's not get catty."

"Yes, all right." His mama came over to Jim for a long hug and squeezed his muscular biceps. She stepped back, crying. "It's been months. I hardly recognize you without your long hair."

"It is what it is." Jim shrugged. "Hair or no hair, I feel like a different person. The old me is in here somewhere."

Sara and Melanie walked straight up to Jim with their arms open. He tried to hug them both at once. Melanie stepped away, moving over to their dad for a hug—Jim knew they hadn't seen each other for at least a year. For now, he let the thought go, because all he wanted to do was hold Sara in his arms. The embrace was blissful, and everyone else faded away. He held onto her until his dad nudged him.

"Here you go, son. You must be thirsty."

Jim guzzled the Coke down. "Thanks for coming, everyone." He hugged his mama again, knowing how difficult it was for her to be around Suzy.

"Melanie and I had to come," she said.

"Thanks." He reached for Sara's hand, and felt a warm blush spread across his cheeks. "Mama, Melanie—this is Sara."

"Here we all are together. Imagine that," his mama said. "And Sara, Jim told me about you. You're as pretty as a pearl. It's good to meet you in person."

"You, too, Mrs. Masterson." Sara reached out her free hand.

His mama took Sara's hand and pulled them both in for a hug before Jim could release his grip. Sara's face blushed while giving him a *what the hell* expression. Inside, he felt a tingling warmth spread through his chest, and his stomach fussed even though he wasn't hungry.

Stepping back, his mama said, "It must have taken ages to get here."

"About four hours. I'm stopping at a friend's place in Macon for the night on the way back."

"Dear, that's a wonderful idea. Before you go, we must spend some time together. Perhaps an early dinner?"

Melanie smiled. "Mama, please. Don't push it."

"Oh, you know me. I'm always in a rush to get to know new people."

"Not always," Melanie said. Jim assumed she was referring to Suzy.

His mama turned away and said jubilantly to his dad, "You're looking well-fed."

"Yes…" His dad cleared his throat. "Just a few extra pounds. Nothing to dishonor the uniform."

Twenty minutes later, after rehashing aspects of the ceremony, Jim said, "I need some time alone with Sara. We'll meet you back here in twenty minutes. There's an ice cream truck in the traffic circle if you want some."

"All right, son. Come on, ladies. My treat."

Jim and Sara strolled off hand in hand, away from his family. He looked back over his shoulder and saw his mama gesticulating. They kept walking until they reached the military museum and ducked around a corner. There, Jim took Sara into his arms and passionately kissed her. They lingered in the moment until one of his brothers in arms came by and catcalled. Sara backed off.

"Hey, Griswold, give us a break," Jim exclaimed.

"I was just playing. No harm, no foul." Griswold kept moving away from them and was soon out of sight.

"Welcome to the military, my lady. It's a laugh a minute."

"It's fine. I can take a little sassing."

"Everyone's full of themselves at this point." Jim's energy level was off the charts, even though he hadn't had enough sleep. "I'll be heading to Fort Bragg in North Carolina soon to live with a bunch of paratroopers. I'm sorry. I wanted to be closer to you."

"We'll figure things out." Sara rested her hand on his cheek. "Where are the others going?"

"Some of the men's destinations were picked through a lottery system, and they're going overseas."

"Being in a lottery sounds scary."

"A little, I suppose. At least I'll be in the States."

"Blaire is lucky to have Adam on the base in Savannah. She told me the Rangers at Hunter Airfield are a rowdy bunch."

"When I can get time off, I'll come see you." He pulled a piece of paper out of his breast pocket with his new address. "I'll be living in a military apartment complex on the base. Do me a favor and pass my contact info to Adam." Jim suppressed his emotions and said, "Sara, it won't be easy spending even more time apart. I'm up for the challenge. How about you?"

"Yes, of course." She hugged him. "We'll keep writing..."

"I'll phone and come to Savannah whenever I'm free."

"I hope so." Sara looked at her watch. "I'll keep studying and then find work to distract me."

"Good. Sounds good." Jim lifted her chin with his hand and saw a tear roll down her cheek. "We are a pair, aren't we? I never imagined our meeting would turn into such a strong attachment." He wiped the tear away with his thumb.

"I'm sorry." Sara looked away from him. Her eyes continued to pool with moisture.

"No, I'm sorry. I wish I didn't have to put you through all this military stuff."

"I thought I understood, but I didn't until now."

"We both have more to learn. Sara—I'm in love with you."

"So am I." She paused. "I mean—I love you, too."

Jim put his hand in the pocket of his dress trousers and pulled out a chain. "This is for you."

Sara examined the two pieces of metal hanging off it, and a sign of recognition spread across her face. "The 1961 penny we found in the park—you saved it."

"Yes, it's special to me because of you. I drilled a hole for the chain and added one of my dog tags. They are a promise of my loyalty."

She pulled the necklace over her head and set it next to her mother's red stone. "I'll keep them close."

Jim took Sara's hand, turned her wrist toward him, and exposed the palm. He ran his fingers over the sensitive skin toward her forearm. A noticeable shiver ran over her. He kissed Sara one more time, and didn't want to stop. They had to go back to the family.

As Jim and Sara approached the family on the bleachers, he felt a tinge of guilt for leaving them standing there with false smiles on their faces. When they got closer, he saw his mother's eye was twitching. Melanie gave him a sideways glance, which wasn't a surprise. He knew it meant thanks for leaving me with these nut jobs. His sister was still a teenager and didn't want to deal with their drama on top of her own.

The stress between his mama and Suzy was palpable, but they were there for him. Otherwise, he knew they wouldn't have put themselves into such an uncomfortable position. They had met once in person and had spoken on the phone by chance. Jim had witnessed his mother's end of those strained conversations. She was being supportive by making the drive for the ceremony, but she was still like a bird with a broken wing in this situation.

"After I leave," Jim said, "you all should visit the military museum over there. It has some interesting history."

Jim ducked away to a cart by the bleachers and returned with bottles of water for everyone. They drank some on the spot, but he soon realized he needed to go over to the buses and encouraged them to come along. His family time was almost over. Piles of gear sat on the sidewalk. He pulled a small personal bag out of the stack while talking to some of the soldiers in his unit. New recruits loaded the bags under the bus. It was time to say goodbye and get on board. His parents, his sister, and Suzy hugged him with all their might.

Sara came last with a kiss and a promise. She placed her hand over her heart. "I'll wait for you."

He hesitated before stepping up onto the bus, then accepted his fate. Going down the aisle, he chose the window seat near the sidewalk so he could see Sara while the bus drove away.

Chapter 11

More Training

A MONTH LATER, WHILE RESTING ON HIS SLEEP-SACK IN THE mountains, he was interrupted when something skittered across the top of his head and into his lap. A fellow soldier had received Jim's letter in error before they'd left Fort Bragg, and took his time delivering it. They exchanged some verbal jabs. O'Sullivan implied, then denied, he'd opened the sweet-smelling letter. Jim looked at the envelope. It was from Sara and was dated before any others he'd received. Her name and address were printed in clear block letters, followed by a smiley face. He brought the envelope to his nose and breathed in her perfume. *What did she call it—Cristalle? Suzy had said if a woman wears perfume, you better know what it is. Was this the scent of orange blossom or something else?* The perfume was special to her, a gift from her aunt, which was more expensive than Sara could afford. One day, he'd have enough money to buy her a bottle.

September 1981
Savannah, still here

Dear Jim,

How is everything? I hope you can write or call soon. I think about you out there every day. I wish you didn't have to go through all this to get funded for college. In the end, you'll be in the FBI. I'm betting on you.

When I close my eyes, I see you standing in front of me after your graduation, looking so strong in your uniform. Thank you for the necklace. The penny and tag are a constant happy reminder of you.

Your mama seemed nice, but like you said, she's so different from Suzy and your dad. Now I understand what you meant when you said she isn't the same as when you all lived in Savannah. Our dinner together after you left on the bus was odd. At one point, she started to talk about Suzy, then stopped abruptly. She seems sad, even in her bright outer shell. I'm not sure if she's looking for friendship from me or trying to be supportive of our relationship. Maybe both.

Anyway, my drive to Macon for the night and Savannah the next day was easy. When I was trying to get back into my studies, two unusual people caught my attention. One in the library and the other in the school cafeteria.

The client at the library was deaf. I didn't realize it until he tried to talk to the librarian in a loud monotone voice. His voice came out muffled, and some words were impossible to understand. The librarian seemed lost when the guy tried sign language. Then he took a piece of paper off her desk and wrote something. It's amazing how resourceful deaf people are. My aunt took me scuba diving a few times in Florida. It was fun, but underwater, we had to communicate with a whiteboard and special crayons. It would have been easier if we'd known some hand signals.

On to the cafeteria story. Whenever I eat there, the smell of canned green beans takes me back to elementary school—not in a good way. To add insult to injury, the woman who sat across from me reeked of garlic. When her neighbor walked away, she stopped reading her book and lunged for the plate and scraped the food into a container. It's heart-wrenching to see a person so desperate.

I could have done something, but I didn't know what. Later, I realized the woman was the bird-lady you told me about. I've seen her in the park several times. She doesn't seem destitute because her hair is always combed. Maybe she's crazy and not poor. Maybe she really lives in a house and doesn't want to be cooped up all day. If the jam-packed cart she pulls around with her is anything like her house, maybe she can't squish into the place except through narrow corridors to her bed.

I went to the park during a study break and found her. When she walked off for a few minutes, I put a bagged lunch on the bench. She came back and ate the sandwich without concern. I mentioned the help center and asked where she lived. Oooh, the stink eye I got was extra evil. She pointed toward the river. I hadn't meant to agitate her.

Some of my aunt's training in psychology transferred over to me and helped me learn to be sympathetic to people's troubles. I miss her. During our last phone conversation, we talked about Cornish piskies (a type of fairy). She said they were once full-size humans and cursed because they weren't Christians. Over time, they shrunk into wrinkled little pranksters. If they feel like it, they can be helpful. I don't know how they got to Wales. It's a strange fable. More later.

Hugs—Sara

Jim put the letter down, realizing he was blessed to have such a compassionate woman in his life. He pulled his hand across his hair, where his bristles had grown out. Yes, he missed his long hair, but he'd gained so many other things.

September 1981

Dear Jim,

I haven't received any new letters from you. I know you said this might happen. I keep hoping you were wrong. Are you getting mine out in the wild country?

Yesterday, I drove to the airport in Atlanta to attend a volunteer orientation meeting for the USO. We've never talked about the place. I bet you know it—<u>U</u>nited <u>S</u>ervice

Organizations. It started somewhere around the beginning of WWII. Six businesses got together and created it to help soldiers.

A friend in Atlanta said I can stay the night when I volunteer. The drive to her place is four hours from Savannah, and it's a pretty dull trek on my own. Next time, I'll listen to a book on tape. The airport's twenty minutes from Mary's place. It took me the same amount of time to park my car and walk across the terminal. By the time I got to the USO's front entrance, my heart was racing. I had to take some deep breaths before walking inside. There were a lot of soldiers at the check-in desk, and some in front of a snack bar. They're on their way to places all around the world. I thought it would be amazing if one of them was you.

The manager appeared and said I was a day early for the orientation meeting, but I hung around. Good thing, too. She's a retired military colonel and liked that I was early, rather than late. The colonel said I'm expected to sign up for a minimum of two work shifts a month. I can do them all at once since I live so far away. The colonel said I didn't have to attend the orientation, because she and the volunteers had covered everything. While I was there, I went up to the security office, read some info about safety procedures, and got my badge without having to deal with a line full of people.

The USO lounge is spacious. Some chairs face the eating area and others the television. Only easy-going channels are shown. Ironically, the sit-com *Happy Days* was on while I was there. The concession counter stocks sodas and a variety of snacks. Everything is free to active-duty soldiers and their families. Individuals and organizations donate money, and occasional meals. There are USO centers on some military bases. They sponsor a lot of activities like movie days, picnics, and a bunch of things I haven't learned about yet. This center has books, magazines, and board games, too.

A volunteer told me that the soldiers like to talk at the snack counter, so I expect I'll learn a lot. Oh, one silly thing. When I was done for the day, I almost forgot where I'd left my car, even though I'd written the space number down. The airport garage must have thousands of parking spots. It took me a half hour to find my car. In the end, I got back to Savannah without any troubles.

—I'll add on to this letter, later.

Hello, again.

It's lunch time. Here's some local news—Mrs. Donnelly is having a small party this weekend. Blaire and I are going early with some homemade crab dip and fried green tomatoes. Things around here aren't the same without you.

Keep your spirits up. I hope you found the photo in my envelope. —XOO, Sara

October 1981

Panama

Dear Sara,

I'm sorry I haven't written. Work continues to control everything. Soon after the previous group returned from the jungle, we were sent out loaded up with tropical survival gear. Helicopters flew us in, and we rappelled out the doors onto a mountaintop—exciting times. Parachuting into places isn't as common as it used to be, but we're trained to do it.

This letter is a rewrite of the original. The first one got muddy. I combined multiple days in this letter since I couldn't get to a post office. Training in the tropics has been a wet mess from the start. Now I understand why the group before us came back muddy and torn up.

All your letters were being held somewhere. When I finally got them, I was happy you included a photo. Thank you.

I'm smiling from ear to ear. The guy next to me grabbed it and then everyone had a peek. They all said you're gorgeous, and I agree. I got it back after a small tumble with the culprit.

Entry 2:

The steep, muddy hills are unforgiving. One man slid about 70 feet, fractured his neck, and had to be airlifted out with a hoist (a wire stretcher with ropes attached to a helicopter). We learned about medical evacuation firsthand. I almost suffered the same fate when I tried to move out of the way. One minute I was slipping off the edge, and the next I was being slammed to the ground on the ridge by my squad leader. Thank God I didn't end up like Smitty. Sounds harsh, I guess. Out here, quick response times give people a chance to survive devastating injuries. We have teamwork and trust going on with this group. The scuttlebutt says he will recover with full mobility to a desk job. Field duty isn't possible after a major injury like his. Smitty is his nickname, short for Smitherson.

Entry 3:

I'm learning how to cross over a river in full gear. At first, everything was fine. My rucksack floated with the waterproof liner, and I kept my weapon dry. But then the murky waters churned up an unexpected fear. Every shadow in the water startled me. I got emotionally stuck until one of the guys shoved me forward. I salute my peers for being supportive. Later, I realized I froze up because all I could think about was Christina floating dead in the Savannah River while Dad tried to help. I know I wasn't there. Nevertheless, Dad's description popped into my mind as fast as the water pulled at me with the weight of my gear.

The next day, I got my act together for a river (rope) crossing. Miller swam across, secured the rope on a tree on the opposite bank. We pulled it tight, tied it to our side, put on handmade harnesses, and pulled ourselves hand-over-hand across. That time I managed okay. With any luck, there won't be any other SNAFU (Situation Normal All F'd up) events. Crude jokes and swearing continue to run rampant throughout the group. You'd want to cover your ears.

We are eating MREs (Meal, Ready-to-Eat). Add cold or hot water over the dry food and eat up, yum. There are resupply stations every few days. Regardless, there's a bunch of stuff we need to carry. The big muscled guys are a bunch of wimps. Not really. Sometimes I can carry stuff that's too much for them, which is weird because I weigh less. So, that's cool. We all have unique skills.

Entry 4:

I'm doing better today. I've never seen so many types of trees—almond, coffee bean, banana, and coconut. Also, odd ones with multiple legs that look like they could walk if they had a mind to. Some others have thick roots above ground. The number of animals is off the charts: sloths, monkeys, and parrots. Someone mentioned there are 10,000 varieties of plants and 1,500 of animals. I'll try to see them all. No, not possible. Too many other things I'm required to focus on.

We've had issues with radio communications. Sometimes we have to keep radio silence and use hand signals. It's tough because we can't always see each other through the brush. We discuss solid advance strategies before we move ahead. Our navigation training from boot camp is critical in these situations.

It's very hot and humid in this place. I drink so much water that I should apply to be a fish (joke). The air smells fresh, even with all the mud getting stuck on various parts of me. No matter how hard we try, everyone's slipping all over the place. Sometimes, the mud is so deep it tries to suck our boots off.

We've also deliberately rappelled down the hills face forward, so we can see our enemy on the way down and when we reach level ground. In regular life, athletes rappel down backward. Imagine running down a hill, holding onto a rope for stability, using one hand with a rifle in the other. It's hard to explain the rigging. If I stay on my feet, I'm golden. The last few feet are tough, because I need to stay extra alert while changing my position. Thank God, no one has had any uncontrolled descents.

In the afternoon, we dug a deep pit and lit a fire to dry our gear (night fires are forbidden. The light would attract the enemy in real combat missions). It's important to wear dry clothes and socks at night to avoid infections.

I put my wet clothes by the fire to dry out with everyone else's and fell into a light sleep with my head on my rucksack and my hands wrapped around my rifle. My stomach was full of delicious MRE chicken pasta. No, not delicious. I would have rather caught a fish and cooked it for dinner. A little later, my ruck started to move out from under me. While I was half-asleep, I figured one of the guys was messing with me. With my eyes still closed, I reached out and touched a hairy, bristly thing. It was a wild pig trying to steal my stuff. We had a tug-of-war while I growled at it. I won. Good thing, too. I need all my stuff. Everyone had a laugh at my expense. To be fair, it was a comedy show. Poor little piggy.

Entry 5:

Today we filtered water to help us learn to deal with fresh water shortages. We collected long sticks and stuck the ends into the ground and tied others to them. I should draw it for you, but it would look like a jumbled mess. From top to bottom, equally spaced, we added three bowl-shapes made from T-shirts. Each bowl contained a different item—top one: moss containing natural iodine. The next, sand. The last, charcoal. The filter system is more of a last resort if you don't have halazone purification tablets and need clean water. The water needs to sit before we can drink it, because the chemicals must evaporate out. The water we processed through the filter system tasted metallic, earthy, and something else I couldn't recognize. Learning how to survive with natural resources is pretty cool. In some ways, it reminds me of building shelters out of sticks in my backyard forever ago. I think I was ten at the time.

Entry 6:

Water, water, water… When the rain gets heavy, it rushes down the mountain in previously eroded V-shaped channels up to three feet deep. One guy showed us how to get out if we fall in either by choice or by accident. When I went in, I had to roll the right way on my back so my ruck would catch on the bank and stop me from rushing down the hill. It was like an amusement park ride, but I was the boat. I got it figured out right up to the part when I had to stand up. It was a challenge, but my buddies helped.

We also learned how to do a fireman's carry and make a stretcher in a hurry. Throwing someone over my shoulder wasn't as tough as I thought it would be once I learned the technique. The stretcher wasn't so easy. We used two long branches and some cloth. It's hard to haul around a soldier twitching in mock pain with a heavy rucksack on my back. Four people, one on each makeshift pole, worked better than two. When we came to a hill, we used ropes to move the stretcher down the embankment.

After resting from this round of exercises, I'll be involved in three weeks of live fire training. I'll explain later. My brain feels drained. One of these months, things will settle down.

I'm looking forward to seeing you then. I'm dozing off. I better stop writing. —XXO, Jim

October 1981
Fort Bragg Exercises

Dear Sara,

I'll be writing in my usual fits and starts. I don't even know what day of the month it is, or if I'm telling you things in the right order.

We're in the middle of the live fire training. The exercises are similar to real combat. It was a major operation to move everyone into place for these war games. Opposing forces dress in different gear, so we can distinguish one team from the other. We're sleeping with the ticks and mosquitoes, and eating MREs. There are swamps and man-made obstacles all over the place.

The goal of these exercises is to develop reactive habits in realistic situations, so we don't freeze up on actual missions. We're continuing to learn how to adapt to unpredictable, demanding circumstances. We'll live through screw-ups here, learn how to improve tactics, and do better the next round.

The auto-response training is meant to reprogram us into behaviors that are not ingrained in us under normal circumstances. We worked on this in boot camp, too. A natural thing would be to pull your hand back if something is hot. An unnatural one would be to throw yourself on the ground and start to crawl for cover if you hear a loud noise. Another would be constantly looking around for danger. A variety of responses will become permanently ingrained in our psyches. At this point, I don't know how this will translate into civilian life.

A goof-ball needed a medic this morning. Mongo slept next to me last night and got up to get dressed while he was still half-asleep. Didn't turn out great. There was a loose thread on his shirt, and he cut it off with his flick-knife. Then he forgot to close the blade and put it back in his pocket. He came back from the medic laughing like a maniac with stitches. That's one way of getting out of training for a few days. He can't risk getting an infection. So, they let him off the hook until he's healed.

The other day, I was under the roofline of a building. There was a torrential rain, and the gutters were overflowing. No surprise, I got soaking wet. I ended up lying in four inches of water for hours, reflecting on my life. Most of the time, my duties don't change because of the weather, unless there are lightning storms. All bets are off then. Lying around in the water was a helluva day. When it stopped raining, we used bonfires to dry everything. My skin was wrinkled from the exposure for hours. The uniforms dry quicker than the socks (4 pairs for the duration).

On one of the drier days during pathfinding, we came across an unexpected metal thing sticking out of the dirt. Turns out, it was a TNT dynamite box from WWII. Erosion made it come to the surface. For an instant, I thought we'd traveled back in time. The EOD (Explosive Ordnance Disposal) came in later to clear it out. Damn lucky we found it with our eyes instead of our feet. We can never let our guard down.

We all got attacked by bugs and poison sumac. The lucky ones only got a few itchy patches. The rest of us had sumac rashes all over. I needed steroids to get the mess under control. Before the meds took hold, it was almost impossible not to scratch through my clothes. I didn't want to do it any other way because infections could set in with my dirty fingernails.

At one point, about 40 of us moved around in groups (a platoon). The tension was higher than usual because all the ambient sounds were gone (no birds, no animals, no wind, nothing—total silence in the forest). Our senses tingled, and we were sure we were going to get ambushed. It felt like the forest itself was uneasy. It's unnerving because we're trying to avoid getting overtaken. If we do, "the enemy" appears in force on foot or in ATVs (all-terrain vehicles) and yells out we're all dead because we're surrounded. Unlike real life, we get to try again.

All for now.
Jim

Chapter 12

Connecting

TWO MONTHS WITH SARA IN PERSON BEFORE BASIC TRAIN-ing, and many months after, through letters and phone calls, had been an ideal way to get to know each other. Now that Jim was on leave, he was in a hurry to get to Savannah. When they first met, he hadn't gone to her apartment. This time, he wanted to see where she lived.

Sara had described the side entrance during one of their conversations, so he knew where to go. He headed around and rang the bell while clutching a bouquet of white daisies mixed with pink roses. No one answered, and he considered trying to call her on a local pay phone. Idling by the door wasn't an appealing idea.

A man with a bolo hat tilted forward over his brow walked up. "Anyone home?"

"No. Who are you?" Jim replied, sounding confused.

"A friend." The man tipped his hat up and winked. He shoved an envelope in the door's mail slot and swaggered away, grumbling under his breath.

A tinge of foolish jealousy spiked up. Getting his hackles up about an unknown man at Sara and Blaire's door seemed ridiculous. "Right. Well, have a good day," Jim called out, before stepping away from the door.

Jim walked around to the front of the house and noticed a plaque on the corner indicating it was a historic home from 1819, Regency Style, without a family name noted. The sidewalk and a narrow strip of grass separated the brownstone from the road. A few off-kilter red bricks popped through the ivy-covered building. The main entrance was an uninviting double door, covered by vertical black bars and a brass latch that wouldn't budge. He reached through, grasped a lion's head, and rapped the knocker two times. Some rustling noises came from the other side. The inner door opened, while the external bars remained closed.

"Hello? Can I help you?" An undersized terrier snuggled up against the man's leg and wagged its nub of a tail.

"Yes, sir. My name is Jim Masterson. Do you know when Sara will be back?"

"Well, hello," the man said in a chipper voice. "That's a handsome uniform you're wearing. I'm Mr. Veasey. She told me you might come by."

"Nice to meet you, sir. I tried the side door, but she didn't answer. Sorry to bother you."

"No, no. Come on in. Sara should be home soon." Mr. Veasey scooped up the dog and unlocked the barred door. His open hand jumped forward. Jim returned the gesture in one smooth motion. Mr. Veasey vigorously pumped his hand up and down a few times before releasing his grip.

"This is Sammy."

The dog's paw lifted on command.

Inside the front door, off to the left, a narrow-railed staircase paralleled the black-and-white tiled hallway. The place smelled like a mixture of dirty laundry, wet dog, turpentine, and paint. The smell was overpowering. He wanted to go outside to get some fresh air, but he stayed in place.

To the right of the hallway was an open living room with canvases leaning up against every wall. An almost completed, three-paneled work of art was propped up next to a drape-covered window. The piece was about five feet tall and wide. A mermaid, in bright primary colors, flooded the center and was surrounded by many overpowering human-like figures with oversized, gaping, tooth-filled mouths. They turned the rendering into a nightmare.

"Oh, I'm sorry. I shouldn't leave you standing here with the flowers. They're nice. I'm sure Sara will be pleased. Let me put them in a vase. I'll come right back." Mr. Veasey placed Sammy on a brown fringed pillow resting on a frayed armchair. "Wait in my studio. It used to be a living room. The art's taken over."

"Thank you, sir."

While Jim waited, he scanned the rest of the room. On an easel a canvas was half covered with an indistinguishable design combining primary-colored paints and pencil sketchings. Back toward the hall, he saw the infamous painting of the two soldiers Sara had told him about. Squinting at the picture didn't comfort him anymore than with his eyes wide open. The men's unsmiling, dirt-smudged faces were normal enough, yet they looked both dead and alive. Their clothes and caps were splotched with primary colors, and they appeared to be walking out of a bog filled with twisted bodies and destroyed military equipment. The background looked like smeared black-and-white dots. Its dull tones radically contrasted the soldiers. A disturbing chill ran up his spine.

Mr. Veasey returned with the flowers in a vase and pointed at the mermaid painting with his free hand. "I've sold many of these types to locals, collectors, and prominent people in New York, Los Angeles, and various resorts around the world. My friend Chuck oversees the marketing."

"Sara mentioned your work. It's an impressive collection." While saying so, Jim wished Sara would show up soon, so they could flee. Mr. Veasey and all his paintings put out disturbing vibes.

The man was proud of his home. He went into a long monologue and explained how he rented out one room in the main house to short-term guests, even though there was no sign out front stating such. Jim listened without absorbing the rest of the man's elaborate description of the home's history and his part in every renovation. At the end of the narrative, he guided Jim out onto the patio and put the flowers on the wrought iron table.

"Stay here. I'll be right back." Mr. Veasey touched Jim's wrist.

The backyard was about twenty-by-forty feet and felt cozy. Red bricks, in a circular pattern, covered most of the ground. By the fence, a flowerbed was filled with a medley of colorful flowers. In the far corner, a large oak tree created a partial canopy over the patio. Long tendrils of Spanish moss clung to the extended branches, not unlike most of the trees in Georgia. Why it was called a moss, when it was related to the pineapple and wasn't even from Spain, Jim hadn't a clue. Except, he knew the legend told of a Spanish conquistador who got it caught in his beard while pursuing a Native American princess; hence, the name Spanish moss.

Mr. Veasey returned with a bottle of sarsaparilla. "Here you go. It's Sara's favorite. I keep a crate in the kitchen for her visits."

"Thank you, sir." Jim finished the tepid drink in a few swallows, even though he still didn't like the caramel and vanilla flavor combination.

"She will love these flowers." Mr. Veasey's voice lowered. "Did Sara tell you I'm hosting dinner here tonight for you? I selected a bunch of things from the farmers' market this morning."

"No, I haven't talked to her since last weekend."

"Oh, dear, I shouldn't have said anything. I suppose she meant to surprise you." Mr. Veasey hesitated, and his eyes glazed over. He flinched, and said, "There will be six of us. You two, Blaire, Adam, and Chuck. He used to be a military photojournalist in the Army and often says each day could have been his last. All considered, he's a pretty calm fellow."

"Goes with the territory," Jim said. "A party. That's very kind of you, sir." Jim hadn't realized Adam was coming. Mr. Veasey was on a roll, revealing secrets. *What else would he spill?*

"I've seen one or two of Chuck's photographs, and he's seen all of my work." Mr. Veasey gazed off for a moment and scratched his head. "Never mind. So, for dinner, we're having burgers for the men's benefit and lots of vegetables on the side to keep the ladies happy."

"Sounds good."

"Adam came by yesterday. On weekends, he's been splitting his time between Blaire's and his mother's house. The base is close by, so it's not an issue. The place can be stifling at times."

"I understand," Jim replied. "Between my regular work at Fort Bragg, and my correspondence courses for a college, I'm tired most days."

"Keep those courses up if you can."

"I plan to go to the University of Georgia when I get out of the military."

"What degree?"

"Criminology. I hope to get accepted into the FBI."

"Very good."

"It'll be good to see everyone, sir." Jim noticed a raised box in the corner and gestured toward it. "Sara told me she does some gardening. Did she plant those?"

"Yes. Good observation." Mr. Veasey strolled over and held up a net, revealing some spinach. "See, it's doing all right. My daughter and I made the box years ago before I—well—never mind. The ground was barren when Sara moved in, and I insisted she revive it. The mesh keeps Chuck's gray tabby cat and any strays out of the dirt. I leave milk out every night. I'm not sure which cat drinks it."

"A very nice setup." Jim rested his hand on a beam holding up a striped awning off the wall of the house. "Where does your daughter live?"

"New York. She followed in my footsteps and became a lawyer." Mr. Veasey hesitated. "That was before I retired and became a full-time artist."

"I'm guessing Sara told you my dad's a local lawyer?"

"Certainly did. Quite a coincidence. I know your father from a previous case."

"Was it about my sister, Christina Masterson?" Jim was fishing for information. He wasn't sure why he needed to ask.

"Yes. It was a tragic situation."

"Her loss still haunts our family." Jim paused in thought. "I wish I knew why people can be so cruel."

"I'm afraid I can't say much about the case. Confidentiality laws and all."

"Yes, right, I forgot. My mistake." He hadn't forgotten, but he said so anyway.

Jim changed the topic. "My dad has a painting on his wall signed *Veasey*. Is it your work?"

"If it's a guitar in Cubist style, it's mine. It was a gift. If your father saw me now, he wouldn't recognize me. I've put on a few dozen pounds and don't wear suits anymore."

"I suspect he remembers you." Jim put his hands in his pockets. "Mr. Veasey, is there somewhere I can change my clothes?"

"Oh. Well. Yes. You should leave your uniform on until Sara gets here. It's so distinguished." Mr. Veasey winked and clicked his tongue.

"Thank you, sir. She's seen me in it before. I'd rather get into something more comfortable."

"As you wish. Let's see—what time is it?" Mr. Veasey pulled up his paint-spotted sleeve to reveal a yellow watch with an hour and minute hand that looked like bones. "Ah, yes, Sara should be back in half an hour. The bathroom is under the main stairs."

"Thank you, sir." Jim tried not to obsess over the watch.

"Go on now. I've been keeping you from changing. I'll leave some cushions by the back door for the chairs. The wrought iron isn't comfortable without them. Bring them along when you're done."

"Yes, sir." Jim found the bathroom under the stairs and ducked his head to accommodate the low alcove ceiling. There was no way a rounder, taller person could manage in such tight quarters. Mr. Veasey was both. The space reminded Jim of vintage shops he'd seen in Portugal with trinkets hanging on the walls. He balanced his bag on the triangular corner sink, closed the toilet, and sat down. His knees hit the sink cabinet, and undressing became an acrobatic task. Laughing at himself, he got up and hopped around while changing into his jeans. Switching his shirts wasn't any easier.

Amid the contortions, he got a glimpse of his new tattoo in the mirror. The green dragon stood out on the left side of his tanned, muscular chest. He'd show Sara, eventually. His face was red from struggling within the tin-can room, and his short hair had one spike sticking up in the middle.

After packing his uniform, he splashed water on his face and smoothed the rebellious hairs down. When he was satisfied, he strutted over to the screen door, scooped up the chair pillows, and stepped outside.

Chapter 13

An Encounter

WHEN JIM STEPPED OUT ONTO THE PATIO, HE SAW SARA by the table. She bolted toward him and wrapped her arms around him and the pillows. The experience wasn't what he'd expected, and they both burst into laughter. She took the cushions and threw them onto the wrought iron chairs. He pulled her back into his arms and swung her around before planting a kiss on her lips. Off to his side, he heard a gate open and someone's throat clearing.

Pulling back from Sara's embrace, he saw the intruders were Blaire and Adam. Blaire's long, wavy hair was dripping wet under Adam's Ranger beret. Adam's hair looked as if someone had gelled it upright. Water dripped down his forehead. Their faces glowed pink, with somewhat of a guilty expression. Jim decided they had been in the apartment, and they weren't just talking.

One day, he and Sara would be together in the same way, but they weren't in a hurry. He knew too well how intimate encounters could leave a lasting impression, no matter what the outcome. He moved his eyes across the garden, hoping to draw himself away from his physical desires. Along part of the fence, he cast his eyes on a trellis covered with broadleaf hops vines. Mr. Veasey could send the seed cones off to be made into beer or do it himself. There was a place up north that made beer from a client's homegrown ingredients. If there was a lull in conversation, he'd be sure to ask.

"Oh, beautiful flowers, Mr. Veasey," Sara exclaimed. She put her nose in the bouquet.

"Not mine. Your sweetheart brought them for you."

"Jim, thank you." Sara hugged him again.

"I forgot the dessert upstairs—and the plates," Blaire said. "Sara, come help me. Guys, we'll be back in a flash."

They disappeared through the gate. A good excuse for girl talk. Jim had a few private words of his own for Adam.

"Are you going to make an honest woman outta her?"

"Don't worry about it." Adam smiled. "One of these days, I'm going to ask Blaire to marry me."

The girls returned with an apple pie and a tub of vanilla ice cream. Sara put them in the mini-fridge by the back door. Mr. Veasey and an unidentified man came outside with condiments on a tray.

"Oh, Jim." The other man extended his hand, and Jim shook it. "We met out by the lady's apartment. I'm sorry, I should have introduced myself. I'm Chuck."

"Nice to meet you, Mr...." Jim breathed a sigh of relief now that he knew the man had no interest in dating Sara. Chuck was a lot older than he seemed outside the apartment steps. He and Mr. Veasey both appeared to be more interested in each other than either Sara or Blaire.

"Chuck. Call me Chuck. Mister is too formal."

"Yes, sir," Jim replied, supposing *sir* wasn't right either.

Chuck snickered and walked back inside. Ten minutes later, he returned with a tray of raw and cooked vegetables, and placed them on the table. He vanished again and came out with uncooked, one-inch-thick hamburger patties.

Mr. Veasey doused the burgers with brown sauce and placed them on the grill, an equal distance apart. He measured with a metal ruler and hovered over them like a vulture.

Chuck whisked his hand across the chairs. "Sit, sit. Relax. We'll prepare everything."

After objecting and trying to help several times, Jim surrendered. He adjusted the cushion on the wrought iron chair, made himself comfortable, and ate a few carrot sticks while waiting for the burgers to fill his growling stomach.

For a time, no one said anything until Adam broke the silence with a question for Chuck. "So, Blaire tells me you were a photojournalist, working right alongside the soldiers' fighting communism in Vietnam. I bet that was interesting."

"It had its moments," Chuck replied. "Some days were—worse than others."

Sara leaned into Jim. "Chuck has lived here a few months since they—oh, never mind. This is our first group meal."

"I don't know if we're getting enough training to deal with combat. I'm pretty sure the war games aren't anything like the real thing," Adam said. "What happened over there?"

"It was brutal, even for a photographer. Hueys and other vehicles got us out of jams or brought us supplies. The fighting soldiers, they had it rougher than me with their search and destroy recon missions." Chuck turned his chin up into the clouds before continuing. "They are still around today, right, men? The Chinooks?"

"Oh, yes—helicopters are still around," Jim responded. "The Chinooks are more for heavy lifting."

"I remember one time when I was with some men, mucking through the marshes. One of them got his foot stuck in something. I was on one side, another soldier on the other. He was supposed to help, but he was high on something, and wouldn't stick his hand in the water. The creed of looking after each other doesn't always apply. A lot of the men smoked marijuana or cigs to keep their nerves in check. Neither appeased anyone that day. I ended up hoisting my camera on my back so I could reach in the water and loosen the roots... flat-nose snakes and leeches all around."

"Never leave a man behind," Adam said.

"Stuff happens—sometimes it's hard to know what'll go on— even when training is ingrained," Chuck said.

Jim traveled back in his mind to the time he froze up in training in the water and had some sympathy for the offending soldier. He gazed at Sara and tightened his lips, knowing he'd told her about the incident while hoping she wouldn't say anything. She didn't, and he was relieved he could trust her. At the same time, he was grateful the episode wasn't in an actual combat zone.

When Chuck finished his first story, he moved onto another about the Vietcong tunnels in Vietnam for a solid half hour. Jim spaced out and fixed his eyes on Sara.

Chuck talked a great deal. At one point, Jim tried again to find out his last name because it continued to be uncomfortable addressing the man so informally. *What was he hiding?* Mr. Veasey probably knew. Jim had never met anyone who could talk so openly about their war experiences. *Had these things really happened around him? Had something gone wrong, and now he chose to conceal his identity, so he wouldn't be found out?* It was impossible to know. Jim chided himself for being suspicious.

He asked, "What was it like, taking photos of hell?"

"It was worse for them than me. I kept out of harm's way, with very few close calls. Somehow, I became addicted to getting into the action through my camera lenses. There were film crews out there too, and they televised it for the world to see. That's about the time the anti-war protesters started up in the States."

"So, you're anti-television?" Adam asked.

"The printed word is a gentler approach. I felt entrenched and detached simultaneously while I was there. My opinion of political agendas and the military aren't glowing. The Vietnam era changed me."

"I'll bet," Adam interjected and rolled his eyes in Jim's direction. "It changed the world."

Chuck talked and talked between bites of his dinner, explaining his experiences while waving his burger around to emphasize points.

"Chuck, Chuck," Veasey said. "Slow down. I can't keep up. Not to offend, but the topics you're choosing are hard to stomach during a meal."

"I suppose they are. Sorry, ladies. How do you like the hamburgers? It's a new sauce."

"Delicious," Sara replied with a mouth full of vegetables.

"So, Adam, you're a Ranger," Chuck blurted after he took a breath. "Do you boys still use beads for pacing and navigation?"

"What are those?" Blaire asked. "Something like Catholic rosary beads?"

"Spot-on, little lady," Chuck said.

"Hmm." Blaire pursed her lips. "It was a guess. I wouldn't know. I'm not Catholic."

Chuck was getting on Adam's nerves. Jim knew this because his friend's eyes narrowed in the way they always did when he was holding himself back.

"Honey," Adam's face relaxed into a smile, "they're easy to make. It's a set of beads on a lanyard that helps soldiers count off steps when they're walking. Kinda soothing to fiddle with the rest of the time. I'd agree they are like rosary beads, except they don't have a cross hanging off one end, and they're shorter."

No one could dish out so much crap and get away with it. Chuck, either your peers or the enemy, would knock you senseless, listening to your incessant rambling. Jim fiddled with a thread on his jeans.

Blaire turned to Chuck. "So, when you were out there in the muck, what did you do if someone got hurt?"

The expression on Chuck's face turned from animated and light to somber. Jim wasn't sure why, because everything the man said so far sounded self-serving. "Like I said, I helped when I could."

"I see." Jim wanted to say a hell of a lot more to this man whose stories weren't entirely believable. Instead, he held his tongue.

"Ever since then, I've gotten to know people through their words and actions. I try to capture who they are in the photographs—politicians, celebrities, mobsters, and military men. Reporting the truth is important, in writing and in photos, even if you need to run for your life after disclosing things the head honchos don't want revealed. Nothing should be off-limits. Photojournalists need to take significant candid pictures. Then there's the trouble of not showing the surrounding events. We can't show it all, and the public can misconstrue the circumstances. One person's photographs can't tell the entire story."

"What about..." Adam tried to get a few words in and failed.

"I'm sure you've all heard about the Vietnam girl running naked through the streets after napalm got on her clothes. And in 1968, the incident titled 'The Saigon Execution'? The Vietcong, child-murdering traitor, got justifiably and ruthlessly executed in the street. Anyone can add a story of their own and be brought to tears without knowing the truth. There are many similar situations. It's hard not to judge the photographer when they snap pictures instead of helping."

"Why?" Sara asked.

"There's no straightforward answer." Chuck danced away from yet another question. "While people make history, we capture the moment. In any case, I started putting myself at risk in the field after my older brother died on an intel mission."

The rest of Jim's burger sat uneaten on the plate. He imagined flies landing on it and then the maggots developing. The words "my brother died" wouldn't leave his thoughts. The circumstances were different. The results were the same—a dead loved one. For Chuck, his brother. For Jim, his sister. Both of those deaths resulted in self-sacrifices. Jim was doing the same thing in the military. The FBI would be no different. He rolled his shoulders to release the building tension. Getting back to the burger, he scooped it up and bit into it, knowing he would carry on with his plans no matter what the cost.

Chuck kept talking. "I found the effect the military had on people in the Vietnam years created dissension in the ranks. Some were drafted into service and others volunteered. Either way, many believe they'd made a mistake. Their lack of commitment became a toxin. They wanted a normal life with a wife and kids. If they already had families back home, they were worried about them sticking around.

"Once the men are home, they stand out in a crowd because of how they carry themselves. They look confident because that's how they were trained. Look closer at their eyes to see the truth. If they stare into the distance and rarely speak, they aren't there with you, but somewhere far away, on a battleground with their buddies. There is something about them that makes me want to reach out and do something, since I understand. On good days, I help; on bad, I pretend I don't see. Make sense?"

Jim replied, "On some level. I hope to never find out what it's like to be disconnected from the present." Jim read the time on his watch, gazed over at Adam, and raised an eyebrow. It was almost time to leave. He had fifteen minutes to get them out onto the sidewalk and down the street. "Well, Chuck—Mr. Veasey—it was good to meet you both. I'd like to take Sara to the beach since I'm leaving town soon."

"Blaire, you and Adam wanna come?" Sara chimed in.

"You bet." Blaire got up from her chair. "Thanks for your hospitality. See y'all later."

"Yes, thanks for dinner, Mr. Veasey." Adam got in the last words without addressing Chuck. On the way out, Adam shook his head and sighed.

The four of them paraded through the back gate onto the public sidewalk. Jim put a finger to his lips and made sure everyone saw. They walked in silence for another block, to keep their hosts from hearing anything derogatory they might say. Once they turned the corner, Adam broke the silence.

"Man, that Chuck guy has a lot to say." Adam reached for Blaire's hand.

"Tell me about it." Jim took Sara's hand.

"He doesn't usually talk so much," Sara said. "Have you ever heard of the expression talk the bark off a tree?"

"Well, sure." Adam stretched his hands up into the air and yawned.

"We'll survive," Jim replied. "Some of it was interesting. Truth be told, I didn't want to listen to him go on about soldiers all night. We need a break from the military." He concentrated on the surprise he had for Sara, brought two fingers to his mouth, and let out a loud whistle. With some of his savings from the last months, and some help from Suzy, Jim had put together something special for Sara. He figured his best buddy would love sharing it with Blaire, too. Within seconds, a horse-drawn carriage with fringe draping down from a covered roof pulled around the corner and stopped.

"Care to take a ride?" Jim asked.

"This is amazing. You're full of surprises. First, the private tour at the museum ages ago, and now this." Sara was beaming.

"Up we go," Adam said, and he helped Blaire into the carriage. Blaire was speechless.

This topped anything else they could have come up with. Jim couldn't have been happier with their reaction.

Sara hugged Jim and kissed on his ear. The sensation sent a shiver down his spine.

Chapter 14

Correspondence

Dear Sara,

How are you holding up? This year has been harder than I expected. Congratulations on your degree! I'm a little early with the good wishes. Better early than never, right? You've accomplished a lot. Your classes at SCAD sounded challenging.

I didn't tell you everything I wanted to in my last letter because I had to sleep. We go through two different cycles. We're on one or the other during the year. They're called mission or support cycles. On support, I can go home on weekends. On missions, we are on field duty, in or out of the country. If I'm still on mission status and there are no impending world conflicts, I'm obligated to stay within 50 clicks (kilometers) of the base during these phases. It's rough being part of the rapid deployment force. Talk to the soldiers at the USO about the 82nd. They'll have a lot of praise, but they won't likely sign up for the job. At least that's what I've heard—what have I done? I've never been so tired and more overworked in my life.

I'm not sure where or if I'll be going on a mission at some point. They (can't say who they are) would love to know more about our area of operations, especially who's going where, so they'd be able to find our weaknesses. I have a right to be paranoid, since my career may be in jeopardy if I tell you too much. This letter isn't much of a concern. Mentioning names are off-limits. However, the ones I've mentioned up to now in letters are okay, since I've never brought up actual dates or specific tactics. All of us were re-programmed to be a little paranoid and hyper-vigilant about what we say and do. The point is to protect the people we associate with. Soldiers talk openly about missions among themselves, but rarely to anyone outside their immediate units.

I talked to Adam on the phone at Hunter the other day. He'd finished working in Saber Hall and said his situation is like mine. If we get deployed, we could end up at the same location. Rangers and the 82nd often work in tandem on missions. We talked about things and agreed his work requires more secrecy than mine. So, Blaire shouldn't worry if he doesn't tell her much. Truth be told, I feel like I burden you with my stories. I'm not sure which way is right.

I'm getting through my latest non-military class. It takes up hours, I could be catching up on much needed sleep. When I mail your letter, I'll mail out a term paper. This might be my last one until I get to the university even though my progress will slow down. Sleeping is more important. Yeah, I know, I put this on myself, but I still don't believe I had a choice, and there is no doubt I'm toughening up daily. I'll be a good FBI candidate when I'm ready to apply, but for now I need to concentrate on my current day-to-day duties.

I'm trying not to stress out. One of the guys—Gunther—didn't help my mindset when he flipped out. He's around six foot four, weighs about 240 pounds, and has been called "a cornfed dude" because he's all muscle and grew up on a farm. To put this into perspective, I'm 160 pounds. Gunther started banging on the door of our building after hours. Jay opened it, and got bludgeoned full in the face with a monster fist. Then Gunther barreled in with the MPs (Military Police) in hot pursuit. The four of them tried to apprehend him and got thrown into a wall. The wall fell to pieces. Turns out he had taken the commander's jeep and gone on a drunken joyride. He freaked out when the MPs were after him and wanted to get into the building quickly. Anyway, Gunther was so out of it he didn't realize the door wasn't locked. Since then, the wall's been repaired. Nevertheless, the event is stuck in my head, and Jay is still out of commission, with a broken nose and jaw.

Later, we learned Gunther was having a flashback (it's like hallucinating without drugs) from some training accident with explosives at the end of his enlistment in the Marines. When his time was up there, he moved over to the Army instead of finding a civilian career. None of us knows why. After the violent episode, they sent him out for a psych eval. They say he's not coming back since he's a detriment to his platoon. He had a .08 blood alcohol level (a high number without being stumbling drunk), and nothing illegal in his system. I heard, before the episode, he hadn't slept in four days. Even a stable personality can lose their mind after being awake for so many days.

I'll be getting a long four-day weekend soon, but I'll be on 'mission' status. Savannah is off-limited this time. I'll read a military textbook and catch up on sleep. I hope we can spend time together soon, but before then I'll send you something sweet. Thinking of you continues to keep my spirits up. Thanks for the new beach picture of you. Your skin glistened in the sunlight in your teeny-tiny bikini—beautiful. You are in every way, outside and in.

Keep the home fires burning. Gotta sign off now. I have ironing to do before I hit the rack for some shut-eye. Will dream of you—love, Jim

P.S. In regard to the article you sent—I believe putting soldiers into a foreign country is only good if the country can't defend itself. Once the citizens become self-reliant, it is a waste of time for the military to be there.

In My Room
Savannah, June 1982

Dear Jim,

I feel like I'm avoiding the military and embracing it at the same time. One moment, I'm turning away; the next, I'm researching and going to the USO. Sounds strange, I suppose. It's interesting to watch the soldiers' behavior when they come to the USO. I hear them carrying on outside the door, cursing and sassing each other. When they cross the threshold into the lounge, they stop. It's like a switch. One of them told me they don't want to offend the volunteers.

There's a TV in the lounge, and cartoons are on instead of the news, so no one gets riled up about current events. It's funny seeing grown men mesmerized by *Tom & Jerry, Road Runner* (beep, beep), and *Sylvester & Tweety*. They aren't exactly peaceful with the characters being abused and then revived to take abuse all over again.

The wind howled through my windows last night and gave me the chills. Some say the wind is full of spirits. It didn't help that I was reading *The Shining* by Stephen King. I picked it up off a park bench, and now I regret my decision. It's worse than my last attempt to read one of his short stories in *Night Shift*, where the Greek god Pan required a sacrifice in "The Lawnmower Man."

This morning, I was thinking back to the times you jumped out of an airplane or a Chinook helicopter. My paratrooper. You know I'm afraid of heights. Blaire went skydiving. She said it was freeing after she got over the idea of stepping out into the abyss and floating down to the ground. Thinking about it makes my head spin.

Chuck is out on the curb, chopping wood. Mother Nature helped by giving him a task. At least three heavy tree limbs fell after the storm knocked out the power lines. The end of one branch was bigger than Chuck's head. After cutting a chunk off, he used it for a chopping block for the rest. No, not his head, the wood. I'm laughing at my words, having read them again. I realize it's a strange picture I'm describing. Mr. Veasey said Chuck has PTSD. It's a new term coined in 1980 and replaces the old term shell shock. What am I saying? Sorry, I shouldn't explain, since you know Gunther has it. So, memories of Chuck's past come back to haunt him, and he gets the related images under control by doing strenuous, productive physical activities. Sounds like a good plan.

At first, Mr. Veasey seemed irked. Most people around here have wood delivered in neat stacks. Chuck's piles looked like a twisted beaver dam. He said hiring someone was a waste of money and he'd rather do the work and blow off some steam. If you ask me, which you're probably not, the guy isn't all there. I forgot to mention that a branch hit the windshield on his car and broke it. You should have heard him cursing like a wild man, so unlike him. He apologized for sounding off— lazy language, he said. Anyway, it's good it wasn't someone else's car. There might have been even more shouting or a stack of insurance problems.

On to something else. Last weekend, I talked Blaire into going horseback riding, since we hadn't been to the barn to groom horses or ride for months. We couldn't afford to go every week anymore, so we stopped and then got caught up in other things. The treat you gave us with the horse-drawn carriage ride motivated us to get back in the saddle. We rode our bicycles over to the barn. Between the bikes and horses, we kept busy for hours. By dinner time, we were plumb worn out, sore and happy.

My double shifts at the USO are working out fine. I picked the busiest time slots to keep me hopping. Last weekend, one of the ladies was spazzing out over a mouse in the sticky trap by the fridge. She said it was a man's job. I ignored her, grabbed the trap, and threw it out. The volunteers are primarily nice women. A few come across as sour-faced grumps. They've been volunteering for a decade and for some reason keep coming back. Perhaps I've misread them. When the lounge isn't busy, I talk to the nice ones a lot. They're all older than me. I don't mind because they're interesting and more worldly. When the activities slowed down, one of them always helps me with some of my troublesome schoolwork.

The soldiers are mostly men, with a few women. Some of the guys like to flirt. Now, don't be jealous. I only have eyes for you. Every time I see a guy with dark hair and blue eyes, I think of you. Most of them don't talk to the staff, but others don't know when to stop. I've learned things about their families, their MOS, and where they are going or coming from. I've never heard of some of the places. The map, tacked up by the front desk, comes in handy. Some of the soldiers stand at the food counter and try to guess each other's jobs by tossing out clues. You can be proud of me now for knowing MOS stands for <u>M</u>ilitary <u>O</u>ccupation <u>S</u>pecialty.

Thinking of you every day. Love, Sara

July 1982
Savannah

Dear Jim,

The letters continue. Between the ones you've sent and mine, we have over 100. We have a record of our year, and I think it's worth putting them into a binder. I have mine in a box for now. I loved your phone call last week.

Your sunflowers arrived today. What a nice surprise. Adam brought them by with the note from you in his handwriting. What's gotten into you? Last month, it was a hollow book filled with chocolates for my graduation and now the bouquet. It'll be wonderful to see you next month. I'm excited.

It took me longer to send this letter than usual. Aunt Deborah came and left since I last wrote. She flew in from Wales for a week. No warning—she just appeared with a suitcase. When I got back from the library, she was sitting on my doorstep. The poor lost thing. It was hard to manage my schedule, but we had dinners together during the week.

Over the weekend, we flew up to DC and toured around. We divided our time between the museums and eating in town. At the National Art Gallery, I had to buy an umbrella to shelter us from a random rainstorm. It was fun walking in the downpour. There were puddles everywhere. I resisted the urge to puddle jump. The rain didn't last long. We slit up and headed in different directions. She walked over to the military memorial. I sat by the Tidal Basin and stared at the Washington Monument reflecting off the surface. When she found me later, I practically jumped out of my skin. I could have stayed there for hours thinking about life, and what it will be like to see you again.

Next thing I knew, we were on our way to the Natural History Museum. I tried to talk Auntie into a paddleboat ride instead. She said if we didn't hurry, we'd be late. I had no idea what she was up to. She grabbed my arm and hustled me along. I don't know how she did it. She'd arranged a behind-the-scenes tour of the ornithology department like you'd done for me in Savannah at the art museum. It was great to see my mentor from my internship. We stood around talking to Mr. B for about thirty minutes, and then he took us on the tour. By the time we left, I felt high on life.

We walked to Georgetown for dinner in half the time it normally would have taken. Auntie kept grabbing my arm to slow me down. She was a little winded after the three-mile walk—I felt guilty. In the end, she didn't mind since I marched her straight past the White House. I'm rather numb after seeing it too many times when I'd lived in the area, but her face lit up.

I took her into a restaurant with a patio outside right next to the C&O Canal, and she got excited all over again. A soda with rum mellowed her. We ate crabs with delicious red spice sprinkled on top. Old Bay—you may have heard of it? The best tangy spice, ever! We spent the night in a no-nonsense local hotel and flew back to Atlanta the next morning. Auntie boarded a plane back to Wales from there. I was already at the airport, so I took a shift at the USO before driving back to Savannah. It was a long week, but I loved my time with her.

One day, I want you to meet her. She said I should visit her in Wales soon. I'm not sure how. Maybe in the summer. My life is a little less flexible than hers.

Guess what your mother did. It's nothing freakish. Well, at least I didn't think so. I got a package in the mail. The return address was from Clarissa Masterson. Well, you can imagine, I was confused because I couldn't remember your mother's first name. At first, I didn't open it until the temptation overwhelmed me. She sent me the most amazing handmade (by her) quilt. I couldn't believe my eyes. I've only met her once! I guess she likes me. Look at the photograph. It's gorgeous. There are birds and flowers all over the fabric. The visit to the bird-man at the Smithsonian, and now this.

See you in a few weeks. Don't faint with disbelief. I won't write again until after I see you. There's a lot I've got to do in advance, so I'll have more free time once you're here.

Love you sweetheart, Sara

Chapter 15

The Beach

JIM WANTED HIS NEXT VISIT TO SAVANNAH WITH SARA TO build up like a musical crescendo. It took him a while to figure out how to accomplish this task without giving away his plan. Keeping things simple seemed best, so she wouldn't guess what was coming. They arranged to meet at the train station during a phone conversation.

By the end of the week, he was ready for his motorcycle journey with the little box snug in his backpack. The registered mail from his mama had arrived just in time for the trip. He covered his clothes with his motorcycle outfit and tied the backpack to the rear seat. After checking and triple-checking both the map and bike, he rode away from his building, past headquarters and around the circle toward the civilian world. Driving by the statue of *Iron Mike* enforced his own commitments. *Iron Mike* was an airborne trooper, and so was Jim.

Each day, he was thankful to be alive. The last large-scale joint operation of the 82nd was over a decade before in Vietnam. There was no way of knowing what would come next. His mind wandered to another statue dangling from a church spire in Normandy, France.

What was the real man's name? Private John Marvin Steele, WWII. He was famous back in the day for going off course while jumping out of a plane and getting his parachute stuck. My parents took me to see the area in France. Back then, it seemed like a message not to join up. Dammit, Dad, you meant the opposite. I'm still annoyed with you some days. Yet, at other times, I'm not because I'm stronger now.

Jim refocused and got on with the drive to Savannah. Two hours in, his body rebelled and his mind drifted again. He imagined driving along the coastline and stopping at Myrtle Beach for a swim or a run.

Arriving quickly in Savannah well-rested and in one piece was more important. He should have realized, but he hadn't planned things out well enough before leaving the base. At the next rest stop, he scanned the map and adjusted his route to Florence, North Carolina. There, he parked his bike at a friend's place, took a taxi over to the train station, and hopped on to the next Palmetto train.

He longed to wrap his arms around Sara and knew their reunion would be as sweet as always. Settling into his seat on the train, he closed his eyes and hoped to dream about her.

Hours later, Jim awoke just before the train pulled into Savannah. When he disembarked, Sara wasn't there. His heart pounded as he paced back and forth with his backpack close to his chest. Every other woman he saw elevated his anxiety, even though he tried to quell his emotions. There were plenty of taxis by the curb. He chose not to deviate from their meeting plans, and fretted over why she was late. When he'd almost given up, she appeared around a corner. Not wasting a moment, he approached her. Much to his relief, she was eager to be in his arms. Jim kissed her forehead and then her lips. They lingered together for a time until a group of loud teenagers approached. With the interruption, Jim took Sara's hand in his, and they walked together down the aisle to the taxi stand.

Getting into the first available taxi, Jim instructed the driver to take them into town. He was bubbling over with excitement. Instead of giving away his surprise too early, he controlled himself and inwardly thanked the military for teaching him how to be disciplined. The afternoon was filled with normal events like strolling through town, dropping by his dad's, and getting some food.

"So," Jim began, "I bought a motorcycle from someone in Fort Bragg."

"You did? I'm surprised. You'd said you didn't like rattling around on Adam's."

"Well, when I saw the bike, I couldn't resist."

"Where is it?"

"Back in Florence, in a family friend's garage. I started to ride down to surprise you, but I got too tired. Work's been busy, and I haven't had enough sleep."

"It's good you stopped. I'll see it another time."

"You want to ride? If you do, I'll get an extra helmet in pink and a jacket."

"Um, pink like Blaire's?"

"Sure, you'll be twins."

"I'm not sure I want to."

"Fair enough," Jim said. "Let me know if you change your mind."

As late afternoon approached, they walked to the brownstone to catch up with Blaire and Adam. After a quick reunion, they all jumped into Blaire's car and headed for the beach to catch the sunset. When they pulled into the parking lot, Sara braided her hair to keep the breeze from pushing strands into her eyes. Out on the dunes, they all pulled their shoes off and walked down by the water.

Adam and Blaire ran down the beach at least a mile in front of them. He and Adam had collaborated. Jim had twenty minutes before their friends turned around. By then he'd hoped to have said what he intended. They walked side by side, with their hands entwined, along the hard-packed sand by the incoming waves. Sara swerved to avoid white cresting water, which splashed and turned in spirals by her bare feet.

"Sara?"

"Yes?"

"We've known each other for—what, a year?"

"Yes, silly. Letters, phone calls, in person. It seems like I know you as well as I know myself."

"Me, too—I mean, I feel the same way. I could stay here forever." Over her shoulder, he saw a ship passing by on the horizon. The sight seemed significant, although he wasn't sure what it meant. "There's one thing you've never asked me. This is awkward."

"What? Sounds scary." Sara stopped by the waves, leaned over, and splashed a bit of water up at him with her open palm.

"Not really. It's a little uncomfortable to discuss." Jim pulled in his breath, counted to five and exhaled. He had rehearsed the lines in his head a dozen times and hoped the words would come out the way he intended.

"What is it?" Sara grasped and squeezed his hand.

"I—there's a reason we've never—there's a reason we've only kissed."

"Ah, right. I figured you were shy or something." She giggled.

"No, that's not it. I took my cue from you." He sighed. If he couldn't talk this through, he would melt away into the water and never return. "It's not because I haven't wanted you. We've been…"

"Oh, honey, where is this going? You're weaving around like a blind bat."

He almost couldn't do this. Adam and Blaire were turning around, heading toward them. "Yeah, I guess. Sara, I haven't—we haven't— because I respected your devotion to your beliefs."

"Right. I wanted our relationship to be strong on many levels." She stopped, turned, and was scowling at him while a tear emerged from the corner of her eye.

He wiped it away.

"We've known each other for so long, but you've been away most of the time."

"Yes," he said.

"I thought something was wrong." She sniffled.

"No, Sara. You've been so tolerant of my schedule."

"And mine," she said.

"Our separation has been tough on us." He pulled her up the bank, away from an emerging wave. They almost fell. "I wanted…" Jim dropped onto one knee and tilted over.

"You okay?"

"Yes, of course." He brushed off one hand and put it into his pocket. For an instant, he feared the box with his grandmother's ring had fallen into the ocean. Much to his relief, it was right where he'd left it. Flicking the box open, he pulled the ring out with the pocket and smiled. "Sara, will you marry me?"

Sara fell next to him and laughed with apparent delight.

He wasn't sure what she was thinking.

"It's a gorgeous ring." Sara's lips were trembling, and she extended her hand.

Jim slid the ring into place. His heart pounded so hard that he thought it might pop right out of his chest.

She looked at her outstretched hand and put it on his chest. The motion shifted his shirt collar to the side. "I see you have a tattoo. When did you get that?"

"Ages ago."

"Ew, gross. Ours are almost identical. I'm teasing. I like it."

"Sara?" Now, he was worrying about why she diverted away from his marriage proposal.

"Jim, I love you." She took his hand, stood up, and pulled him with her. Next thing he knew, she'd run her hands up around the back of his neck and kissed him. A moment later, she stepped back and said, "Yes, of course I'll marry you, on one condition."

"What, my love?"

"You take me to bed tonight and show me…" Her cheeks reddened, and she momentarily shied away.

He took her into his arms and kissed her deeply, to show his consent. "Mm, you're delicious—I have a condition, too."

"What?" Sara replied.

"Before I take you to bed, remove your makeup. It's like a mask, and I want to see all of you."

"You sure you don't want to wait until our wedding night to see me unmasked?" Sara giggled at her joke and slid her hand under his shirt.

The sensation of her touching his bare chest sent a ripple of electricity through his body.

"I'm sure. I don't want any last-minute surprises." Jim was laughing, too.

"On a serious note, let's combine forces with Adam and Blaire. She told me they got engaged last night."

"We're not sleeping with them." Jim smiled.

"Oh, stop. Of course not."

"I heard he was going to ask."

"And you didn't tell me?" Sara pushed him away.

"Oops, sorry. I was focusing on getting to Savannah to make my grand proposal—Blaire didn't tell you they were engaged?"

"Well, she, yes, she did. Never mind." Sara grabbed Jim's hands and ran around in circles, pulling him with her.

"Jesus, woman, stop. You're making me dizzy."

"Where are we going to live?" she said.

"On base or off. You can check it out, and we'll decide. Both places have access to community activities."

"Okay, let's think about it. Whoa, I'm going to be Mrs. Masterson." She kissed him. "We can have a small double wedding with Adam and Blaire."

"Whatever you want." Jim hugged and released her. "Speaking of—here they come."

Adam and Blaire were running straight toward them. Blaire arrived first and glared wide-eyed at Sara. "Well, did you say yes? Are we going to jump the broom into married life?"

"Of course," Sara replied.

Blaire was so excited. She fell into Sara's arms, squealing, and jumping them both up and down. Jim and Adam started to laugh.

"Whoa, look at that," Adam said. "I didn't know we had such an amazing effect on them."

"Okay, okay." Jim chortled. "Sara wants a joint wedding."

"Anything they want. I'll be there," Adam said.

"Yep, me, too." Jim shook Adam's hand before giving him a bear hug. "Great. Who's going to put it all together while we're off soldiering?"

"I'm betting on my mama, since she loves organizing parties."

Back and forth, they debated on whether to share the news with their families right away or celebrate on their own. Spending their entire weekend on arrangements wasn't at the top of anyone's list. They could talk to Adam's mother later. The rest of their families could be phoned in the days ahead.

On the drive back into town, Jim slung his arm across Sara's shoulder and she snuggled in close. No one said anything along the way. If the rest of them were like him, they were absorbing the gravity of their engagement and upcoming marriage.

After Adam had parked the car across the street from the café, they walked in and found a place to sit. Jim thought about the first time he'd eaten there with Sara.

"How about at The Marshall House?" Blaire blurted. "My mama would want Charleston, but I feel more at home here."

"The Marshall House sounds perfect," Sara replied.

"I don't know. It's haunted." Jim raised his hand up in the air, wiggled his fingers, and grimaced. "Woo-hoo, poltergeists and specters beware. Why not—so is most of Savannah. Look out, spirits, here we come."

Chapter 16

A Wedding

SEVERAL MONTHS LATER, JIM AND ADAM STOOD SIDE BY SIDE on the sidewalk across the street from the Marshall House, which took up most of the block on East Broughton Street. The red brick inn, with green wrought iron balconies and window shutters, was more imposing than either of them recalled. On the roof, an American flag flew in the breeze. Two separate porches on the fourth floor were decorated with a profusion of white flowers. There he saw two separate groups of women leaning over the balconies, talking across the expanse. Jim recognized his own mama and Adam's, but he wasn't sure about the others. His confusion ebbed when the ladies waved in their direction and said something he couldn't quite make out beyond his and Adam's names. Then he decided the mystery women were Aunt Deborah and Blaire's mother, Mrs. Fairmont. Jim and Adam saluted for effect.

Jim's timing was spot-on. Spending the night in Adam's quarters at Hunter, getting dressed, and having lunch across the street from the inn got them there on time without having to deal with family members fussing over them. It was also a better tactical plan than milling around somewhere else or arriving late because of unforeseen complications. To avoid any embarrassment, Jim brought peppermint gum to freshen their mouths before the ceremony.

"It was a mistake not to come and rehearse before the wedding," Adam said. "I know my mama wanted us to."

"More thrilling this way, if you ask me," Jim replied. "Besides, we couldn't take any more leave, and we need all the time we can get for our honeymoon." He punched Adam's arm and then wiped a fleck of dust off where his fist had landed.

"Noooo! We wouldn't want that." Adam put his arm around Jim's shoulder, bending him forward and knocking his cap off. Jim grabbed it in mid-air, put it back on, and pulled on the sleeves of his dress uniform to straighten it.

Ignoring what just happened, Jim said, "It's good we already took care of the moving arrangements. Getting Sara's belonging to Fayetteville took some doing. She'll start teaching in September."

"Yeah, man, I know. I was there when her stuff was moved," Adam said. "I've already moved my things into the apartment. No more living on base."

"Yeah, I know. I was there," Jim said. "We're two nervous cats."

"Like the four-legged one on the porch, pacing?" Adam flicked his chin toward the right.

"Funny." Jim peered past the feline to a long-paneled window with shifting glass. "Okay—there's someone looking this way through the porch window."

"Where? I don't see anyone. I'll wager it's the sun reflecting off the pane."

"Could be a ghost from the cellar. Soldiers and guests haunt this place."

"Well, aren't you cheery?" Adam guffawed. "Come on, man, let's get married. The ladies are waiting. This is going to be an exciting night."

"Oh, stow it," Jim exclaimed.

"Plan to," Adam joked. "Do you have the marriage licenses?"

"Yes." Jim reached inside his jacket to double-check.

They crossed the road when the traffic ebbed. To release some jitters, Jim started to march, and Adam fell into the cadence up the porch steps to the front entrance. While their feet strode up and down in place, the door opened on its own. They took off their caps, tucked them under their arms, and continued inside across the large black-and-white marble tiles shaped in squares, diamonds, and swirls. It reminded Jim of a dream world. Their polished, black dress shoes and pressed blue trousers reflected in the mirrors embedded in the long reception desk.

A young woman glanced up from a pile of papers, smiled, and gestured toward a room across the hall. "Mrs. Marshall is your guide.".

"I don't understand," Jim replied.

"The portrait behind me is Mrs. Marshall. Our fearless leader likes to walk the halls." The young woman sheepishly smiled and winked. "Congratulations on your marriage."

"Thank you." Jim stared at the portrait, and the figure's eyes seemed to shift over his shoulder. The receptionist must have been joking, because Mrs. Marshall had been dead for years.

Jim and Adam turned on their heels, soldier fashion, marched into the room, and down the aisle flanked by chairs filled with guests toward a brick wall draped with white linens to soften its stark appearance. He recognized his guests on the right and a few of Adam's on the left. The group included about thirty choice friends and family members. Some were in uniform and others in suits or dresses.

When Jim and Adam reached the front, they pivoted and took two steps to either side of the aisle. To keep calm, Jim mulled over a few things. So far, Mrs. Donnelly's organizational talents were perfect. Sara and Blaire had wanted to keep things simple, and Adam's mother had kept everyone on mission after many negotiations with the families. Not a straightforward task with Aunt Deborah in Wales, his eccentric mother in Florida, and Uncle Jorge in Portugal.

It had been two months since their engagements, and Mrs. Donnelly had pulled strings to get them into the Marshall House banquet room. The chairs she'd selected were painted bamboo. The front two rows were reserved for family members with draped ribbons and a few flowers. Soon, the military chaplain, Chaplain Scythe, would step into place between them and the ladies would walk down the aisle. Choosing this officiant made sense because Adam knew the man, and Jim didn't want to be hemmed in by religious doctrines within a church. The chaplain was flexible about their wishes and was able to fit them into his schedule.

Jim turned his head toward a window by the porch and saw a silhouette facing in their direction. Chiding himself and blaming nerves, he refocused on the ceremony. The pianist in the corner began to play. The family walked into the room two by two: Blaire's parents, Aunt Deborah and Jim's mama, Suzy and his dad, and lastly, Mrs. Donnelly with Uncle Jorge. Jim wasn't sure how Adam's mother had decided who sat where, but having her enter the room last made sense. She could make sure everything progressed according to her plan. Each member slid into place in the front row. Jim flexed his knees, preparing for the next procession, and noticed Adam had done the same. In unison, they exaggerated deep inhales and exhales.

At the other end of the aisle, Sara and Blaire came into view side by side with a single lace ribbon entwined within the braid that wrapped around each of their heads. Their gowns were identical champagne-colored lace with V-necks, and nipped-in waists with the fabric flowing down to above their ankles. Underneath were flat shoes with lace tendrils covering the bridge of their feet. They both clasped a few sprigs of baby's breath and two pink roses in their hands. Jim knew they were antique gowns from the 1920s; Sara had told him so. But he never imagined how warm inside he would feel when he saw her beauty with fresh eyes. His nervous jitters melted away when she came up beside him.

Chaplain Scythe began:

"We are gathered here today… Do you, Sara Cosgrove, take James Masterson to be your lawfully wedded husband… Do you, James Masterson…

"Do you, Blaire Fairmont, take Adam Donnelly to be… For sickness and health until death do you part…

"I now pronounce you—two married couples. Mr. and Mrs. Masterson and Mr. and Mrs. Donnelly."

Kisses and embraces followed the exchange of promises. The newlyweds paraded back down the aisle into the lobby with the guests close behind.

Without delay, the staff closed the banquet doors and thumped around inside. Mrs. Donnelly ducked inside to manage the situation. Twenty minutes later, she reappeared and said, "Everyone, attention please. The room has been transformed. Go on in and find your name cards hanging on the small trees by the door. Flip them over and you'll find your table number. Blaire, Adam, Jim, Sara—y'all go first." She kissed each of the newlyweds on the cheek before flinging the doors wide open.

Jim's jaw dropped, and Adam was speechless. Sara and Blaire were on the edge of tears. The staff had turned the room into a magical place. Silver buckets around the room held branches with tiny white lights. A semi-circular table, for the family and the couples, stood where Chaplain Scythe had officiated in the front of the room. The main table, and six others, were covered with white linen cloths and clusters of flowers. Twelve chairs were by the main table, and six were around each of the smaller ones.

Everyone collected their seat assignment cards and settled into their corresponding chairs. Chaplain Scythe sat in the middle of the head table. Jim and Adam sat on either side with their brides. Mrs. Donnelly had mixed up the seating at the main table in such a way that Suzy and his mama were at opposite ends to avoid unnecessary confrontations or any discomfort between the two women. Uncle Jorge and Aunt Deborah were with his mom and his sister, Melanie. Suzy and his dad were next to by Mrs. Donnelly.

The staff entered with bottles of champagne and circulated among the guests. When they were done, Chaplain Scythe led the celebratory toast.

The meal began with a few oysters. They reminded Jim of the party at Mrs. Donnelly's house when he and Sara met in Savannah. "Sara?" He slipped an oyster into her mouth.

"Hmm, a delicious aphrodisiac." She swallowed it down and gazed at him.

"It is, it is." He kissed her and then someone tapped him on the shoulder. Looking around, he couldn't figure out who had interrupted them. Then he spotted something out of the corner of his eye. "Sara?"

"Yes, darling?" She ate another oyster.

Jim pointed toward the window. "Did you see that?"

"No. What?"

"Never mind. I thought I saw someone I didn't recognize."

"All right." She popped a third oyster in her mouth and stood. "I need to say something to Blaire without talking over the chaplain."

While Sara busied herself with Blaire, Jim stood and ambled over to the window to confront the stranger. None of the other guests seemed to notice the man, even though he wasn't dressed for the occasion. A headband held his long hair in place, and a scraggly goatee draped a good six inches down his chin. The man's clothing was straight out of the '60s: a tie-dye shirt, a long wooden bead necklace, bell bottom jeans, and canvas sneakers spattered with red spots.

"Excuse me, sir, this is a private party," Jim said.

The man's eyes were glassy and unresponsive.

"You need to move along, sir." Jim gestured toward the door.

"My son," the man said, and raised his finger.

"I'm not your son."

The apparition disappeared through an open window.

Jim tried to maintain his composure. The oysters and champagne must be muddling his brain. He walked back to the table and sat down, thinking some solid food might help.

"Jim?" Sara came behind and whispered in his ear. "What on earth were you doing over there? Your arms looked like a scarecrow's, waving in the wind."

"Nothing, nothing. Don't worry."

The rest of the meal didn't get better. Trying not to eavesdrop on Aunt Deborah and his mama was impossible.

"At my place in Wales, there are a lot of spiritual things taking place," Aunt Deborah said. "Imagine living in cob houses or yurts with moss roofs. My place has a wood stove for cooking and heating the room. There's a vegetable garden in a greenhouse to extend our growing season.

"My neighbor has this brilliant gadget called a Rocket Stove, which takes twigs and turns them into heating fuel; the ashes go back into the garden. It's more like a luxury campground with some innovative devices to combine ancient techniques with the modern world. It's a communal living situation, but everyone has their own tiny house."

"I'm not sure how I'd manage year-round," Jim's mama said.

"Sorry, I should have explained better. I'm there six months out of the year in a supportive role for the locals who want counseling. The cliff walks and woodlands are lush and feel like they're straight out of Emily Brontë's novel, *Wuthering Heights*. I realize her book takes place in England, so saying Wales is a bit of a stretch." She paused long enough to eat a few forkfuls off her dinner plate. "As I was saying, the rest of the year I live in Jacksonville, Florida. Before that, I raised Sara in Charleston."

"Fascinating." His mama encouraged her to continue.

Aunt Deborah proceeded to tell his mama a mythical tale about second sight and the Otherworld of fairies. To top it off, she brought King Arthur and Merlin into the scene.

"Oh, darling. I can't believe it," his mama said. "In the last few years, I've become interested in the stratosphere beyond our known world. I flew down to South America and learned about vision quests. Shamanism and all things spiritual helped me get through the loss of my baby girl."

Right, Mama—going from a Catholic to alternative concepts. Leaving Melanie and me alone for two weeks to travel and indulge in recreational drugs. Tell everyone at our wedding. Thanks for your restraint.

"Yes, I'm so sorry. Sara told me what happened. Truly a tragedy." Aunt Deborah reached out and squeezed his mama's hand.

"Deborah, we must have known each other in a former life. We are getting on so well."

"Reincarnated, hmm. We could be. Were we men or women before?" Aunt Deborah laughed at her perceived joke.

"Yes, well, who knows," his mama retorted with an impish smile.

"It's good you have Melanie and Jim. We shouldn't talk about unhappy things today."

"So true," his mama replied.

"Let's focus on this joyous day for the newlyweds."

Jim stopped listening to the women's conversation when Uncle Jorge stood up with his glass of champagne and tapped it with a spoon. "Everyone, attention please. My name is Jorge, Jim's uncle. Since I came all the way from Portugal, the families requested I give the speech. I like to talk a lot, so they gave me notes to curb my tendencies."

"Here, here," Jim exclaimed. "It's so good to have you, Uncle."

"Thank you. Every summer, Jim's family came to my home in Sintra. My wife, Yara, would love to be with us. I know she is watching from heaven. All those departed are celebrating this happy day with us." Uncle Jorge rubbed his eyes. "Sorry. Today will be in all our hearts forever. I have known Jim and Adam all their lives. They have been to Portugal many times during their childhood and have become fine young men. I have no doubt their brides are as wonderful as they are beautiful. These two couples—Adam and Blaire, Jim and Sara—are destined to be together.

"For those of you who do not know, they met at a student party Mrs. Donnelly hosted. She is also hosting this wedding, but I don't think I was supposed to tell. These wonderful young people have stayed together even when the men went away to the Army. A dedicated group.

"There is a Portuguese tradition to make a monetary donation to the newlyweds in the bride's shoe."

"Uncle, no!" Jim called out. "You'll embarrass our brides."

"It is already arranged. I will not ask Sara or Blaire to remove their shoes. Mrs. Donnelly has put two decorated ones by the door. I hope each guest will contribute. I know all of you wish them nothing but love and long lives. Drink with me in toasting them."

The celebration over food and drink carried on for an additional two hours and concluded with cutting cakes—one for each couple—and throwing the bouquets. Sara threw hers straight into Melanie's arms. Jim laughed because his sister was too young to marry and didn't even have a young man on her radar. Blaire's bouquet landed in Aunt Deborah's outstretched hands.

The excitement settled, the newlyweds thanked everyone for coming and scooted out of the room toward the familiar carriage waiting outside. The driver was the same one who had picked them up months before near Sara and Blaire's brownstone. The carriage took them around Forsyth Park and around the historic district, returning an hour later.

Back inside the Marshall House, the newlyweds walked up the stairs together, and separated into their adjacent suites. Inside, on a table, sat fluted glasses and a bottle of champagne with fresh raspberries and blackberries on a plate. On a second one; brie cheese and savory unleavened crackers. Jim didn't want any of it. He faced Sara, clasped both his hands around hers, and spread their arms apart like he was ready to take her flying.

"You are a vision of loveliness." He pushed their hands down to his sides and kissed her. This would be their first night together since the night of their engagement.

"I know it's silly. This time I'm nervous," Sara said.

"It's okay." Jim felt the goose bumps on her arms and kissed them.

"I'll be right back." Sara disappeared into the bathroom.

Jim wanted to help her relax. So, instead of standing in the middle of the room doing nothing, he undressed and slid beneath the covers.

When Sara returned, she sheepishly smiled and dropped her gown off her shoulders. It fell to the floor. Before Jim could respond, she was under the covers, kissing him and trailing her fingers over his tattoo and down his chest. Their lovemaking began tenderly, evolved into a thirsty passion, and ended in an exhausted sleep.

In the middle of the night, Jim awoke, hoping to entice Sara with kisses. The brass doorknob rattled, and the keyhole glowed. He resented leaving the warmth of Sara's body. Rolling out of bed, he tucked the quilt around her and threw on a hotel robe while walking across the room. The doorknob kept rattling.

"Adam? Is something wrong?" Jim cracked open the door on the chain. No one was there. "Not funny." He closed it and double-checked the lock.

A minute later, water was running in the bathroom. Sara was still lying on her side, facing away from him. Her breath was steady and smooth, so he knew she was asleep. The nightlight helped him see there was no one there, but the tub was filling up. Jim twisted the handle to quiet the noise and made sure the stopper was out of the drain. While Jim pondered the situation, he squinted at the tub. On their own, the two tub handles turned, and the water came on again.

Hearing ghost stories was completely different from experiencing the sights and sounds. Jim recalled cemeteries with cold air blowing by on a hot day. Such things were more tolerable than the hippie at his wedding and the moving fixtures on their wedding night. Jim stepped into the hall and left the door open in case Sara woke up to something worse. He stepped over to the suite beside theirs and knocked.

"Adam, Adam?" Jim called out, and stood there waiting.

The door opened. "Hey, man." Adam stood there in a matching white robe with the hotel's insignia. "Well, don't we look posh? I'm busy. What were all those kids doing stomping through the halls at this hour? Look, there are a lot of small, gray footprints down the red carpet."

"What? I didn't hear or see any kids. The old typewriter down the hall is clacking away. Yesterday, someone downstairs said Mr. Harris wrote Uncle Remus's stories on that machine." Jim rubbed his forehead. "Jesus. I came over here to ask you if your bathtub came on by itself or anything else unusual. Like your door rattling?"

"No. If I hadn't heard the invisible people in the hall, I'd say you're crazy." Adam laughed. "Now, we both are. What's that smell?"

"Lavender?" Jim replied.

A horse whinnied.

"Wait, hold on." Adam disappeared into the room and returned. "Nope, no horses outside. A few cars, though."

"I'm guessing we're sensitive to these noises, because no one would stay here if this happened every night. It's distracting."

"Unless they like ghosts, then they'd flock here. Blaire fell asleep while we were talking. Sara?"

"She passed out after..."

"Ah, man, this marriage thing... We're going to have a great life."

Chapter 17

Months Gone By

BY NOW, JIM AND SARA HAD SETTLED INTO THEIR APARTMENT outside of Fort Bragg. Each day was uncomplicated and blissful, right until Jim had to sleep in the barracks for a two-week drill sequence. After a couple of days away, Jim wanted to hear Sara's voice and further explain the situation. His fellow soldiers were running around in organized mayhem.

When things calmed down, he called, but she didn't pick up. He left a brief message on the answering machine and then began a letter. He wrote fast and planned to mail it before it was too late to tell her what was happening. The words he wrote were almost unimaginable. His time was fragmented. During work breaks, he wrote bits and pieces of the letter. While scribbling, he saw some of his buddies out of the corner of his eye. They were shouting.

Late October 1983
Base, Fort Bragg

Dear Sara,

I'm writing like a crazy man because I don't have a lot of time in between tasks. I had said I'd be home soon, but there have been some developments that will extend my time away. Try not to worry. Be aware, you might hear things on the news. Know, they won't have all the facts. The descriptions will be myopic. Please keep what I'm going to tell you private for now. I feel it's important you understand what's going on.

The alleged drills are ramping up quick, and I think they'll turn real this round. We're dealing with preparing for DRF-1 (division readiness force-1). Everyone is buzzing around, getting their gear ready for the C-141 jets standing by to take us into the world. We never have enough time for everything. My gear was ready yesterday by chance, so I'm ahead of schedule. All the equipment must be clean for the D-MET (division maintenance evaluation team). Those men inspect everything with a fine-tooth comb.

Hold on…

Where was I? Let me clarify. I've told you variations of all this in person, I think. Truth is—I need to organize my thoughts and you're the lucky recipient. The 82nd is called the RDF (Rapid Deployment Force). That's why we train to jump out of airplanes. The tough part is getting ready for the jump. It takes half a day to prepare and minutes to get out of the plane. Ironic, right? So, if something happens anywhere in the world and the U.S. needs to send troops, we'll be the ones to get dropped in. The Navy SEALs or Marines often are the first to go in. Other times it's us because we can get in faster than boats. If it turns out we're called up to be part of a multinational peacekeeping force, they'll send my battalion of about 1,000 men in.

Here's the breakdown. There are three battalions in our brigade. If some international things kick off, the country will need a battalion to go. This will probably happen.

Oops, hang on…

I'm back. I tried to write this all at once, but it wasn't possible to sit still long enough under the current alert level. Right, what was I saying? I don't know. Things have radically changed in the last two hours. We were just informed we're going to Grenada. Finally, all our training will be put into good use.

See you when we come home.

Love you (oh, yes, I do… la, la… I am attempting to sing a song by James Brown). —Jim

Chapter 18

Homecoming

November 1983…

THE HELICOPTER SET DOWN. JIM WASN'T SURE WHAT HE would experience when he stepped back on U.S. soil after returning from combat in Grenada. The hours on board with the rumbling engines and cramped quarters numbed his senses even further than they already were. Losing brothers in battle was worse than any emotion he'd ever experienced. Adam's death hit him harder than losing Jay or O'Sullivan. There were too many injuries and losses between arriving in Grenada and leaving after mopping up. He'd left at the end of October and now it was early November. The time away felt like an eternity. Thanksgiving was coming, and he didn't feel grateful for anything. After going over the events in his head at least a half-dozen times, all the pieces weren't fitting together.

He wasn't sure how to deal with the encounter he would have with Blaire. She'd likely been informed. Sara probably high-tailed it out of Fayetteville to comfort her best friend as soon as they heard. Dealing with Blaire's grief on top of his own would be a challenge for Sara.

Jim grabbed his gear and headed toward the exit. His bicep twitched from the wound. He had to stop and adjust the bandage and take another pill to ease the pain. Stepping out onto the tarmac, he breathed in the Carolina air—one, two, three deep breaths—to release the cricks in his neck and shoulders.

Going home wasn't an option until the AAR debriefing was complete. Their superiors had to hash through what they'd done right or wrong, and what could be improved. Hours later, he tried to telephone Sara in Fayetteville. She didn't pick up the line, so he left a message on the answering machine. The thought of dialing Blaire's number in Savannah made his gut seize, and he hoped Sara, not Blaire, would answer the phone. Sure enough, Sara answered, but with some panic in her voice until he reassured her with the words, "I'm okay, I love you."

Sara said in rapid sputtering, "Blaire went into labor before she knew anything about Adam. I dropped everything and drove down to Savannah to support her. The doctor said, for a first-time mother, the delivery was one of the easiest he'd seen. We were only in the delivery room for an hour. Dustin was born healthy, even though he arrived two weeks early."

"It's good you got to her in time. Is her mother there?" Jim asked.

"Yes, she came in from Charleston the next day. We didn't hear about Adam's death until after we'd left the hospital. An officer, and an enlisted man Blaire didn't recognize, came to the door with the news."

"Ah, now I understand."

"Anyway, that's why I'm in Savannah. I decided to stay longer and take extra days off from my students to support Blaire. She has other friends, but none of them can understand her grief like we can. Dustin is keeping her from completely falling to pieces."

"I can't leave Fort Bragg yet." Jim tried to keep his voice even.

"I'll come home tomorrow afternoon," Sara said. "Blaire's mother has everything covered for now."

"Thanks. We can regroup and go back to Savannah when my leave papers are issued." Jim sighed and paced back and forth until the phone cord twisted into a knot. "I'll pick you up at the train station."

An hour after their conversation, Jim tried to start their car. It didn't light up and his frustration almost boiled over when hooking up the jumper cables produced no results. He didn't have time to fool with the engine. Taking a deep breath, he arranged for it to be towed to the local garage and then borrowed a friend's Buick to pick up Sara the next day.

After a restless sleep, he walked out to the car and potato-sacked himself into the driver's seat. Picking up Sara at the station would hopefully improve his mood. When she emerged and crossed the platform, he hugged her a bit too hard. His bicep hurt, but he ignored the pain and breathed in her scent.

"I have to say it again." Sara choked out, "I'm so sorry I wasn't here when you came home from Grenada."

"It's fine. It couldn't have been any other way." Jim relaxed his grip, ran his hand over Sara's back, and leaned down to kiss her. For an instant, her warmth grounded him and a flicker of joy passed through his heart. He was home in her embrace, but sadness and guilt for losing Adam was at the forefront and overshadowed everything.

They'd settled into the car, and he drove north. The conversation was disconnected and hollow.

Jim said, "Someone called last night, asking if we were planning to show up at the military ball. I said no."

"Good. I can't imagine going," Sara said. "Getting dressed up isn't a big deal. However, the receiving line and dancing? No, I can't manage."

"My thoughts exactly." Jim winced; his bicep was sore. He'd changed the bandage once, but avoided examining it too closely since the bullet had torn a red, four-inch-long angry groove in his arm. "Spending last night alone in our apartment didn't do me any good. I should have tried to sleep in the barracks. There are empty beds now."

"Jim…"

"I tricked myself into falling asleep by saying *peace, peace,* a hundred times while pretending a shroud was coming over me inch by inch. A few hours later, I woke up in a frenzy over a random noise."

"You've lost a dear friend under horrible circumstances. Between his death and everything you must have witnessed; how could you not be upset? It might be good to talk it out."

"I'm not so sure." He fidgeted with the knobs on the radio, changing the stations over and over while thinking of the failed communications on the mission. Sara's hand touched his, and he took his off the knobs. The restless, faraway aura did not abate. He moved his hand onto the console between the seats and tapped his fingers.

"Jim?"

"Going to the ball would also mean seeing a chair bent over a place setting at the table to honor and mourn the dead. I couldn't hold myself upright the way my commander would expect. Then there are the medals for valor. I don't think I deserve one."

"Oh, I see," Sara said, with a hitch in her voice. "I'm sure you're wrong. We should go."

"Maybe. So, how's Blaire?" He hesitated. "All alone in Savannah?"

"What? Her mother is there. We talked about her on the phone before I came back on the train."

"Right, I forgot for a moment." Jim moved his hand off the console and onto the wheel. One hand twelve inches apart from the other at the 9 and 3 positions. Why did he care? A tornado was going off in his head.

"We're all upset." She'd grabbed a tissue out of her bag, flicked it up and down, and blew her nose.

Jim reached across the console and touched her cheek. "I'm sorry things turned out this way."

"This isn't your fault." The warmth of her hand on his made him realize how cold he felt.

"What is life going to be like without Adam? We've known each other forever. And now he has a son without a father. And poor Blaire…"

Sara was staring at him; he could sense her eyes penetrating his soul. "This is all too serious to discuss in the car."

Jim proceeded mechanically along the road while his mind rattled around in his self-imposed solitude. The mission wasn't what he'd expected, even though he'd been well trained. At the time, he was in the immediate "present" because there wasn't any other choice. But now, instead of doing the same thing, his mind was stuck in the past. If he could move his thoughts forward, the future would look brighter. His emotions kept taking over and reliving the mission. It was as if his heart hadn't quite made it home with his body. Yet Sara was by his side, and she was his anchor in his upside-down world.

As Jim drove along the road, a dog ran onto the highway and the left bumper struck it. He saw it in time, but didn't swerve the car.

"Stop," Sara cried out.

"Dogs run in the road every day—I'm not going back." His words emerged like an angry bear.

"No, they don't," Sara snapped. "What's happening to you?"

"What, um, I don't..." The brakes screeched, the car slowed down, and he turned it into the grass in the median strip. A vehicle veered around them, with the horn blaring. Jim shoved open his door, ran back to the dog, and dropped to his knees. The dog's chest was heaving and his pulse was weak. Running his hand over its coat; it came away bloody.

"Rest easy. I'm sorry, guy." Without warning, Jim started to weep. The emotions he'd been holding in during the mission flooded out. The shield he'd attempted to put between his heart and his mind collapsed.

Chapter 19

Confession

THE CAR DOOR SLAMMED. BEFORE JIM COULD PULL HIMSELF together, Sara came up behind him. He could sense her hand reaching toward his shoulder even before it connected.

"Jim?"

"I'm sorry. I didn't mean to be so callous in the car." He wiped his nose on his sleeve.

"Why, Jim? Why?"

"No dog tags. We can't leave him." His words tumbled out, and the tears overflowed again and plummeted down to his chin.

"Jim—Jim?" Sara said in the softest voice he'd ever heard. "What are you saying?"

And then it struck him. He wasn't mourning the dog, but Adam. He put his arms around Sara and cried with his face hidden in the crook of her neck. After an unknown amount of time passed, he reined in his emotions.

"Sara, thank you." He sat on the ground and stroked the dog's ears while his hand trembled. The blood was the dog's and Adam's all at once. He rubbed it off on the grass. "Poor fellow, I'm sorry. Your family will miss you."

"Let's call the sheriff's department. They'll take care of everything," Sara said.

Jim raked his finger down his cheeks. With a tremor in his voice, he said, "Adam—he's really gone. I saw him lying there after the bullet—I, I saw—I tried to save him, I couldn't. He wasn't conscious for long. I have his ring. He loved her so much. Now he'll never come home."

"She'll appreciate having the ring back."

"If the men saw me collapsing like this, they'd kick my ass. My commanders never seem to flinch, yet here I am, crying like a baby. I'm such a wimp." Then he realized he didn't recall what Adam said right before he slipped away.

"No, no, you're not! I'm here, I'm here. Lean on me. Come on, Jim. You're right—we can't stay by the road like this."

A few minutes later, he let Sara help him to his feet. They walked back to the car.

Sara drove while he sat in the passenger seat. "Let's go to Clark Park and walk. There's a pay phone by the parking lot. We can call the sheriff from there."

"Okay." On the way over, he thought about the mission and what he could tell Sara. He had to be honest with her while censoring parts.

At the park, they got out of the car in unison. Sara pulled some coins out of her purse, left Jim standing by the car, and walked over to the pay phone. He watched her pick up the receiver and drop coins in the slot before diverting his attention to the car. A few pieces of the dog's bloody hair were attached to the fender. The sight made him cringe, but he resisted falling back into despair. Five minutes later, Sara returned, and he grabbed her hand. They walked toward the main asphalt path in the park.

"Done? Everything okay?" Jim asked.

"Done. They'll collect the dog and see if they can find the owner."

"Thank you. I should have made the call."

"Darling, it's fine. You've got enough to contend with right now."

The covered bridge wasn't too far away. When they arrived, Jim stopped and pulled Sara into his arms. Holding her felt like a breath of fresh air. His mission was over, but he couldn't let go of the images.

"Jim, tell me what happened."

"Anything I tell you must stay between us. I shouldn't tell you anything. We're not supposed to…"

"But you're going to."

Her words lifted him up. He felt supported and a little stronger than he had been a half hour before when he was sitting in the ditch with the dead dog. To calm his simmering nerves, he traveled back in time to their first meeting on the train when the burdens in his heart were lighter.

"I wasn't planning to." He took a few more steps. "But, yes, I'll try. Except, there are a lot of blank spots. Some things are firsthand, some hearsay. Commanders, like General T and Colonel S, don't communicate with enlisted personnel. The colonel had been back in our ranks for about a week before the mission. Everything channels down to us on a need-to-know basis.

"I heard there were up to 7,000 military personnel involved. There were a lot of problems in the field and not enough advanced planning. Someone screwed up the timing and dropped a group of Marines into the water in the dark. Some of them drowned. They hadn't been trained properly. Wrong place, wrong time. It was a helter-skelter affair."

"Sounds like an awful start. Did anything good come out of the mission?"

"Some men are already calling this mission the Rucksack War because of the limited supplies and time involved. The civilians we helped were grateful. Sorry, that didn't answer your question."

"Well, helping people is something to hold on to." Sara jogged ahead a few paces and stopped while he caught up.

"What was that about?"

"Just had to release some tension. So, now, tell me. I'm ready for the rest."

"Okay. Various military branches were going to go on the mission. It took much longer than it should have to get everyone organized. There were a lot of disagreements on procedures and tactics. And problems with equipment. By the time we arrived in Grenada, we were using tourist maps to get around, which jeopardized the mission and put civilians in danger."

"Lordy, not good."

"I didn't shoot any civilians, thank God—no collateral damage on my part. Wiping out innocent people can't be easy for any soldier.

Wrong place, wrong time for all concerned. Everyone's trained to follow orders and avoid asking why."

"Sorry, I'm going to. I heard some things on the news. In the letter you sent me before you left, you said they'd leave out parts."

"Yep, that's always the case. For security reasons, the government shouldn't be telling journalists anything until after the mission. It's true we were getting hundreds of U.S. medical students out of the country, so they wouldn't become hostages like the people at the U.S. Embassy in Beirut.

"We were also over there trying to stop Fidel Castro and the Communist Party from encroaching on the U.S. The airport at Point Salines was supposed to be for the tourist industry. Instead, it was laid out like a military strip."

"Until now, I'd never heard of Grenada. Now everyone knows it's off the coast of Venezuela, below Cuba."

"I didn't learn about the country's politics until after our debriefing." Jim sighed.

"The Caribbean should be a vacation spot, not a war zone."

"Well, it wasn't exactly a war. It was an intervention. An operation the government labeled Urgent Fury and said it was connected to the Cold War." Jim's eye twitched, and he rubbed the nerve into submission.

"I'm ashamed. I know about so many things, but not this. Why is it called cold?"

"It's okay." Jim pushed Adam out of his thoughts again and continued the history lesson. "Yep, there's the word war again. George Orwell came up with the term, Cold War. The U.S. and Soviet Union are trying to avoid direct military confrontation and at the same time expand their influence over other nations by providing military and economic support. If we go head-on into battle, it could turn into a nuclear disaster and leaders want to avoid getting to that point. Since the Caribbean nations asked for our help, the operation was launched. I hope I'm saying this right because my brain's mushy."

"Hmm. I get it." Sara sighed. "Military actions—Vietnam was a military action with over 50,000 soldiers killed. No matter how I look at this, it's still a war."

"I guess. Anyway, it took us almost a day to get down there, with fuel stops in Puerto Rico and Barbados. Various military branches arrived at different locations, on different days, and on different transports. Our two battalions got there after the Rangers. We crossed paths with them during the operation.

"The prime objective was to destroy a regime planning to export terror and undermine democracy. The island is too close to our borders to let them do whatever they want. Our government feared more terror would arrive on U.S. soil, so we intervened."

"Most people don't have a true understanding of what's going on in the world," Sara said. "President Reagan explained a fair amount. He said the Caribbean nations requested U.S. help. He also said, since Grenada was once part of the British Commonwealth, Margaret Thatcher wasn't too pleased she hadn't been told anything until after the mission began."

"It was probably right to get involved the way we did. I'm not sure why Thatcher got her feathers into a knot." Jim paused for a few minutes, trying to decide what to say next. "The governor was being held in his compound on the island. One helicopter crashed on the way to the rescue. The pilot died and five others were injured. At another point, a hotel caught on fire. I don't know what happened to the occupants. Then an explosive device dropped into a psych ward by mistake. The surviving patients were walking through town, mumbling and babbling. They looked like zombies. The nurses and some other soldiers were trying to corral the lost souls back to safety."

"Sounds horrible. I'm sorry. Go on."

"There were hundreds of combatant detainees—I helped march them into holding areas. They were questioned, but not tortured. I'm sure it would be better to be dead than tortured and starved. I don't know what happened to them after they were detained.

"Later in the day, we found large amounts of military supplies in a storage area with Cuban and Soviet insignias—some of our soldiers blew them up so they couldn't be used against citizens. There was some false info going around about a mass grave. Everything was so confusing. I was out there, following orders like a robot through frosted lenses. All the details will come out in the future in some military manual. I'll never be the same. The old Jim…" There it was, all laid out. He hadn't intended to say so much, but he couldn't stop. It was better than getting into what happened to Adam.

"How can any soldier come out of combat unchanged?" Sara squeezed his hand. "Thank you for explaining everything. I hope talking helps?"

"A little. I'm stringing this all together and avoiding explaining what happened to Adam because I want to claw the fragmented pictures out of my mind."

"I'm sorry for all the trauma you've been through. How did he…"

"I keep trying to sort out the details. The worst parts are all jumbled."

They walked off the bridge and continued along the asphalt path. A breeze struck up, and she hugged in closer to his side. In the distance, a waterfall in the park hummed. The leaves from the trees were in piles on the ground with hues of yellow, orange, red, and brown—the life stripped out of them. Jim could relate.

"Several hundred were wounded, and more than a dozen were killed in action. I heard nine helicopters crashed. It wasn't like Vietnam because our engagement lasted a short time, but it was the biggest operation since. Even with all the training, no one was fully prepared.

"When I met up with Adam, he said the Rangers dropped in by parachute and hit the ground running because they were being fired on by the enemy. It didn't take long for the Cubans on-site to surrender. Adam's group cleared the runway so my division could land in a C-141 plane." Jim didn't mean to sound so aloof. It was the only way the scene could continue to unfold. He didn't want to breakdown again. "Adam's group and mine met up, and headed to the area where the students were supposed to be. We went into the building, and it was empty. Next, we got on the radio and were told the students had been moved to the other side of the island. We realized the empty building we were standing in was a trap. Insurgents were nearby, and they ambushed us. Our men were there with Adam's."

Sara bumped his arm.

Jim flinched in pain.

"Oops. Sorry, I didn't mean…"

"It's all right. A bullet grazed my arm. The sound rushing by was worse than the impact. The pain came later. It's going to leave a scar and remind me of the mission every day. I deserve at least this after not being able to help Adam."

"You should have told me before; I would have been more careful." She moved over a little. "Think of it as a reminder of your friendship. It tells a story, kind of like a tattoo. I'm relieved you didn't get hurt worse."

"Yeah, this is nothing." He adjusted the bandage through his sleeve. "Adam got a direct hit when he deliberately stepped in front of me."

"I'm sure you would have done the same."

Jim's pulse elevated. He took some long breaths. "Jay and O'Sullivan are dead, too." A knot came up in Jim's throat, and he swallowed it down. "The bullet skirted the edge of Adam's flak jacket and pierced his chest. I took off his jacket and put pressure on the wound. He bled out. It seemed like an eternity, but it was minutes. All I could do was attempt to comfort him with bullshit words of encouragement. If our team hadn't called his team into the building, this would never have happened."

"You can't blame yourself. Never, never."

"Well, logically, you're right." Jim continued with the story. "When Adam was gone, my team leader had to pull me away from him and out of the building. Right after, the place erupted in flames from incendiary mortars.

"Not being able to stay with him and say one last goodbye tore me up. I went berserk, like an enraged beast, with my heart pounding and adrenaline rushing through my veins. I started firing at the enemy with pure hate—nothing like I've ever felt before. It was like a bear trying to protect its cubs, with no concern for self-preservation. My reaction surprised me.

"The medics collected Adam's remains later and took him to the USS Independence offshore—the wounded and the dead were transported there before anywhere else.

"On the transport home, I kept asking myself; What kind of God allows war? Or have civilizations screwed themselves up so much God simply consoles us after disasters? Who is to blame? The politicians? It isn't the civilians. Could I have saved Adam?" Jim's voice trailed away. "I'll never get over what happened."

"I'm so sorry. Thank you for confiding in me."

Jim moved forward with Sara in silence.

Finally, she said, "We can't tell Blaire the details."

"Yes, I agree. It's bad enough he's gone. Now I get why some soldiers say 'it should have been me.' If it was, I wouldn't be in pain."

"Hey, I would be without you."

"Sorry. My dad had some of the same feelings about Christina's death. Why did God protect us and not them?" Jim's ears rang, and he thought he was going to collapse again, but he persevered. "I don't understand why horrible things happen. Why…"

"I don't know, sweetheart. I don't know," Sara said quietly. "The wounded—are they over at the local Womack hospital?"

"There, and places like Walter Reed in DC. The medical brigade deals with everyone on-site and then each military branch handles their own wounded."

"You need to sleep tonight. If you'd like, I can help you relax with a massage and…"

"Tonight, I sure hope so. Tomorrow, I need to go camping in the woods alone, since I have a few free days before work starts up again."

Sara interrupted his brooding. "No, not alone. It's not a good idea right now."

Jim didn't respond until they'd walked farther along the tree-lined asphalt path. "You're probably right." He rubbed his eyes. "How's the baby?"

"Dustin acts like any other newborn—sleeps, cries, nurses, and poops."

"Nice image." Jim chuckled.

"Blaire's keeping busy taking care of him. She'll go back to work in six weeks. When her mother leaves, Mrs. Donnelly will help. Things will get easier for everyone with time. Didn't I mention some of this on the phone?"

"I suppose you did. Sorry."

"It's okay." Sara spoke in a soothing tone, which helped him continue. "There's a lot going on. Jim, we're going to get through this."

"I hope so." Jim's mind wandered over to the word *gratuity*. "We were told everyone on the mission would receive a commendation medal, but no extra leave or income because we were doing what we were trained for. Blaire will get a sizable death gratuity. It's like life insurance money. The term *gratuity* nauseates me, and the hundred thousand dollars will never heal any wounds."

"That's for sure." Sara shook her head.

Jim wanted to change the subject for a few minutes. "This path we're on is called the Cape Fear River Trail. Kind of ironic."

"Sure is. They named it after a film in the 1960s, or maybe it was the other way around. Gregory Peck is in it."

A dog ran by them. Jim couldn't figure out why they were so prevalent wherever he went. Perhaps they were trying to tell him something. Some of the dogs in Grenada were so hungry they were gathering around dead human bodies. Those dogs ended up dead too, because fellow soldiers shot them out of disgust. Jim's perception of dogs had changed since he and Sara were thinking about getting a puppy. But if they did, it wouldn't be like the starving ones.

"What's with the dogs running amuck?" Jim's jaw tightened. "I'm feeling really bad about hitting the other one."

"I know, but get back to Grenada."

"Yeah, right, okay." Jim swept his hand across his head from front to back. "Did I tell you communications were all F'd up on the mission?"

"Only about maps. Tell me."

"So, we all knew what was supposed to happen, but the radio guy needed to clarify crap when things go sideways. The trees can interfere with transmissions of rucksack antennas. There's a set of codes each operator knows. A relay system takes off from one operator to the next on the same channel. The codes can change as we go, and if one system fails, we're screwed. The local radio tower was taken over by the enemy. In the end, someone had to use a pay phone to reach support crews on the ship."

"Pay phone?" Sara sounded confused.

"Yep, on a public street."

Putting his hand in his pocket, he pulled out Adam's ring. The pocket came out along with it. He sniffed emotions back. "The last time my pocket inverted was the day I left Orlando and met you. Curious. What does this mean?"

"It means whatever you like." Sara stopped, stood on her toes, and kissed his cheek. "Or change is already here, so more is coming?"

"Sara, I'm going to apply for a transfer. Pull some strings. See if we can live in Savannah on the base or somewhere else. Fort Bragg feels wrong. I need to leave it behind."

"We could, but you'll still have your ghosts. I mean memories, no matter where we are."

"Yeah, escaping is futile."

"Either way, we can still help Blaire down in Savannah."

"It's really been my home all along," Jim said.

"And it's mine now, too." Sara rubbed his back. "Before I forget, I need to tell you something else. A few cars on base were vandalized while you were gone. I don't understand why."

"Stuff happens." Jim scowled.

"I'd like to be near Blaire, but I thought the base in Savannah was full of Rangers."

"Maybe I should train to be one."

"Oh, Jim, no. Wait a bit before you decide."

"You're right. I'd feel like I'm betraying their memories by talking about taking one of their spots. None of them can truly be replaced. I'd be like a shadow going in so close behind them."

He pointed at a sign: Waterfall This Way.

"Yep, I see it," Sara said. "You're trying to distract us with a waterfall?"

"Well, yes. It's thirty-five feet high."

"And the park is seventy-six acres. No waterfalls today." Sara flicked his wrist hard with her finger. "Ranger? You're not serious?"

"It would mean a longer military commitment."

"What about school and the FBI? It's what you wanted."

In his mind, he fumbled about before answering. "You're right. I finished some courses done during my enlistment. I'll try to get transferred without extending. We'll see. If we move, what will you do about your teaching?"

"I'd get my license reinstated in Georgia, or a new one somewhere else. You know we'll never get Savannah out of our hearts."

"Let's see what my boss comes up with." He was relaxing after unloading everything. "If the transfer doesn't come through, we'll make do and move back to Georgia later. I've got two years of duty left."

"We'll make it through this. I love you, Jim."

Chapter 20

Memorial Service

THE FRIDAY BEFORE ADAM'S SERVICE, JIM TOSSED THE WEEKend travel bags into the trunk and drove back down to Savannah with Sara. Jim and Adam had agreed if anything ever happened to one of them, the remaining soldier would make sure the other did not have a big send-off. Mrs. Donnelly agreed to honor her son's wishes.

Sara wanted to see Blaire before anyone else. Mr. Veasey and Chuck were out of town, so they didn't have to bump into them this time around. Jim pulled the car beside the curb and grabbed his beret as they got out. To stretch their legs after the drive, they started walking around Forsyth Park. Memories of Adam were everywhere.

Two laps later, their emotions overwhelmed them and they headed back to the car. Jim threw his beret onto the back seat to avoid triggering Blaire's emotions. Adam often made a point of putting his beret on her head, first thing, when they'd been apart. Jim and Sara walked around to Blaire's door. He rubbed his palm on his trousers, took a deep breath, and pushed the button. The bell chimed beyond the threshold and mixed with the sound of a baby crying. Five minutes passed before the door swung open. The light in the corridor backlit Blaire and turned her into a shadow.

"Jim, Jim." Blaire clung to the bundle in her arms.

He leaned in for a gentle hug and released her before he got lost in his own emotional despair.

Sara reached out and touched his arm, before hugging Blaire. "We love you, sweetie."

"Blaire, it's a relief to see you and little Dustin," Jim said.

"Yes, yes—I named him Dustin Adam. He was born the same day

his daddy….." Her voice dipped down and choked on a sob. "Jim, I am a mess. I can't believe I'll never see him again. If it wasn't for Dustin, I'd be in even worse shape. I—I cry every night."

Jim's heart broke a little more. "Blaire, I'm sorry he's not coming home."

"Somehow, I knew I'd lost him when our son was born. Sixth sense, I guess."

Jim brought the ring out of his pocket, along with a dog tag. "These are his. Sara bought a necklace so you can wear them."

Blaire held out one hand. It began to shake. More tears emerged, and she bit her lip.

Jim put the keepsakes in her palm and closed it around them. "I was with Adam to the end. Everything happened fast. He said to tell you he loves you." As Jim said the words, guilt flooded through him. Adam said no such thing, while shock and death overtook him.

"Oh," Blaire said in a whisper. She rocked Dustin, even though he wasn't restless.

"Let us know how we can help. Anything you need. Okay?" Jim said.

"Okay." Blaire choked out the word.

"I'm betting Adam is looking at you right now from heaven," Sara said, and rubbed her eyes.

"Thank you. I love you guys." Blaire sniffled. "I feel so raw."

"Is there anything we can do for you in the apartment?" Sara asked.

"My mama is helping with baby chores and cooking."

"Are you sure we can't help?" Jim responded.

"Yes, I'm sure." Blaire stroked Dustin's head. "Go around to the patio. We'll be out—in a few minutes. We're having dinner at the Donnelly's house. Can you drive us?"

"Of course," Sara said.

"Thank you. Truth be told, Mama's helping almost too much. Mrs. Donnelly, and the base wives, will chip in when she leaves. Everything's moving too fast. I need to slow down and heal."

"Yes, I understand," Jim said. "We'll plan on coming down often if we can't get transferred here."

"I hope you can." Blaire hugged Jim again. "Go 'round. The patio is open."

Jim and Sara left. Turning the corner to the familiar gate, he pushed it open, thinking of their times in the garden with Adam.

"Jim, before we got here, I talked to Blaire on the phone. She told me Adam won't be buried at Arlington National Cemetery, even though he's eligible."

"Yes, I heard," Jim replied. "Adam's mother wanted him close, so she and Blaire could visit."

"I'm glad they're doing it this way. DC is too far away."

Ten minutes later, Blaire appeared in the garden with her mother and Dustin. Jim had only met Mrs. Fairmont once at their wedding. They exchanged condolences and awkwardly chatted about meaningless chores on the way over to the Donnelly's house.

During dinner, Jim's mind seemed to leave him. There he was, sitting across the table from Blaire's mother, staring down at the dinner plate filled with food. To him, it resembled gray brains mixed with red bits. It was proper food, but his mind had wandered off to the mission and death again. When Sara said his name, he startled himself back into the current reality, and wondered how long he'd drifted away.

In the end, it turned out to be comforting to spend time in Adam's family home. The evening reminded Jim of the time they'd been together when he'd gone down to The Warehouse Bar and Grill. That night, he'd found Sara again at Mrs. Donnelly's party. Fate; he guessed it was fate. Those events should remain at the forefront of his mind, not the tragic mission.

On Adam's behalf, after dinner, Mrs. Donnelly gave Jim her son's motorcycle. He wanted to refuse, but couldn't. Thinking of the pink helmet in the side bag brought a slight smile to his face. She said she would do almost anything to push time backward before Adam died, to prevent the heartache they were all experiencing.

The Cemetery

Blaire's mother hadn't left her side since Dustin's birth, and insisted on driving them separately to the cemetery, with Jim and Sara following behind. Driving up to the wrought iron gates of Greenwich Cemetery wrenched Jim's soul. Sara sat with her hands clasped together in her lap, her thumbs raking across each other, and he presumed she was quietly worrying about how the day would affect everyone concerned. His eye twitched, and he rubbed a bead of moisture away that was gathering in the corner. The collar of his dress uniform felt unusually constrictive. Thoughts of ripping the jacket off and shredding it into a million pieces came to mind. Anger, sadness, and remorse teamed through his veins. If they hadn't entered the military, Adam would still be alive.

Mrs. Fairmont stopped the car in front of the stone-faced office. Jim pulled in behind her and watched her go inside. Not moving to follow her, Jim waited until she emerged and waved a map in his direction. She got back into her car and drove off. He didn't follow right away, but watched her car meander down the road. Several cars pulled up behind him. Jim tapped his fingers on the steering wheel, feeling he should move forward for the other people's sake while not wanting to deal with the next step of saying goodbye to his best friend. The anxiety turned his stomach.

"Jim, you've gotten this far. We need to keep moving," Sara said in a soothing voice.

"I know, I know." He forced himself to move the car forward down the lane and parked behind Mrs. Donnelly's car.

"Adam's remains were buried weeks ago, away from everyone's view to soften the blow, but it didn't help Blaire." Sara observed.

Jim looked out the car window toward the gravestone. Mrs. Donnelly stood next to Blaire in a long, black dress. They hadn't seen her by the office and assumed she had arrived before everyone. Next to them sat a stroller, with Dustin propped up in a clump of blankets. Blaire shook, as if the temperature were below zero. Her shoulders twitched back and forth, and her fingertips clawed up and down on her cheeks. Before Jim and Sara could get out of the car, she rushed over to a tree and vomited.

"We need to go to her," Sara said.

Jim turned his head and focused on Sara's feet, then swallowed hard. They both took in a full breath, sat up tall, and rushed out of the car to help. Before they reached her, she'd taken her position next to Adam's mother. Jim and Sara surrounded Blaire and pulled her into a group hug until she stopped shaking.

In the background, two men in uniform stood near some young palmetto plants and oak trees covered with Spanish moss. Jim approached and saluted. They returned the salute. One man had a bugle hanging by a leather strap on his shoulder. The other had his hand on a rifle with a cap perched on the muzzle. Both symbols are to honor the dead. Jim invited them to join the family, but they declined. They'd arrived early to pay their respects and preferred to stand at a distance. The first man explained he had played "Taps" while his buddy propped up the rifle by the gravestone. As he spoke, he plucked a palmetto leaf from the plant and wove it into a rose shape around a Purple Heart medal. He handed it to Jim and asked him to place it alongside the family's flowers in honor of Adam's bravery.

For a minute, Jim was taken aback, and then noticed the man's insignia. He, like Adam, was a Ranger. The Purple Heart had been given to this Ranger when he was wounded. He said he wanted Adam to have it. For this man, giving it to Adam meant more than holding onto it. Jim saluted in thanks before going back to the family.

Blaire had a Gold Star dangling from a lanyard on her wrist to acknowledge the loss she had suffered. The star seemed like such a little thing to honor Adam, but it was important. Jim placed the Purple Heart by the graveside flowers and explained why he had it. She smiled and nodded at the soldiers.

Twelve family members encircled Adam's stone and held hands while a cousin prayed aloud. Stepping back from the group, his cousin walked around the family headstone and spread her hands across the top. As the cousin spoke of Adam's life and his contribution to the military, Jim rubbed his fist across his cheek to erase his tears. He flinched when Sara touched his side, but was grateful to feel her presence.

The ceremony felt like the longest thirty minutes of his life beyond the death itself. Once the group disbanded, he and Sara walked among strangers' graves to remind themselves others had also lost loved ones. For reasons he couldn't explain, this produced a calming effect. Although he doubted it would last.

They walked back to the car, and Jim opened the door for Sara. He glanced over at the grave one last time and saw a familiar face. The man from their wedding, still dressed in a tie-dye shirt and bell bottom trousers, had come to pay his respects.

"Hang on, I'll be right back." He closed the car door and walked over. "I've seen you before. Why are you here?"

"My son," the man said.

"I'm not your son."

"My son." The man's arm raised, and he pointed. "Adam."

"What?"

"He is transcending." The apparition disappeared before Jim could respond.

Transcending? Transcending. Adam's transcending?

Taking deep breaths, Jim shook his head, saluted the headstone, and walked away. Jim began to question his own sanity.

Back in the car, he started the engine. Looking ahead, he noticed the other cars were gone without him even realizing. He'd been too self-absorbed. Taking a moment in the stillness, he uttered one last goodbye to Adam.

Fayetteville, North Carolina

Back in their apartment, Jim's sleep patterns were erratic, while Sara slept undisturbed throughout the nights. Whenever he lay down, he could only sleep for a few hours at a time. Some nights, he woke up in a sweat without knowing why. Other nights, he had nightmares about the military and losing Adam, with Christina coming into his line of sight sometimes. During one nightmare, his dad was in the background in his Marine uniform among a crowd of combatants. Jim shot him, then realized what he'd done, and sat bolt upright in bed. Nothing made sense. He surmised a psychoanalyst would know what they meant. Yet, he had no intention of getting medical help.

Going back to sleep once he woke from a nightmare had become a reoccurring challenge, and this night wasn't any easier. Often, he'd tried to spin the nightmares into something less menacing, but it rarely worked. Each time he woke up, it took a while to pull himself back into the current reality. This time, he trudged outside to look at Adam's motorcycle. Hauling it behind them on a trailer from Savannah was the only choice. Adam's mother couldn't stand to look at it in her driveway. The constant reminder wasn't helping Jim, either. But sitting on the curb looking at it was better than falling into another nightmare.

His thoughts were plagued, not comforted, by the way Adam's dad's ghost seemed to be watching the living without being able to offer any protection. *Would Adam watch over Dustin?* Whether the answer was yes or no, their presence never stopped a life from being taken.

Jim surmised that being without his own dad would be worse than dealing with his misguided advice. Joining the military wasn't one of his better ideas. He decided right then to stop being angry at his dad for the suggestion. Jim could have refused. And his entering the service would not have kept Adam alive. Even so, the regrets and guilt still hung around. He thought, *why did Adam have to take the bullet for me?*

Chapter 21

Chaplain

AFEW WEEKS LATER, JIM WALKED BY AN OPEN DOOR ON the base. A plaque on the side of the doorjamb indicated it was the Chaplain's office. Below it, a table with a bowl of wrapped chocolates and butterscotch candies. Jim hesitated. The chocolate wasn't easy to resist.

He took a piece, unwrapped it, and popped it into his mouth. It had been at least seven years since he'd attended Mass or entered a church.

He thought, *Should I go in for counseling? The military talks about God and country. I never stopped to think about how the words are accepted by non-believers.*

The chaplain, with his white collar tucked beneath his khaki fatigues, interrupted Jim's quiet reflection. "The chocolates are my favorite, too."

"Yes, sir."

The man talked freely, but there was something about his eyes. They seemed different from any other man of the cloth Jim had encountered. Milky and piercing, yet warm. The chaplain appeared to be about the same age as Mr. Veasey's friend Chuck. Vietnam came to mind. There was something else familiar about this man.

"Come on in. A man of faith, I presume? I find people without it take the world on their own shoulders and it's a heavy burden to carry."

"I'm afraid I've lost some of mine." Jim followed him into the room, not knowing why. The space smelled like licorice. Talking about his spiritual collapse receded into the background. The man reminded him of Father Mulcahy from the *M*A*S*H* television series.

"I'm new here, came last month from Hunter. They are both nice bases compared to my Vietnam years."

"I'm sure." Jim couldn't figure out why the chaplain was so forthcoming with information. At first, he thought it was the man's way of making people more comfortable. Jim felt the opposite, and then knew why the chaplain seemed familiar. "Sir, I just realized you officiated at my double wedding in Savannah. Masterson and Donnelly?"

"Ah, hmm."

"Chaplain Scythe?" Jim figured this was a promising development.

"Yes, my formal title. You looked familiar when you walked in. I couldn't place you right off. How are you?"

Before responding, Jim paced around the room, eyeing the books on the shelves. Some covered a variety of religions, others were military manuals, and the rest were action-suspense authors he recognized.

"I'm okay, sir." Jim pulled back his shoulders to emphasize the point.

"You don't look certain."

"Well, I'm sure we've all been through a lot. I'm no different."

"Seen my share of crap, dealing with my own traumas. Helping others with their concerns helps me with mine."

"Yes, sir."

Jim put his hand on top of a stack of brown books without titles. The spines were all the same color.

"They're blank, ready to be filled with words. Please, take a copy and write down your experiences. Write whatever you like. I recommend leaving it on your nightstand with a pen. Write in it after a dream when you first wake up. My entries are about pleasant dreams and nightmares. Once a week, I read them with my morning coffee. It's purging. Try it out. Please, take one."

Jim hesitated, but took a journal and pressed it against his hip. With a wry smile, he said, "Thank you. I'm not a great writer. If you think it will help, I'll give it a try."

"The more we write and talk about things, the easier it is to get through whatever weighs our spirits down. It helped me with my flashbacks of people's physical wounds and their suffering."

"I imagine you've seen a lot of suffering."

"Yes, well, goes with the territory." Chaplain Scythe sat down at a desk. "It helps to be around military and non-military people to balance our lives. I'd also suggest volunteering in the community. If you're interested, I sponsor confidential group meetings twice a month where the soldiers talk about their experiences."

"Thanks for the journal. I'll think about the meetings." Jim responded without taking much stock in the chaplain's suggestions and doubted group meetings would help his career. "I need to get to work. It's good to see you again." Saluting, he backed up toward the door.

"At ease. You don't need to salute me in my office."

Jim thanked the chaplain again before hurrying away. He didn't need to report for duty for another half hour, but he had been caught off guard and didn't want to talk anymore.

Days later, after a series of night shifts and daily activities with Sara, Jim was in front of the chaplain's office again. He helped himself to a second piece of candy, peppermint this time, and composed his thoughts.

"Hello. Good to see you again," Chaplain Scythe said.

"Hello, sir." Jim wanted to keep things formal to maintain military etiquette.

"Coffee?"

"Yes, sir. I've just come off Mids."

"Always exhausting."

"I suppose. I haven't slept well since our mission in Grenada."

"Sounds normal." The chaplain passed him a mug of warm coffee with a picture of a dragon on it. "The last time we met, you seemed conflicted. Anything I can help you with?"

"Well…"

"In confidence, of course."

"Faith and duty."

"Right up my alley." The chaplain seemed to find this cliché humorous.

"Here's the thing—I was raised Catholic, with an all-knowing God who is everywhere, even if we can't see Him the way we see each other."

"Yes." The chaplain nodded.

"My mama was a secretary at our Catholic church. So, my sisters and I were very involved, too. When I was a teenager, we moved away from Savannah to Orlando, and everything went catawampus. Our traditions were gone." Jim tried to sound matter-of-fact, but the words came out deflated. "Mama got into shamanism, séances, and other things, attempting to connect with other worlds. She hopes reincarnation is a thing."

"Ah, other planes of consciousness."

"I suppose. When we moved to the RV park in Orlando, she started putting fairy statues all over the grounds." A nerve twitched in his neck. "When people showed up for revival meetings, I ended up with my nose in a Bible to avoid them. One group sat around a circle with incense, candles, and wine, praying to Dionysus. Mama said it was to honor the female deity. Some days, then and now, I'm not sure I believe in anything beyond this world. Witnessing all her experimentations didn't do much for my faith."

"Why did she change her path?"

"This is difficult to talk about, too." He plunged ahead. "Our little sister was murdered when we were children. Mama took Melanie, my other sister, and me away from Dad and our home in Savannah. Once we got to Orlando, she gave up going to church." He considered talking about Aunt Yara, except her death had nothing to do with the move to Orlando.

"I'm sorry."

"Thank you, sir. It's been years." Jim sat down when Chaplain Scythe gestured to a chair.

"Because of everything, I wrestle with faith and religious practices."

"I've read about many peoples and faiths over the years: Buddhists, Jews, Muslims, and—of course—Christians, since I am one. Each group has a unique approach to life and death, but one thing is sure." The chaplain paused and leaned up against his desk. "There is a God, or a force we call God. I like to keep an open mind about religion."

"What about people who believe in nothing but life on Earth?"

"In some ways, they become their own god. I don't envy anyone without faith in a higher power. Life's a lot harder without help. Statistically, depression runs rampant when we're on our own."

Jim paused for a long time. "I never thought of it that way. And the Bible?"

"I, for one, believe none of the holy books are wrong—they are all just different. God is watching over us. Whether we choose to listen to His guidance is something else altogether. We are imperfect."

"Sounds too simple." Jim shook his head. "These days, I'm having trouble with the sixth commandment—Thou shalt not kill."

"Masterson, think of it this way. If a person was being chased down the road by a man wielding a big stick, would you try to help? If you had the training, you would. Think of the Good Samaritan concept from the Bible."

"I'd want to help, even if I wasn't trained. Civilians get hurt in war, too. They lose the ones they love or get killed as collateral damage."

"Yes, yes, that happens in wars. Then there's the kill or be killed concept."

"I don't understand where you're going with the commandment."

"Let me put it a different way. When on a mission, you may not see the innocent civilians you are protecting, but you are protecting them. The point of the military is to have a powerful force behind the people."

"Aw." Jim wasn't sure how else to respond.

"Back to the Bible."

"All right. Should we take it at face value?" Jim asked.

"The Bible has its share of conflicts to learn from. Wars or military actions are about political policies, human rights, and religion. Some biblical verses are straightforward, but others need interpretation. Thou shalt not kill may appear direct, yet I don't believe it is. When you're on a mission, you do your duty and follow orders. People die, sometimes at your hand. God is the ultimate judge. We have to live knowing we are in His good graces while doing our best in this world."

"Sir. Donnelly and I stood side by side when we married Sara and Blaire. I lost him—my best friend—on our first mission. Adam died in front of my eyes. How am I supposed to go into combat again? I know about death after my sister died, but I didn't see it happen. This is different. Some days, I'm having trouble functioning."

"I'm sorry for your loss. Many soldiers are conflicted after missions." The chaplain stopped talking. He exhaled forcefully, and the air blew into Jim's face.

"I was all right with the concept of combat before I experienced it firsthand. Now it's harder, instead of easier, to justify killing a human being."

"I understand."

"I'm struggling. So, the Bible says we live forever through our belief in Christ. If it's not all literal, maybe we live forever because we live through our friends and descendants. It would be interesting if parallel worlds exist, and we couldn't see beyond the borders other than encountering transitional ghosts or sensing something invisible watching over us."

"Before, I believed ghosts existed because they had traumatic deaths. I'm not sure anymore."

"Mm-hmm, not very comforting." Jim angled his head left and then right to relieve the tension. "There must be a lot of ghosts roaming around in this world."

"Yes, I see your point."

"Eating the forbidden apple in the Garden of Eden represented man violating God's rules. What about the immaculate conception of Mary followed by Jesus's birth? For me, it's a far stretch and bends reality. Fine Christian, I turned out to be."

"You've been through a tough time, losing both your sister and Donnelly. Your faith in humanity is being tested. I believe God has a reason for everything, even if we don't understand."

"So, destiny?"

"Of sorts. The longer you live, the more questions you'll have."

"Sometimes I think everything is based on fate and there are no choices, only illusions of choice. My wife believes our life evolves and changes as we make decisions. And each choice alters the next event for us and everyone around us."

"The premise doesn't work well when you're following military orders."

"I suppose not." Jim looked at his watch. "Thank you, I've got to go now."

"I hope our conversation has helped a little. Don't carry a ruck-sack full of guilt around with you. Surrender your worries to a higher power."

"Thank you. I'll try."

"Come by any time."

As Jim departed, he vowed to overcome his angst and find a way to move forward with better attitudes. He owed this to Sara, to Adam and to his wife and son. Yet, he wasn't sure he wanted to talk to the chaplain again.

Chapter 22

Jim's Journal

It's my day off. Time to give journal writing another try. So far, it has all seemed like weeks of scribbling without any resolution.

I had to get away from my normal routine, to breathe and regroup. Now I'm sitting in this stupid-ass library, staring out the window at the terraced rock garden beds. They are beautiful. I can't appreciate them because I'm in an off-beat mood. Blaire's not working here today, so she won't see me moping around. Today I feel raw and want to bawl my eyes out or smash my head into a wall. My mind is either zoned out or racing.

This area of the building is so quiet. I can hear even the slightest noise created by everyone around me. A movement of a chair, a cap being popped off a pen, a whir from an air conditioning unit, a librarian moving books across a desk, a random yawn, and a child asking a question loudly then being told to hush.

Now I'm hearing the faint ringing and whirring in my ears. It never leaves me while I'm awake. I try to focus on anything but the buzz. Too much exposure to weapons wiped out frequencies in my ears. My brain tries to fill in the lost signals. Sometimes it helps to listen to music to drown out the noise.

I need to take a writing break.

While I was on my feet, I walked left, then right. I couldn't grab a hold of any one concept, couldn't do anything sensible. I picked a book up, put it down. Grabbed another and did the same. A pointless fidget. I am writing again.

I feel bad for Sara. We've been married almost two years and are going through so much crap. Adam has been dead for six months. And Dustin is six months old. The little guy reminds me of his father every time we're together. Even so, I'm glad Blaire moved up to Fayetteville when my transfer to Savannah didn't go through. Helping her with Dustin when she's working evening and weekend shifts is great. He smiles whenever he sees me.

Yes, I have a beautiful woman to spend my time with who understands my moods. Most days, she says the right things. There are times when nothing works. On those days, it's like I'm in a glass box looking out at the world and no one can get in. We can touch with the glass between us, like at a prisoner's visitation, but without any completed connections.

Any minute, things could change; my world could shatter. Sometimes, I see everyday events in real time without being able to connect to them or to the people around me. They become invisible, camouflaged. It feels like an out-of-body experience. Other times, I recall everything from Grenada as it plays out in front of me like a movie scene.

Last weekend I sat with Sara, Blaire, and their friends while they talked about… I don't know what. They must have thought I'd gone nuts sitting there without saying a word. At that time, I was able to listen; nothing else. So unlike me. They talked about day-to-day stuff. What they ate at family cookouts or the beautiful weather. It's so superficial. They're scared to talk about anything significant when Blaire and I are around. I zoned out after I'd heard enough of their mundane trivia. There must be a way to get them back to talking in-depth about world events, philosophies, and everything. The pussyfooting around Adam's death doesn't help. They should know better because half of them are military spouses.

Work's keeping me busy. The random shit I must do gets on my nerves. Maybe our team might be sent out to "save" the world again. Even so, I must keep track of my FBI goals and my desire to help people. I seem to say this a lot. It would also be good to keep telling myself how lucky I am to have Sara. How lucky I am to be alive!

When I enlisted, I felt bold and determined to get training, to get experience beyond my job in Orlando. The imaginary place Mama tried to settle us into, so we wouldn't linger on our sadness after Christina's murder, didn't bury our sorrow. For a time, the fanciful things distracted us so our emotional wounds wouldn't fester and destroy us. It was a bandage, not a cure. Baby sister, I will never forget you. And now I add Adam to my sadness, along with the other soldiers. I miss them all. And Aunt Yara, too. Trying to hang onto the good memories isn't working these days. Will time tip the balance?

I always go back to Mama's decisions. The ones she never asked us about. Her religious shift away from Catholicism into shamanism didn't help me or Melanie. What did she and Dad say to me when Christina died? Some creep gunned her down, and they didn't know why. Hmm, it turned out they knew. Why did they lie?

I was nervous every time I left the house for a long time. It was good they didn't tell Melanie how Christina died. She was too young to understand. Keeping the truth from me at the time was a mistake. Ha, now I'm talking to you both on paper and neither of you will ever see this. Finding out the truth about Christina so long afterward brought the pain back to the surface and solved nothing.

Death is inevitable for us all. How we get there matters. Loss is loss, and it shows how vulnerable humans are. I like thinking we live forever like the priest said at Mass when we were kids. Back then, I imagined he meant we lived in our bodies without end. Nice image. It made every day happy and innocent. Thinking a body takes its last breath and moves onto some other place sounded easy until I watched men die in combat, with blood seeping from unnatural openings in their bodies. There are people who overcome seeing such things, and others who can't.

Even after thousands of years, the military still can't tell which of us will become stronger with the reality of battle, while others fall to pieces. If they could have figured it out, I wouldn't have gotten in.

My hauntings feel like a never-ending pit. At first, sleep lets me escape for a while until my nightmares start and take me back to the places I'd rather not go. Sometimes, I wake up in a cold sweat; other times, I wake up restless or exhausted. I guess I'm doomed to four hours of sleep at a time. This isn't a new revelation, but writing it out has gotta help.

How can men sound so sane and proud when they tell war stories far worse than mine? Vietnam must have been a hellish experience in and of itself, even before U.S. citizens started protesting at rallies against soldiers. Could dark humor and pride be part of the answer to bring some emotional peace to a soldier? Until recently, I'd forgotten about Adam's father being one of those protesters. It's odd that Adam enlisted, knowing his father's history. I should have said something, but he'd already enlisted with the recruiter. There wasn't any point in reminding him at that point.

Awake or asleep, I continue to struggle with morality and loss, even with Chaplain Scythe's counsel. In combat, it became abundantly clear: every minute of our lives is precious. Now, I'm fighting myself.

Over and over, I ask myself, with no clear answers, why does God allow such violent devastation to come into our lives for the sake of differing ideologies between tribes? There are so many people in the world trying to integrate with each other. It's a great idea until we don't agree and can't come to peaceful resolutions or worse, don't talk at all. Weapons are raised, instead of voices. A mighty convoluted way to diminish the number of people in the world.

I think the military wasn't a good choice on my part. Learning to be disciplined and physically fit came at a price that I didn't expect. How could I have been so naïve? Going to college with a bank loan and then transitioning into the FBI would have been better. When I get in, I'll go for something investigative, so I can avoid shooting at people.

Yes, I helped innocent and unarmed people, but the cost was high. In self-defense, I shot at people who shot at me. At times, I missed on purpose because the concept of ending another person's life was hard to bear.

Logically, I realize my experiences were nothing compared to what other soldiers have experienced. It still hurts, no matter what.

There must be a way to emerge out of my cocoon. More exercise? More writing? No, I'm done for now. Writing is exhausting.

Chapter 23

Drawings

BACK AT HOME, AFTER DINNER, JIM CONTINUED TO BE AB-sorbed in his own thoughts when he fell into bed. After so much reflection, he hoped to sleep better. Four hours later, he was wide awake. Wandering outside, he took some deep, cleansing breaths. Half an hour later, he gave up and went back inside and lay on the bed next to Sara. Sleep still didn't come. He got up again and walked into the kitchen with the light of the moon reflecting through the window over the sink. The light glistened off a small divot in the glass, which hadn't been there before. He stared into the night, search-ing for something unknown. Something dangerous. He checked the locks on the windows and doors.

Minutes later, Sara walked into the kitchen in her silk robe and turned on the light. Jim snapped to attention. He felt off balance and shifted his glance from her to the magazines on the floor next to the couch. "Are you going to read those?" He pointed to the pile. "Or should we pitch them?"

Her chin tilted toward the offending pile, and she wrinkled her nose. "Jim, you're picking on me. The one on top is mine. The rest are yours. You don't need to grumble at me. I'm on your side."

"I'm sorry. I can't sleep." He realized he'd sounded gruff and changed his tone.

"Maybe a different mattress would help? Or gentle music in the room while we're sleeping?"

"I doubt it." He paced the room like a caged tiger. "I'm wrapped too tight tonight."

"Yes, I noticed."

"This is the second time I've woken up."

"I'll get dressed. We can go for a walk."

"No, I'm better off staying inside right now. I was sleep deprived in boot camp without combat. Now it's worse and harder to manage, along with my duties." He continued to pace. "I'm sorry about dinner. I couldn't eat it and didn't explain. When the red juices dripped out of the edge of the steak, I saw human blood and death. Of Adam and the others…"

"Oh, now I see. I will cook different things. All right?"

"Thanks. I've been disgusted by beef too many times. I should quit trying to eat it."

She came close and wrapped her arms around his waist. "You smell like spice—a little clove mixed with nutmeg?"

"Yes, yes, it is. You fell asleep, and I couldn't. I ordered carry-out from the new Indian place and ate it out front. I'll take you there sometime. Between the food and the two other times I couldn't stay asleep, I'm beat. I feel like I'm in the middle of a psychotic adrenaline rush."

"So much restlessness," Sara said.

"I wish I could fix my sleep patterns."

"Fix? You're not broken physically. You're broken emotionally and in mourning." Sara pulled out a pitcher of cold milk from the refrigerator and made hot chocolate. "Here you go."

"Thanks. Add some whiskey? No, never mind." He took the mug from her outstretched hand. "I don't want to wallow in liquor. I tried one night, and I short-circuited while you were sleeping. I thought I was tripping into an alternate dimension, which was odd, since it was only whiskey."

"Honey, I'm sorry. It must have been awful. I wish you'd woken me." Her hand came up and stroked his hair. "Something has to change," Sara pleaded. "You're quieter than you used to be. It's like you're withdrawing into a dark cave."

"I'm sorry, too." He stroked her cheek. "I told you a lot after our Grenada mission was over. More has come to light, or dark, since then. That's all I can say."

Jim's journal lay open on the counter to a series of drawings. He could tell from Sara's glances she'd seen it, but she hadn't said anything. Before he could talk about them, she turned on the radio. The first song filled the room. They listened to the words that reflected on life—wanting to change things—to heal, to toughen up. Jim rubbed at his eyes to suppress the emerging puddles. Freezing time with Sara, and going back to the days before Adam died, would be a blessing. God brought him to Sara. At the right time, God would intervene and help Jim again. Or at least that was what he hoped for.

"Jim, you've been through a lot. We need to go somewhere—somewhere you can feel safe. How we'll pay is a mystery."

"When we got married, my pay increased, and I've been squirreling it away." His voice trailed off as he said, "Add it to yours, and we should be able to come up with a nice getaway."

"Oh, I didn't realize you had." Sara squinted. "A break should help."

"Can't hurt." He'd get another pay increase when they had children, but he couldn't imagine being a father. In his current mindset, he wasn't ready for the added responsibility. He hugged Sara and drew her in for a kiss. "Hey, at least I'm not like Gunther, who was hallucinating, and punched poor Jay in the face for no reason.

"It's hard for me to even understand. One night shortly after Christina died, Adam slept over at our house. He said I got up in the middle of the night and walked out the door. Curiosity got the better of him, and he followed me. I walked to Forsyth Park and talked to a statue about Christina, came home, and fell into bed without any memory of the event."

"Did you ever do it again?"

"No one else ever said I did."

"This is all so complicated." She pulled back. "What if—"

Jim cut her off. "I'm not bad enough to act like Gunther. Yes, my nightmares are warped versions of my missions, but others are bizarre fantasies with talking creatures. I can't even put any of it into words. So, I…"

"The drawings. What are they about?"

"Yes, drawings." He pushed the journal across the counter for her to see.

"I'd hoped writing would help, but these?"

"Yes, I've written a lot. The drawings are a recent development."

"The other night, you were on the floor by the bed, doing push-ups, counting, and saying, 'Yes, Drill Sergeant.' I said 'Masterson' a few times to play along. You came back to bed, but I don't think you heard me." Sara paused and sipped her cocoa. "On a different night, you sat straight up in bed, talking gibberish and sniffing at the air like a pup. You stopped and lay down without realizing I was there. It took me a while to fall back asleep."

Jim took a swig of the hot cocoa. "I wish I could figure out how to control myself."

"I read that sleep deprivation magnifies anything we worry about and then it takes even longer to heal from trauma. Mix in feeling weak and guilty for things beyond your control, and you have a messy pudding." Sara's eyebrows furrowed. "We'll figure it out. Thank God you have a calm disposition."

"Yeah, you too."

"I realized getting angry isn't going to solve anything. Your brain's trying to sort things out and it can't. Short-term versus long-term memory. Things got into your head in a rush and they didn't all get stored. In trauma, this can create these types of complications. At least, the book I read said so."

"My reactions became ingrained during training and combat. I regret they've spilled out at the wrong time."

Sara squeezed her lips together while she looked at the drawings. "When I am over at the USO, I work with someone who has PTSD. The person exercises a lot and meditates to help relax. Between those talks and what I read at the library—I understand enough to be patient."

"Back to the drawings. I'm not sure how I drew them. I mean, I was barely awake. When I've tried other times, the drawings look like a five-year-old's scribble scrabble. All crap and worthy of a trash can."

"Well, these are amazing."

"Thanks. They're straight out of a good dream." Jim stroked her hair. "You sound like a therapist."

"You've never seen one. How would you know?"

"Movies."

"Of course." Sara's index finger traced the first, second, and third creature's outline. "This one—with the snake head and donut hole through its belly—the body looks like a horse with a pigtail. What do you think the pyramid in the background represents?"

"No idea. It's weirder than the rest. And these dreams were in color. Not the usual black-and-white. In this one, I think the snake head represents evil temptation, like the snake in the Bible with Adam and Eve." He paused when he mentioned *Adam* and a knot came into his throat. "The body itself doesn't mean anything. The hole in his side—it stands for missing a heart, a soul—being in pain. The pig's tail makes me think of my training when the wild boar tried to take my rucksack away."

"And the statue drawing? I'm guessing it's because you like statues and no other reason?"

"Maybe, except the chin looks like a bird beak, like the ones doctors wore to prevent the spread of diseases. It has real flowers in its arms. Why? I don't know." He paused again. "The other four-legged thing, I can't decide if it's a lion or a dog or some of both."

"Who's Danica?" Sara traced the swirling script on the bottom of the pages.

He traced the name on the same path, their fingers touching. "Beats me."

"I don't understand." Sara clenched her hands around the edge of the open journal. "Who is this woman?"

"It might not even be a person."

Sara squinted at him. "These are like an artist's visions I saw in college—um—thinking—a painter—Henry Fuseli. It's called *The Nightmare*."

"Your artistic knowledge is unlimited."

"Why thank you, sir. But, no, not really." Sara smiled. "He created paintings of dreams and supernatural events. I checked out the book at some point in school and left it lying around."

"I don't remember it." Jim rubbed his head. "There's another one I want to put on the page, but I can't draw when I'm fully awake. Can you help?"

"Sure." Sara grabbed a pencil and artist's eraser out of a kitchen drawer. "I'm ready."

"Okay. Right before I fell asleep, I was thinking about the Army Airborne symbol of the Sky Dragons. That's probably how I fell into the dream."

"Hmm, or from our tattoos. Does the dragon breathe fire?" she asked as she sketched.

"I didn't experience fire coming out of the dragon in this dream. It would fit with—with Adam's... I don't want to say it—his charred body. If I don't speak the words, it'll take me even longer to heal."

"Oh, dear. Okay, I'll leave out the flames." Sara smudged the beginnings of the flames away.

"Now, for the interesting part. There was a person facing away from me, sitting on the ground, hugging the dragon. There was an

X-shaped fabric draped across two red, blood-like marks starting at her shoulder blades and extending down her back."

Sara continued to draw.

"Yes, it looks about right. You could be a criminal sketch artist. One more thing. The dragon had a glowing orb around its body."

"These are beautiful and haunting," Sara exclaimed.

"Yeah, they sure are."

Sara scrunched up the edge of her robe. "Too bad marijuana isn't legal. I heard it's relaxing."

"Um, no. It would show up in a random pee test at work, and then I'd be out the door even if it was legal. Thanks for the help."

"Go on back to bed. I'll be there in a few minutes." Sara nudged him along.

He slogged off to the bedroom and collapsed diagonally onto their bed. *I wish I could sleep forever. I need to heal, but is it even possible?*

Chapter 24

Night Crawl

JIM SHIVERED WITHOUT KNOWING WHY, THEN SOMEONE SPOKE to him in a faraway echo. The voice got louder. He jarred himself into reality. Someone was saying something from the open window of a vehicle.

"What's going on?" The man driving the vehicle inquired.

Leaning in, Jim realized it was a friend from the military police division. A second later, he noticed he was standing there in a pair of briefs. *What happened to the rest of my clothes? And why am I miles away from our apartment, barefoot and shirtless?* He lifted one foot and rested it on his opposing knee. The underside was red, but not cut or bruised.

"Good evening," Jim said, playing it cool.

"Why are you off base, dressed in your skivvies?" Marshall scratched his receding hairline. "Did your roomy lock you out? Or have you been drinking?"

"Nooo, I must have been sleepwalking," Jim said. It was good this MP had pulled up next to him. He knew others wouldn't be so cordial.

"It's okay. You must have a lot on your mind. I just went off duty. I'll give you a lift home."

"Thanks." Jim pulled open the passenger door.

"Take the blanket off the seat and get in. Where are you living these days?"

Jim sat down and wrapped himself up. "Westover, apartment six."

"Right, off we go."

"Marshall, a question." Jim pointed at a car across the way with a boot secured to the tire and multiple tickets behind the windshield wipers. "What's with the car over there? It's been around for a while."

"Yep, it has. I checked into it yesterday," Marshall replied. "It was someone's…"

"Was?" Jim asked.

"Was. The guy went AWOL. By the time they found him, it was too late. He was dead. Shot himself in the woods."

"Christ. Anyone we know?" Jim pulled the blanket tighter around his midsection.

"Don't think so. Crebs was his name. The car is being removed later today." Marshall abruptly changed the subject. "Remember one time when we shared drinks and laughed over names—among other things?"

"Hmm, let me think. Ah, got it. An orthopedist named Bonebreak, and a neurologist named Brain. What about them?"

"Nothing, really… it's a random thought. I don't know how you know the specifics after all this time." Marshall clicked on the turn signal. "We took turns driving when the guys had too much to drink."

"Rowdy crowd. And they loved to fraternize with single women. It's good we had each other's back."

"Yes, for sure. And we still do. We should get together again, for old time's sake." Marshall pulled in front of Jim's place.

"I'm married now. Sara's okay with me going out with the guys. Here's my number." Jim scribbled it on a piece of scrap paper and got out of the cruiser. He hustled up to the front door, which was conveniently unlocked. It was likely his fault because he doubted a sleepwalker would lock a door on the way out.

For better or worse, Sara was awake and sitting on the kitchen stool in her bathrobe, tapping one finger after the other on the counter as if she were playing a piano. *Tap, tap, tap.* The drumming noise conveyed her distress.

"Jim, you look…" Sara eyed him with one eye squinting and the other raised. "I was about to get myself together and go look for you. Or call someone. Your wallet, shoes, and jeans were still on the chair when I woke up. At first, I imagined you'd been called to work and rushed off wearing something else. Your uniforms were all accounted for in the closet. I knew you would have woken me before disappearing on a mission."

"You know it," Jim said. The statement helped, but not enough. So, he added, "Sleepwalking."

"Where do you think you were?"

"I don't know." Jim scratched his head.

"I'm worried. Waking up and being restless is one thing. Wandering off completely oblivious is frightening. Next thing I know, you'll disappear altogether or end up like the crazy runner I saw pass by our place last week."

"What? Who?" Jim added, "I smell burnt coffee."

"Yesterday's dregs, I suppose."

"Sorry, what were you saying about the runner?"

"He was in short-shorts and a torn T-shirt. His hair and beard were scraggly. The guy waved at me and said, 'Good morning.' There were a bunch of people following him—other runners or reporters. I didn't know what was going on. You better not turn into a ragamuffin like that. Never mind, I'm not making sense. It's disturbing; you came in the front door in your underpants! Things are going to hell around here."

"I'm sorry," Jim said. Her eyes were red, as if they were on fire. The surrounding skin was swollen. "You've been crying."

"I've stopped." Sara rubbed her cheeks hard with her palms. "Sleep deprivation and worry would turn me into a growling monster. I don't know how you manage."

"Well, I was a monster once."

"You mean the time you were thrashing around in bed and whacked me in the head right after you returned from Grenada?"

"Yep."

"The aspirin took the edge off." Sara sighed. "It took all my willpower to get back in bed with you two days later."

"I still feel awful about it." Jim rubbed her shoulder.

Sara blew her nose, and the unusual volume made him twitch. She threw the tissue into the wastebasket, filled a glass of water at the sink, and gulped it down. "Go put something warmer on, so we can talk properly."

"Yes, ma'am." Jim took a quick shower and donned a green robe. Going back into the living room, he found Sara on the couch, hugging a throw pillow as if it were a life jacket.

"You in your red robe and me in my green. We're ready to celebrate Christmas."

"Really? You're so precious."

"Sorry. I'm trying to lighten the mood. Not working?"

"Not really." She sighed. "Several weeks ago, I found you outside working on the motorcycles in the middle of the night. Then last weekend, you were staring at the full moon from the front steps. The moonlight hit you, and the shadow behind you bounced off in two directions. Are you going to turn into a shape-shifting werewolf next?"

"Oh, that's silly," Jim crooned, joining her on the couch and pulling her into his arms, along with the pillow. She stiffened in his arms, backed off, and tossed the pillow over his head. He tickled her side and drew her back in. This time, she snuggled into him and relaxed against his chest. "Sara, you know I have combat nightmares. I wake up, pull myself out of the turmoil, and pace. I don't want to disturb you."

"Well, you can wake me up. Sometimes you do anyway. You grind your teeth or mumble. Then, I can't sleep and get up. I read for a while on the couch before I go back to bed. Maybe you should read about PTSD the next time you're in the library. It might help."

"Yes, I should get some more information. Next time I wake up, I'll let you know," Jim whispered. "We could have a nice cuddling to get me back to reality. We both sleep better after…"

"Oh, I can never say you're not a romantic." Sara pulled out of his arms and her facial expression changed into a grimace before she sat back and gazed into his eyes. "Sounds nice. However, it's a short-term solution."

"The sleepwalking bothers me the most. I'm not in control. Hey, it could be worse. I heard about a guy who had an imaginary friend and screamed all kinds of things in the shower. And whenever he played basketball, he shouted at people who weren't there."

"Sounds psychotic. No one ever said being in the military would be easy. Last week, I drove over to a women's social meeting at the community hall. One of the women said her husband was running around the house, shutting all the blinds because he was sure someone was watching him. He kept seeing things in his peripheral vision and there was nothing there. Don't worry—I didn't say anything about your nightmares or anything else."

"Peripheral vision stuff can be an issue for any military person. At times, it feels like someone's near me. Then I turn around and no one's there. The brain can add in things. Also, there's the issue of someone real being there and needing to decide what to do next. I could side-step, defend myself, or simply say *hello*. The training drills beat the observe-orient-decide-react behavior into all soldiers. In regular life, we can't act like that. I'm trying to relax when I'm awake and not be easily startled by phantom or real people appearing in windows or around corners."

"You're jumpier when you haven't had enough sleep," Sara interjected.

"Tell me about it," Jim said. "At work, I heard someone talk about imaginary blood running down a wall. The guy wasn't on drugs; I asked. Luckily, it only happened once. No one wants anyone on their team who can't keep a grip on reality."

"Would you consider getting counseling?" Sara asked ever so gently.

"A good thought, but no. Only soldiers who've gone off the deep end get therapy. If we can't solve things on our own, the bad juju goes on our record. The base chaplain, the one who married us, told me about meetings he sponsors with soldiers to talk things out. He suggested I join them. I'd rather not. It's supposed to be confidential. Over time, I bet the information would leak out."

Jim went back into the kitchen and aimlessly rummaged through the drawers. Realizing he was hungry, he pulled the jelly jar and bread out of the fridge and tried to make a sandwich. Then he couldn't find the peanut butter. But when he did, the knife got stuck in the jar. "I can't even feed myself!"

"You're tired." Sara moved to his right side. "Here, I'll do it."

"Thanks." When she was done, he picked up the sandwich and a dollop of jelly leaked onto the counter. She wiped it away with a sponge without commenting.

While he ate, he stared at the ledge of urns behind the sink. "The plants are looking a little worn out, just like me."

She kissed him on the cheek, put her hands on his belly, and moved down until she reached his groin. "You and the heartleaf plants will be all right with a little tender loving care. They've wilted before and gotten strong again. It's a nurturing thing."

"Ah, you can nurture me anytime." Jim enjoyed her touch. Married life with Sara was a dream come true on so many levels. She teased and fondled until he released and relaxed.

"If you need to, run around the neighborhood before bed in the evenings. I can go with you, and after…"

"Nice idea. We'll have to learn to adjust our strides so we can stay side by side."

"Alrighty then, it's a date." Sara paused. "Oh, and I've been thinking."

"Oooh, never good." Jim laughed. "Can we stay on track? The bedroom's over there."

"Not yet. We need to talk some more."

"While I recover?" he teased.

"We could go to Sintra and take Blaire and Dustin." Sara reached over, took a glob of jelly off his cheek, and licked it off her finger. "What do you think?"

"Uh-huh, okay. The trip might do her good, too. So, what are you proposing?"

"We can go for a couple of weeks over the summer when my students are on break."

"It's a good idea. Let me know what works for you, and I'll ask for some time off," he replied through a sticky sandwich mouth.

"Also, if we have time, we can visit Aunt Deborah in Wales. She's always talking about how relaxing it is by the ocean cliffs."

"A change in scenery and spending time with our families is a great idea." Jim's thoughts took over. *Being surrounded by Uncle Jorge and Cousin Peter couldn't hurt. Maybe it would also help if we encouraged friends to come to our apartment more often.* Out loud, he said, "I'll be back." Walking over to the hall closet, he pulled out a box of Cristalle Chanel perfume and gave it to Sara. "I'm sorry I've been so difficult to live with lately."

"Oh, how sweet, thank you. We'll find a way through all this." She opened the box and rubbed a dab on her throat. "It's still my favorite."

Jim leaned in and smelled the perfume. "Delicious."

"It'll be great to get to know your uncle. Meeting him at our wedding didn't give us much time." She nudged him away. "And there's something else on my mind. When we get back, we should get a dog."

"Little lady, you come up with the best ideas." Jim kissed her. "Thank you for being so understanding when I short-circuit."

"Glad to be of service." Sara snickered and began massaging his shoulders. "A dog would be a good companion and could sleep next to our bed at night."

"Uncle's dog sleeps with him."

"No, the floor's fine."

"Having a dog close by might help me sleep all the way through."

"I like the idea, but not on the bed," she emphasized the point.

"Okay, okay," Jim conceded. "I often found Buddy in the barn sitting in front of Rolan's stall. Sometimes, they'd be touching noses. Until I met Rolan, I'd never seen such an enormous, tri-colored horse."

"Tobiano."

"What?"

"Never mind. It's another way of defining the color. The pair of them sound happy," Sara said. "When we met in Savannah, you mentioned Rolan to impress me on our first beach walk."

"I guess I did." He smiled at the recollection. "Best day ever."

"Tell me more about Buddy."

"Okay." Jim pulled her closer and wound a strand of her hair around his finger, let it go and watched the curl unfurl. "Buddy is a cross between a Labrador and a boxer. He's quiet, too, hardly barks, and he's loyal beyond reason."

"Yes, we should have a dog like him."

"It'll take time to find a good one and go through the training. The last time I was at Uncle's place, there were probably a dozen egg-laying chickens wandering around, eating insects. Anyway, Buddy never ran after them. He did go after Uncle whenever he rode Rolan into the woods."

"I'm not sure how you got to chickens and horses when I brought up a dog. Never mind for now. There are other things to worry about. I know you'll pull through, and Uncle will help." Sara stood, took Jim's hand, and led him to the bedroom.

PART THREE

Chapter 25

Travels

ACCORDING TO JIM'S CALCULATIONS, THE TRIP TO PORTUGAL was going to take ten hours in airplanes and another forty minutes by train from Lisbon to Sintra. Add the transfer times, and they'd be traveling for at least fifteen hours.

They arrived at the airport, checked in at the counter, and found their departure gate. Jim settled down next to Blaire and Sara in a long row of chairs in the waiting area. A few minutes later, Dustin's pacifier tumbled toward the floor. Both Jim and Blaire tried to catch it and bumped shoulders. He recalled the first time he and Sara met on the train. How they'd touched hands while retrieving a ball of yarn. Even though he hadn't realized it at the time, he'd fallen in love with her on the train. So much had happened since then. Sara supported him, and her sublime strength kept him from unraveling.

The first flight to Philadelphia was tiresome, from lugging bags around to dealing with Dustin's antics. The women passed him back and forth to stop the boy's fussing. Sitting on Jim's lap seemed to calm him the most. Entertaining a baby under these circumstances was exhausting. Once they transferred planes, it would be closer to Dustin's usual bedtime, and everyone could get some rest.

Following a short walk through the terminal, they struggled through the aisle of the second plane with the carry-on bags. Jim watched Dustin's body swing from side to side within the pack on Blaire's back. A cinched band kept him secure. It didn't stop him from trying to escape. Dustin kept grabbing onto Blaire's ponytail, clenching and unclenching his fist among the strands. Meanwhile, his other hand flew into the air without apparent purpose, as if he were riding a bucking horse. When he wasn't wiggling, he seemed to love watching the world with wide eyes while babbling or cooing and moving his tongue around on his newly erupted two front teeth. Blaire turned sideways and Jim wiggled Dustin out of the pack, so she could settle into her seat and buckle up. Dustin was the only one who didn't miss Adam. One day, Jim would tell him everything about his father.

It was always fun to watch Dustin until the crankiness started from under or over stimulation, from hunger or fatigue, or from whatever else sets a baby off. Sara had talked about having one of these tiny human creatures at some point, but he wasn't in a hurry. He still had too many things to work out before getting serious about the added responsibility.

In the plane, they sat behind a bulkhead. A flight attendant handed Jim a bassinet to clip onto the pull-down shelf mounted on the wall. He wasn't sure why she'd designated him for the task. After the flight took off, it didn't take long to settle Dustin down into a nest of blankets with a bottle to soothe him to sleep. Blaire had prepared ahead, because she didn't want to nurse him on the plane.

Halfway through the Atlantic crossing, the cabin became stuffy and claustrophobic, with the air circulation vacillating between cool and warm. Looking around, Jim realized no one else seemed to notice. No one was pulling at their collars, pushing blankets off themselves, or signaling the cabin crew. Blaire and Sara were asleep. Jim's restlessness increased. His body heated up like a whistling kettle. First, he tapped one foot on the floor and then the other. Next, he wiggled his shoes off without using his hands, since he didn't have enough room to bend over to take them off. This effort distracted him for a short time. He moved his heels up and down. Pulling out the drink tray from the compartment on the side of his seat, he tried to read an in-flight magazine. Nothing helped his anxiety.

Trying an alternative tactic, he stared out into the abyss through the cabin window and took deep, long breaths. As the plane lowered its altitude, his anxiety converted into a glassy-eyed stare. Moonlight reflected off the wing in between a smattering of cirrus clouds. Long ago, Uncle Jorge had taught him the Latin names of clouds.

What would his uncle be like when they arrived? So much had happened since their last meeting. Aunt Yara had been a rugged woman with a gentle heart. Her name meant Water Lady, and reminded Jim of the water tunneling alongside the labyrinth of walking paths winding around the Portuguese gardens of Quinta da Regaleira.

The estate was steps away from his aunt and uncle's home. Each visit, he would walk from their place through the circular stone tunnel into the gardens. Closing his eyes, he imagined what the place had been like a decade before, when life had still been innocent and full of happy delights. During those times, the light sparkled through the canopy of trees and unseen animals scurried beneath shifting, low-growing foliage. The statues and buildings with organic themes and stippled stone were his favorite. Quinta da Regaleira had always been a magical place, although he never explored at night for fear of goblins and spirits.

In recent years, he'd read the tunnel's entrance was made of an eight-foot-tall megalithic stone like the one in Cornwall known as Mên-an-Tol, or the crick stone. The one in Sintra was a larger version, and he hadn't been able to figure out how it got there. Legends said going through such circular rocks during certain phases of the moon brought out its powers. Jim wasn't sure what they were.

On this visit, unlike the others, Aunt Yara would be there in spirit. Her death was as horrible as Adam's, but a car, not a bullet, had ended her life. While Jim sat there, his imagination started working too well. Outside the plane's window, the clouds uncoiled and the sky seemed to melt away. He saw Aunt Yara's crumpled body, lying on the ground with black car tracks across her middle and blood seeping out of the corners of her mouth. Her blood morphed into images of Adam and Christina's faces.

The reality of Adam's wounds—the hole in his chest and the blood. *How many times would he have to see this? Or feel the guilt of not telling Blaire the truth?* Adam had said nothing about his love for her. Shock had taken over his ability to speak coherently. He focused on the vent blowing air from the ceiling and took a long breath to re-center his mind.

Dustin muttered something that somehow came out clearer than the expected baby jibber-jabber. It sounded like, *don't worry.* Jim chuckled, but it came out tormented, off-key.

Another image intruded. He recalled once being told the path of memory was bizarre. In school, he'd blanked out during a math exam and couldn't solve anything. Needless to say, his combat experiences were unforgettable. It didn't seem fair. He wanted to forget about death as easily as a math equation. Childhood was long gone. Jim prayed Dustin's life, unlike his sister's, would be long and full of good times. He wondered what Christina would be like if she survived. He wondered if his parents would still be together if they hadn't gone through so much trauma.

Struggling to stand up, he folded his shoulders forward and climbed over Sara and Blaire while they slept. In the aisle, he paced, and hoped to settle his nerves. It seemed absurd that being on this commercial plane would rattle the empty spot in his soul. Maybe it wasn't so strange. The last time he'd been on a long flight was in November, after the Grenada mission.

So far, this trip magnified his loss yet again and caused him to rehash everything. He wished he'd brought his journal instead of leaving it on the nightstand. The deceased men had been brought home in body bags and could be patched up enough for their families to view them and say goodbye. Their loved one's felt closure in a way Adam's mother and Blaire could not. Adam's body and face had been burned beyond recognition. They had to imagine the old Adam—tall, strong, and full of life.

Mrs. Donnelly's words spun through his mind for what must have been the hundredth time. She had told him to look after Adam. Although it was an impossible request, he still felt responsible for failing them both. Rationally, Jim knew she would never blame him for her son's death. On an emotional level, she probably felt he could have done better. He kept thinking he should have died instead, but he knew everyone reacted this way after combat. Every time he reviewed the events, there didn't seem to be a way around what happened. Both Sara and Blaire agreed, even though they couldn't understand the way fellow soldiers could. He needed to let the guilt go.

In a whisper to no one in particular, Jim said, "God is in control, even if I will never understand His reasoning. Why one person dies before the other when they're still young continues to be an unanswered question. The elderly going in their sleep is kind. Death any other way feels cruel."

The man in the aisle seat looked at Jim with an inquiring eye.

"Oh, sorry. I was talking to myself louder than I thought."

"You all right?" the stranger asked.

"I will be, thanks." Jim stopped pacing up and down the aisle and crawled back into his seat. Blaire and Sara woke up in the commotion. Dustin twitched and cried out. Jim easily calmed him down with a few *tut tuts* and *there, theres*.

Portugal

The Aeroporto Lisboa was not much different from any other European hub, except this one had large pipe-like support beams and an open floor plan with a breeze running through to dissipate the air on hot summer days. A kind staff member expedited them through customs because they had a baby in tow. Jim hadn't realized how many things they'd need to lug around. Blaire had done her best to keep the number of items to a minimum. They entered the main concourse. The bright light coming through the floor-to-ceiling windowpanes almost blinded Jim.

Before leaving the terminal, Jim trotted over to the money exchange and swapped dollars for Portuguese escudos. Outside the airport, a commuter bus sat by the curb. They stuffed their bags into a holding area and found seats.

As the bus moved along, they talked among themselves about how much time to spend in Lisbon. Savannah was large enough for Jim's liking, with a hundred thousand people spread across many miles.

Lisbon was massive by comparison, with a population of around two million crammed into a smaller space. They decided not to push their luck with Dustin beyond taking the time to find an outdoor spot for lunch by the Tagus River.

Even though many tourists swarmed to Lisbon to soak in the sun and history, Jim had never entirely liked the city, but he enjoyed the food. It was a seaside town, so it was not unusual to smell salted or rotting fish. Visiting Portugal during the warm season was far better than any other choice they could have made, and Sintra was his favorite town. He recalled the only Christmas his family toured Lisbon on the way to his uncle's. Back then, it was raining, and the uneven cobblestone streets were slippery. Bits of paper trash stuck to the sidewalks in spots and indiscernible clumps of dirty gunk backed up in random street corners. The gutters emitted a putrid aroma that could only be masked by cologne or perfume.

This visit to Lisbon wasn't any better than the visit during his youth, except it wasn't raining this time and it was warmer. All the vendors were selling merchandise on the streets and in shops. It would be difficult to get a moment's peace with merchants hawking their wares. Jim reminded himself to stay calm. Crowds put him in a heightened state of awareness and made him uncomfortable. The volume of tourists and local voices was almost deafening. The fight-or-flight instinct set in. His heart rate elevated, his vision became myopic, and he wanted to duck into the nearest alcove. He tried to take his mind beyond his concerns and examine the classic architecture and landscaping flanking the river while pointing out the details to Sara and Blaire. Bringing real-life architecture off the pages of Sara's school books excited her beyond Jim's expectations. She was mesmerized and wide-eyed.

The four of them settled down in the outdoor seating area of Café Martinho da Arcada. Blaire threw a small blanket over her shoulder and nursed Dustin. If he fussed, the clientele would be tolerant under the circumstances. Jim talked to the server in Portuguese and ordered their food. While they waited, he refocused his mind on Cousin Peter and shared his thoughts with Sara. He'd forgotten how much she loved to listen to just about anything he had to say. He'd been way too quiet of late.

After Jim ate his meal of *bacalhau lagareiro* (cod dish) and the women finished a plate of *sardinhas assadas* (fresh sardines), they all hustled over to the Lisbon train station. Sara took Dustin while Blaire folded up the umbrella stroller. With one fluid movement, she maneuvered him into the carrier on her chest, facing forward with his little legs pumping. There wasn't any point in putting him back in the stroller until they got to Uncle Jorge's place. The paraphernalia she carried seemed to come out of a bottomless bag.

Up on the main level, Jim bought tickets for the regional train to Sintra. They pushed through the turnstiles and spent the next ten minutes wandering around. Sara took photographs of the large tile murals on the walls while they waited.

The train pulled into the station with its brakes squealing. Jim remembered them being quiet and hoped this was a fluke and not a sign of danger. The doors slid open, and he proceeded down the aisle with the women close behind him to the available seats. The doors closed, and the train zipped out of the station.

Along the way, Blaire and Sara gazed out the window at the scenery. They made remarks about the brick row houses and the laundry hanging off clotheslines. Jim found the view rather dull compared to what they would see in Sintra. He hoped this train would carry them into a new normal, or at the very least, provide them with a solid footing to launch from. In some ways, it was like the day Sara changed his life when they met on the way to Savannah years before, except on this journey he carried remorse and terror within his soul.

During the train ride, Jim nodded off. He was brought back into consciousness by a pulling sensation. Opening his eyes, he saw Blaire's hand on his sleeve, and Dustin's underneath hers. Jim tussled the baby's curly hair as the train arrived in the station. They disembarked, the doors closed, and it shifted back toward Lisbon. Sintra was the last stop on so many levels. If Jim couldn't heal at his uncle's, he wasn't sure he ever would.

Seeing the train station brought him back to the times he'd come with his parents. The building still had alternating red and white bricks arching over the front doors. Outside on the cobblestone streets, tour guides wove between the crowd, seeking out new clients with a persistence that rubbed on Jim's nerves. Small tour buses lined the road. Peter didn't seem to be anywhere among the horde.

When the crowd thinned out, Jim only saw two older gentlemen sitting at a stone table playing chess. About the time he started worrying about transportation, a carriage appeared. The sign on the side said, The Masterson Party. A familiar face jumped out of the driver's seat.

"Peter. You're a welcome sight." Jim bear-hugged his cousin and introduced everyone. He gestured toward the rig. "Is this a new addition to the family business?"

"Good to see you," Peter replied. "No, I borrowed the carriage from a friend."

Peter and Jim crammed the luggage into the box behind the passenger compartment. Blaire swaddled Dustin in a blanket and held him close. The ride up the narrow winding street jostled them about. Along the route, Jim pointed out the narrow staircases between buildings, statues, six-pointed stars engraved in the cobblestones, and palm trees. When they left the central part of town, the land turned into a wooded wonderland with numerous varieties of trees and vegetation. Peter pulled in front of his father's house. They unloaded the luggage by the front door. Jim knocked. Uncle Jorge didn't answer.

Peter held out his palm and winked at Jim. "*Escudos* for me?"

"You're a clown. No tipping. It says so on the back of the seat."

"I have to return the carriage." Peter clapped Jim on the back. "I'll see you later." Peter climbed into the driver's seat, grabbed the reins, and the horses clattered away.

They walked around the property, toward the barn and gardens. Jim saw a man cloaked from head-to-toe in a baggy white outfit. Smoke billowed out of a can in his hand.

Over by the barn, Buddy barked a greeting. He moved slowly into a standing position, strolled over to Jim, and licked his hand. The dog was no longer young and appeared gray around the snout. His hind legs were stiff, and he stretched them out while Jim rubbed his head.

"*Jiminho, pare aí, não é seguro,*" a voice shouted in Portuguese through a mesh hood. It was Uncle Jorge.

"Hello." Jim waved his hand in a quick, twitchy movement and laughed. "*Jiminho?* Little Jim? Uncle, I'm all grown up. Can we speak in English? No one…"

"*Eu sinto muito,* hello." Uncle Jorge's voice sounded far away within his disguise. He raised one of his hands, which was covered by an oversized glove, and waved them away. "Welcome to my home, ladies. Please stay over there. We should talk from a distance."

"Hello," Blaire and Sara said in unison.

"The bees are calm today," Uncle shouted and ambled a little closer. "There are thousands out here."

"Have you counted, Uncle?" Jim said with a huge grin across his face.

Uncle took his hood off, and his forehead scrunched up with his entire face. "I know because I have to register my hives and create lists—too many lists. These bees are for honey production. Many bees in Portugal pollinate plants. Has the baby ever been stung?"

"No," Blaire responded, taking a few steps back.

"It's all right. Show the ladies the bee observation tubes at the other end of the barn. Less chance of getting them stuck in their hair, clothes, and so forth. I'm almost done. I need to finish this."

"All right, Uncle. It's great to see you, too." Jim stood in place and listened to the humming radiating from the hives.

"Stay, Jim," Sara said, and started to move away. "We can go on our own."

"No, no," Uncle Jorge called out. "Someone has to take you. It would be rude otherwise. Jim knows the way. There are six horses in the barn. You can visit them and see the bees. We have chickens, too."

"Okay, Uncle."

"I'll meet you in the house in ten minutes."

Jim guided the group to the end of the barn to show off Uncle's bee tubes. He was sure Blaire and Sara would have preferred to visit the horses.

The glass observation hive was full of honeycombs and buzzing bees. They were entering and exiting through a tube in the exterior wall. Jim paused long enough for them to watch the queen bee laying eggs while another bee rubbed thick pollen off its legs. Each bee moved from cell to cell while others waggled their bums. The pollen was thicker than what covered the cars in Savannah on a spring day.

"So," Sara said, "tell us about Peter."

Jim chuckled, knowing full well this was for Blaire's benefit, rather than Sara's. "We haven't written or talked in five years. Back then, Peter was finishing up his degree at the university in Coimbra. He was obsessed with guitars and his studies. When he graduated, he went out with his friends to bars, singing and strumming guitars. Didn't seem unusual until he said they were wearing their graduation robes with multicolored ribbons streaming off them to represent their university accomplishments. When they'd finished, they burned the ribbons in a vat."

"Interesting," Blaire said. "And odd."

"Tell her about the bats in the library," Sara said.

"Ah, I forgot about that." Jim rubbed his head. "He wrote me about the ancient university library, where bats come out at night from the upper corners of the walls to collect any insects feasting on the books on the built-in oak bookshelves."

"Interesting from a distance," Blaire said.

"I hope you'll be okay after spending so much time away from Peter," Sara said. "He was very nice to us during the carriage ride."

"He didn't sound as rough-edged as he was when we were kids. I don't know if that's a good or bad thing."

"It's not fair to assess him too quickly," Sara interjected.

"You're right. He's a smart guy, and he's always been good-hearted."

Jim opened a door in the back of the building and took them to the chicken coop.

Through the window, they could see six nests, each containing a bundle of eggs. The mother hens were nowhere in sight, although he heard their clucking.

"Stay here. I'll be right back." He plodded outside to the enclosure and saw them rolling around in the dirt. Returning, he found Blaire and Sara standing in front of a horse's stall. Blaire was helping Dustin stroke Rolan's snout.

Jim leaned into Sara, nudging her. "Oh, no chickens and bees for you?"

"Yes, hmm, no."

"While we're away from Uncle, I should mention he likes to talk. Blaire, he's an interesting character."

As they walked out of the barn, two colorful magpies landed on the garden fence.

"Well, good afternoon," Blaire said.

"Why are you talking to birds? A new thing?" Sara asked.

"I'm feeling superstitious. If there are two, I have to talk to them to ward off bad luck. They are supposed to be the souls of the departed. Who knows? Never can be too careful."

Chapter 26

Bees

JIM LED SARA AND BLAIRE INTO THE HOUSE. THEY TOOK A quick tour of the living space and then headed into the bedrooms. It was quite apparent whose room was whose because there was a labeled card on top of each set of folded towels on every bed. His room with Sara's was on the first floor. Blaire and Dustin's room was upstairs opposite Uncle Jorge and Cousin Peter's individual rooms. Since Uncle Jorge said he'd be in soon, they didn't unpack. Instead, everyone headed back to the living area to wait for him.

Sara and Blaire tried to settle onto the couch. Jim took the armchair. Dustin had other ideas. He squirmed around, trying to get out of Blaire's lap. Being confined for twenty-four hours had gotten everyone into a fidgety mood. The jet lag and time zone changes were taking their toll.

Thirty minutes, not ten, had passed since they'd gathered in the yard. Jim began to worry. The outer door swung open, and a figure came into view. The sun backlit the large bear-like silhouette with indiscernible features. The shadowy creature lumbered in the door and gave itself away. Of course, it was Uncle Jorge.

"Isn't he the adventurer?" Uncle Jorge closed the door behind him and pointed at Dustin. "I didn't travel until I was a teenager." His English was clear and concise, with hints of a Portuguese accent. Smoke trickled out of the metal bee can like a genie's lamp. Uncle Jorge gave the billows a quick squeeze. A puff of clouds emerged.

"How are your bees, Uncle?"

"They are healthy like a horse. I brought in some honeycombs." Uncle put a bucket on the table by the door and took off his bee hood. Above the table was a framed photograph of three bees. The worker was the smallest; the middle sized, the drone; and the largest, the queen. Jim knew this much about bees and little else.

A bee clung to the sleeve of Uncle's suit, with its wings splayed. He placed a gloveless finger in front of the creature, and it crawled up onto the back of his hand. "Look at this worker, so placid. The others were a little unruly today and needed a strong dose of smoke to calm down. Precious things. They pollinate my vegetables, and I get lots of produce."

"Aren't you worried about getting stung?" Sara asked. Before Uncle Jorge could respond, a black-and-white striped butterfly landed on her blouse. "Oh, it's beautiful."

"Yes. It's rare to have one fly inside." Uncle paused and took a breath. "Back to the bees. To avoid their wrath, we must keep calm. They sense fear. Education is the key. They get angry when they get stuck between tight places. Not to worry about drones, they can't sting."

"Good to know," Blaire said. "Except they all look the same to me."

"This little worker bee has things to do. So pitiful on her own in the house." Uncle opened the door, blew on his hand, and the bee flew off with the butterfly. "The buzzing hives are music to my ears. Now that I'm free from the bees, I want a hug from everyone. Especially these beautiful women. We didn't have enough time together at your wedding."

"We'll make up for lost time while we're here," Sara said. Both she and Blaire took turns hugging Uncle Jorge.

"Jim, I know you're allergic to bees," Uncle Jorge said.

"You should have told me," Sara said.

"I reacted one time here and never again." Jim rubbed his cheek, recalling how his face had swollen up like a tomato. Back in the day, his mama had rushed to the rescue with Benadryl. "Even so, I stay away from them."

"Good choice," Uncle Jorge said. "I thought you were a goner until your mama stepped in."

"It was nice to meet her at our wedding." Blaire sighed.

"Sadly, my sister and I only speak one or two times a year." Uncle Jorge covered his mouth for an instant before continuing. "She changed a lot after the family..."

"Let's not talk about Mama now," Jim interrupted, and refocused on Dustin. The little tyke looked happy enough.

"Agreed," Uncle said. "I like *Apis mellifera carnica* bees since they rarely sting. The ancient Druids believed the bees symbolized the sun goddess and celebrated their lives. During many festivals, then and now, mead is the drink of choice. It contains fermented honey."

The corners of Jim's mouth turned up in a tiny smile in an effort to show some support. "There sure are a lot of flowers around the pond and in the olive grove for them." Jim made a mental note to show Sara and Blaire the surrounding lands over the days to come.

"Yes, it's amazing. They finish one area in bloom before going to the next. If a solo bee must travel too far to find new flowers, it'll go back to the hive and do a waggle dance to tell the rest where to go. The nectar from different types of blossoms creates different flavors of honey. I collect it in separate batches throughout the season."

"Oh my, you sure know about bees," Blaire said with genuine interest. "I love clover honey."

"Your hair is the color of honey," Uncle said.

"Yes, I suppose it is," Blaire said, and turned the conversation in a new direction.

"I brought a chocolate chip cookie recipe with me. I can make a batch while we're here and add honey instead of sugar. I had planned to bring some cookies on the plane, but decided they would have broken or been eaten along the way."

"How nice." Uncle Jorge walked around the room in his bee suit, looking like a deflated balloon, and took one of Blaire's hands between his. "I am heartbroken over losing Adam. Of course, you are devastated. I will leave an empty seat at the table to honor him. I did for Yara for a long time."

"Yes, well," Blaire said awkwardly. "The first few months were the hardest. I miss Adam every day, but Dustin keeps me occupied."

"Yes, I understand. I'll get some of last year's honey for everyone. Dustin, he's too young. I hope this year's batches are good. They change every year." Uncle Jorge strolled in and out of the kitchen with his voice melodically rising and falling as he opened and closed the oven door. "The queen, who is larger than the other females, spends her days laying eggs while being attended to by the workers."

"Interesting," Sara said.

Uncle strutted back over to the front door by the bee smoker, peeled off his one-piece bee suit, and hung it on a hook. "Any time I go to the beehives to take care of the colonies, I wear protective gear. I am an apicultor—a beekeeper."

"I see," Blaire said.

"Uncle, are you cooking something?" Jim asked.

"I am making a stew." Uncle Jorge gestured toward the oven. "Go see the covered pan. And a *queijada de Sintra*—cheesecake with cinnamon on top."

"Sounds good. Next time, can we help?" Sara asked.

"Of course." Uncle put a jar of honey on the counter. The label said *Mel do tio Jorge*—Uncle Jorge's Honey. Under the words was a sketch of a wrinkled, bearded man. Next to the jars sat a gallon jug of something resembling tea, along with glasses for everyone. Beside it was a bowl of pickled olives, also labeled from Uncle's crop. He placed three spoons on a plate. They all got the hint and tasted the olives, which were tart and sweet with a hint of salt. Next, they moved to the honey, dipped in their spoons and licked them clean.

"It's all delicious," Sara exclaimed. "You're a master."

Uncle Jorge went straight back to talking about bees. Jim wasn't sure everyone was interested, yet they all appeared to be captivated. They intermittently nodded and smiled.

Uncle pointed at the smoker. "I light a small fire with rags or pine needles in the box. And when it gets going, I blow the smoke out the nozzle with the bellow bag. I check the hives now and again without always taking any honey."

"Uncle, you are always a wealth of information." Jim couldn't help laughing. Sara had once said this about him in Savannah. He and his uncle shared this trait.

"Thank you. I like to learn about many things." Uncle Jorge turned toward Dustin. "Blaire, I put the fragile things away. Jim warned me the little man was crawling. I have a basket of toys for him in the corner with some cardboard books."

"The stuffed rabbit caught my attention," Blaire said with a bright, tired voice and handed it to her son. "Thank you."

"Very good. Seeing Dustin reminds me of a story. Long ago, my wife gave Jim a bucket of honey. He stuck half his hand in for a taste. We had to pull it out. Ah, we had a good belly laugh." Uncle Jorge turned around, headed over to his bookshelf, and slid out a copy of *Winnie the Pooh*.

"Great, thanks for bringing that up," Jim responded sarcastically. He hadn't any recollection of a jar on his nose. Then with heartfelt sincerity, he said. "Blaire, I can get a copy for Dustin when he's older."

"Oh, thank you, Jim." Blaire gently took the book from Uncle Jorge and flipped through the pages. "I wish I could understand Portuguese."

"You'll learn some while we're here," Jim replied.

Uncle Jorge described in detail the orchids, lilies, lupines, and other flowers throughout the property. He went on to talk about the vegetables, consisting of cabbage, leeks, tomatoes, and beans. Then he changed to discussing the olive grove and the vineyard. The fruit, vegetables, and chicken eggs provided them with an abundance of food throughout the season. They canned the vegetables they couldn't consume, and either sold the remainder or gave it away.

"Jim, do you remember our trip to the Alhambra in Spain?" Uncle Jorge asked.

"Yes. I was ten years old. My dad has a framed photograph Aunt Yara took in my room." Jim also couldn't forget the visit because Aunt Yara had been hit by a car a month later.

"It was in the summer. Christina and Melanie were too young to go."

Memories were flooding into Jim. "The open courtyard with the twelve white lions surrounded a white basin. Aunt Yara said the filigree walls reminded her of her mother's lace curtains."

"Everything seemed to have a purpose in the Alhambra," Uncle Jorge said. "To feed the belly or enlighten the soul. The gardens are precise."

"Yes, right," Jim said wistfully.

"Long before you were born, the place inspired us to grow flowers and to start an apiary to keep bees," Uncle said.

"It's wonderful here," Sara said.

"Thank you." Uncle Jorge moved over to the table and shuffled some books around. "Excuse me, I need to change into dinner clothes. We'll eat the stew I made—*caldeirada de peixe*—with fish. And then the cheesecake for dessert. I will tell you more stories later."

"When's your son coming back?" Blaire asked.

"Pedro is performing at the Tivoli Palacio de Seteais hotel with a friend. I'm surprised he didn't tell you before he drove away." Uncle adjusted the band around his ponytail. "Mm, perhaps he will play his *guitarra Portuguesa* after dinner."

"Pedro?" Sara's eyes squinted with confusion.

"Remember, I call him Peter," Jim explained.

"Oh, right, Peter Pan," Sara said. "I'm sorry, I shouldn't tease."

"It's all right," Jim replied.

"Sounds like a great way to keep his name in my head," Blaire said with a giggle. "Is he a lost boy?"

Jim answered with a shrug. "Around here, he is Pedro. Either name is fine."

"Why? Sounds confusing," Blaire said.

"It's how it's always been. I don't know why," Jim said. "It's like my dad calls me James Michael."

Peter appeared out of nowhere with flushed cheeks.

"Hello, hello," Peter said in Portuguese, with the largest smile Jim had ever seen on his cousin's face. "Good to see everyone again."

"How was everything?" Uncle asked in Portuguese.

"Exceptional." Peter responded. "We should speak in English."

Peter engulfed Jim in a hug. At first, he stood stock-still, then returned the embrace.

"And who are these beautiful ladies?" Peter asked. He was obviously playing with them since they'd already met a few hours before. "No, let me guess. You must be Blaire, with little Dustin?"

"Hello, again, Peter," Blaire said.

"I'm sorry, I should behave better. I'm sorry about Adam. He was a good friend to all of us."

"Thank you." Blaire smiled weakly.

"And Sara, it's a pleasure." He leaned in and placed one kiss on each of Sara's cheeks. "I am now the cousin. My driver's hat is gone."

Jim watched Blaire and Sara's reactions, and they seemed captivated by Peter's demeanor.

"Pedro, thank you for bringing them with the carriage," Uncle said.

"Yes, thank you," Sara said. "It was a special treat and reminded me of our rides in Savannah."

"Son, congratulations on your event today." An enormous grin spread across Uncle Jorge's face. "The palacio is the best hotel in Sintra. It's an honor to perform there."

"Yes, the place is beautiful and so are the people," Peter said.

"What's it like?" Blaire bounced Dustin on her hip.

"Little Dustin is a happy child." Peter tickled the baby's side. "The hotel was a palace years ago in the eighteenth century. It's on the UNESCO registry. Every room is elegant, and the staff has kept up the royal standards."

"Your costume is elaborate," Jim said. "I thought it was just for our carriage ride?"

"No, no, I wear it for work. It's required. The black top and trousers." Peter held up his hand to reveal a billowing sleeve. "I used to wear a long, black cape when I was at university in Coimbra. This is nothing."

"Tell us more," Sara said.

"If you insist. The grounds have a series of hedgerow mazes the guests often get lost in. We performed outside. The interior is supposed to be fit for a king, with Moorish architecture inside and out. I was told the master chef makes the best food in Portugal."

"We?" Blaire asked.

"My vocalist sings alongside me, and I play my guitarra. The hotel management was so pleased, they invited us back for their regular Saturday luncheons, not just for ceremonies like today."

"Guitarra?" Sara asked.

"A guitar. Mine is like a mandolin—round shaped." Peter tossed a lemon to his father. "From the hotel."

"Can you play for us after dinner?" Blaire asked.

"Yes, I would be happy to." Peter smiled at Blaire. "Before it gets dark, I want to show you the estate gardens. The owner is away for two weeks. I'm helping clean and paint some of the rooms. We can walk around without disturbing anyone. Would you like to go?"

"Oh, yes," Blaire said enthusiastically.

"You all should go," Jim said. "Peter can give you a fresh perspective without us. Uncle and I can stay here. We'll take care of Dustin."

"I would be honored to be your guide," Peter said.

"Thank you," Blaire said. "It would be good for Dustin to be without me for a little while."

After the tour of the gardens and the family meal, Peter brought out his guitar and plucked away at the twelve strings, which looked like six at a quick glance. Blaire bounced Dustin on her lap during a series of energetic melodies and songs. On cue, when Peter lowered the pace and volume of his music to a melancholy fado, Dustin fell asleep. The variations in the music, combined with Peter's baritone voice, hung in the air long after everyone retired for the evening.

A Day Later

Jim got out of bed to the sounds of pans clanking in the kitchen. Stretching, he noticed the sun was up, so he'd slept more than usual, with a minor interruption in the middle of the night when he was awoken from a pseudo-nightmare. It was a twisted scene of a dozen soldiers trying to protect kids at an elementary school from an alien invasion. The platoon corralled the kids into vans, while everyone else was held at bay on the sidewalk. Soon after, bees appeared in an enormous cluster without attacking.

Looking over his shoulder at the lump of covers in the bed, he decided it must be someone other than Sara making all the noise. He let her be, got dressed, and left the bedroom. In the kitchen, he was surprised to find Sara and Uncle Jorge. The lump in the bed must have been her pillows under the quilt. Briefly, he popped back into the room to make the bed. Buddy's nose peeked out from under the covers. The mystery solved.

"Come on, good boy," Jim encouraged.

Buddy jumped off the bed, nuzzled Jim's hand, and followed him into the other room.

"Morning, everyone. Sara, did you let Buddy in the bed?"

"No, it was his idea," Sara replied. "You were curled into a little ball when he jumped up. Did he fool you?"

"Yep," Jim said. "I thought you were the one rolled up in the quilt, snoring."

"Nope, sorry." Sara giggled.

"Jim, how did you sleep?" Uncle Jorge said in Portuguese while looking at him with wide eyes. "Did the tea I gave you before bed help?"

"What? I'm sorry, what did you ask?"

"How did you sleep after the tea?" Uncle repeated in English.

"I had a jumbled dream of soldiers, children, and bees. It was not my usual type." Jim went to the sink, cupped water into his hands, and vigorously rubbed his face. "None of it made any sense. At least no one got hurt, which was a refreshing change from my *normal* combat nightmares. I didn't wake up again in a cold sweat, and managed to fall back asleep."

"Good, good. That's a start." Uncle sat down with a cup of coffee. "Some vitamins could help, too."

"Thanks, I think," Jim said skeptically.

"Sara, can you check in the garden for some fresh peppers and onions? Also, eggs?" Uncle Jorge asked. "Take the basket by the door."

"Of course, Uncle Jorge. Here, darling." Sara handed Jim a towel to dry his face. Then she went out the front door with Buddy.

"Jim, help yourself to some coffee," Uncle said. "Blaire will be down soon. She's bathing Dustin."

"What were you saying about the tea?" Jim asked.

"I added some things to help you sleep," Uncle replied.

"I didn't realize you'd doctored it."

"I couldn't tell you without disrupting the results." Uncle sounded pleased. "It's a remedy from a friend. I don't know if it will work every time."

"What's in it? No belladonna, I hope? It can churn things up. I already have enough crazy in my head."

"In Italian, belladonna means beautiful lady. No, I used chamomile and dried roses soaked in boiled water. Next time, you could try my tea blend with lemon balm, ashwagandha, chaste tree berry, and passion flower. I have a different one with chamomile flowers, passion flowers, rose petals, and Saint John's-wort. Another of chamomile, peppermint, and snake herbs. Or you can try my tinctures." Uncle Jorge held up a small brown glass bottle. "They are mixed with alcohol to preserve them. One has wild lettuce to help you sleep. Take a drop or two at a time under your tongue if you want to try this instead of the tea. What do you think?"

"Odd. Snake plant? I'm skeptical about any of that stuff. It's good you didn't tell me before I drank my tea. When we came here, I figured your place was what I needed to unwind. To reconnect with a calmer reality. The tea could be part of the therapy, I suppose. I'll call you my mystic doctor."

"Mystic? No." Uncle Jorge sounded a little offended. "They're not addictive. Don't worry, Sintra will help you."

"I'll try not to. I don't want to start hallucinating."

"I heard of an anti-malaria drug that can cause those," Blaire said. "Let me think, it's called mefloquine."

"That's reassuring," Jim said.

"Nothing in the tea will turn your head upside down," Uncle said.

"Good to know." Jim cleared his throat. He needed a few minutes away from the house. "Excuse me. I want to say hello to the horses and see if Sara is okay."

"I will put some jasmine in your room. The aroma can help you relax."

Chapter 27

Connetions

ON THE WAY INTO THE BARN, JIM SAW SARA IN THE GARDEN, putting some brightly colored vegetables into the basket. He waved and called out, "I'm going to visit the horses."

"Alrighty. I'm almost done here, then I'll get the eggs."

"I'll catch you on the other side of the building." Jim walked down the barn aisle. The horses' noses came over the wooden stall doors to greet him. A few whinnied hellos. Seeing them again filled him with indescribable joy.

An orange tabby cat rubbed Jim's leg on the way to a dish of dried food. Then a gray one, he knew to be named Pascal, strolled in, and balanced on his hind legs, begging for attention. Jim reached behind Pascal's front legs and picked him up while the rest of the cat's body hung limp. Up against his chest, Pascal wrapped its front paws around Jim's neck. This one was an old friend and the only cat he'd ever known who gave hugs. At the opposite end of the building, he put Pascal on the ground and he trotted away with his tail straight up in the air.

Sara was bent over, rooting around in the straw under the hens.

Jim asked, "Where'd you learn to collect eggs?"

"Aunt Deborah. She has a flock in Wales," Sara replied. "I visited her in my sophomore year of college."

"Ah, should we make time to go over there for a day or two?"

"Blaire won't mind. This morning, I asked Uncle Jorge if Aunt Deborah could come here or if we should go there instead."

"You did?"

"I'm sorry. I hope that's okay?" Sara stopped rooting around, stood up, shook her hands off, and loosely hugged him for a second without using her hands. "Egg hands."

"No, no, it's fine. We are all family now. What did Uncle say?"

"Since they met at our wedding, he sounded thrilled at the idea. If she comes, he said he'd make a reservation at Peter's hotel for her since the house is full."

"Let's see how things go over the next few days and decide," Jim replied.

"When I talked to Aunt Deborah before we left, she said it's up to us and not to worry either way. She's within earshot of a phone about five o'clock every day if we want to call. I gave her Uncle Jorge's address."

"Sounds good. Our three weeks here will go by quickly."

"And we're here for healing."

"Aunt Deborah's time shouldn't interfere with anything anymore than being around Uncle or Peter," Jim reassured Sara.

"Good. I wanted to make sure," Sara replied.

"Go on back in the house. I need a little more time outside alone. Do you mind?"

"Of course not. See you later." Sara hugged him again and headed toward the house.

After another twenty minutes passed, Jim wandered back across the yard and into the house. The basket of eggs was on the counter, but Sara wasn't around. Uncle Jorge was sitting in a chair with a cup of coffee and a newspaper. Next to him were two extra cups and a kettle. Jim settled into a chair and poured himself a cup of coffee.

"Uncle, where's Sara?" Jim sat in an armchair.

"She went upstairs for a few minutes."

True to his word, Sara reappeared and kissed Jim and Uncle on the forehead before she playfully pulled on Jim's sleeve and balanced herself on the edge of the armchair.

"Uncle Jorge, sorry to interrupt. The photograph over there…" She pointed at the poster-size print on the wall by the door. "The flowers aren't like anything I've ever seen before."

Uncle Jorge placed his newspaper on the side table and smiled. "It is special to me."

"Sara worked at the Smithsonian, so she knows a gem when she sees it," Jim stated matter-of-factly.

"Jim, shush, now. You don't need to get into my history. It was years ago, in high school." Sara touched his arm and turned to Uncle Jorge. "The flowers are half one color and half another. Like when I put a carnation in dyed water and the color creeps halfway up the petals."

"There is no food dye. Yara took many photographs to get this one. We saw some things about color studies done by a scientist named Karl von Frisch when we were in Coimbra, long before Peter attended school there, and put the techniques to good use."

"It's extraordinary," Sara exclaimed.

"Thank you. When Yara and I were walking around our pond, she took the photograph of the flowers from a bee's perspective with a special ultraviolet lens. These colors are more vivid than anything humans know. We can't see white in its true shade, and bees can't see red."

"Your wife—Aunt Yara." Sara chewed on her lip before speaking again. "Jim told me you'd lost her when he was a kid. I wish I could have met her."

Uncle Jorge walked over to the wooden shelf over the tiled fireplace, picked up a framed photograph, and showed it to them. Two people were sitting on the back of a black horse. Each was dressed in multicolored patched clothing with a tiny hat upon their heads. The man straddled the horse, and the woman sat sideways behind him on the horse's rump. Both riders were smiling with excitement. The horse was adorned with tan-fringed harnesses and its tail was tied up in a bundle. It appeared completely at ease with the riders.

"This is my favorite picture of Yara and me. It's hard to tell since we look much younger. We traveled to a friend's hacienda in Spain and dressed up one summer morning. I didn't really want to, but Yara loved the idea. Their horses were very cooperative. The photographer kept asking us not to smile. He gave up when we couldn't stop. Every time I look at it, I'm filled with love."

"What a wonderful woman," Sara mused.

Jim caught Sara looking at him the way she always did, right before a kiss. Yet, this time, she would save her kisses for behind closed doors. Jim knew neither of them would ever want to be separated the way Uncle Jorge or Blaire were forced to by the death of their spouses.

"Everything in this house is a memorial to our life together. Her presence has never left me. I am not resentful anymore. Do you see the crest above the door?"

"Yes. I wondered..." Sara didn't finish her sentence.

"Sometimes it moves sideways, off-balance. I laugh when it does. This happens when my days aren't going well. It could be a ghost."

"Which one?" Sara asked. "Jim told me they tickled his feet when he was little."

"Is the cholera girl still haunting the house?" Jim asked.

"No, she moved on. She stayed a long time, poor child."

"So, who moves the plaque?" Sara asked.

"Could be my wife's wicked sense of humor coming from the Otherworld." Uncle Jorge wagged his finger. "The crest is the coat of arms of the Portuguese nation. It's been modified over the centuries. The five shields in the middle with the white pockmarks represent damage done during fighting. The five castles represent the victories over the Moorish people and Portugal's independence. The items behind are meant to represent two laurel branches tied together with a scroll. There's nothing written in this replica. Inside the real one it says: This is my beloved famous motherland."

"You and your history," Jim said lovingly. "At my old job site, there are plaques to honor the people who contributed money to the park."

"I think you liked it there more than you'll admit," Uncle said and continued his story. "I keep the property the way Yara and I set it up years ago. Even if it doesn't sound like it, I live in the present, with cherished memories of the past."

Blaire walked into the room with Dustin and sat down on the floor with her back against a wall. "There's no doubt love is powerful. Losing someone is harder than I'd ever imagined."

Dustin wiggled out of Blaire's arms and crawled over to Jim. He reached down and helped Dustin stand up.

"Keeping busy helps," Uncle said. "Most of my days are filled to the brim with community related activities and my own property maintenance. People pay me, or give me goods, in exchange for my work on their cars or shoeing their horses. During the high season, we give tours on horseback. For some reason, there are fewer people this year. I keep busy. I don't want to waste a minute of life—it's too precious. I allow myself to think about Yara in the evenings."

"You're a strong man," Blaire said. "If it wasn't for Dustin, I don't know how I'd manage."

"You would, you would. Humans are stronger than we think." Uncle Jorge ran his finger along the edge of the nearest table, which was embedded with small tiles. "She made this from broken pieces we found during our travels."

"It's beautiful." Sara grabbed her camera off the kitchen counter and took a picture of both the table and the ultraviolet flowers. "Sorry, I hope you don't mind?"

"No, I don't," Uncle Jorge said. "I used to dream of Yara at night, with flowers floating behind her figure. Sometimes, at night, I walked in the woods of Quinta da Regaleira. Back then, the Well of Souls— the Initiation Well, *Poço Iniciático*—was boarded up. The well made all kinds of creaking sounds, like singing. In the spring, the area surrounding it grew the most unusual flowers and some yew bushes. The flowers bloomed for a few seasons after Yara died. Then one year, they stopped. I never found out why. The yews remained; they are sacred, along with the cypress trees by the cave's entrance nearby. All trees are important in one way or another. The evergreen trees were connected to pagans. To win them over, Christians started decorating trees to help them convert to Christian ideas."

"Tell us more about Aunt Yara," Sara requested.

"Yes, of course. Here's another horse story." Uncle Jorge appeared to hold his breath before he began. "Horses and Yara were one and the same. Sometimes, we rode in more remote areas in Sintra. On one trip, the horses didn't want to load into the trailer. Yara coaxed them in with a bucket of carrots and apples. It took some time, but she won. They did too, with the treats. I closed the back ramp and Yara ducked out of the side door. The drive didn't take long. It sounded like Rolan and Marco were arguing. Yara worried the trailer would tip on the curved roads. We checked, and they were swinging their heads back and forth over the hay. At the park, when we opened the ramp, they backed out fast.

"We rode for a while through the woods. It was getting late when we came to a field. Yara realized she hadn't asked Peter to feed the horses at home. She wanted to race across the field. We started, and halfway, she screamed in pain and pulled into a full stop. Marco had been so excited, he kicked out during the race. His rear hoof struck her foot. She was so angry and refused to rest. We were off full speed again until we reached the woods and slowed down for the rest of the ride.

"Back by the trailer, Yara's foot hurt. She pulled Rolan over to a bench and slid off onto her good foot. I found a stick to help her hobble around. I loaded the horses on my own, and we started for home. Yara wanted to stop for a drink without checking her foot. When we got home, she insisted on feeding the horses. Over two hours had passed since she'd been kicked and her foot was numb. We got the boot off and the outer side looked like a *banana-da-terra*."

"Banana-da-terra?" Sara asked.

"Your pronunciation is good. It's a plantain and not as sweet as the bananas you have in the U.S." Uncle Jorge continued the story. "The swelling had a small crescent shape in the middle, like the moon. Her foot was a little broken."

Jim smiled at his misuse of the word. A little broken was still broken. He chose not to correct his uncle.

"She used an ice bag and a slipper. It took her a week to see a *medico*. God, even now, I still love her. Stubborn and strong."

Blaire got up, walked across the room, and lifted Dustin into the air. He didn't want to leave Jim, and let out a growly, squeaky cry. She handed him a cookie, and he quieted.

"The connection with your wife is so beautiful," Sara said.

"I dreamt of her often. Those times comforted me."

"You were lucky.," Jim said, while continuing to look at the photograph.

"Time," Uncle said. "Time heals. The memories never leave. They become more distant and manageable."

"I'll have to trust you. Losing Adam—no one should have to see the horrors of combat," Jim said. "Sorry, Blaire."

Blaire's head snapped up. "What did you say? I wasn't paying attention. Dustin is distracting me with this book." She held it up and began reading out loud. He pulled at the pages, and it was only a matter of time before one of them came away from the binding.

Jim continued talking to Uncle Jorge in a quieter voice. "When Christina died, it took a long time before she became a manageable memory. My combat nightmares are harder to handle."

"Your time here will help," Uncle Jorge said.

"When I die," Jim rubbed his head, "will I go to heaven or hell?"

"Hell, of course." His uncle roared with laughter.

"Seriously?"

"These days, you have one foot in both worlds. But, joking aside, heaven I think, unless you are reincarnated."

"Nice idea, except Christians don't believe in reincarnation. If we don't believe in an afterlife with Christ, I don't know where the priests think we're going."

"Maybe, just dead."

"Then I'm a deviant Catholic." Jim sighed. "With the things I've seen, I'm not sure I can get back to traditional thinking."

A bee flew past Jim and crawled onto the table. Uncle Jorge slid a piece of paper under it. "Wait." He got up, pulled open the front door, and blew the bee out into the wild. "There's a price to the answer to your troubles. Do you want to know?"

"I want to know."

Uncle Jorge walked into the kitchen, brought back bread and honey, and sat down again.

Jim took a bit of raw honey out of the pot with a knife, spread it on a piece of bread, and took a hungry bite. "Now, this tastes like a bit of heaven."

Sara stole a nibble of Jim's bread. She said, "Yes, I think it is from heaven."

"Glad you like it," Uncle Jorge said. "After living here for some years, my wife taught me a lot about different ways of seeing the world. She had a friend, Luanna, who was a psychic. The woman could tell complete strangers about their lives. More than once, while we were riding in the woods, Luanna would stop fast, jump off the horse, and walk to some unmarked site. One time, Yara ventured out with her while I held onto the horses. Yara told me extraordinary things when they returned."

"Like..." Jim had to know.

Uncle Jorge reached out to a cassette player by his side and turned it on. A familiar song filled the space. Jim and Sara were instantly captivated.

"Uncle, the words. Slowing down time. Innocence. Recovery." Jim bit his lower lip. "The timing of this song—it's uncanny. The night we decided to come visit you, Sara turned on our radio and the same song played."

"Nothing here happens by chance. This is only the first song of a collection I've recorded for myself. I play them again and again, when I'm thinking of Yara." The second song on the recording started. "My favorite. 'Fire and Rain' by James Taylor. Your name isn't why, and it doesn't match Yara's circumstance. I listen anyway."

"It's sad, but poignant," Sara said.

The song ended.

Jim asked, "What were you going to tell us about Luanna?"

"Ah, yes. One summer day, Yara touched Luanna's arm during an encounter. It was ice cold. The next time, Luanna said there was an invisible beast within an old stone foundation. There were many more strange things she never explained."

"After all the ghost stories we've heard in Savannah, I believe you," Sara said, with her voice dipping to an almost inaudible pitch.

"I haven't seen Luanna in years. She disappeared after Yara's death. I could have killed the drunk man myself after what he did. It's better I didn't. Yara wouldn't have approved. The man is in prison. Prison for a lifetime is more torturous than a quick death."

"I miss her," Jim said. "The last time I was here, she was riding a horse through the woods with the tourists. I tagged along on a gray pony, and Aunt Yara was riding Rolan. I was mad I couldn't."

"The gray pony is gone," Uncle lamented. "And so is Christina. She was such a precious child. I believe the afterlife, heaven, is a parallel world to ours. I like to think, even now, that Yara and your sister are sitting together on the pony's back flying around in the Otherworld, having a wonderful time."

"Really?" Jim said. "It's a nice idea, but I find it difficult to believe."

"Most times, we can't see the other place. Then there's the in-between where souls wait to crossover. They are the ghosts. Jerusalem has a well of souls. It's different from the one here. There must be many places like these. Read John 4:1-26; it talks of the well of eternal life."

"Nice thought. Now. I wish I hadn't started this conversation."

"You did. Too many of our loved ones have left this world to the next. There are many unexplainable things happening in Sintra. Sometimes some of heaven leaks out into our realm, and sometimes hell. Science, magic, and faith are interconnected. Different ways of looking at similar phenomena."

"And reincarnation?" Jim needed the conversation to go back to the original question.

"Yes."

"Yes, what?"

"I believe in reincarnation. I'm more of a Buddhist in those matters."

"So, you're a Catholic-Buddhist?" Jim tapped his fingers on the table. A bad habit he acquired from Sara. "Uncle, I don't think…"

"Stay here long enough, and you'll change your mind." Uncle Jorge winked. "There's a reason Buddy sleeps in my room every night.

Let us talk more tomorrow about these things. Have some tea before you go to bed."

"Yes, Uncle."

"When you try to sleep, concentrate on what the wise man Henrique José de Souza said: '*Conduz-me di ilusório ao real, das trevas á luz, da morte á imortalidade.*' It leads me from illusion to reality, from darkness to light, from death to immortality."

Chapter 28

Surprise

A DREAMLESS, FULL NIGHT'S SLEEP WAS A WELCOME RELIEF. Jim rolled over toward Sara and stroked her hair. She opened her eyes, stretched like a cat with her hands above her head, and folded her arms and legs around him. An hour later, they got out of bed and dressed.

Jim followed Sara into the kitchen to find Dustin banging a spoon on the table while Blaire fed him with a second one. Old and young looked at each other, and Dustin stopped banging his spoon. Uncle watched while sipping his coffee. Peter stood by the stove, making a family-size Spanish tortilla using the farm's eggs and linguica sausage.

"Good morning, everyone," Sara said brightly.

"Good morning, good morning," Jim added.

"You two sound chipper," Blaire said.

"I slept a little longer than usual," Jim said. "It's a beautiful day."

"Good to hear," Uncle said. "I finished working on Senhor Salinas's engine this morning. My day is free. Sara, you are still sleeping—half alert. Look over by the door. You are missing a surprise."

"What?" Sara said. "I don't understand."

Silence overtook the room.

"Hello? Hello?" a voice said from the shadows.

"No, it couldn't be." Sara glanced at Jim with tears in her eyes before scooting over to the corner. "Aunt Deborah, Aunt Deborah. Oh, my God, you're here. I can't believe it!"

After a crushing, tear-filled hug, Aunt Deborah and Sara came across the room with their arms around each other's waists. Dustin saw them in the full light and his hands flew up in the air, and he broke into tears. Moments like these made Jim wish he understood why babies cry.

"Come and sit down. Jim and I were working out how to come see you in Wales."

"We decided over the phone that I should come instead."

"I didn't know you two kept in touch after our wedding."

"Surprise!" Uncle Jorge exclaimed.

"Sometimes things just happen," Aunt Deborah said. "I should have told you."

"It's all right. It's so good to see you. So, tell me."

"Jorge and I started writing each other," Aunt Deborah continued. "Later, we added phone calls. So, here I am. It seemed like the perfect time since you all are here, too."

"I am sorry if it is not," Uncle Jorge piped in.

"No, really, it's fine. I'm happy," Sara said, and shifted the conversation. "The other day we were talking about the estate next door. Since you're here, Aunt Deborah, we should go out exploring. You've gotta see the gardens and the Initiation Well. Uncle Jorge, I barely remember it from my walk with Blaire. I'm sorry, the jet lag must have fogged my brain."

"My mind's clear. Wales is a half day's journey from here and on the same time schedule," Aunt Deborah said. "It's nice to get away for a while to experience something other than wood cook-stoves and rudimentary plumbing."

"I'm sure." Jim reached out to hug Aunt Deborah. "It's nice to see you again."

"It's so good to see you all."

"Rudimentary plumbing?" Blaire asked.

"Yes, a sawdust-lined outhouse and a solar-powered shower."

"She likes roughing it." Sara poured a glass of water for her aunt.

"I am happy to see you in person, Deborah," Uncle Jorge interrupted. "It's been too long since we met in Savannah."

She clasped her hands around his. "I completely agree, Jorge."

"As I said on the phone, I booked a room for you at the Sintra Tivoli Palace Hotel. It's very nice, and Peter is working there tonight."

Aunt Deborah scolded Uncle. "I need to pay you for the room. You shouldn't have."

"Ah, let him. It makes him happy," Jim said.

Uncle Jorge wryly smiled. "Jim, Sara, I'm sorry. I had planned for you to stay there for a few nights. Sadly, they don't have any extra rooms. They gave yours to Deborah at my request. Next summer, I'll make sure you get in."

"Uncle, you've done enough," Jim said.

"I want to do this. You will let me?" It was more of a command than a question.

"Thank you. You're a sweetheart," Sara said.

Uncle didn't miss a beat. "Will you accompany me to dinner, Deborah?"

"I only have a few days here. Sara, do you all mind?"

"No, you should go. We'll make dinner here while you're gone. After Dustin's in bed, we can chat all night."

"Thank you." Aunt Deborah and Uncle Jorge appeared effervescent, like two teenagers.

"I hope you'll enjoy your stay with the hotel's delicious food and beautiful surroundings," Uncle Jorge said.

"I'm sure I will. It's quite elegant. The landscaping is exquisite and the mountain views are breathtaking. Inside, there are sections of the wall that I thought were wallpaper. It turns out a French painter named Jean-Baptiste Pillement created the masterpieces in the 1700s." She took a breath. "They have horses on the property, and so do you. Thank you again for booking a room there. It's more extravagant than I'm used to these days."

Jim's brain was churning in a good way for a change. Uncle Jorge should have a new companion, and Aunt Deborah might be the one.

"Aunt Deborah, do you want to lie down a few minutes before we go exploring?" Sara asked.

"No, no, I'm ready when you and Jorge want to go. I'd like to walk."

"All right. Before you go, I want to finish a story I began before you arrived," Uncle said. "Sara wanted me to talk about the local well. I will explain. The place is called the Initiation Well. I call it *o poço das almas*—the Well of Souls. It is close to an area on the estate called the Threshold of the Gods. There are many statues to see. One of my favorites is Hermes, since he's the messenger of the gods. A lot of the architecture on the grounds was inspired by spiritually based groups.

"The well is many meters deep. Regardless, it was never filled with water like traditional wells. It's the shape of a water tower, but it is buried. If you look down inside from the top, it's dark and hellish. From the bottom up, it's heaven's light. On the inside of the cylinder, there is a set of spiral stone stairs, with archways facing into the center. On the floor, there is a rose set on a star pattern, representing the first owner's coat of arms."

"Who was the owner?" Aunt Deborah asked.

"Carvalho Monteiro started putting the estate together in the early 1900s," Jim replied. "The well is known to be the *axis mundi*, or axis of the earth. It's intended to be the umbilical cord connecting one world to the next. The chapel is also worth visiting."

"My, my, Jim, you have a good grasp of history," Aunt Deborah said.

"Thank you."

Sara continued. "Monteiro and the architect—Italian, Luigi Manini—were inspired by the 1320 poem of Dante Alighieri's called the *Divine Comedy*. The overall styles of the grounds are varied—Roman, Gothic, Renaissance. Oh, and Manueline architecture after King Manuel for the sixteenth century or late Gothic period. Dante's *Comedy* talks about nine levels in various degrees of hell and paradise."

"Comedy?" Blaire said.

"Doesn't sound like it. The classic definition of comedy begins with despair and ends with happiness," Sara explained, and pointed at the plaque. "Uncle Jorge has a Portuguese coat of arms over his front door. It shifts periodically. I don't know if the one in the well moves."

"But both plaques have ghosts connected to them," Jim said.

Uncle Jorge interrupted. "Let's not talk about ghosts today. We don't want to alarm Deborah."

"Alarmed? No. I've seen my share of mystical things in Wales."

Uncle continued his explanation. "All the architecture at the estate was designed with nature in mind and reflects the beliefs of groups like the Knights Templar, the Rosicrucians, the Freemasons, and likely various other mystical groups. Some say their descendants and followers still visit the estate. Who knows. Historical truth can be elusive."

"Who are these groups?" Sara asked.

"The Rosicrucians were a German anti-Christian brotherhood who emphasized the study of nature and its hidden forces. Their symbol was a rose cross. The Templars were Christian monk-like warriors who were eventually disbanded by the Catholic Church because they became too powerful."

"The Freemasons, known best for their stonework in cathedrals, go back to King Solomon, and there are millions of them throughout the world. For a while, the Freemasons performed their initiation rites on the estate, and then people started calling it the Initiation Well. There is a lot of information available on the subject, although some of it is conflicting. We could research."

"I will look for clues while we are here. I don't know what I can find at home," Sara said.

"Very good. There are some books on these groups on my shelves; some English, others Portuguese. You're welcome to read anything I have. There is a connecting dark cave between the Well of Souls and a lesser well. Some say you might see nymphs. The stepping-stones from one to the other can be slippery. There is a portal at the base, with statues of lizards and a guardian goddess to greet visitors. It's twenty-seven meters up from there unless you walk around the grounds to the top and go down the well's stairs."

"Sounds spooky," Sara said.

"Go in with positive attitudes and it can transport you," Uncle Jorge said. "The owner is fine with us wandering around. There are subterranean tunnels connected at the base. I don't know if they are blocked off or not. It takes hours to explore the labyrinth of caves, grottos, and lakes. There are many water vessels, statues, mythical elements symbolizing both the physical and spiritual aspects of life throughout."

"Yes, I'm sure Aunt Deborah will be captivated," Jim said. "Everything here has a deeper meaning than what you'll see. Keeping an open mind is the only way to experience it all. Right Uncle?"

"Yes, *Jiminho*."

Peter appeared in the doorway. "Anyone want to go for a ride?"

Blaire raised her hand.

Jim and Sara stood. She said, "This is my Aunt Deborah."

Peter extended his hand. "Ah, yes. Very nice to meet you."

"You too. Your father and I were going to walk the grounds, but we can wait."

Uncle Jorge said, "We can go tomorrow. The horses need some exercise. If Deborah is fine, we will take care of Dustin."

"I would love to."

"When you return, everyone can try my Port wine from the Douro Valley. During the wine's fermentation process, when the sugar levels are right, brandy is added to fortify the mixture to create the drink." He took a breath. "I'll get some Madeira out, too. It's made off the coast of Africa on the Portuguese Madeira Islands. A lot of it started being shipped to Savannah, Georgia hundreds of years ago."

Uncle pointed to the Port bottles lined up on a shelf by the kitchen. Each bottle was equally spaced. "The bottles have different levels of sweetness, color, and aroma to be savored, not rushed. The alcohol content is about twenty percent. When you are riding, I will prepare a plate of cheese and fruit. And Port wines to taste."

"Sounds great, Uncle." Jim then whispered to Sara, "If you don't like the Port, he probably has some green sangria."

She presented him with a sour face.

Blaire kissed Dustin on the head and passed him over to Uncle Jorge. Peter gestured to Blaire to go out the door first while ignoring Jim and Sara.

They followed behind. Sara cupped her hand around her mouth and whispered, "Do you think Peter likes Blaire?"

"Looks that way."

"I'm not sure she's ready to get involved with anyone."

Together, they strolled toward the gable roofed stone barn. Above the entrance, a cluster of horseshoes had been fastened with the opening facing the heavens. On the wall next to the door were intertwining circles carved into the stone with a large 'X' over them. Jim thought about the Nazar—the all-seeing eye. He didn't want to walk around the outside of the building to see if they were still on the window sills, and guessed Uncle had also crossed them off in frustration after Aunt Yara died. She had once told him they warded off evil spirits.

Chapter 29

A Ride

WHEN JIM HAD VISITED THE HORSES THE DAY BEFORE, or at any other time in his life, he hadn't really focused on any of the building's details. This time, he was more observant. The aroma of the newly delivered hay hovered in the dirt aisle. Each stall's half-door, with bars and half-walls, separated one horse from the next. The doors' glossy finish peeked through, but most were dull from age.

The sound of slurping water came from the first stall on the right. A horse on the left, presumably Vida, as noted on the plaque, rubbed her mane on the partition. Then the distinct whinnying of Rolan's voice echoed through the barn. His stall was toward the end of the building, and he wasn't going to be ignored while Blaire and Sara peered into another stall with a yearling.

With Peter's help, Jim, Sara, and Blaire each brought a horse out of the stalls. Rolan, of course, was for Jim. Ever since he'd been tall enough, they'd ridden together. Today was no different. He knew Uncle loved Rolan more than the rest of the herd. At one time, he had a miniature horse with colors that almost identically matched Rolan.

Sara led Vida to the far end of the barn, tied the rope on a ring, and waited for the others to join her. Mateo was for Blaire, and Marco for Peter. Vida's yearling was sounding off his objection to being far away from his mother. A high-pitched call emerged from behind its stall. Jim walked over and reassured the colt with a treat and a stroke between his ears before going back to Vida.

Everyone spaced their horses about five feet apart to provide enough room between them for grooming. Peter disappeared and returned with brushes and hoof picks. The task used to be boring and laborious when they were kids. Now, it felt therapeutic. The muscles in Jim's shoulders relaxed.

Once the horses were spick-and-span, Jim went back outside to the outer building with Peter to collect the gear from the tack room. Jim went over to the labeled saddle racks. He put one saddle on top of the other and tossed two saddle pads on the pile. Next, he threw two bridles over one shoulder and wove his arm under the pile of saddles. The collection teetered under his chin and the smell of leather brought back fond memories of sitting with Aunt Yara, treating the leather with eucalyptus oil and beeswax.

Moving the tack would have been easier if everyone had grabbed their own. Jim and Peter wanted to out of courtesy. Back in the aisle, Jim noticed Blaire was watching Peter with a keen eye while her foot made patterns in the dirt. Blaire took one saddle from Peter. "Whoa, these saddles really do have deeper seats than we're used to."

"They're more secure than English saddles, more like American cowboy ones," Peter said.

"I don't know. They are a little different from American ones." Blaire was flirting.

Out of nowhere, Uncle Jorge came running pell-mell down the barn aisle, with Buddy in close pursuit. They ran right toward Jim. Uncle Jorge's hands were straight up in the air, vibrating. Buddy would have had his front paws up too if he could.

At first, Jim wasn't sure what to make of it.

Uncle shouted, "*Abelhas! Abelhas!*"

"Uncle, Uncle, are you stung?"

"No! No. From the window I saw *um enxame* of bees surrounding a new queen. It's attached to a grapevine in the garden."

Jim whispered to Sara, "He's found a swarm of honeybees to catch."

"Where's Dustin?" Blaire said with alarm.

"He's asleep. Deborah is inside. She's keeping watch while I capture the bees. Move the horse out of the way." Uncle Jorge's voice boomed, and the horses pranced in place.

Sara moved the offending Mateo out of the way. Uncle Jorge rushed into a stall filled with Nuc boxes for starting new hives, larger boxes for already established colonies, and various items relating to bees.

"Hey, slow down, Uncle. You're going to break something. What's the hurry?"

"A lucky find." Uncle spoke so fast, the words jumbled together. "The bees feed extra royal jelly to some of the larvae to create a new queen. The old queen took flight with some workers in a swarm to start a new life. They are clustered. I need to catch them and put them in a fresh box."

"You're not in your bee suit." Jim worried about Uncle's frenetic behavior.

"They are calm when they relocate."

"You're not."

"I won't get hurt."

"Uncle, please, wear a hat." Jim grabbed one from the stall with the bee boxes. Shoving it on his uncle's head and rolling it down over his shoulders produced little resistance.

"Go back to the horses, go ride. I'll be fine." Uncle Jorge trotted back down the aisle and out the door with his arms wrapped around the box. If he did get stung, Aunt Deborah would patch him up.

Until now, Jim hadn't investigated the four storage stalls. In the second one, hay was stacked in rows halfway up to the ceiling. In the third, a wooden rack held farm and garden tools. In the fourth, blacksmith supplies were shelved, along with boxes of horseshoes labeled by size. Pulling himself away from the paraphernalia, he went back to the horses and riders.

It was time to get on the trails. Together, they walked their horses out of the barn. Peter held Mateo while Blaire mounted. With small gestures and quiet words, he could calm any beast. Jim was watching his cousin and almost forgot about helping Sara. All he needed to do was hold the side of Vida's halter while she hopped onto the saddle. After helping her, he grabbed onto Rolan's reins, put his foot in the stirrup, and swung up into the saddle. Blaire and Peter took the lead on the trail. Jim and Sara followed. There was enough room on the path to proceed in pairs.

"There's something going on with them," Sara said in a hushed voice.

"Sara, you're so cute." He restrained a laugh. "It's a good thing."

"I think so," Sara said. "I'm sure Adam wouldn't want her to be alone."

Jim focused back on Peter and overheard him discussing the terrain like a professional guide who cared deeply about the land and its history.

"There was an earthquake in 1775. It brought a tsunami into Lisbon on All Saints' Day. The surrounding areas rattled, causing death and destruction in its path from the fires and collapsed structures. Many sites are still buried, even in Sintra, and are waiting to be dug up by archaeologists."

Peter tended to be in tune with people's feelings, but this time his cousin was slipping. Jim knew Blaire didn't want to talk about loss. About the time he thought he should force the subject in a different direction, Peter switched to a more lighthearted discussion of the cacophony of birds they heard singing. And he made sure to mention the domestic-sized wild cats wandering about. Jim stopped worrying. Blaire was in good hands.

She appeared to be completely taken in by his cousin's charms throughout the ride: a nod here and there, a shake of her blonde hair, or a flirtatious giggle. Jim relaxed and listened to the rhythm of their voices, along with the twittering of birds. Silence in the out-of-doors always made him nervous. Even so, he kept his eyes peeled for movement within the forest.

As the trails narrowed, they adjusted their position to a single-file line.

Peter, going back to his tour guide dialog, turned in the saddle and called out, "Keep your heels down and your toes up. And no pulling on the reins. They don't like their heads jerked around. You might be tempted when we come to the hills."

As they traversed the path, they leaned forward in the saddles up the hills, and leaned back when they went down. On occasion, they'd go from walking to trotting and back to walking. The horses knew the routines well, and might have been able to take the trails blindfolded or in the dark. Jim knew Uncle and Peter had taken them out many times with tourists on the same three-hour loop, using either these horses or some of the other ones Uncle kept in the fields by the olive grove.

As they rode, Jim thought of traveling through life's challenges and hoped to come out on the other side of the dark places that often consumed his heart. He breathed in the warm air, catching the scent of humus from the composting leaves, and proceeded down the trail behind Sara. The fragrance was intoxicating and invigorating in a way that resembled the feeling of endorphins rushing through his veins after a run. He thought, *Appreciation for the good should be greater after experiencing the bad.*

Moving forward, he became acutely aware of the rocks and roots in front of Rolan. By a root sat an oversized toad with the back end of a lizard sticking out of its mouth. Rolan didn't seem to care and stepped gingerly over the obstruction. Continuing to the river, Rolan stopped and tossed his head up and down. He refused to move forward, even though the other horses were leaving him behind. *Why would Rolan act this way after traveling this route so many times?* After looking up and down the stream, Jim noticed a branch caught on a cluster of boulders in the water. It created a chilling image of a trapped animal. No wonder his four-legged friend refused to ford the placid waters. With some verbal encouragement and heels into his sides, Rolan moved forward with a jolt into the river and bounced onto the opposite embankment. Jim was relieved he had his heels down or he would have popped off the saddle.

The group traveled ahead for an additional hour before circling back to the barn. The horses knew the way home and Jim settled into the saddle. By the time they returned to the barn, the horses had cooled down. They each got a light brushing before being put back in their stalls with a portion of their evening hay and grain.

Inside the house, as promised, Uncle had set out the platter with each cheese labeled: *nisa, terrincho, pico,* évora, *azeitā,* and *Sāo Jorge.*

"Uncle? *Sāo Jorge* cheese? Named after you?" Jim grinned.

"Yes, I'm a saint." Uncle laughed at his own joke. "It's a tangy, cow cheese from Azores."

Behind the platter sat a collection of glasses and Port wines: Quinta do Noval, Rebello Valent, Warre's, Ferreira, and Sandeman.

While they sampled the assortment, Uncle said, "When you were riding, I captured the bee swarm. They'll have their new hive set up soon."

"Well done," Jim said.

"And the wines and cheeses are delicious," Sara said.

"How was your ride?" Aunt Deborah asked.

"It was relaxing, but Rolan resisted going through the river. Everything worked out okay in the end. I haven't ridden since I joined the Army. I'm sure I'll be sore tomorrow."

"Speaking of, I'll be going back to Wales in the morning." Aunt Deborah's head dropped down a notch. "I'm sorry I can't stay. Everything here is wonderful."

"We'll all miss you," Uncle Jorge said. "Next time, you can stay longer and we can go riding together."

The Wee Hours

Riding had helped Jim relax. The relief was temporary. When he went to sleep, his visions of combat woke him around three in the morning. To clear his mind, he went outside. There he found Blaire sitting on a bench.

"You startled me. Why are you out here so late?" Jim asked.

"I must have caught your ailment. I woke up about a half hour ago and couldn't go back to sleep. Walking it off isn't an option because I need to be near Dustin if he wakes up. He doesn't always self-soothe. This seemed like a good place to collect my thoughts."

"What's on your mind?"

"As if you didn't know—Adam, of course."

"I'm still struggling with his loss," Jim said.

"I know. I'm wondering how he'd feel about me being attracted to another man."

"Oh, I see. Well, he'd be jealous." Jim took Blaire's hand in his. "No, I'm sorry. I know he'd want you to have a full life, even though he can't be with you. He'd want Dustin to have a father. I know he wouldn't want you to go through life alone."

"I know you're right, but…"

"No, Blaire. No. It's time. You have Dustin, work, and friends. If you are interested in another man, it's okay."

"Thank you, Jim. This means a lot coming from you."

He tried to lighten the conversation. "Is there someone in particular?"

"Yes. You know it's Peter. He's interesting and kind."

"Yes, true. There are all sorts of things he does for Uncle Jorge. I mean, for his father."

"Then there's his music and taking people out horseback riding."

"That too. As long as I've known him, he's been great with people. I've always respected him. Back then, being five years older than me seemed like such a big deal. Now, the age difference doesn't faze me."

"Oh, I guess he's just being nice to me."

"Hard to say for sure."

"And he's older than me?"

"Not by much. Don't worry, Adam's probably smiling at you from heaven. You need to learn to relax and have fun again."

"So do you." Blaire got to her feet. "Loss is part of life, but Adam left too early. I will never forget him, no matter what happens."

"Neither will I."

"Thank you for your help tonight and all the days since Adam's death. I need to go inside and try to sleep. I want to be alert when Dustin wakes up."

"Goodnight, Blaire." Jim sat on the bench for an hour before heading back to bed.

Chapter 30

The Shop

THE NEXT NIGHT, WHEN UNCLE JORGE STARTED DINNER, Sara offered to help. They began making *carne de porco a alentejana*, a pork dish with clam and tomato sauce. While they were distracted, Peter took Jim's arm and coaxed him out the front door.

"I have a question."

"Okay," Jim responded.

"I'm enchanted by Blaire. Do you think she'd like to see my workshop?"

"Yes! She likes you. The problem is, she's afraid to dishonor Adam's memory. I told her not to worry."

"Thank you. Let's go inside, and I'll invite her. I want to go before dinner."

"I'll come along—to help her feel more at ease." Jim put his hand on Peter's shoulder. They went inside, and Peter extended the invitation.

Blaire agreed to go and scooped up Dustin. The trio walked outside and down a narrow dirt path to the workshop a quarter of a mile into the woods. All along the way, Dustin babbled and pointed in various directions.

Peter's shop exterior was stucco and painted a deep brownish-yellow, with one door in the front and a chimney above the roof. The tile on the surface was covered with a thin layer of green moss. Inside, the walls were stone, some bare and others covered with off-white canvas. There were two tables: one with a work in progress, the other with some saws and a ventilator pulling air and dust through a pipe to the outside. In the back corner, there was a collection of stacked planks.

Blaire began to ask questions. Peter was more than happy to oblige. She was good at stroking people's egos when she set her mind to the task. Jim had seen her take this kind of interest in Adam. He worked at accepting his own words from the night before about moving on.

She seemed to enjoy listening to Peter's English. His Portuguese accent with the off-beat vowels and missing consonants was melodic. Jim hadn't worried about his own Americanized pronunciation of Portuguese, because the locals had always understood him.

Time would tell if Blaire and Peter's connection would be a stepping-stone to healing, or something long term. Jim didn't know when he'd become so introspective on romance. The process was almost like meditating, to let his mind escape from thinking about death. A strange, nonsensical approach, but it helped. He refocused on Peter's voice, as he displayed his collection and all the associated paraphernalia like a proud peacock spreading its wings. The level of Peter's involvement within the musical world had increased tenfold since his university days.

While Jim leaned on the doorjamb, he studied the tools hanging off hooks in many rows on the wall. Underneath them, a band and table saw. Below those, a series of unmarked drawers going down to the floor. Averting his eyes, he focused on Blaire. She walked around, running her free hand through the sawdust and over the edge of the table in sweeping playful motions. She stopped on the far side of the room, with a self-contented smile on her face. Jim hadn't seen her this engaged in a long time.

"Peter," Blaire said, ever so sweetly, in an elevated Southern accent. "Why didn't you tell us you were so talented with wood?"

"I'm still learning." Peter laughed. "It seemed better to show you. A master who lives in town trained me. We talk or visit every week. He taught me how to put guitars together. The cuts, the curves, the strings, and how to select the right wood. Making guitars is a spiritual experience."

"Never thought of it that way." She pointed toward a labeled shelf.

"Where did you get them? I have never seen these types of wood patterns before."

Dustin reached for the shiny guitar pegs on one of Peter's disheveled-looking guitars. Blaire grabbed his hand.

"No, it's all right. It's my first. See the rubber band across the strings?"

"Yes, and the pen and paper clip. What are those for?" Blaire asked.

"It reminds me I once had less than I do now." Peter put his hand on Blaire's lower back. "He won't do it any harm."

"Thank you," Blaire said.

Peter smiled and continued explaining. "I lost my capo and made this to help hold the strings down to make the sounds I wanted—low 'e' in this case. Also, the paper clip through the hole replaces a fastener I lost. It keeps the string in place for display."

Blaire placed Dustin's hand on the strings by the paper clip. He grabbed at the sturdier strings down the neck along the fret and attempted to close his fingers around them. "Your daddy tried to learn how to play."

A *click, click* sounded out with Dustin's effort.

"The body of my guitars are rounded or heart-shaped for fado."

"Fado?" Blaire asked.

"This music started in the 1700s. Fate decided two lovers couldn't be together. Ever since, the music has been filled with sadness. The best fado performer today is Amalia Rodrigues. The sound this type of guitar makes is higher than a classical guitar. Sometimes I use nylon strings, other times traditional steel. The nylon goes out of tune faster and the steel slips on the pegs. No situation is perfect." Peter touched the back of Blaire's hand. "It'll take some time for Dustin to develop the calluses needed if he becomes interested when he's older."

"And years of practice." Blaire's mouth turned up in a restrained smile. "Tell me about the different woods you've collected."

"I label them all, so there's no confusion. Some are good for guitars, like Brazilian rosewood, and others aren't. Rosewood is rare and can put up with lots of handling." He stroked the labels while he talked. "Wood from the linden tree, the maple, walnut, and mahogany. In a guitar, the sounds they make vary a little. Some instruments will have inlaid designs made of contrasting wood combined with gold threads. The types of wood are endless. I won't tire you with them all."

"You're not. This is a treat. Where did you get the wood?"

"I am glad you are interested. I will explain. A local craftsman retired from woodworking and gave them to me. Each piece is big enough to make a guitar. I would have to break tradition if I used them, since they are not the usual style for Portugal."

"You can be a trendsetter."

"I don't know if it is a good idea. I will try. The older guitars I have are from all over and need repairs. I plan to restore and sell them for a profit."

"Maybe I should learn to play," Blaire said. "How did you get interested in restoration?"

"My mother used to restore things over at the Palais de Regaleira at the far end of the garden. The building was a mess back then, but the rosewood and mahogany furniture sparked my interest. The pieces have an unconventional, layered appearance. It is one of my favorite places. A long time ago, it was inhabited by the Moorish people. A more recent owner, Carvalho Monteiro, was a creative genius. We went to the same university in Coimbra. I wasn't even born when he attended…

Jim interrupted. "I can smell dinner all the way out here. Let's go back to the house."

Chapter 31

Into the Night

THE CHIMES OF THE GRANDFATHER CLOCK IN THE CORNER woke Jim. He knew it had been in silent mode the previous nights and wondered why it was sounding off. It was impossible to see its face in the dark. He counted three strikes and didn't know if he'd missed a few before he fully woke. Yet again, he'd slept only a few hours. His hopes of sleeping soundly back in the safe confines of Sintra vanished.

He touched Sara's arm, and she let out a soft moan without reacting to the chimes. The rest of her body was wrapped tightly in a blanket cocoon on the far side of the bed. If it hadn't been wedged against the wall, she would have fallen onto the floor. Thankfully, he hadn't been deprived of a blanket. There were two on the bed and she'd claimed one. Inching his way out of bed, he banged his ankle on the rough-hewn logs of the mattress frame and held back a curse. A crescent moon brought a small amount of light into the room, just enough to find his way to the chair where he'd left his clothes. Putting them on took longer than usual in the dim light.

As he moved out of the bedroom and across the living area, the floor squeaked. He stopped. The silence returned, and he realized there wouldn't be enough light from the moon to venture outside. There wasn't a flashlight handy, so he slowly crossed the room toward a nightlight by the front door. Halfway across, he knocked a chair over and a thud echoed through the space.

Sara was a sound sleeper these days, so she probably didn't hear the noises, even though he was only a few yards away from their bedroom. He didn't know how Uncle Jorge or Peter would respond. He didn't hear them calling out or moving around upstairs. Blaire and Dustin's room was further into the house, so they likely weren't disturbed either.

Stealthily moving across the room, he reached the table. Underneath it was a lantern and a set of matches. Jim pulled up the glass cover and lit the wick. Before he left, he patted his shirt and jeans to make absolutely sure he was dressed. He snorted in a pseudo-laugh at his antics on the night he'd gone out sleepwalking in his underpants in Fayetteville. Sara hadn't found his midnight prowling amusing then and wouldn't under any circumstances. Grabbing the lantern handle, he ventured out into the night, closing the door behind him.

Outside, the smell of boxwood bushes overtook his senses, yet he knew there weren't any around. His eyes and nose watered. The hair on his neck prickled, and he was sure something or someone was watching him. Then he heard a bird call and flapping wings. An owl launched out of a tree and passed overhead. If that wasn't startling enough, he heard a bell tolling and what sounded like a loon calling out in the distance. The loon didn't make sense, because they didn't live in Portugal, which made its wolf-like sound more disturbing. He wandered toward the tunnel with the lantern held high. A fountain he didn't recall dripped into a puddle, and sounded like a spring rain. Further jolting his senses, he noticed an animal standing motionless by the entrance. It reminded him of the dog statue at Morrell Park in Savannah. Yet this enormous animal was something else, and Jim wanted to run for his life. Instead, using all his restraint and military resolve, he ignored the creature and walked over to the barn and closed himself inside.

To distract his racing heart, he thought about the little ghosts in Uncle's house. At night, they used to like to slam kitchen cabinets or tickle people's feet, while laughing in childlike voices. Going up the stairs produced an eerie sense of being followed. Because of this, Jim had always slept on the main floor when he was a kid. They were gone now, but no one knew why.

The distraction worked. He dismissed his fears, switched on the barn lights, and hung the lantern on a hook by the door. Rolan's head stretched out of a stall and whinnied. Jim strolled down the aisle, put his hand on the horse's neck, and pushed over a spike of hair that stood up like a bristle brush. A small cloth bag hung off a ring on the wall. Reaching inside, Jim pulled out a curry brush and ran it over Rolan's coat in a circular motion before leaning into the horse's neck and inhaled. There was nothing like the smell of grasses mixed with dried mud on a horse's coat.

When he and Rolan had ridden together years before, he'd felt lost in the forest's magic and was unencumbered by adult responsibilities. Christina's death began the breakdown of his innocent childhood. Because of the tragedies he'd experienced, he knew life should be grabbed by the reins and experienced to the fullest, because each day could be the last. A cliché perhaps but, indeed true. The military conditioning caused him to be stoic and nonreactive in many situations. But in the barn, he could let down his defenses and mourn losing Adam without human witnesses.

Jim brought Rolan into the aisle, then clipped a rope onto the gentle giant's halter. The horse's long, wavy mane needed combing, so Jim got busy releasing the kinks until the mane lay flat. He brushed the horse's body with the curry and began to talk, knowing he would not be judged or scolded. From time to time, Rolan snorted or gave Jim sideways glances. This release of information and emotion was far better than pouring out his story to Sara in Fayetteville after the dog's death, or talking to Chaplain Scythe on base, or any journal entry. Rolan could hear he'd felt guilty about Adam stepping in front of him and taking the bullet. Rolan could hear he'd lied to Blaire when he'd told her Adam spoke of her in his last dying breaths. Rolan could hear he'd considered suicide. He'd talked until there were no words left.

His old friend was shiny and clean, while Jim was covered in dust. After wiping himself off and putting the tools away, he hugged Rolan's neck and put him back into the stall. Turning off the lights, he grabbed the lantern and swung it back and forth as he walked out of the barn.

The dog-like creature was still standing by the tunnel in the shadows. It seemed to snap to attention when Jim got closer, and it moved into the darkness of the 100-foot tunnel to the gardens. An intense desire to follow came over Jim. His heartbeat sped up again. Raising the lantern, he walked into the eerie space. He knew from his childhood wanderings there was nothing to fear. Nothing looked the same as it did a few days before when he'd taken a stroll for old time's sake. During that visit, the floor was covered with uneven stones and dirt, the walls and arched ceiling with blue and white decorative tiles. Since then, the walls had change and were now covered with moss. Water dripped from the ceiling. Would he find the garden be different, too?

He brought the lantern down by his side. On the ground, he saw footprints other than his own in the damp soil. They looked like dog tracks, but bigger. Spreading out his free hand to gauge the size, he saw the impression was at least five inches long. A shiver went up his spine. He'd never seen a dog with such enormous paws. It was more likely a wolf. For an instant, he considered going back to the house. *Soldiers don't turn back* reverberated in his ears. At the end of the tunnel, specks of light danced in the air and parted as he moved forward into the open. There were no bonfires or fireflies nearby to explain the phenomenon.

Turning 180 degrees, he looked back at the stone wall flanking the sides of the opening and saw the alcoves. One was empty; the other had a two-foot-tall, indistinguishable, two-legged form filling up the space. It was half white, half smoke colored, and patterned like the yin and yang symbol. Otherwise, it resembled a mythical pixie without wings. On its feet sat some green lichen. The military taught him how to pay attention to details and keep them cataloged in his mind. He was sure the pixie was a recent addition. If not, his subconscious was playing a trick on him.

He walked on through the garden paths and heard a powerful rush of water passing by him, but he knew it was the underground piping system that moved water from natural springs and local storm drains into ponds all over the property. The sound of the moving water felt hypnotic as he progressed down the long path. Without realizing how much real time had passed, Jim found himself in the heart of the garden.

When he arrived at the Promenade of the Gods, the melodic sounds were replaced by silence. A quiet so complete that he became concerned and began to scan the area. The names on the plaques at the base of the statues were familiar. Each statue was as unique as the gods they represented: Hermes, god of travel; Pan, god of the woods and nature with a body of man and goat combined; Aphrodite, goddess of love with her human body wrapped in a meager flowing cloth; Dionysus, god of wine with a cluster of grapes in one hand and a wine challis in the other; and Orpheus, the greatest singer with a strung lyre across his arm. Jim laughed out loud at the next figure. Vulcan, not from Star Trek, but the god of fire, carrying a blacksmith hammer for metalwork. Metal—not heavy metal music. His mood lightened with the associations. Emotional ricocheting wasn't a wise idea now or at any time. Yet, he couldn't stop himself.

As he continued down the aisle of statues, he muttered to himself, "Demeter, goddess of crops; Fortuna, goddess of good luck; Flora, goddess of flowers." Flora had moved. He'd seen her closer to the tunnel on a different day. Now, she held a bouquet of stone flowers across an arm that morphed into living blooms with a black and white butterfly gathering nectar from one of the flowers before it flew away.

Jim looked over at the main house on the grounds and wondered if anyone menacing would come out of the building and chase him away. The gargoyles felt menacing in the low light. Hues of natural green and brown lights drifted within the gardens. The moon, now full, reflected off the porcelain-colored statues—another impossibility, since the moon was a crescent when he'd left Uncle's house only a short while ago. One statue, he didn't recognize by name, was wrapped in a toga. It looked like his drawing of a human figure with a beaked mask over its face. A plague doctor from another time. The scent of lilies hovered in the air. Some of the finely chiseled statues looked the way they should. Others had hollowed eyes, with faces resembling melting ice cream. He didn't know why ice cream was involved, except it was often his comfort food of choice.

One animated, milky face came to life and said, "No one can see into this parallel world unless the king gives permission."

"What did you say?"

"When the mortal world is too much to bear, perhaps this one is better."

"What?" Jim seemed to say the word without moving his mouth.

The statue said nothing more.

Jim moved on. His sleepless nights of wandering in the States had never been like this.

While he walked, he envisioned the dream that woke him. He'd experienced it before in a different way. In this one, he was running and everything was in slow motion, with multiple shades of gray streaking past in a red fog. His uniform snagged on something and ripped, but he kept going. Next to him, Adam and other soldiers were pressing forward. The scene morphed into a building. They were firing weapons out toward the road. Adam fell, and a hissing sound followed. Blood flowed out from his friend's flak jacket. A flash in the dim light turned into flames. Adam vanished. Jim woke and carried the trauma with him. If he could recall happy memories, he knew he could heal, but the horror and guilt kept cropping up and haunting him. His mind could never quite clear up the details, and he suspected this was why he was haunted.

As Jim proceeded, another face appeared within a stone face. It looked like a young version of Adam. Jim knew this warrior statue was called Queluz, even though the plaque's letters were worn thin. The figure was six feet tall and seemed so much bigger when they were children. Jim smiled and rubbed his eyes. It spoke, and the voice was his friend's, but not exactly. The sound was childlike, a version of Adam. "You're not dreaming. It's me, man. I'm in transition. It takes time to morph my soul back into a body. It's like stuffing a mass of sardines into a small can." The disembodied voice hiccupped out another remark. "Remember the good times—not how I died. So many good times."

"I'm trying," Jim replied. "Sardines? Not liking the image."

"I'm almost back to you. That's why I am like a child. I'm leaving here and evolving into my son more and more each day."

"What?"

Adam's face flashed away, and Queluz's warrior face became stone again.

The latest tea concoctions must be playing with my mind. Could I be asleep and not out in the garden at all? I'll take a boring night of wandering over what's going on. Animal statues are all over the place, some in plain sight and others with the tops of their heads showing. Are any of them on the prowl? Walking, walking. I have to keep moving.

Pulling his hands across the back of his neck, he tilted his chin to the heavens and let out a scream that emerged like the call of a wild banshee. The release freed him, at least for a few minutes, until he saw a statue of Saint George holding a staff with a cloth banner fluttering in a breeze. Under his feet; a dragon. Neither had been there before. The stone face began to glisten with water droplets, and its eyes moved left and right behind holes that resembled a mask. A mask hiding a soul. Jim's skin prickled with goose bumps. The staff pivoted due west, and Jim walked west.

About a half-mile down the path, he saw two parallel drag marks in the dirt. At the end of the tracks, there was a bench and an unlit lamp post straight out of his books about Narnia with filigreed twists and turns. It also resembled the harbor light from the riverside in Savannah, where he'd met the old dog.

For no particular reason, he sat on the bench's wooden planks, and they flexed with his weight. With all the crazy things that had been happening, he half expected the boards to talk. To tell him he was hurting them, and he should stand up and go home. Instead, Uncle's lantern flickered and died.

A breeze picked up and musical notes sounded off in the trees. The branches above him moved across each other like a bow pulling across a violin. The sounds were initially comforting. Then they changed to ominous whispers, accompanied by unseen squeaking of birds or reptiles. Seeing them would be better, but he knew the trees were the source of life. Being under the trees was better than being out in the open. Comforted by this, Jim nodded off to sleep. When he awoke, Uncle's lantern was gone.

Another statue caught Jim's eye. It hadn't been there before he sat down. This childlike figure was smaller than the rest, three feet tall or less, and vaguely reminded him of the pixie by the tunnel. An image appeared where its stone face had been. It jolted him more than seeing Adam's ghost. This face was the clearest one he'd seen. It was Christina. Her face was full of life and giggles. At first, he decided this night couldn't be anything other than a cruel dream, but then he recalled seeing her face after a long day at work before going into the Army.

In an uneven, childlike voice, Christina said, "Hi, brother. You'll see me again soon. I won't remember, but you will. I will be your tiny baby when I return. This, and Adam's return in Dustin, must remain our secret. You can only tell Sara; no one else. A vow you must keep."

"This is unbelievable."

"Promise." The image scowled.

"I do," Jim replied.

Christina nodded and disappeared.

"No, come back." His appeal faded away with her.

Chapter 32

A Collapse

NOTHER HOWL CAME FORTH. THIS TIME, IT WASN'T JIM. In the clearing, a gray wolf appeared. It was massive and as big as the paw prints suggested in the tunnel. It sauntered toward Jim, then stopped about ten feet away and sat on its haunches. They stared into each other's eyes. The encounter soothed Jim. The wolf appeared to be waiting for something Jim couldn't understand. Why was a pack animal all alone? Why was Jim all alone? Both were trained to work with others in teams for a common cause. Was the wolf a figment of his imagination? Was he fabricating every mystical event? The wolf statues from his youth, meeting Sara and talking about reaching the level of Wolf in Cub Scouts, and having dogs all his life were in his subconscious and may have created these new experiences.

An undetermined amount of time passed, and something changed in the wolf. His snout tilted upward, his head turned left, then right, his nostrils flaring in and out. There was a distinct smell of smoke in the air. The wolf stood and ran down the path from the direction Jim had come. A force pulled him to his feet, and he followed. The wolf almost outpaced his maximum stride, but he knew it could move even faster. The wolf arrived at the tunnel, went in, and vanished.

Jim continued through onto the other side. He looked ahead and saw flames kissing the barn's rooftop. Uncle Jorge was shouting from inside the building. Adrenaline took over, and Jim rushed to the entrance. The noise of the stalls being thrown open in the aisle caught his attention. Before he could react, Marco and Mateo burst through the dense smoke into the open air and almost ran him over. Marco's mane was singed, and Mateo's tail stood straight up with anxiety. Vida came next, with the yearling tucked by her side. They were whinnying and squealing in terror. The sound was unlike anything he'd ever heard before.

"Where are you, Uncle?" Jim called out.

"Here, over here."

Jim followed his uncle's voice.

Uncle Jorge was in a stall, trying to coax Rolan out the door. The horse's eyes bulged with fear and the whites of his eyes flashed. Uncle pulled off his shirt and put it over Rolan's ears and eyes to create a blindfold. They walked forward. Rolan was too wide to get through the door. Something they couldn't see through the smoke blocked it from fully opening. Rolan pulled back, yanking Uncle with him, and cowered in a corner of the stall.

Uncle regained his balance and murmured to Rolan while Jim attempted to free the door. It wouldn't budge. The barn groaned, and Jim heard a loud snap. An impulse seized him. He grabbed Uncle, pulled him out of the stall, and shoved him toward the exit, leaving Rolan behind. Uncle moved along and then froze in place.

"Jim, look…"

"No time, Uncle." But then he did. The smoke parted. There was a wisp of something—no, someone—a woman. One hand was out-stretched, beckoning. In a flash, she was gone. Jim shook his head, then went back and tried to free the stall door one more time. Another loud popping, cracking noise from above rang out through the building.

Jim grabbed Uncle, heaved him out of the building, and they both tumbled onto the ground. The roof's trusses collapsed, with Rolan inside. Jim had saved them both from suffering the same fate. He stood up and helped Uncle to his feet, and led him away from the barn toward the house. Once there, Uncle collapsed by a tree in a state of shock. Ash covering his hair and shoulders. His face was pale, and his clothes reeked of smoke.

Peter bolted through the main gate. Close behind, the fire *bombeiros* drove onto the property in their red, yellow, and white striped truck. They unrolled the fire hoses toward the pond behind the barn. The truck pumps began thumping. Gallons and gallons of water surged through the hoses in lumps and rolls. The men held on tight, opened the valves, and the flow surged out. The water shot up into the air and arched down onto what remained of the barn roof and smoke billowed out.

Jim hovered over his uncle, trying to calm his own nerves. He wasn't afraid during the rescue; now he was, and threw up the contents of his stomach a few feet away from where his uncle sat, motionless.

He went back over and said, "Uncle, I'm sorry I had to fling you out of the barn."

Uncle Jorge said nothing.

A great sense of relief swept over Jim after saving his uncle from certain death. He couldn't save the horse any more than he could have saved Adam, his sister, his aunt, or anyone else he'd loved or served with. The situations were dissimilar. The association was clear. Death was still death.

Peter hurried over and wiped his father's scuffed-up knees with a red rag. There were many colored scraps of fabric in a covered bin near the house. It wasn't clear why Peter had selected a red one. The sight of it reminded Jim of blood and death, which didn't help his current state of mind. With Peter's consent, Jim left them to take a moment to pull himself together. He needed to go to his uncle's prayer spot by their cemetery. The walk would give him some space away from the crisis and allow Peter to comfort his father.

It took a few minutes to find the right trees behind a row of graves. The clothesline was still there, stretched between two trees. Safety pins held the squares of prayer fabric in place with prayers written across them. Written words were often more powerful than spoken. Jim needed to write a prayer on one of the old scraps of cloth, even if it meant sharing a few words with an unknown writer. Looking around, trying to figure out what he'd used to write the words, he spotted a box behind a tree. The latch and hinges were stiff. Inside were pieces of cloth, some pens, and safety pins. Soon after scribbling a prayer asking for inner strength for all concerned, he was interrupted by a commotion of people. He attached his cloth to the line and hurried back over to Peter and Uncle. They were on their feet, watching the streams of water flooding the barn.

People were rushing in from town. Jim didn't recognize any of them and surmised Uncle and Peter would. Some people had blank expressions; others reacted with pity or tears. Jim heard someone shouting about standing between the house and barn to watch for floating embers that might catch other things on fire. A few men moved toward the barn to help. The bombeiros waved them away. The roar of the fire, heat, and smoke combined with shouting people created a surreal chaos.

Uncle Jorge appeared to be coping with the interlopers, yet his face remained blank throughout the conversations. It was strange to watch Peter and Uncle console the gatherers, rather than the other way around. The scene didn't make any sense. Why did everyone else sound so distraught? It wasn't their barn that had gone up in flames. Some of the people said they would come back another day to help with cleanup and promptly disappeared. A few stragglers stayed behind.

"Uncle? Talk to me," Jim said.

"How did you know?" Uncle Jorge asked.

"Know? Know what?"

"To help me?"

"I was in the estate gardens." Jim paused. "A wolf, um, alerted me to the smell of smoke."

"Ah, *Canis lupus*... I've seen him."

"He's massive."

The bombardier fire chief appeared with a report in Portuguese. "Senhor, I'm sorry we couldn't save the barn. One of my men let the chickens out of their coop right after we arrived, so they are fine. There is a lot of water in the saddle room. Some of the equipment is wet..."

"My fish? In the pond?"

"I'm sorry, senhor. There's a small amount of water left in the middle." The chief paused. "Many fish are flapping around in the mud. I know you value them, too. I sent some of the towns people out there to collect the ones they can in buckets and return them to water in the middle. It's a slippery task."

"Should I help?" Peter asked.

"Yes, son, go. Try to save them."

Jim couldn't figure out why Uncle had sent Peter away. Had he gone mad? Then Jim understood.

Uncle said, "My wife's—"

"Your wife—I . . ." the chief said.

"The horse inside was hers," Jim responded without thinking.

"I'm sorry, senhor. The building came down. The horse is with God."

Uncle Jorge broke into tears, which flowed down his flushed cheeks and into his beard. He dragged his hand from his forehead down over his vacant eyes, closing the lids like one would do for a corpse. Unlike the dead, his chest heaved with sobs, and his shoulders drooped like a deflated balloon. Without speaking, he spoke a thousand words of sorrow.

The chief's eyes opened wide when he realized his mistake. "The horse didn't suffer. I am sure of it. I don't know why some horses won't leave their precious barn, even in a fire."

Uncle's hand moved up into fists, grasping toward the sky in anguish. He slid back down by the tree, pulled his knees to his chest, and wrapped his arms around them. The poor man looked like a small child who had lost everything.

"Crap, what?" Jim felt totally confused. Uncle Jorge was a strong man, and he'd never known him to succumb to emotions in this way.

The chief leaned in toward Jim and whispered, "I misspoke. I was the first one on the street when his wife died. He's connecting her to the horse."

"Oh, I understand." Pain rippled through Jim's heart. He knew how associations could tear at a soul.

Jim sank down next to his uncle. The chief moved back a pace.

"She was in the aisle," Uncle whispered.

"Who, Uncle?"

Uncle Jorge tilted his head upward. "Yara. I saw her ghost. She was wearing the long gown I buried her in. The one from our riding portrait."

"Uncle," Jim asked, "the photograph in on your mantel?"

"Yes. I would have stayed to die and be with her. You pulled me out. Why did you pull me out?" Uncle put his head in his hands.

"Senhor, can I take you to the hospital?" the chief asked. "The smoke, the shock..."

"No." Uncle Jorge uncurled his body.

Peter trotted back from the pond and helped his father and Jim to their feet. "Fish all accounted for."

Uncle coughed a few times. "Why did I scratch the symbols away after Yara died? Why?"

"Uncle, you're not making sense."

"She said they would ward off evil. Why? I need..."

"Papa, those marks are from superstitions," Peter said. "Let's go inside."

As they approached the house, the front door swung open. Somehow, without any logical reason, Sara, Blaire, and Dustin had slept through most of the crisis. The house seemed to have been wrapped in a protective blanket.

"Oh, no, the barn!" Blaire exclaimed.

"I can't believe you all didn't hear anything," Jim said.

Dustin balanced on Blaire's hip with an impish expression on his face. Jim almost recognized it as one of Adam's expressions implying, *we have a secret.* Then he leaned toward Jim and reached out.

"Come here, little man."

Sara proclaimed, "The house must be enchanted. Otherwise, how could we have missed the smells and sounds?"

"Who knows. Go into the house." He passed Dustin back to Blaire. "Take Uncle with you. Peter and I will dry off the saddles and figure out where the chickens went."

"Come on, Uncle Jorge," Sara encouraged. "I'll make some chamomile tea." She escorted the group inside.

Jim turned back to the devastation, with Peter by his side. A slight breeze came up; the billowing smoke cleared to trickles, and clouds poured down rain in short-lived bursts, perhaps to express their sorrow. Sara reappeared with two raincoats, handed them over, and retreated to the house.

The beehives in the garden were untouched. The barn's stone walls were intact; the stout six-inch hardwood support posts were still upright, though charred black with indentations. The lucky horseshoes lay on the ground beneath the main entrance. The roof was gone, and a single beam of light came through the clouds and landed on a spot where the barn aisle had been. At the far end of the barn, the chickens were pecking at the rubble and collecting dead bees from the observation hive by the remains of their coop.

Who was the woman in the aisle Jim and Uncle saw just before they'd gotten out of the barn? Jim didn't want to believe they'd seen the ghost of Aunt Yara. Seeing ghosts must be a bad omen. He wanted to tell Peter his mother was still present, but wasn't sure this would be comforting.

"I'm going to work on the saddles," Peter said.

"Right. I'll look around the building. I'll be with you in a minute."

A pile of hay in the middle of the skeletal structure smoldered and smelled pungent. A tiny flare-up emerged to start the blaze again. Jim grabbed a bucket of water from under the remaining spigot and tossed it onto the spot. The flames went out. Then he realized the hay smelled of burned grass, which wasn't too harsh. It was the pungent odor of charred flesh turning his stomach. A smell that etches into one's soul and never leaves.

In a corner, at the other end of the building, a pile of ash and debris surrounded Rolan's remains. Their favorite horse lay on his side with the hair on his body singed off, his side split open with a beam resting across his chest, and his head more bone than flesh. Rolan, Adam—both burned beyond recognition. The bile rolled up into Jim's mouth. He turned away before further defiling the area and left the scene.

Chapter 33

Remnants

INSIDE, AFTER PETER AND JIM HAD DOWNED A STIFF DRINK, they began to relax. Uncle Jorge finished his third drink of Aguardente de Medronho. The brandy calmed his spirit and loosened his tongue. He described the significance of the barn beyond his business ventures. It represented his wife even more grandly than anything else. While he spoke to no one in particular, he gazed out the window. "When we moved onto the property, the barn was a dilapidated old building. The exterior shell was intact. The interior had collapsed. Yara and I worked together to restore the place for our horse business with help from some local builders. The grotto stones strengthened the outer walls."

"Papa, we can rebuild."

"It will never be the same—nothing will be."

"We must go on," Peter said, with a hand on his father's shoulder. "We need to arrange for Rolan's burial."

"I know, I know. This loss is another heartbreak in our lives. I want no part in the task. Please hire a crew."

"Yes, yes, I understand," Peter said. "We'll need many people to help with all the mess."

"I'll take care of today's meals and make some extra casseroles," Sara said. "Blaire, can you help me?"

"We're going to be busy," Blaire replied.

"Jim and I can post a task list outside for everyone to access," Peter said.

"What will you write?" Uncle asked.

"Details about setting up a place for new hay and grain storage, tending to the horses' needs, piling up useful timbers, checking on the vegetable plants and beehives."

"We should leave the bees to Uncle Jorge," Sara said.

"You're right," Jim agreed. "I'll build a new chicken coop. You all can help with a temporary shelter for the horses. Let's work out the list together."

"I am grateful for any help," Peter said. "Tonight, and for many years since Mama left, Papa has been known as a *saudade*."

"That's a tangent," Jim said.

"What is a *saudade*?" Blaire mispronounced the word. It sounded like sauce-dad instead of sau-da-di.

"It means someone who longs for the people and experiences that once brought them great pleasure. Papa often says to parting friends, *Vou ter saudades tuas*. It means you will be missed. For him, the meaning is far deeper and spiritual."

Jim pulled the conversation back to the business at hand. "Peter, I'm concerned no one will show up to help. Can you go into town and ask your friends?"

"Good idea. I'll ask them to come in two days. We need time to plan and buy supplies."

"I'll keep an eye on things while your father tries to relax. When you get back, we can organize tasks."

"I won't be long," Peter said. "I'm sorry your trip here has come to this."

While Uncle rested, Jim sat on the bench outside the front door, reading a Portuguese magazine. However, concentrating on the text after hours of unrest was impossible. He peered over the top edge of the magazine. As far as he could see, no one was coming onto the property to interfere with Rolan or the barn's remains. Brushing up on his language skills was part of the ruse if anyone inquired.

His thoughts rolled back in time to the story he'd told Sara about horses refusing to leave a barn in Savannah, whose spirits remained in the new structure and continue to haunt it. *Would Rolan be with Uncle in this same way?*

In the background, Jim heard pots moving around in the kitchen. He gave up his 'guard duty' and he went inside.

During their evening meal, Jim breathed a sigh of relief when Uncle started talking about other things, like olives and grapes.

"I'm blessed to still have a house and garden to tend to. The rest of the horses will graze across the property until I can make reconstruction plans. The olive grove and vineyard will keep income rolling in."

"Olives?" Blaire asked.

"Yes, yes. We have small trees on the other side of the woods with a reasonable harvest. The olives are more plentiful in warmer temperatures like Ěvora."

"Where is Ěvora?" Sara asked.

"It is three hours to the south and east." Uncle pointed in each direction.

Jim loved that Sara, in her usual way, tried to continue this vein of conversation to help Uncle escape the current situation. "I like olives. Can we eat them straight off the tree like apples?"

"No, no… they are bitter. I have a group of pickers come each year to harvest the crop by shaking the trees onto cloth under the trees."

"How are they prepared after they're harvested?" Blaire asked.

"Good question. Curing requires a brine of salt and water to get the oleuropein bitters out. It takes a month at home; I don't know how factories do this."

Soon after Uncle finished talking about olives, he explained how he leased his land to a vigneron, who grows grapes for red wines: Arinto, Jampal and Malvasia. Jim admired Uncle for his determination to get through the bad times.

Sara popped out the front door without an explanation. A half hour later, he started to worry, and went outside to track her down. She didn't seem to be anywhere within his range of sight. On his way to the barn, she came out from the woods with two horses on lead ropes.

"What are you up to now?" Jim asked. "Why is your shoulder tilted?"

"Oh, um—I came out to get some air and then decided to check on the horses. I'm sorry I didn't say anything. I thought I was going to cry."

"It's okay. I figured you needed some space."

"Yes. Yes, I did. Your poor uncle. I didn't want to fall apart in front of him." Sara winced. "He's doing everything to avoid talking about his trauma."

"A coping mechanism," Jim said. "And your shoulder? What happened?"

"I messed up. While I was walking, I decided it might be good to get your uncle in front of a horse to comfort him." Sara's face turned into a scowl. "Ouch, my shoulder hurts. Never mind. I caught Marco and tied him to a tree. Mateo didn't cooperate. He yanked my shoulder hard when I grabbed his halter, then ran off. Jim, I fell. I'm all right, but something else happened."

"We better get you some ice, or do you need a doctor?"

"Ice, yes. Doctor, no. Jim, I need to tell you something else."

"Oh, God."

"No, it's not bad, not entirely. There I was on the ground, and I saw—something you'd shared with me at home."

Now it was his turn to scowl. "Sara?"

"The woman and the dragon. The creature had a glowing rope-like figure eight symbol stretching from end to end…"

"The alpha and omega. Incredible." Jim was aghast. "Sintra and Savannah are haunted.

"The world is haunted. Never mind for now. We need to stay focused on helping your uncle with the fire mitigation and not worry about spirits."

"Easier said than done." Jim rubbed his ear. "Is that why the horse bolted?"

"Maybe—I don't know—he came back on his own." Sara massaged her shoulder several times. "The dragon was on the edge of the field. A young woman came over and helped me up. Well, I'm not sure how she did. I don't recall her hand touching me. She had a strange-looking baby in one arm—it was tiny, maybe six inches long and iridescent. She told me to be careful with my baby. I didn't know what she meant, but I smiled to humor her."

"Christ," Jim exclaimed. This didn't sound any easier than his own experience, and it wasn't the right time to share. "Then what?"

"Nothing. She walked off toward the dragon and got on its back. It breathed out little golden sparks, and then they disappeared. Jim, they were like the ones in your drawings."

"This place. No, the world is full of surprises." He turned and knocked on the front door.

Uncle came out and smiled when he saw Sara holding Marco and Mateo. Uncle ran his fingers through Marco's long mane, pulled off the singed pieces, and hugged the horse's neck. "You're all right, my love."

Chapter 34

Recovery

EVERAL DAYS LATER, PEOPLE POURED ONTO UNCLE'S PROP-
erty with prepared food, shovels, and a tractor to clean up the
debris. Jim helped Sara heat up the casseroles she and Blaire
had made after the fire. Intermittently, he peered through the front
window to monitor the guests. There were a few people nosing around,
others getting busy, and still others dropping coins and bills into a jar
Sara had set out by the garden gate.

Jim and Peter went outside and pulled two long wooden tables
out from behind the house into a clearing for the casseroles and donated items. Whatever didn't fit there could go into the refrigerator
in the house for Uncle to distribute later.

Over by the cemetery, men were preparing Rolan's grave. Jim
couldn't imagine how they'd get him out of the barn and into a hole
deep enough for a man to stand in and wide enough for a horse. The
tractor was doing most of the digging. When it was done, it backed
away, and the men jumped in with shovels. The dirt came flying out
of the hole and only the tops of the men's heads were visible. Peter
went out to check on their progress.

Back inside, with his head hung low, Peter said, "The men told me
to keep everyone in the house and away from the windows. They're
going to pull Rolan out of the barn with chains and we shouldn't
watch."

Since Jim had seen the devastation up close, he knew it was best
for everyone to stay away and remember Rolan riding down the trails
or frolicking in the fields. Jim tried to force the charred image out of
his mind and envision the evening he and Rolan had been together,
"talking" in the barn. For a moment, he thought of the lantern. He'd

hung it in the barn and then taken it with him, but it had disappeared when he'd dozed off in the forest.

Jim took it upon himself to walk the grounds with a skeptical eye. It seemed too many people were socializing while leaving the hard labor for the larger men. Guests roamed around, chatting among themselves. Some sat on chairs scattered on the premises, talking about things he couldn't interpret over the cacophony of voices. Most of them were speaking in Portuguese dialects.

A lady with red, talon-like nails sat on a bench by the garden. Jim was close enough to see and hear. Not close enough to engage in conversation. She sucked the *pastel de nata*—a small custard tart—off her fingers, then dug some out from under her nails. The image, although not flattering, reminded Jim of the overgrown goldfish in the fountain back in Savannah. Something about this hungry woman was familiar. She looked like Aunt Yara. Jim knew she didn't have a sister, so who could this be?

Farther across the yard, there was a teenage boy with a red scarf around his neck, coming out of the new chicken coop Jim had built the day before. The boy's blue, upturned shirt bulged with lumpy masses. Over at the serving table, he grabbed something and sat on the bench next to the woman with the red nails. Before he took a bite, he pulled one egg after the other out of his shirt, and placed them in a basket Jim hadn't noticed.

Someone behind Jim said, "*Olà, João.*"

Jim spun around toward the familiar voice. It was Tomãs. They'd known each other since childhood.

"Hello. It's so good to see you," Jim said in Portuguese, and stuck out his hand.

"Where have you been?" Tomãs pulled Jim into a bear hug. "It's been at least six years since you were here."

Buddy came up next to Jim's leg.

"I wish. It's been more than nine years. Buddy was a puppy on my last visit."

"Sí, you are right."

"I went into the Army, and it took over my life."

"I understand. I served for two years." Tomās rested a hand on Jim's shoulder. "A requirement here. Where is our friend, Adam? We had such good times together when we were children."

A light-headed moment washed over Jim. "Adam—is—gone. One of our missions ended his life."

"I am so sorry."

"Thanks." Jim felt compelled to change the subject. "I'm married now. Let's go inside. I'll introduce you to Adam's wife and mine."

They walked toward the house and went inside.

Sara popped up from the other side of the kitchen counter and slid a tray of *pasteis de bacalhau*—codfish cakes—onto a trivet. She said, "Hello. You two are chummy. Who's this?"

"Tomās, this is my wife, Sara."

Blaire came around the corner with Dustin in her arms. "Olà."

Jim gestured in her direction. "And this is Adam's wife and son; Blaire and Dustin."

Dustin smiled and reached out his hand.

"Olà." Tomās briefly mimicked a manly handshake.

Tomās bowed in Blaire's direction. "I'm sorry for your loss. Your husband was a good friend, and I'm sure his son will grow up to be a fine man."

Before they could exchange any more conversation, someone knocked on the door and pushed it open a few inches. A worker stuck his head around and reported the horse had been buried and the grave marker was in place.

"I'll go see what they did." Sara walked out the door.

"Wait," Jim said, but she didn't stop.

"Let her go alone," Blaire said.

Sara returned five minutes later. She said, "They put a pile of basalt stones over the grave and placed a wooden cross behind it. Best I can understand from their broken English, they are going to pull the charred wood out of the barn and spread it in the fields. No payment required."

"They are good people," Tomás stated. "The wood will feed the soil."

The oven timer went off. Before Blaire could respond, Tomás put on the oven mitts and pulled out the sheet of cod cakes. Together, they arranged the fish on a serving plate. Blaire took them outside, leaving Dustin on a blanket on the floor. In the meantime, Jim served up several bowls of *soupa de marisco*—seafood soup—for them to eat. The space was heating up from the cooking. Sara reappeared, leaving the front door propped open with a chair at an angle to keep Dustin from crawling away after lunch. Blaire put Dustin on her lap and spooned tiny portions of the soup into Dustin's mouth. Jim laughed out loud at the image of Dustin opening his mouth like a baby bird and making little num-num sounds of appreciation in between bites, with the broth dripping down his chin.

Jim liked the concept of souls transitioning. The visions he'd experienced were changing his perspective. *If reincarnation exists, everyone would be comforted by the knowledge, while not being thrilled about being a helpless child all over again. If everyone dies without returning, where would new souls come from? There couldn't be an unlimited number in the universe.*

Jim stepped outside again and saw the boy who had been carrying the eggs, still sitting on the bench. His head kept twitching left and right. Jim moved closer and asked in English how the young man knew Uncle Jorge and what he intended to do with the eggs. While Jim waited for a response, he noticed there wasn't an imprint in the ash where the red-nailed lady had been sitting. The boy remained mute. Jim tried another approach in Portuguese.

"Where did the lady with the red nails go?" Jim held his hand up and pointed at his fingernails.

The boy's eyes stilled, and he squinted up at Jim. "Senhor. I don't know what you mean."

"She was here?" Jim gestured at the bench.

"No, senhor." The boy's eyes darted around. Without another word, he stood and walked away like a skittish squirrel.

Jim turned his attention back to the bench. The woman had re-appeared. A glint of light sparkled in her hair. She said, "Nothing is ever as it seems. I hope the wolf was helpful."

Before Jim could respond or question her intentions, he was dis-tracted by two men grabbing the boy before he had a chance to walk twenty paces. They turned him around, slightly off-balancing his pro-gression, and pulled his hands together behind his back. One held him while the other walked back toward Jim. The woman in red stood, smiled ever so slightly, and vanished.

"Senhor. I am sorry to disturb you," the man said in Portuguese and flashed a badge to identify himself. "Where is Senhor Jorge?" The familiarity of the request was off-putting since the man wasn't using Uncle's last name.

"Did you see a woman walk away from the bench?" Jim responded in Portuguese and was pleased they understood.

"No, senhor. My name is Officer Borges. I am the investigator on this case. Are you in charge today?"

He reached out and shook the officer's hand.

"Yes, I am. My name's Jim Masterson. My uncle stepped away before his horse was buried. Why is the teenager being arrested?"

"We have evidence connecting him to your uncle's barn fire, and to another one."

"Arson?" Jim rubbed his temples.

"We found suspicious black residue near what's left of the hay. This is likely where the fire started. It is the same type as the other fire in the area this week."

"I understand. Thank you for your help."

"Please, tell Senhor Jorge to come by the station. I have more in-formation. He needs to make a formal report."

Uncle Jorge came around a corner. "Olà, Borges. What have you learned?"

"Olà, senhor. I was telling Jim there were signs of arson and an-other barn burned down the same way. It's tragic all around. This was a case of pyromania, but it's a complex situation. The teenager we just arrested had a twin sister, who died in a barn."

"How terrible," exclaimed Uncle. "Why did this become my loss?"

"His sister was with a helper who was preparing the horse for an event using electric clippers. The horse spooked and slammed her into a wall. She didn't survive, and he released his rage by burning barns."

"None of our clients died. It's strange he attacked my place," Uncle said.

"I feel his pain. My sister was killed, but I would never hurt an innocent bystander. Why was the boy here today?" Jim asked.

"It's a strange thing. We suspect he felt guilty for causing you pain. Classic arsonists like to watch their work go up in flames for the thrill of it and some come back to see the ashes after. This boy's motivation doesn't correspond with those cases."

Jim looked across the yard. The boy was twisting his shoulders within the other officer's grasp and said something.

"Excuse me." Officer Borges walked over to his partner and returned after a conversation. "My associate told the boy his actions killed a horse. He confessed to blocking the stall door and said it looked like the horse who killed his sister. Now he realizes his mistake and says he was possessed. He is heartbroken and sends apologies."

"Uncle, when I saw him today sitting on a bench, he looked familiar. I'm sure I saw him in the shadows during the fire. At the time, I didn't see any reason to single him out."

"The boy needs some serious help," Uncle said. "However, I will need funds to rebuild."

"Yes, we shall deal with him," said Officer Borges. "He's fifteen, so he may be granted leniency and community service. Or you could recruit him to rebuild your barn for retribution."

"No, I don't think so."

"Gentlemen, I must go."

"Thank you for your help, Officer Borges."

The officer bowed his head, rejoined his partner, and took the boy away.

By the end of the day, everyone was worn out. The crowd of helpers went home after a successful day of cleaning up the debris and addressing the chores on the list Sara had posted. They'd built a lean-to for the newly delivered hay and a box for the grain storage.

Back in the house, almost everyone except Jim sauntered off to their bedrooms. With an enormous sigh, he collapsed onto the couch. Fifteen minutes later, he went into the bedroom to check on Sara, who was asleep and still in the clothes she'd worn all day. He didn't want to bother her, and meandered into the kitchen.

Blaire appeared with Dustin and left him with Jim. The little guy didn't seem tired. Taking care of him felt like such a natural thing to do. Sometimes, Jim read to Dustin, but he didn't on this occasion because he didn't want to fall asleep in the middle of a page. Instead, he carried Dustin around, examining books and trinkets on the shelves while talking nonstop about the details of each item. *Babies must absorb information somehow.* If Jim's night walks weren't delusional episodes, he was sharing events with Adam through Dustin. The idea warmed his soul. His words droned on until Blaire appeared and took Dustin upstairs.

Jim showered the smoke smells from his hair, fell into bed next to Sara, and closed his eyes.

Chapter 35

The Chapel

JIM AWOKE WITH HIS FISTS CLENCHED BY HIS SIDE AND PEERED at the ceiling in the dim light while deciding whether or not to go for his usual late-night walk. *A soldier should not hide from creatures of the night. I could snuggle close to Sara to release my tension, but the act wouldn't solve anything.*

Instead, he pushed the covers off his naked body and tucked them against her to keep the drafts away. He slipped into his jeans, a button-down shirt, his watch, and a pair of sneakers. On the way out the front door, he saw, and grabbed, a long-stemmed flashlight resembling a police nightstick that could be a weapon, too. Even if the oil lamp hadn't disappeared, it was no longer an appealing source of light. It was too soon to be playing with flames.

There hadn't been any bits of lantern casing in the barn, but he was still suspicious. *Could the boy have stalked him through the woods without his knowledge?* If so, missing the fact was an insult to his military training. He couldn't imagine why the boy would have gone to those lengths. There was no point, so he dismissed the idea and went out into the night.

The sky was dotted with clouds, and the moon created shadows all over the ground. Seeing his surroundings this time would be easier than before when he'd glimpsed the animated faces in the statues. He continued to question his mental faculties. Yet, the wolf was real. There was no doubt it led Jim back home to save Uncle Jorge from certain death.

Uncle said he saw Aunt Yara's ghost in the barn. Jim had seen something, but he wasn't certain. His uncle was convinced she appeared in the house when the coat of arms moved over the doorway. And perhaps there were other things Uncle hadn't mentioned. There were so many mystical things in the estate's gardens he had described from recorded history. Encounters with ghosts or spirits, whether by seeing or sensing them, were not unheard of in the world. Knowing this somehow comforted Jim.

Down in the yard, the tunnel had changed again. The ceiling dripped water. The sound of droplets striking their corresponding puddles resonated throughout the space. Holding the light up, he saw movement on the walls. At first, it looked as though the moss was pulsating. A small lizard's eyes blinking in the light with its mouth opening in silent objection at being disturbed. At the other end of the tunnel, dust motes drifted across the lantern's light. Stepping out, he turned back to the entrance. The statue was no longer in its alcove.

He decided to make his way to the chapel, which he knew was situated along a path near the Initiation Well and not far from the estate's main house. Jim liked Uncle calling it the Well of Souls.

The chapel was slightly larger than the ones he'd seen within massive cathedrals like Notre Dame in Paris or the National Cathedral in Washington, DC. As he moved forward in the night with the flashlight, he focused on the images he could recall of the chapel, Capela Da Regaleira, to calm his nerves. On the inside, he knew a twisted staircase led above and below the main sanctuary's altar. The world

above and below. The pentagram, the sun wheels, the metal gate closing off the lower entrance, and a spiral horned creature.

During his childhood, he'd found the exterior flying buttresses
of cathedrals comical, yet he'd experienced a sense of awe he could
never explain. Even now, he felt an emotional charge at the architectural feats of master builders. The tiny Capela Da Regaleira in Sintra
mimicked the styles on the exterior of grand cathedrals with Gothic
spires and statues within niches. Jim's favorite part of Gothic architecture had always been the narrow, triangular peaked stained-glass
windows that told stories through colorful pictures. The panels were
a brilliant way to teach scripture to people who couldn't read.

As he moved along, he thought about the military again. He
knew he'd joined to pursue his goals of becoming an FBI agent, but
the price he paid was too great. The guilt he continued to carry over
Adam dying in front of him was still traumatizing. How would he manage being exposed to death in the FBI on a regular basis? Working in
Orlando was far easier. Yet, who said life was supposed to be easy?
His previous employer brought people joy in the midst of life's realities. Fighting crime was more important, and he needed to accept the
baggage that came along with the job. He had wanted to let go of his
connections to mystical things his mama had brought into their lives.
The task wasn't any easier than vanquishing nightmares. And now, he
wanted to keep the magic.

The hairs on the back of his neck prickled when he got closer to
the chapel, and he wished he had a battle buddy rather than proceeding
alone. His ears rang in the unnatural silence, which was soon replaced
by a branch cracking and a cricket-like chirping. Hoping there was
nothing to fear, he tried to find the source. Nothing came into view.
Likely, his imagination was acting up, and he took some deep breaths
and focused on getting to the chapel. Refocusing his mind, he thought
of Sara. A positive adrenal energy flowed from the depths of his soul
and out through his tear ducts into an all-encompassing, silly grin.

He ran the last quarter mile with the flashlight beam bobbing.
This time, he was not running to shed anger like he had when his dad

said, "Son, enlist in the Army." Instead, he felt gratitude for the life he still had, the life that was not taken from him in combat. Life should be danced through and not wasted on remorse. He reminded himself that people lost should be remembered by the happy times after a period of mourning. Christina, Aunt Yara, and Adam would scorn Jim's reoccurring gloomy attitudes and would never want him to wallow in grief. As he ran, he pushed his sorrows into the shadows and continued moving forward.

The three-story chapel appeared to have moved closer than Jim knew to be true. He hoped his own momentum had distracted him from the realities of time, and his watch concurred. The stained-glass window on the side of the marble building glowed. The main door was open, and above it a triangle surrounded the all-seeing eye. Toward the front of the chapel, he saw unattended, lit candlesticks on the altar. Statues flanked both sides of the entrance. When he was younger, he'd seen figures in and around churches. None of them had been like these. For now, he didn't look too closely. Instead, he turned off the flashlight, put it down by the door, and strolled into the chapel. Halfway down the aisle, he sat on a pew for a moment of reflection. Once his breath had regulated from the run, he walked down the stairs to the crypt.

He crossed the black-and-white floor tiles, representing the conflict between good and evil, and gazed at a picture on the wall of Carvalho Monteiro. It was strange to see the Brazilian, the old owner of the property, in the bowels of the chapel instead of in a more prominent location. While looking into the portrait's glass, a shadow—not Jim's—passed by. Turning, he bit his lip. A man appeared in a straw fedora hat, with a white beard, and a long woolen coat. With all of Jim's experiences, he knew the figure was a ghost. The ghost of Senhor Monteiro. Without thinking, Jim followed the apparition up the stairs. Monteiro drifted past the altar and disappeared through the chapel doors. Jim didn't know why Monteiro had shown himself. A spirit guide, perhaps? It was time to venture outside and examine the statues.

On one side of the door, he saw a winged horse with realistic sea-glass green eyes instead of the customary stone. A spiral of gray moss hung down from the horse's snout. The horse transformed into a scaled creature and shook off the moss. Jim stepped back under the eaves of the chapel's door.

On the other side of the door, a woman with two blood-red marks down her back straddled a long-snouted dragon. A warm mist came from the dragon's nostrils and landed on Jim's cheek. He wagered these were the same pair Sara saw in Uncle Jorge's field. Except this time there wasn't a premature baby in her arms. The dragon snorted and twitched its shoulders when the woman dismounted. The exchange was curious rather than alarming to watch.

These three beings, they could no longer be called statues, moved forward down the winding pathway until the horse took flight and disappeared above the tree-filled mountainous terrain.

Jim's eyes widened like saucers in a cartoon. He shook his head and smirked at himself. Stepping farther into the shadows didn't serve a purpose, so he moved out into the open air. The clouds above had parted. The moon, in its glory, would not hide him this night. Not knowing what to do with the woman or dragon, Jim ignored them and walked forward a few paces with his shoulders back and eyes darting.

Off to the left were more figures. Each living being was well known in their stone form. By day, a plaque stated their names and positions in history. They, too, came to life and moved out of order into a cluster by some trees.

The wolf stepped off his pedestal, which read Guinefort, and approached Jim. He recognized the brown and gray fur from their stare-down on the night of the barn fire. During this transformation from statue to flesh, its coat was wiry. The fear melted from Jim's adrenaline-filled heart. Succumbing to it could cause mistakes and lead to panic.

Guinefort moved behind him, sat next to his leg, and pushed under his hand, which landed on the wolf's head. Without thinking, Jim stroked its ears. It didn't seem right to be allowed to touch things from a parallel dimension, but somehow, he could. They waited there together and watched the others.

In some ways, it seemed like the characters from C. S. Lewis's *Chronicles of Narnia* had revealed themselves in front of him, turning from stone back into flesh after being transformed by the wicked witch. In Lewis's story, there were fauns, centaurs, and cyclops to contend with, but none in this scenario. The characters had never been flesh before, yet they must have been. Perhaps he had created this scene because of his experiences with such stories. His intent to escape such fantasies had failed. This wasn't a dream. And he knew Guinefort, except, until now, he hadn't known the wolf was also a transformed statue.

Six characters he recognized, and three he did not, moved toward the dragon. It shuddered and the scales down its spine twitched. Its voice boomed in Jim's direction. "I am Tatsuya. This is the angel Armisael." A small stream of fire and cluster of firefly sparks burst out of his mouth and nose.

Jim couldn't turn away, even though he wanted to bolt. Instead, he moved back a step and realized the sparks looked like the ones he'd seen by the tunnel on a different night. The dragon must have been nearby then. Without thinking, Jim bowed.

Together, Tatsuya and the rest of the figures paraded up to the top of the Well of Souls, where a brownish-red coated lion, with open wings spanning at least six feet stood, larger than any bird or lion Jim had ever seen. The regal creature looked like one of his newer drawings. Before he could adjust to the scene, the winged horse reappeared and landed on the other side of Guinefort.

In a soothing, wispy voice, Guinefort said, "Do not be afraid. Stand in front of the king and wait for the reason we have revealed ourselves."

With a nudge from the wolf, Jim continued to move toward the lion, who appeared to be waiting for something Jim couldn't imagine.

Jim tried to deduce possible reasons for these mystical visions. *Could my mama's shamanism be infiltrating my mind with animal totems? If not, could they be a result of Uncle's stories or ghost stories from Savannah?* His feet started to move again, without his consent. He continued walking without knowing why. The motley crew of five—a winged horse, Tatsuya the dragon, Jim the mortal, Guinefort the wolf, and Armisael the wingless angel—would be a picture he could never have imagined in any place other than in fairy tales.

At the top of the hill, Jim moved with them to the edge of the Well of Souls. The lion blinked several times and his eyelashes folded down onto his cheeks with each movement. A dimpled grin spread across the beast's face like a mischievous Cheshire cat. The expression was more menacing than anything else. A far cry from the friendly face of Aslan in Narnia. An enormous mane surrounded this lion's head and glowed in the moonlight like an angelic crown. Jim bowed again.

By Jim's side was the top of the open well. The opening was wide and deep like a grain silo, and buried in the ground just like Uncle had described. A stairwell ran around the inside wall. Ornamental ropes and statuesque figures were embedded in the stone. Ropes hung down, with small patches of a green moss-like substance clinging to them. Stone stairs had a filigree wrought iron railing along the edge to prevent visitors from falling into the pit. The pit of despair, or hope. Jim didn't know which. He'd never paid much attention to the place until they'd come to Sintra this year. Now, he needed to understand the well and its meaning beyond Uncle's description. This place didn't look like Dante's Inferno.

Jim's thoughts were being heard.

Angel Armisael's words floated from her lips in a wisp of fog. "The beings you see on the stair walls are representations of spirits or souls. When a person's body dies, each row of steps takes the traveler further back into their lives. At the bottom of the steps, there is a stone path through the water where travelers cross to a new life. Sara and Blaire saw this when they visited. We saw them cross, but the stones were dormant."

"What do you mean?" Jim smoothed down his hair. "What's flicking in and out over the railings?"

"Patience." The lion breathed out a frosty breath. "There are two ways you can cross here. The first way is to pass from this life to the next in an ethereal spirit after you leave your human body. The second is if you are conflicted in this life. Passing through the well will bring you peace while your current physical body is still living on human lands. You can make the crossing in your current form if you are chosen, and the path has been activated." The lion's paw rose and pointed to the expansive landscape of trees and foliage surrounding the well. And then his body transformed from his glorious figure into a bedraggled creature without explanation.

New blossoms of evening primrose, white Brahma Kamal, and moon flowers opened in front of Jim's eyes. The flowers Uncle said had disappeared after Aunt Yara died were back.

"I must be dreaming," Jim said.

"You are dreaming while you are awake. It is complicated," Armisael said. "Your sister, Christina, and your friend Adam have seen your pain. They want to help. We decided to show you."

"I'm not sure how to deal with this," Jim exclaimed.

"What you have seen and are seeing is not impossible. There is more to both our worlds. They are parallel and invisible to humans."

Jim's thoughts spun in a state somewhere between disbelief and awe.

"I *know* you saw a shadow of Christina and Adam in the statue on your last visit to this realm. I *know* you dream of Adam and your sleep is…"

"Yes, but—why did Sara see some of you, too?"

"We are here to help. She needed to see, so she will not question your sanity." Tatsuya had become an emissary for the lion, who was now silent and staring intently at the dragon. "Adam is almost done with his transition into Dustin. Your sister—how do I say—will be sewn into a new casing when your child is born."

"My child? When?"

"I cannot say more of this. It is forbidden."

"By whom?" Jim felt like he was on the edge of a jagged cliff. Yet, his feet were firmly planted on the ground.

"The king and his son, Guinefort."

"How is this possible? A lion and a wolf?"

"They take whatever form they wish, to help whomever they are connecting with."

"Hmm, is the lion a version of the Grim Reaper?"

"Man's invention," Armisael said. "Many names are used. They all have the same meaning. Malak al-Maut, Thanatos, Mavet, and Dullahan. It all depends on what part of man's world you happen to be in and which century. You have learned enough for one night. Go back to Sara."

Armisael put a warm hand on his cheek, but he didn't feel the expected pressure of her hand.

As instructed, Jim turned and ran the two miles back to the tunnel like a hunted beast toward the comforts of home, forgetting about the flashlight he'd left behind at the chapel and depending on his night vision. He hoped Sara would still be in bed and he could curl up next to her without a word. He wasn't ready to explain everything. Telling her what happened would be a challenge.

When he arrived back at Uncle's house, he pondered again over his level of consciousness during these bizarre events. Up by the door lingered an unknown woman. She wore a sheer, flowing floral gown, and might have been from the forest. He had never seen this ethereal creature before. There was something familiar and soothing about the woman. On top of her head was a fitted cap covered with what he presumed were lilies and hyacinths. A sweet smell surrounded her form.

"You surprised me," Jim said. "Who are you? Where did you come from?"

"Many questions. I'm always here. Most times I am behind you, so close you cannot see. A breath away." Her lips moved ever so slightly, like a ventriloquist.

"Always? Even when I'm…?"

"Always."

"Are you a ghost?"

"Some might call me so. We are not supposed to meet like this. I'm Danica, your guardian angel."

"Danica? You? The pictures I drew, or Sara and I drew, had your name after each one. I had no idea why I wrote it. I never heard your name before."

"I am Danica, yes. Revealing myself was part of the grand plan to help you."

"Wow. So, does everyone have a guardian?"

"Yes, everyone."

"No matter what they believe is beyond our world?"

"Everyone, everywhere."

Jim wasn't buying into this explanation. He opened the door and walked inside. The Catholic teachings of his youth must be invading his senses. *No, no,* he scolded himself after what he'd been through in the garden. It all had to be real on some level. Sara had once suggested he study other theologies and places of worship in Savannah to see which ones suited him better. At the time, he doubted any of them could help him. God seemed elusive after what he'd seen in Grenada. The angel, and the events of the night wanderings, were slowly changing his understanding of God and the life in the hereafter.

In a rush, he quietly closed the door. For a millisecond, he thought he'd escaped. The woman was standing next to Uncle's blue and white tiled fireplace. The dark wood mantel was an inch higher than her shoulder. Jim turned back toward the door to see what would happen. She was there, moving like a switch of a light back and forth, from one spot to the other. He saw no visible movement of her feet.

"Why can I see you now? Am I dead? Asleep? Why am I being exposed to all these things in Sintra?"

"More questions," the angel said. "Your unresolved pain is why we are all revealed. You saw some of us when you were a child. If you could successfully conjure us up in your memories, you would likely brush the thoughts away and call them foolish games of make-believe. Any adults who talk of such things are usually not believed or are thought to be mentally deranged. Right now, you are still in the world of humans while going through the experiences we allow. Sintra is open to these alternate visions. Other places you live or have lived are blocked by the confusion of a disconnected, chaotic world."

"Disconnected from what?" Jim's mind scrambled for his own answers. If Sara or Uncle entered the room, would they see him talking to himself and not this *being*, this *spirit?*

"The planes beyond the human realm. Go to bed and wake refreshed."

Jim did not hesitate to follow the angel's orders. Perhaps, once he could process everything, tomorrow would be a better day. He trudged down the hall and collapsed on their bed into a deep and dreamless sleep.

Sara was still asleep when he awoke. He kissed her cheek and rolled toward the edge of the bed. Something hard was under the pillow. Reaching into the folds, his fingers touched and pulled out a wrought iron, old-fashioned skeleton key. At the top of the stem, a blue tassel was woven through a hole in the middle of an engraved heart. He imagined this key would go into a lock he hadn't seen in the gardens. Perhaps the key's sudden appearance further proved the visions were real. For the longest time, he stared at the blue tassel. It was the color of Adam's porch ceiling in Savannah, haint blue. Until these nights of magical visions, such things were pure fantasy. Thinking through everything was too difficult, so he drifted back to sleep, hoping the color would indeed ward off evil spirits.

Hours later, the sun hit Jim's closed eyes and woke him from a blissful sleep that contained not a single nightmare. Sitting up and stretching, he was surprised he was fully dressed, and the key was still under the pillow.

Chapter 36

The Key

AN ORANGE SUNSET GLOWED OUTSIDE THE LIVING ROOM window while everyone relaxed with a glass of Port wine. Dustin crawled across the floor, clutching the key with the blue tassel. He rolled sideways into a sitting position and put the key's teeth in his pursed lips. The shape his mouth formed almost looked like something out of *Alice in Wonderland*. Jim exchanged scowls with Dustin, gently tugged the key out of his mouth and put a spoon in its place. For reasons Jim didn't understand, the transaction made him want to wander through the estate after everyone was asleep. The challenge would be finding a keyhole. It felt like an eternity before everyone retired for the evening.

Jim woke and got out of bed around four a.m., out of habit rather than from a nightmare. This was a welcome change. He guzzled a glass of water, threw on some clothes, and took the key and a flashlight with him to the tunnel. It was time to go hunting. The key could be connected to the shape-shifting statues. It was still difficult to believe both the two- and four-legged manifestations were not a product of an inflated imagination. The key was solid and real.

On his way through the tunnel, there was nothing unusual to fixate on this time. At the exit, he moved the flashlight around on the wall and noticed the statue was back in the alcove pointing toward the wall at a four-by-six-inch keyed door. Pale vines hung down on either side like a drawn pair of curtains which could have been closed to conceal before. Within the vines were tiny glistening drops of something resembling water, but they were gelatinous to the touch. He put the flashlight on a rock at an angle and the beam reflected off the wall. Pulling the key out of his pocket, he turned it over in his hand several times. The old skeleton key didn't go in easily. Finally, it relented and turned three times counterclockwise before opening. A hissing sound burst forth, along with a cold mist that seeped out around the cracks.

Inside the small box sat several items. Jim recognized each pristine item without knowing how the artifacts could be intact. *How did they find their way into this hiding place?* The first: a silver chain with a locket. Pushing the clasp, it popped open. Inside was a portrait of Uncle Jorge on one side and Aunt Yara on the other, each with a lock of hair covering a portion of their faces. The second item: a folded-up piece of paper wrapped around a baby carved in stone. On the paper, he recognized colored crayon figures drawn by Christina, depicting the two of them on either side of their childhood Yorkshire terrier, Buttons. Under each image, their names were written in her primitive handwriting: Jimbo (no one else called him that), Buttons, and Christi (she couldn't quite spell out her entire name). In a silhouette, behind them, was an angel. The last time he'd seen this drawing in his closet, he hadn't noticed the angel. The third item: the engraved knife Adam had placed on the bar in Savannah during their reunion.

What was Jim supposed to do with these treasures? The despair and feelings of loss crept in again. His sister, his aunt, and his best friend all died too young. Too early. They should have been around for many more decades. It wasn't fair. They had so much more life to live.

He'd never told Sara, never allowed himself to admit that he'd considered ending his own life when Adam died in battle. Turning the gun on himself right after would have ended his troubles. Then everyone he loved might have been tormented, too. Adam and he were supposed to protect each other, and Jim had failed. He must have told himself this a hundred times, knowing he should let the guilt go. The punishment should be death. No one else viewed his failure the same way. Soldiers die or live; it was a fact. There's no getting out of death when one's time is up.

He put most of the objects in his pocket, but kept the knife out. Flicking it open and holding it in the light, he saw a thin layer of oil coating the razor-sharp edge. Moving it over his wrist, he considered his options. Hesitating, he folded the knife and put it in his other pocket, away from the fragile items.

Buddy came bounding into the back of Jim's knees, knocking him to the ground. It was a strange time of night for Uncle to let Buddy out. They tumbled farther into the garden and came face-to-face with the wolf. Jim got to his feet, and Buddy hid behind his leg.

The wolf began to utter a sound, beginning with a snort, which turned into a laugh and finally human speech. The wolf bowed. "Guinefort, at your service. I am your animal spirit guide. Now you know. These items prove your experiences here are real."

"The night of the fire, you were there." A long pause ensued. "A talking wolf, statues morphing into animals and humans. I need a sanity check."

"You are perfectly sane."

"Good to know you think so." Jim shifted his feet and took the opportunity to ask questions. "Tell me, why does the woman on the dragon have two fire-red scars down her back?"

"Ah, a complex situation. She once had a full set of glorious angel wings. One assignment went terribly wrong. This happens sometimes. She and a demon were sent to pick up the same soul. They battled until her wings were damaged beyond repair. She acquired and saved the soul, so the sacrifice was worth the loss. Afterward, her wings were removed, and she was given the dragon to continue her work."

"It's all hard to believe," Jim said.

"Many things are for humankind."

"You all should be invincible and self-healing," Jim said.

"Things are not always what they seem. Sometimes the loss is a lesson or a punishment. It is not for me to understand her complete story." Guinefort's mouth moved into a smile, his teeth showing on the sides of his jaw. "Humans see one color while bees see another. It's the same for all realms. All the worlds."

"How do you know I had a conversation about bees recently?" Jim scowled. "Never mind. Nothing seems to be what I thought it was in Sintra or in Savannah, or anywhere else. Maybe my guardian angel told you. This all explains any ghost encounters I've had or heard of."

"It's good we could help."

"Yes, oddly. Unbelievably. You and the others have helped me. I'm more myself than I have been in months. Maybe years."

Guinefort growled in a low tone. "Now you know, you don't have to feel downtrodden about death. You can be at peace while only missing the familiar form of a loved one. Christina and Adam are returning to you in a new form. Your Aunt Yara is waiting for the right moment to let go of her concerns and become human again."

"I'm still not sure I understand."

"Did you sleep well for the first time in many moons?"

"Yes. Why am I?"

"Because you are coming to accept the truth. Sara saw, but in a smaller dose. She wasn't meant to see all we have revealed to you. We gave her enough to believe you when you explain there is something beyond your known world."

"Were the pictures we drew from my dreams, and the visit from Armisael after Sara wrenched her shoulder all a part of it?"

"Yes, that is right. You are still repeating questions; you must have faith." Guinefort went over to Jim's free hand on the opposite side of Buddy and nuzzled it. "Let's go for a walk. Stay close. The night is becoming foggy."

Jim laughed. "In more ways than one—the fog has lifted from my life. I have you and the others to thank."

Guinefort nodded. "Leave the man-made light here. Let us go."

"Poor Uncle, I have lost three of his lights."

"They are things. Loss of these is nothing."

They walked together through the haze. Buddy seemed to understand what was going on and stood proud, like a prince beside the wolf, who was at least six inches taller and thirty pounds heavier. Jim imagined the three of them in a drawing side-by-side and couldn't help smiling. The two canines appeared to be previously acquainted, but it seemed improbable. *How could a mystical wolf be connected to a mortal dog? Yet, how could Jim be connected to a world he shouldn't be able to see?* Jim's only reasonable choice was to trust his senses. He patted the outside of his pocket where he'd refolded and placed Christina's gift, along with the locket.

Walking on, a trance-like haze came over him and the mortal world. Soon, down the pathway, the immortals morphed into flesh again as they had done the night before. They clustered nearby, along with the wingless Armisael and her dragon, Tatsuya. The beings spoke among themselves of spirits they had obtained from the day before. Jim heard their words, but didn't grasp their meaning. In all probability, they were not permitting him to assimilate the information. Up the hill, by the well, Jim could see the king pacing back and forth.

Guinefort said, in a matter-of-fact and almost bored tone, "They do not take souls before they are ready. Armisael and others either fly on horses or dragons or by their own wings to collect souls as they depart the humans' realm."

"Why is one still a statue?"

"Smart boy. You have never encountered this one in your past lives, so it remains solid stone in your presence. Hmm. The others you have lived amongst in one form or another."

Jim opened his mouth to ask another question. Guinefort answered before the question was uttered. Telepathy was added to Jim's list of the wolf's capabilities.

"The ones who ride may or may not have their own wings."

"Wait," Jim exclaimed. "What if a soul isn't ready? What about people like my sister and friends who were shot?"

"They were ready whether they knew it or not."

"Not comforting," Jim grumbled.

"All souls are brought to points over the globe to be judged. The ones who have reached their predetermined goals become angels. Some are guardians, like the one who allowed you to see her at your uncle's house. The souls who have not achieved their goals are reassigned a new body to begin again. All except the evil ones, who go elsewhere."

"Where?"

"We will not talk of the place." Guinefort said nothing more.

On this visit, wingless Armisael did not speak to Jim. She mounted Tatsuya. The dragon took off like a jet and vanished across the western skyline. The other shape-shifters—Hermes, Pan, Aphrodite, Dionysus, Orpheus, and Vulcan—moved away like summoned zombies with their hands stiffly hanging by their sides.

"You must travel across the stones to be healed. You have been told of this," Guinefort said, and led them to the crossing. He nudged them on.

Jim was about to say something when Guinefort vanished. At the end of the watery path, a horse with white wings stood with his neck arched and nostrils flaring. Without hesitation, Jim moved forward across the stones, with Buddy following behind. When they reached the other side, a lightness came over him, and he felt elated. The clouds shifted among the inky-black sky, and the horse's front hoof began pawing at the ground before moving farther into a grass-covered clearing.

Jim and Buddy walked slowly toward the horse. As they got closer, Jim talked in a low voice and outstretched his hand, hoping it wouldn't bolt. It held still. He stroked its white neck and wings, while wondering why it allowed a stranger to be so close.

Before Jim could do anything else, and without warning, the horse moved sideways and whinnied the words, "You lie."

Jim couldn't imagine what he was lying about. Then realized the horse wasn't addressing him at all.

A bird came out of nowhere like a bullet, with its talons and hooked beak aimed right at the horse's wings. The sound emanating from the creature's body combined the rush of wings with a crow's caw. Its wings, multicolored gold and red, resembled a mythical phoenix. Without thinking, Jim implemented his military training, reached for the bird, and wrapped his hands around its throat. Releasing one hand, he grabbed Adam's knife from his pocket, flicked it open, and slashed the bird's throat. A bluish-red blood flowed onto the ground and spread out into a pool larger than expected for a bird no heavier than a chihuahua dog. The bird shape-shifted into its true form with demon horns and a gnarled, wart-covered body. One more bird appeared, and he killed it too. The horse's wings wouldn't suffer the same fate as Armisael. Thinking of the phoenix comparison, Jim surmised the birds would come back to life and attack again, but they lay still.

"Thank you, young human," the horse said. "In the years to come, I will recollect how you saved me. You are brave and true. I am sorry for all that you have had to endure. You are forgiven." The horse reared, flapped its wings, and flew off into the east.

Amidst the commotion, Jim slipped on some blood in the underbrush and lost his footing. Unbeknownst to him, the clouds had concealed a steep hill. Down he went. He bumped along the ground while trying to grab passing trees and bushes. Defeated and bedraggled, he landed hard at the bottom of the ravine. His head fell back against the earth and he dropped into unconsciousness.

Disoriented, Jim awoke with his head throbbing. The sun broke through the trees and stunned his vision the way a weapon flash or an old-fashioned camera bulb would. Shielding his brow, he felt moisture on his forehead, an egg-sized lump, and two bloody gashes.

"Jesus, what happened to me?" Buddy was licking Jim's face when a shadow of an enormous griffon vulture passed overhead. "How did we get down here? I remember walking across the stones to be healed. And the winged horse absolving me of any guilt. It felt like I'd gone to confession and received absolution from a priest. I remember the horse flying off after I saved it from the bird demons. Then I slipped on blood, but I don't remember how I got here." Jim tapped on the face of his watch. The second hand stood still. "Broken. Ugh. So much for military equipment being indestructible."

Buddy did not respond. Instead, he nudged under Jim's arm. But as Jim tried to stand, his right ankle buckled beneath him. Buddy appeared to understand what had happened and trotted off to a nearby tree where he found a four-foot-long branch. Genius, Jim thought. The branch teetered left and right on either side of Buddy's head while he carried it between his teeth. Jim smiled at the scene despite his predicament, then sat awhile before attempting to stand again, using the branch as a crutch.

Once more, he attempted to envision the tumble. The trauma must have wiped it out of his mind. "Buddy, it might be God's way of shielding pain. If so, why hadn't He protected me from my nightmares and flashbacks?" Jim unbuttoned his shirt and winced when he pulled it and the T-shirt off. Adam's knife was still in his pocket. How it got back into his jeans before the fall, he couldn't recall. When he opened the blade, it was clean, without a trace of demon blood. He cut and pulled at the T-shirt, creating a long strip of fabric. Grabbing two short sticks to use for splints, he pushed them into the side of the shoe and bound his foot without looking at the damage. Taking his shoe off would relieve the pressure, but he knew not to succumb to the urge. Every part of him was sore. Cringing with the effort, he put his remaining shirt back on to protect his skin from getting scratches when he started moving through the woods.

While struggling to his feet, he sensed a presence near a tree. The vision was none other than his sister, in what looked like a holographic image. She spoke to him, scolded him for the times he thought of taking his own life, and said, "Never consider such a thing again. Life is full of joy and misery. Seeking joy and holding onto it is imperative."

Before he could respond, she vanished. *What was he supposed to feel after seeing her again under these circumstances?* Accept whatever life had to offer; this was the only answer.

Leaning against a tree, Jim recalled two other falls.. The first was back in Ireland when he'd been riding a bike up a steep hill ahead of his parents. Going through an S-turn, his front tire slid sideways, tipping the bike over. A stranger grabbed him before he tumbled down an embankment. The second was in the Army when Smitty went off the cliff instead of him. Jim decided today was his turn to suffer the consequences of a fall. Stumbling off the cliff into the clouds almost seemed suicidal. He felt blessed not to have been killed. The thought made him realize how ironic this was considering he'd contemplated killing himself in Grenada and several times afterward. The recent events had transformed his life and vanquished those impulses.

Continuing forward from one tree to the next, he took breaks while supporting himself on the tree trunks. To distract himself from the pain in his foot, he counted the trees along the way and identified them by name: holm, cork, and Pyrenean oak, then alder, and ash.

Resting, Jim took time to reflect upon more of what he'd learned from Guinefort and Armisael. When he'd asked about Adam and Christina, Armisael said that the supreme God doesn't always determine who dies and when. Fate sometimes plays into the timing. Humans make choices based on what happens around them. Their choices or their family's lead them down a path. His sister died because of a chain of events beyond her control. Adam and others died because of where they chose to be. The words sounded very much like what Sara had suggested months before.

A rustling sound in the woods distracted his thoughts, and Buddy took off running. Jim reached for his invisible rifle. It seemed odd, because he knew he wasn't in a combat situation. The fall must have scrambled his mind along with his ankle. Again, he hobbled forward, hoping Uncle's house wasn't too far away. At the pace he was traveling, it would likely take hours. He hopped from tree to tree on his makeshift cane for forty-five minutes. About the time he wanted to sit down for a nap, Buddy returned with Sara. He watched her slide off Vida's saddle and lead the horse by the reins for the last few yards.

"Jim! Oh my God! Your head's all scratched up and your ankle— what happened?"

"Don't worry, I'm okay. I had a tumble. Besides, I'm not sure you'll believe me when I tell you what's going on."

She sighed and hugged him.

"Ouch, take it easy. I bruised my back. How'd you find me?"

"Buddy pawed at the covers and pulled them clear off. If that wasn't enough, he jumped on the bed and started whining. You were nowhere to be found. The front door was ajar. I figured you'd wandered off again and something had happened."

"Is Dustin all right? He could have crawled out of the house."

"I checked the bedroom. They were still asleep when I left." Sara touched Jim's cheek. "Right after that, I saw the photo on the mantel of your uncle and aunt on the horse, and it reminded me I could grab Vida from the field and start searching. Buddy led the way. So, what happened?"

"I woke up and went walking. After some encounters with… I fell. I must have been unconscious for a long time. The sun hit me, and I guess it woke me up."

"Well, I'm amazed Buddy came to the rescue. You're at least a mile into the estate."

"Whoa, Buddy, you're awesome." Jim rubbed Buddy's ears. "Sara, thanks for listening to him, and coming out here."

"Buddy is the hero of the day."

"We need to talk, Sara."

"Let's rest a minute." Sara took his hand and helped him over to a log. "Did you take any of the sleep herbs last night?"

"What? No, I didn't. My late-night walks in the woods are surreal. I should have told you about them before."

"It's all right. You're telling me now. Go on."

"The first time, things got weird. I thought I saw Buddy by the tunnel in the middle of the night. When I saw the footprints, I knew they were too large to be Buddy's. Later, I found out it was a wolf. At one point, he sat about ten feet across from me. When he took off, I followed, and he led me back to the barn where Uncle was fighting the fire. You know how that turned out."

"Hmm. Perhaps a coincidence? Jim, the animal's description sounds more like another one of the pictures we drew after your dreams back home."

"I know. Wait, hang on, it gets stranger. The ghosts of Christina and Adam spoke to me through statues and holographic images.

"Last night, I got in the middle of an attack that reminded me of the devil monkeys in the *Wizard of Oz*, but it was a mythical phoenix turned demon. It had vicious claws and multi-colored wings. I saved the horse from losing its wings the way the Angel Armisael had before we met her. Remember the one you saw with the tiny baby?"

"Slow down, slow down," Sara pleaded. "How do you know how the angel lost her wings?"

"The wolf, Guinefort, spoke to me. He's the one who led me to the barn fire."

"Good thing he did. You saved Uncle Jorge."

"Look at these." Jim pulled the trinkets from the wall out of his pocket. "These are from Adam, Aunt Yara, and Christina. I'm amazed they didn't break when I fell."

"Oh, Jim, your head is full of all sorts of things. If I didn't know better, I'd say a concussion produced all these illusions." Sara scrunched up her lips. "No more falling of any kind. Do you hear?"

"Yes, but I'll be all right. Everything in this place is beyond anything I've ever experienced." Jim's ankle spasmed and throbbed.

"You've had a midsummer night's dream. Like in Shakespeare's play."

"Ah, perhaps, but I was awake." Jim sucked his cheek in. "I need to tell you something else. Since I left Grenada, I've been fighting a demon far worse than you thought. After Adam stepped in front of me and took the bullet, I almost turned my gun on myself. I have thought about ending my life since then, because of the guilt and nightmares." Jim paused, letting his words sink in. "Now, I never will. My experiences here have changed my perspective."

"Oh, Jim." Sara leaned in, then stopped. "What did the spirits tell you?"

"It's quite a lot to take in."

"Can't be any worse than what you just said."

"True. This is good news. Except a spirit that appeared to be Christina, said I'm allowed to tell you something if we vow to keep the information between us. Not even Blaire can know."

"What is it?"

He took a long breath before he revealed the secret. "Adam's soul is in Dustin, and Christina's soul will morph into our baby one day."

"Incredible." Sara put a hooked finger to her lip, then said, "Secrecy isn't a problem. No one would ever believe us if we explained the things we've seen here."

"Some people might, but I won't be telling." Jim felt a physical release after confessing everything to Sara. Not wanting to allow himself anymore thoughts of gloom and doom, he continued. "Anyway, right before the bird attacked, the winged horse said I saved him like Adam saved me. And I should live without guilt. From now on, I will be free of nightmares."

"This place sure has been full of mystical happenings. How can we know what's real and what isn't?"

"We can't. It's about faith."

"Well, then, we'll rely on faith. Come on, let's go home." Sara pointed at a nearby tree stump. "Can you get over there? I can bring Vida close, and you can get on without hurting yourself anymore. Your ankle looks bad."

"It's a sprain. I don't think it's broken like Aunt Yara's, and she managed."

"I bet Uncle Jorge has a proper splint and crutch hidden in a closet."

Jim stood, and with a little help from Sara and the makeshift cane, he stepped onto the stump. Sara brought Vida around and mounted. Jim grabbed a strap on the saddle, put his good foot in the stirrup, and swung up behind her onto Vida's rump.

Sara boisterously laughed.

"What is it?"

"I imagine we are a sight." Her voice went down an octave. "You rumpled and bruised. Me in my pajamas. We're nothing like the photo of Uncle Jorge and Aunt Yara riding in tandem in their finery."

Buddy barked in what Jim decided was agreement.

"The winged horse also said that in time, by design, we will forget all the things from the Otherworld we've experienced." Jim's voice came out strong and echoed off the trees. "Also, what humans believe through religion is both right and wrong. Everyone is judged at the end of their lives."

"Hmm. I'd say our trip to Sintra was well worth it, even if you did mess up your ankle."

"I agree."

"Do you need to go to a hospital?"

"No. No hospital." Jim was now inadvertently whispering in her ear.

"Yep, after the fire, Uncle Jorge didn't want to go to the hospital. I didn't either after the horse yanked my shoulder out of whack. We're a stubborn lot."

"Yes, I suppose we are," Jim said.

"I can't imagine ever forgetting my encounter with the wingless angel or her dragon," Sara said.

"I'm sure we will remember the fire, and spending time with Uncle, and Aunt Deborah surprising us."

Sara squeezed his thigh. "Jim, are you really all right?"

"I'm going to be fine. I won't be walking about in the middle of the night anymore."

"Good, that's good." She paused long enough to cause him to worry. "Jim, I have something to tell you."

"What is it?"

"The birth control pills. It seems I'm part of the one percent who gets—"

"What?"

"I went to town yesterday and bought a kit. I'm pregnant."

"A baby. Wow!"

"Yes, wow. A surprise all around."

"Is riding okay?"

"Of course. Don't worry about me."

"A baby! This is amazing!" Jim's thoughts were reeling.

"I'm sure Armisael was trying to tell me after the fire. I didn't understand then. I'm betting we'll have a baby girl. She and Dustin will grow up together."

"Since the spirits said we'd have a baby, I can't say I'm surprised. It'll be amazing to have Christina's spirit around every day, along with Adam's in Dustin."

"Yes, I'm still trying to digest the concept."

"So, when's our baby due?"

"Next February or maybe March." Sara smiled. "I'm glad you're okay with this."

"Better than okay." Jim laughed. "I never believed in reincarnation, but now I do. Poor Aunt Yara, after seeing her spirit in the barn fire, I can't imagine where she'll go next."

"With Uncle Jorge until he passes," Sara said. "Or maybe she'll move on if he marries again."

"I think Aunt Yara would be happy if he did." Jim sighed. "We're going to have a baby."

Sara laughed and pulled his arms tighter around her waist. "Yes, Jim, yes."

He slipped his fingers around her belly and laced them together with the knowledge of a new life growing inside. Sara urged Vida forward, and they rode back home to Uncle Jorge.

Author's Notes

This book is to honor a dear friend, although his name was not Jim. In real life, my friend endured what outwardly appeared to be a minor concussive event during a combat mission in Grenada from which he never recovered. His extraordinary experiences, and the stigma of therapy, made it impossible for him to seek treatment. As a result, his post-traumatic stress disorder (PTSD) devastated his everyday life.

Many ideas within this novel evolved during my volunteer work at a USO where I spent countless hours with military personnel. Additional concepts were revealed through significant research, including travels to Portugal, Florida, Georgia, and North Carolina. I don't profess to have firsthand knowledge of the military information I've included in my novel. My hope is that the choices I've made are thought provoking (see the resource pages ahead).

Note

Dear Reader,

I hope you enjoyed my novel. Please consider posting your review on websites such as Goodreads and Amazon to encourage my future projects.

Thank you,

Elsa

Acknowledgments

Sending special gratitude to the soldiers who contributed to my research. Especially to those who gave their valuable time to discuss their experiences. I am especially grateful to my family for their love and support, along with the hours they spent discussing events, editing, and creating artistic drawings to help my vision.

I am thankful to the following individuals who took the time to read my drafts and provide constructive suggestions.

From my Wyoming Critique Group

- Scott Morton, author of Civalia
- Marcia Meredith Hensley, author of Staking Her Claim: Women Homesteading the West

From my Maryland Critique Group

- Eileen Rodberg, author of *The Message Was Clear*

From a Michigan Book Club

- Suzanne Haynes
- Alice R. Champion

As well as Mary Nell Meyers for the information she provided after learning about beekeeping through her father, John Romanik, who was renowned in apicultural circles in Maryland.

Louise Capon, poet and educator

Linda Robinson-Reitsma, educator

Book Club Discussion Guide

1. When you hear of something devastating happening in the world, do you feel the trauma those people have felt, or do you move on to another portion of the day?

2. When you are told an outlandish story, are you skeptical or do you take it at face value?

3. Jim lived by other's rules and codes rather than his own, what happened to his heart?

4. How do religious beliefs create conflict in Jim's life?

5. Did Jim's commitments and loves mold him for better or worse?

6. How was Jim conflicted or at peace with his decisions?

7. Why do you think he lost sleep over the consequences of his actions?

Main Character List

Jim Masterson (Protagonist)—son of James Senior and Clarissa Masterson

Adam Donnelly

Sara Cosgrove

Blaire Fairmont

Death & Guilt (Antagonist)

Additional Characters

Throughout: various animals, statues, and mythological beings, ghosts, and historical figures. Some referred to by name and other not. Noted below in order-of-appearance.

Part One

Bird-lady	Woman in Forsyth Park
Suzy	James Masterson Senior's girlfriend
Christina	Jim's youngest sister
Mrs. Donnelly	Adam's mother
Liana	Housekeeper at the Masterson's
Rex & Buttons	Family dogs
Tobias	Horse in Savannah barn

Part Two

Mr. Veasey	Leases lodgings to Sara and Blaire
Chuck	Photojournalist, Mr. Veasey's partner
Mrs. Fairmont	Blaire's mother
Aunt Deborah	Sara's aunt
Melanie	Jim's sister
Blake Adam Donnelly	Adam's father's ghost

Soldiers Noted:

Drill Sergeant Morgan	Chaplain Scythe
Gunther	Brinkley
Crebs	Jay
Griswold	Jorgenson
O'Sullivan	Smitherson

Part Three

Uncle Jorge	Jim's uncle and Peter's Father
Aunt Yara	Jorge's spouse, Peter's mother
Peter/Pedro	Jim's cousin
Buddy	Dog. Lab, boxer mix
Luanna	Psychic friend of Aunt Yara's
Tomás	Friend of Adam & Jim
Pascal	Gray cat
Guinefort	Wolf
Danica	Guardian angel
Armisael	Wingless angel
Tatsuya	Dragon

Horses at Uncle's barn: Rolan, Marco, Mateo, Vida, plus unnamed

Fire bombardier (brigade) with Officer Borges and visiting townspeople

Resources

Aftershock: The Untold Story of Surviving Peace by Matthew Green

Lethal Warriors: When the new band of brothers came home by David Philipps

Until Tuesday: A Wounded Warrior and the Golden Retriever Who Saved Him by Luis Carlos Montalvan and Bret Witter

Achilles in Vietnam: Combat Trauma and The Undoing of Character by Jonathan Shay, M.D., PH.D.

Why We Sleep: Unlocking the Power of Sleep and Dreams by Matthew Walker, PhD

The Sleep Revolution: Transforming Your Life One Night at a Time by Arianna Huffington

Dreams and Sleep by Trudi Strain Trueit through Scholastic books

101 Questions About Sleep and Dreams: That Kept You Awake Nights…Until Now by Faith Hickman Brynie

The Power of Habit by Charles Duhigg

The Brave Ones: A Memoir of Hope, Pride, and Military Service by Michael J. Macleod

63 Days and A Wake-Up: Your Survival Guide to United States Army Basic Combat by Don Herbert

The Essential Herbal for Natural Health: How to Transform Easy-to-Find Herbs into Healing Remedies for the Whole Family by Holly Bellebuono

Life *Inside my Mind: 31 Authors Share Their Personal Struggles.* Edit by Jessica Burkhart

The Garden of Good and Evil by John Berendt

Haunted Savannah: America's Most Spectral City by James Caskey

The Tales of the Alhambra by Washington Irving

Why Zebras Don't Get Ulcers: The Acclaimed Guide to Stress, stress-related diseases & Coping by Robert M Sapolsky 3rd Edition

Dutch: A Memoir of Ronald Reagan by Edmund Morris

The Rucksack War: U.S. Army Operational Logistics in Grenada, 1983 by Edgar F. Raines Jr.

history.army.mil/html/books/055/55-2-1/CMH_Pub_55-2-1.pdf
Also available in print.

The Magic Zoo by Peter Costello

The Covert Missions of the Military's Elite Fighting Force A Magazine by History Channel - 2017-1-20 SIP (Author), Meredith Media Group(Contributor) January 20, 2017

Films

The Face of War. Interpretation of Marie Colvin, journalist. Film seems to combine two books *The Face of War* by Martha Gelhorn and *The Front Line* by Marie Colbin.

Generation Kill. Mini-series created by David Simon and Ed Burns in 2008. Combat in Iraq. Based on a non-fiction book by Evan Wright.

More Than Honey. Documentary film on bees directed by Markus Imhoof. Released in 2013.

Internet (A Sampling)

U.S. Invasion of Grenada: A 30-Year Retrospective
by Stephen Zunes. truthout.org/articles/
us-invasion-of-grenada-a-30-year-retrospective

TED Talks: Sebastian Junger

Atonement After Iraq by Dexter Filkins in The New Yorker 22
October 2012

President Reagan's speech; www.youtube.com/watch?v=WsDCcP-
fj-Yw, www.britannica.com/event/Cold-War

Georgiaencyclopedia.org/articles/counties-cities-neighborhoods/
savannah

Mefloquine (malaria drug) was formulated at Walter Reed Army
Institute of Research (WRAIR) in the 1970s shortly after the end
of the Vietnam war (Wikipedia). Can cause hallucinations when
mixed with other meds - drugs.com/sfx/mefloquine-side-effects.
html

Depts.washington.edu/oldenlab/
global-perspective-on-crayfish-invasions

Vietnam Photograph www.bbc.com/news/
world-us-canada-42864421

Chalet of the Countess of Edla, Sintra

Jungle warfare training. YouTube.com/watch?v=JiV-1dnrmVY

Parks in Sintra, Portugal. www.parquesdesintra.pt/en/
recreation-and-leisure/horse-riding-tours

Fado music example -www.youtube.com/watch?v=on9lKHZc5jA

Vultures of Douro Valley. https://mossyearth.com

Native trees of Portugal. www.keelayogafarm.com

Otherworld Gnosis: Fairy Ointments and Nuts of Knowledge
by Dr. Norman Shaw psychedelicpress.co.uk/blogs/
psychedelic-press-blog/otherworld-gnosis-shaw

Current café in Savannah. www.sentientbean.com/visit

About the Author

ELSA WOLF

Elsa has spent a life-time traveling and enjoying adventures. She is a George Washington University graduate with a theatrical background. While living in Maryland, she raised a family and operated an equestrian business. During her free time, she volunteered at the USO to support our soldiers. Now living in Wyoming, she continues to research and write while exploring the world. For more information, visit www.elsawolfbooks.com

Buried Truths, A Daughter's Tale
Keep Me Forever

ElsaWolfBooks.com